"Where is my daughter?"

Brenna barely got the words out, winded as she was from running and panic.

Her gaze went to the crime-scene techs milling around the car wreckage in fireproof white suits, two of them prying open the trunk with a crowbar, her heart pounding. *Please, please, please . . . No, not Maya. Not Maya in the car . . .*

"My daughter is a thirteen-year-old girl. She was with the woman who was driving this car."

"We haven't seen anyone, ma'am," one of the uniformed cops informed her.

"What was found in the car?"

"I'm going to have to ask you to step back, please."

She then heard a creaking noise, someone shouting, "Got it," and saw the trunk sprung open, a cloud of black dust rising out of it, hanging in the air. She held her breath.

The techs stepped back, covering their faces. One shouted, "We have something!" and Sykes moved around to the rear of the car. He backed away, shaking his head . . .

No . . .

"Ma'am!" someone said, because she was running to the wrecked car, legs pumping, breath cutting through her lungs.

By Alison Gaylin

STAY WITH ME
INTO THE DARK
AND SHE WAS
HEARTLESS
TRASHED
HIDE YOUR EYES
YOU KILL ME

ALISON GAYLIN

stay with me

A BRENNA SPECTOR NOVEL OF SUSPENSE

HARPER

An Imprint of HarperCollins*Publishers*

This is a work of fiction. Names, characters, places, and incidents are products of the author's imagination or are used fictitiously and are not to be construed as real. Any resemblance to actual events, locales, organizations, or persons, living or dead, is entirely coincidental.

HARPER

An Imprint of HarperCollins*Publishers*
195 Broadway
New York, New York 10007

Copyright © 2014 by Alison Gaylin
ISBN 978-0-06-187826-8

First Harper mass market printing: July 2014

HarperCollins ® and Harper ® are registered trademarks of Harper-Collins Publishers.

Printed in the United States of America

Visit Harper paperbacks on the World Wide Web at
www.harpercollins.com

10 9 8 7 6 5 4 3 2 1

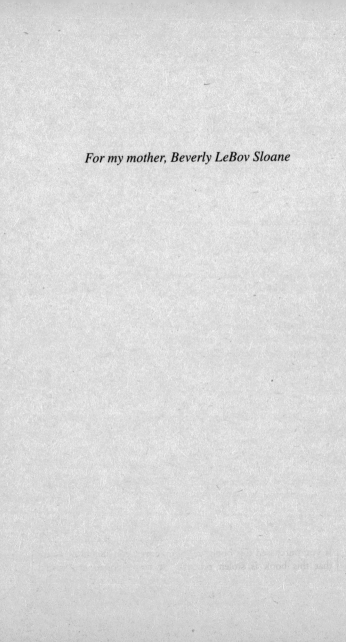

For my mother, Beverly LeBov Sloane

Acknowledgments

As ever, I am so grateful to the wonderful Deborah Schneider, and to everyone at HarperCollins—particularly Lyssa Keusch, a great editor and a true friend.

Much appreciation as well to Josh Moulin and Marco Conelli for their police and technical know-how. And to Marcelle Harrison for her knowledge of City Island.

Thanks to Jackie Kellachan and Nan Tepper at The Golden Notebook for their smarts and for their support of local authors.

And to James Conrad, Chas Cerulli, Paul Leone, Anthony Marcello, Jamie and Doug Barthel, Abby Thomas, the fabulous FLs (enablers in the best sense of the word), and so many more friends (you know who you are) for the writing feedback, drinks, pep talks, and drinks. I continue to love you all.

Thank you Shel and Marilyn (aka Mom and Dad), Dennis, Betsy, Sydney and Sam, Ken and Jessica, and Mom for being the best family anybody could ever ask for.

And always, my two loves, Mike and Marissa.

Part One

I want to die in a movie. I want to lie on my back with a movie star fireman hovering over me, pounding on my chest, begging me to live. He shifts in and out of my fading vision but I can still see his eyes. They are blue and soulful and shiny with tears. There's a white light behind him and it is very, very bright, making him look like an angel. I am weak. I know he's the last thing I will see, and I take comfort in that.

The fireman may be my husband. Or maybe my Long-Lost Great Love. He may even be some stranger who pulled me from a burning car just three minutes ago. I haven't figured that part out, because it doesn't matter—not really. All that matters is this moment, when my life slips away and I am the fireman's WORLD!

"Stay with me," he says. Just like they always say to dying people in movies. "Stay with me, sweetheart. Stay with me, please."

It's the most loving thing anyone has ever said to me. It is the most loving thing I have ever heard.

From the diary of Clea Spector, age seventeen
September 20, 1981

Prologue

"You can be first."

"Uh, no. That's okay."

Lindsay Segal pointed the bottle of blackberry brandy at Maya in such a way that it reminded her of a microphone. "Go on. It won't bite."

Maya thought it might, though. The mouth of the bottle was less than an inch away from her nose, and it breathed on her—an awful, cloying smell, like cough medicine gone bad. Maya's stomach clenched up. She was thirteen years old. Outside of a glass of champagne at Craig Sapperstein's bar mitzvah last October, she'd never had a drink, never wanted one. But the blackberry brandy wasn't a drink so much as a dare. Lindsay had swiped it from her parents' liquor cabinet—a gift from three or four years ago, faded red bow still stuck to the side like a warning label—and brought it into her bedroom under her sweatshirt. "Check this out," she'd said to Maya and Nikki and Annalee, producing it from the folds of the sweatshirt, unveiling it like a magic trick. Maya had just frowned, but Nikki and Annalee had oohed and aahed—as though this sad, sticky bottle were the one thing they'd been waiting their whole lives to see.

Maya still didn't quite get Lindsay, Nikki, and Annalee. But that was understandable. Until this past Monday, she hadn't known them except by legend. Maya was just a freshman, after all, while they were juniors, *big-deal* juniors—all of them popular in that mean-girl way, all with skintight skinny jeans and perfect shiny hair to toss and that live landmine quality—unpredictable and powerful and don't-get-too-close-or-you-will-die.

Back in September, Maya had watched the guy she liked rush up to Lindsay after chorus practice, watched him gather her into his arms and swallow her face, right in front of everybody. *Ugh.* But at the same time, *Duh.* Guys like Miles Torper always fell for girls like Lindsay. Hell, any guy who had half a chance would fall for Lindsay. It was just the way life worked.

Maya had hated Lindsay for a couple of weeks, shot Miles angry looks whenever he caught her eye in art class. But Maya couldn't stay angry at Miles. He was too funny, too talented, too . . . *Miles.*

And anyway what was the point of hating Lindsay? Lindsay didn't even know she existed.

Until a week ago.

The weird twist in Maya's life was, she was now friends with *Lindsay Segal*—something she'd never thought she wanted until it had happened. Well maybe "friends" was too important a word to choose after just six days of hanging out. But the thing was, it felt that way. Important.

Is that your painting on the wall in the cafeteria? It's

awesome, Lindsay had said. *Listen, after school we're going shopping at that new Forever 21. You want to come?* Lindsay Segal, complimenting Maya. Lindsay Segal, assuming Maya liked the same kind of clothes she did. Lindsay Segal, *Miles's* Lindsay Segal, inviting Maya to *shop with her.*

It had been like jumping into ice-cold water on a hot summer day—a shock at first, but then perfect. Maya had said yes. Of course she had. And she'd said yes to helping Lindsay with an art project and yes to hanging out with her and her friends during study hall. And just two days ago, on Thursday, Maya had said yes to sitting at her table, *The Table*, at lunch. Maya the only freshman at The Table, Maya turning her back to her best friends Zoe and Larissa, trying not to feel their sad eyes on her. *They'd do the same thing. I know they would.*

You're having lunch with us, Maya? Miles had said from the end of the table, surprise all over his face. *That's awesome!*

And now, here she was at Lindsay's apartment. Invited for a sleepover. *No parents*, Lindsay had said. *Just us girls.* And Maya had said yes. Of course she had.

"Come on," Annalee said. "We can't wait for you all night, Maya."

Maya looked at Lindsay. "Why do you guys want me to drink first?"

"Because . . ." Lindsay grinned. "You're the *guest.*"

Maya stared at her, at the dead-calm eyes.

"And anyway, Miles said you liked to party."

"*What?*"

"Check it out. She's blushing."

"Shut up, Nikki." Lindsay set the bottle on the floor between them, the grin relaxing a little. "Sorry, Maya. That was rude of Nikki."

Maya cleared her throat. "Miles . . ." Her voice cracked on his name. "Miles said that about me?"

"He didn't say it in those words. He said you're grown up, especially for your age . . ."

"He was talking about me? To you?"

"You're into him," Nikki said it with a little too much eagerness in her voice. "Admit it. Watch out for her, Linds."

"Shut. Up."

"No." Maya looked at Lindsay. "He's just in my art class. That's all. That's how I know him."

"I believe you."

"Good, because—"

"Different," said Lindsay.

Maya stared at her. "Huh?"

"Miles said you're different from other girls—like, in a good way."

Maya's breath caught. Her palms began to sweat and she felt the rush of blood to her cheeks—another blush. She hated herself for it. *Could he really have said that? To her?*

Annalee said, "So you know . . . since he thinks you're grown-up acting and different and all . . . I mean he hardly says nice things like that about anybody."

"That's why we invited you," Lindsay said. "The way Miles was going on about you, he made us think you were . . . you know. Like us." Lindsay tilted the bottle to her mouth and took a long swig from it, her throat moving up and down. Once she was done, she put it down without so much as a wince. "Sorry." She ran her tongue over her upper lip. "I just couldn't wait any longer."

Maya glanced at Nikki and Annalee. Both of them were gaping at Lindsay with such awe, as if she'd just done some amazing gymnastic feat. She half expected them to start clapping.

She turned back to Lindsay. "I am," she said.

"Excuse me."

"I am . . . Like you."

"Prove it."

Maya took the bottle.

"Awesome. Now, chug, girl!"

Maya closed her eyes and thought of Miles. She thought of his lips, forming those words. *Different from other girls.*

She thought of his lips.

Maya raised the bottle to her mouth and tilted her head back, just as Lindsay had done.

For about a second, it wasn't bad, but then the taste barreled in, catching up with her, so much worse than the smell. It seemed to Maya like something not meant to be swallowed at all—cleaning fluid, or kerosene. There was a vicious burn to it, too. It ripped at her throat as it went down, then thudded into her stomach. *Oh no . . .*

Maya gagged. It was all rushing back up, so much faster than it had gone down. She let go of the bottle, put a hand to her mouth. *No, no, not now, please . . .*

"Hey, don't drop it." Nikki caught the bottle before

it tipped over. Maya's head swam and swirled—the whole room did, as though it had been filled with water and someone had pulled the stopper out.

"Oh no, seriously?" said Annalee. "She's gonna boot."

"You called it, Linds."

"No, no . . ." Maya tried to say. "I'm fine." But she couldn't get the words out. She was on her knees, doubling over.

"Oh yeah, she's so grown up." Nikki started to laugh, and Annalee yelled, "Gross," and Maya realized she was puking blackberry brandy, all over Lindsay's pink shag rug.

"Yep," Lindsay said. "I called it."

Maya spotted a trash can by the corner of the desk, but it was too late. She stared at the mess on the rug. Why had none of them given her the trash can?

She blinked hot tears out of her eyes and wiped at her mouth with the back of her hand. The hand trembled. *No one getting me water. No one asking if I'm okay.*

"Well, I guess you're not one of us," Lindsay said. She started laughing along with Annalee and Nikki.

"I'm . . . I'm sorry," Maya said.

Which made those bitches cackle even more. *Why did I come here? Why did I think they were my friends?*

Maya needed to stand up. She needed to stand up and think of something funny to say, anything to say, anything to fix this. She grabbed the side of Lindsay's desk and pulled herself to her feet up and that's when she saw it—the green light at the top of Lindsay's dark computer. The webcam was on.

"Wave to Miles!" Lindsay said.

"No . . ." Maya stared at the screen saver—fireworks

exploding in a night sky. The screen in sleep mode, but the webcam on the whole time, the webcam connected to Miles—Miles hearing everything, seeing everything.

"Gotta keep my man entertained."

Nikki said, "You should so post it on YouTube, Linds."

Maya was moving—out of the bedroom, into the living room, to the front door where she fumbled with the locks, that cackling laughter following her, those bitches' laughter. It wasn't until she was down the hall and pressing the elevator button that it she really started to feel it. Shame. Like a giant wave sweeping over her, the awful memory of it, that laughter swirling in her head.

A setup. The whole week had been a setup. *Different*, she'd said. And Maya had believed it. She'd allowed herself to believe it, just as she'd allowed herself to believe that these girls would want to be her friends.

Just as she allowed herself to believe that Miles . . . *Miles.*

Maya didn't let herself cry until she was safely in the elevator and she'd pressed the lobby button and the doors closed in front of her. She began to whimper, tears spilling down her cheeks, choking her. Soon, she was sobbing.

She managed to pull herself together by the time the doors opened again, but still she was a mess and she knew it. The doorman was talking to some woman. "Here's another one of my baby," he said. "Isn't she an angel? Those eyes just melt my heart." He was showing her a picture on his phone, and neither one of them looked at her.

"That is a very sweet dog," the woman said.

Maya let herself imagine she was invisible, a ghost.

Maya stepped out blindly into the freezing night, shoulders hunched, mouth dry. She pulled out her phone to text her dad that she was coming home. When she clicked it on, though, she saw a new text.

It was from her mom:

Honey, can we talk? Call me anytime.

Maya almost started crying again. She turned her phone off and shoved it deep in her back pocket and kept walking.

Maya would walk off this awful shame. She would walk back to Dad and Faith's and if they tried talking to her, she would say she was tired. She'd go straight to her room and lock the door and fall asleep in her own bed and wake up in the morning and tell her dad that she wanted to be transferred to a different school, where she would change her name and speak with a British accent and never drink with anyone, ever again.

It sounded dumb, but it was a plan anyway. And everybody needed a plan. Even girls walking through the streets of Chelsea on a dark, cold night after ditching a sleepover, girls steeped in shame and dehydration, freezing because they'd forgotten their coat, girls who had never done anyone any harm, who didn't deserve this feeling, who wanted to cry and cry and never stop.

Girls who would never make it home.

1

Nine hours earlier

The waiting room still smelled the same—stale coffee and Pine-Sol. Or maybe it was the memory she had just pushed out of her mind that was still tugging at her, the smell of it lingering. It was never easy for Brenna Spector to unweave the past from the present, but it was especially hard here, in the waiting room of her former child psychiatrist, which—outside of the collection of *Nick Jr.* magazines and *Teen Vogue*s in the rack next to the huge blue beanbag chair—hadn't changed at all since the last time Brenna had been in here: April 29, 1988, *a rainy Friday . . .*

Brenna unzipped her bag for what felt like the thousandth time this afternoon. She slipped her hand in, touched the cover of the journal. *Stay here.*

No doubt Dr. Lieberman believed his young patients found the lack of change comforting. But while Brenna was sure that this was true for the majority of them, it was quite the brain assault for someone with hyperthymestic syndrome. Brenna had been afflicted (or "blessed," depending on your opinion) with the condi-

tion since she was eleven, and it forced ("enabled"?)
her to remember every single day of her life down to
the date and in perfect detail, with all five senses. Most
anything could trigger a memory so vivid, it was as
though she was reliving it. But going back to her childhood shrink's office after twenty years and having it
look and smell exactly the same? Come on.

Brenna couldn't decide whether it felt more like a
bizarre experiment being conducted on her by a sadist,
or the world's worst episode of *Punk'd*. But either way,
the place was throwing more flashbacks at Brenna than
whole season's worth of telenovelas, and she wished
she could wait anywhere else in the building—the
lobby, the stairwell, the janitor's closet. Anywhere.

Brenna had to be here, though, because her daughter
needed help. Said like that, it sounded dramatic, but
the fact was, Brenna's life was dramatic. At least, it had
been lately. For more than ten years, Brenna had been
a private investigator specializing in missing persons
cases—a job that, for a long while, had been mostly
dull and research, spiked with occasional bouts of
revelation and danger. But ever since this past autumn,
Brenna had been on something of a revelation/danger
streak, which had clearly taken its toll on Maya.

At least that's what Brenna had assumed.

A week ago, over dinner, Maya had taken a bite of
her chicken Parmigiana and scrunched up her face in
a way that had made Brenna think maybe she hadn't
cooked it long enough.

"You okay, honey?"

"Yeah. It's just . . ."

"Yes?"

"I think I need to see a shrink."

"You want to see a psychiatrist?"

"You used to see one when you were a kid. How about him?"

"But why?"

"I . . . I just want to talk to somebody."

Maya hadn't gone into any more detail than that, and Brenna hadn't pushed. Brenna had never said, *You can talk to me*, because even if she hadn't remembered her own adolescence as acutely as she did, Brenna knew the situation well enough to understand that as far as this particular topic was concerned, the idea of confiding in Mom was about as appealing to Maya as anesthesia-free liver surgery with a side of Brussels sprouts.

Two weeks earlier, in Brenna's apartment, Maya had been held at knifepoint by a crazy person. She'd pretended it hadn't affected her, but really, who wouldn't want to see a shrink after that? Who wouldn't have nightmares? And who the hell would want to talk to her mother about it, when, if it hadn't been for her mother's aforementioned revelation/danger streak, there wouldn't have been a crazy, knife-wielding person in the apartment to begin with?

So Brenna hadn't asked questions. The following day, after Maya had left for school, she'd picked up the phone and tapped in the same number she'd last dialed on her mother's robin's egg blue rotary on May 4, 1988. *I'm a former patient of Dr. Lieberman's*, she had said to the unfamiliar-sounding receptionist over the phone. *And my daughter needs help.*

Maya had been in with Dr. Lieberman for forty-five minutes. And at the risk of sounding like Brenna's own mother, who unreasonably expected her daughter to have developed a newfound "appreciation and acceptance" of her perfect memory every time she walked out of a session, Brenna hoped Maya was cured. She hoped, during those forty-five minutes, that Lieberman had said something—anything—to bring her back to her old self, that reasonably well-adjusted kid she was before the night of December 21, the kid whose deepest, darkest secret was the worn childhood copy of *The Very Hungry Caterpillar* she'd stolen out of a to-be-donated-to-the-library box and kept hidden in the back of her bookshelf.

I'm sorry, Maya, Brenna thought. *I'm so sorry . . .*

She'd had no idea crazy DeeDee Walsh would show up at her apartment when Maya was there alone. If Brenna had known that, she would have dropped the entire case, forgotten all about it, no matter how much it had to do with finding her sister. Nothing—not even Brenna's twenty-eight-years-missing sister—was worth rushing back to her apartment at 8 P.M. on December 21 after receiving crazy DeeDee's text. Nothing was worth the feeling of unlocking her own door with that texted picture in her mind—DeeDee's knife at Maya's throat, *Brenna's hand shaking as she slips the key in, her heart pounding up into her neck, sweat trickling down her back . . .*

Stop. Stay here. Brenna reached into her bag again and touched the journal. She pulled it out and opened it, slowly turning the pages, not reading them so much as looking at the letters, the soft indent where the pen had moved against the thin paper, the swirls at the ends of the Ys and Js. She imagined her sister's hand, Clea's hand, holding the pen, and that kept her here.

Ironic, wasn't it? Clea, whose disappearance had been the traumatic event to trigger Brenna's hyperthymesia in the first place. Clea—well, an artifact of Clea, anyway—keeping Brenna in the present.

The journal had turned up in Brenna's mailbox four days ago, in a padded brown envelope with no note, no return address, and a Los Angeles postmark. She'd known who it was from and what was inside. She'd even seen Xeroxed versions of the handwritten pages. But still, when she'd opened it, Brenna had gasped. *Her journal.* The journal Clea had kept for years, before and after Brenna had watched her get into that blue car at dawn, a man she couldn't see behind the wheel but whose voice she could hear, deep and resonant.

You look so pretty, Clee-bee.

A man whose name was Bill. Brenna had learned this from the journal, which began when Clea was thirteen years old and ended one month after her disappearance at seventeen. So strange that he would have such a prosaic name, this shadow that haunted Brenna's dreams, her life. Over the years, Brenna had called him so many names in her mind—The Big Bad Wolf, He Who Shall Not Be Named, Voldemort—never Bill.

Clea hadn't revealed his last name in the journal, or why, two weeks after running off with this man she'd more than once referred to as My Great Love, she'd hit the road and started hitchhiking on her own. *I'm free now*, was all she had written on the topic. *Free and alive and hopeful, at last.*

Brenna still couldn't bring herself to read parts of the journal. (When you remember everything you read word for word, you need to be careful.) But the pages Brenna *was* able to read consistently surprised her.

Clea had loved so many boys—loved them deeply and thoroughly and with every inch of her heart and soul—yet when the journal was being written, Brenna hadn't known about any of them. There was her sister in her pink room with the pink shag carpet, Clea with her Elvis Costello records blasting and her Adam Ant poster on the wall. There was Clea, repeatedly telling Brenna to "stop snooping on me, weirdo." And there was Brenna, always snooping, always spying, thinking, *I know her better than anyone. Whether she likes it or not, I do.*

It had taken Brenna twenty-eight years and the strange emergence of this journal to finally realize that she *hadn't* known her sister better than anyone.

She hadn't known her sister at all.

Was Clea with one of those boys now? Was she alive and well, or had she perished twenty-eight years ago, one month after her disappearance, her life ending with this journal? Brenna was beginning to doubt she'd ever be able to answer that question. As close as she'd come to finally finding her sister, she still knew nothing about Clea—not from an investigative standpoint anyway. In her journal, Clea never mentioned last names. And on top of that, Clea was so given to bouts of fantasy, Brenna never could be sure which entries were real and which were 1980s-style fan fiction . . .

But Brenna did have this journal, which for whatever reason was enough to yank her out of her memories. She didn't need any of the things she used to rely on—rubber bands snapping against her wrists, reciting the Pledge of Allegiance or the Lord's Prayer, digging her fingernails into her palms or squeezing her eyes shut like someone in the throes of seizure. All Brenna needed now to stay anchored in the present was the weight of this journal in her hands, the blue faux leather cover, gold-embossed with "My Diary." All she needed was her sister's handwriting, the loops and swirls of it, the bright blue and purple and red ink and all those capital letters and exclamation points, all that barely contained teenage excitement, running up and down the pages. Proof of life, Clea's life.

Maybe that was enough.

The waiting room door pushed open. Brenna closed the journal and dropped it back into her bag and looked up at Maya, Dr. Lieberman standing behind her, a benign smile taped to his face.

"All better?" Brenna winced. "Did I really just say that?"

Maya said, "Yes. Out loud. Unfortunately."

Lieberman smiled. "Your daughter takes after you."

"Don't tell her that. She'll cry."

Maya said nothing. Brenna watched her face. Ever since Maya had asked to see a shrink, Brenna had found herself doing that—staring at her daughter the way you'd stare at a kaleidoscope, looking for the slightest shift in the clear blue eyes.

Lieberman patted Maya on the shoulder. "She has your dry sense of humor, Brenna—that's what I meant," he said. "Maybe next week, we'll get past the jokes and start talking."

Like his waiting room, the doctor had changed very

little in the past twenty years. He still had the pinkish cheeks, the toothy smile, the kind, easy voice.
Lieberman had always reminded Brenna of an oversized rabbit come to life, and that was even more pronounced now, with his hair gone mostly white.

Brenna looked at Lieberman's tie. Mustard yellow,
with little hot dogs and hamburgers all over it. Yep, the
fashion sense hadn't changed, either.

"That okay with you?" she asked Maya.

Maya cracked a smile. A hopeful little smile, nothing sarcastic about it, and for a moment, Brenna was
dropping her off for her first day of kindergarten—
Maya in her pink corduroy jeans and her purple and
pink plaid T-shirt, her pink sneakers from Old Navy
and her furry orange coat—an outfit she'd chosen herself. *Maya hugging Brenna good-bye on the steps of
PS 102, Maya smelling of strawberry shampoo, soft
yellow hair at Brenna's cheek, the glass doors looming
so big behind her . . .*

"Chamomile," Dr. Lieberman was saying to Maya,
his voice yanking Brenna back from that morning,
that sweet, pink morning. It had been September 4,
2001—exactly one week before the attacks—but at the
time, it was just another date for Brenna to remember,
one among thousands jammed into her head and significant only as a start. A good start.

My daughter, growing up . . .

"Yeah," Maya said. "I like all kinds of tea."

Brenna turned to find Maya watching her.

"Try a cup of chamomile before you go to sleep,
with a teaspoon of honey and some milk," Dr. Lieberman said.

Brenna cleared her throat. "Why?"

"Maya's been having a little insomnia," he said. "Nothing to worry about."

"I didn't know that," Brenna said to Maya.

Her gaze dropped to the floor.

"See you next week," Lieberman said. "Same Bat Time, same Bat Channel."

"Huh?"

Brenna said, "That line wasn't even timely when he said it to me."

"When did I say it to you?"

"December 8, 1982; February 21, March 9, and September 16, 1983; February—"

"Okay, okay." Lieberman sighed. "I am officially retiring the line."

"You've said that before, too."

Lieberman smiled, shook his head. "Some things never change."

"Most things," Brenna said.

"That right?"

She gave the waiting room a pointed once-over. "Yep."

Lieberman shrugged. "I'll have to take your word for that."

"You can't sleep?" Brenna said, once she and Maya were in the elevator and heading down. It had been the first thing she'd said to her since leaving Lieberman's office, Brenna trying dozens of different ways to make a phrase out of what she'd been thinking.

Maya shrugged. "No big deal." She gazed up at the blinking numbers and, for some reason, smiled. "It's only been a couple of nights."

For several seconds, Brenna watched her daughter, a lump forming in her throat. "Maya?"

She looked at her.

Just say it. "You can tell Dad."

"Huh?"

Brenna cleared her throat. "You can tell him about what happened . . . on December 21."

"December . . ."

Brenna closed her eyes. "It was wrong of me to tell you to keep that from him," she said. "You can't keep things from your father, even if those things make me look irresponsible."

"Mom."

"I shouldn't have left you alone that night. That never should have happened to you. You were in my care and I let you down."

"Mom."

"Your father should know that."

"*Mom*," Maya said. "First of all, you saved my life."

"But I never would've had to if—"

"Secondly, that freak is in jail right now. No one's going to hurt me anymore."

"Maya . . ."

"Thirdly, I'm not telling Dad."

The doors opened, the last word, "Dad," echoing in the quiet lobby. It was a cold winter Saturday and gray light pressed through the windows, the whole city still tired from the holidays, everything sad and hungover, the year still too new to matter. Brenna had always hated January, for these reasons and more. "Why not?" she asked.

"Faith's a reporter, and she got the same story every-

body else did. I was at a friend's, I came home to find
you and DeeDee fighting with each other, Trent called
the police and they saved the day. That's a good story.
Why needlessly freak them out with extra details?"

"It's not extra details, honey. It's the truth."

"It's *my* truth," she said. "I can tell who I want."

As they headed for the door, Maya placed a hand on
Brenna's arm. Brenna turned to her. "Maya, your father
deserves to know . . ." she started to say. But Maya's
expression stopped her. "It's *our* truth, Mom," Maya
said, very quietly. "And it's not why I wanted to see Dr.
Lieberman."

Brenna never found out why Maya had wanted to see
Lieberman because Maya didn't want to talk about it
anymore. "Whatever I say is going to sound stupid,"
Maya explained to her on the subway. "And then you'll
remember it forever."

"Hey," Brenna tried. "I remember, but I don't judge."

Maya rolled her eyes, which wasn't fair.

"I *don't*," Brenna said.

But really, Maya didn't have to be fair about this,
and Brenna didn't want to press her. Even if she did
manage to yank a reason out of her, Brenna deep-down
knew it that it all boiled down to the knife attack—*how
could it not?* And if Brenna's thirteen-year-old daughter wanted to protect her from the truth, then there
wasn't much Brenna could do about that, was there,
other than to let Maya *believe* she was protecting her?

The subway jerked to a stop at Christopher Street,
and Brenna and Maya sauntered off—no hurry, really.
The subway was a pleasure on weekends—always a

place to sit, no pushing . . . "So," Brenna said. "Devil's food?"

They were on their way to Magnolia Bakery, where the handoff was scheduled to take place. It was Jim and Faith's day to take Maya, and because Maya had been getting increasingly annoyed at Brenna's insistence on accompanying her for every handoff (*Mom. It's daytime and I'm a teenager! I can walk to Faith and Jim's apartment by myself!*) Brenna had been suggesting the most bribe-worthy of meeting places. Last week, the handoff had happened at Urban Outfitters, and it had come with a very cute sweater that Maya claimed she would "wear forever." Before that, it had been at the Apple Store.

"I might try something different," said Maya, who hadn't tried a different cupcake flavor at the Magnolia Bakery since June 21, 2008 (Coconut cream. She'd hated it.).

Brenna turned and looked at Maya and caught her in the middle of yet another inexplicable smile. "Maya?"

The smile melted away fast, Brenna thinking maybe she'd imagined it, maybe she'd just been reading in . . .

"Mom?"

"Yes?"

"Why don't you ever want to talk to Dad?"

"Jeez," she said. "I thought we were talking about cupcake flavors."

Maya stared straight ahead. "It's a legitimate question. I'm not saying you guys have to . . . like . . . go bowling together. But why can't you be in the same room?"

Brenna swallowed. "I hate bowling."

"Not funny." Maya tended to walk fast when she got agitated, and now she was speeding up Bleecker Street at what felt like thirty miles an hour, Brenna rushing to keep up with her.

"We're not late," Brenna said, "and even if we were, Faith would wait. There's no need to run a three-minute mile."

"*Mom.*"

"What?"

"I asked you a question."

"Can we walk a little slower please?"

Maya stopped abruptly.

Brenna sighed. "It's my condition, Maya," she said. "Your father . . . he's a good guy. But being in the same room with him triggers too many memories."

"Are you always going to use that as an excuse?"

"It's not an excuse," Brenna said. "It's a fact. A pathetic fact, yes, but your dad . . ." Brenna's phone vibrated SOS in Morse code—a text. Brenna plucked it out of her pocket and glanced at the screen. *Where are you?*

It was from Nick Morasco. She hadn't spoken to him in two days, hadn't answered his texts or returned his calls. And the last thing she'd said to him was "Can you please leave?"

It hadn't been his fault, either. Well, not really.

Brenna closed her eyes. "You don't know how lucky you are," she said to Maya, "to have your father in your life."

"Unlike your own dad, right?"

"Right," said Brenna, who still couldn't open her eyes.

"So why can't you talk to Dad? You have way crappier memories of other people, but you don't refuse to look at them. "

Another text. Brenna took a look at her phone:

Are you okay?

"It isn't the crappy memories that are hard, honey," she said. "It's the good ones."

"Okay, Mom."

"I mean it, Maya. Maybe when you're older, you'll understand."

"No," she said. "I meant, okay, Mom, there it is." Maya pointed at the bakery, which loomed just across the street, an unruly line forming in the front. "I can take it from here."

"I'm not going with you? I was sort of looking forward to seeing Faith. It's been a while."

Maya said something, too quiet for Brenna to hear.

"What?" Brenna said, but then she looked closer at her daughter, followed her line of vision.

Maya repeated, "Faith couldn't make it today," just as Brenna saw him, toward the end of the line. *Jim.* Maya said, "I . . . uh . . . She called my cell and explained. Some interview got postponed or pushed back to today or something . . ."

Jim was wearing a deep green jacket she'd never seen, but it was the same color as the T-shirt he'd worn on July 9, 1997, pushing the stroller through Central Park, the air thick and sticky and almost solid, smelling of hot dogs and wet sidewalk and sweat . . .

Jim slips his arm around Brenna's waist and pulls her close to him. "She's out," he whispers in Brenna's ear, his breath soft at her neck as she looks down at their daughter, their sleeping, quiet daughter, her hands thrown up on either side of her head, surrendering to sleep . . .

"Finally," Brenna says. She pulls Jim into a kiss . . .

Maya gave Brenna a quick, tight hug. It brought her back. "I'm heading across the street, Mom," she said. "You can stay here."

Brenna nodded, feeling Jim's gaze on her. She reached into her bag to touch the journal, rid herself of the memory. Then, without meeting that gaze, she raised her hand in a wave as Maya rushed up to greet him, greet her father, greet this man whose now grayish hair had been shorn into a buzz cut on July 9, 1997, who'd worn a deep green T-shirt that said, "Lone Star Roadhouse" on it—*that tired, frayed thing that Jim refuses to throw out, a relic from a Nils Lofgren show he went to in college, and it feels like tissue under Brenna's palm, his skin so warm beneath . . .*

Brenna ran her hand over the journal. *Stop.*

She'd walk the rest of the way to her Thirteenth Street apartment. She needed the winter air and the movement and the city noise, anything to keep her from going back to that Wednesday in the park, or to February 4, 1998, or December 30, 1996 . . . any date from those years when Jim was hers and their daughter was small and the future stretched out before them, a long, open road . . .

Once she was a safe distance away from the bakery, Brenna put her hands on her knees and bent over, breathing as deeply as she could. She breathed the rest of the memory out of her, shutting her eyes tight, thinking only of the journal, of her sister's loopy, love-struck handwriting.

Brenna walked the rest of the way to her apartment. The cold air burned her skin, and she welcomed it—the slap in the face she needed.

By the time she got to her building, the near run-in with Jim was, if not forgotten (what was ever forgotten?) not that big a deal.

She got a text from Maya:

R U OK?

Brenna smiled. *I'm fine,* she typed, which caused her daughter to reply with a colon-and-parenthesis smiley face—an inside joke. Maya knew how deeply Brenna despised colon-and-parenthesis smiley faces, and for that reason texted them to her as often as possible.

Stop that.

[:)]

Brenna sighed. She scrolled back to Nick Morasco's last text, which ironically said the exact same thing as Maya's, only without teenage abbreviations, but so much harder to respond to.

Are you okay?

Brenna stared at the words, thinking back again to two nights ago, his hand at the small of her back as she read the police papers—thirty-two-year-old police papers, with her father's name at the top.

Morasco had given them to her, saying, "You can read them or not. Either way, the information is yours." And for two weeks, she'd kept them in a drawer, thinking maybe she wouldn't ever read them. If she didn't read these papers, she'd never have anything to remember.

But that didn't happen. It was a Thursday and Nick had worked late that night. He'd shown up after midnight and he and Brenna had gone straight to her room and locked the door and made love for an hour and she'd felt so sated and secure after, as though nothing could ever hurt her. Brenna had gazed from her bed to her bottom dresser drawer. She'd thought about the papers inside and figured, *Now's as good a time as any* . . .

The screen of her phone blurred a little, Morasco's text softening in front of her eyes: *Are you okay?* That was the question of the hour, wasn't it? And Nick asking. Detective Nick Morasco, who'd never been anything but honest with her . . .

Brenna typed: *I don't know.*

Morasco's text came back fast: *I'm here if you need me.*

Brenna swatted at her eyes. *I'm not going to think about it.*

She took a long, jagged breath, not thinking of Morasco or of her father, not thinking of her mother and the conversation they still hadn't had but needed to, she supposed—*did they really need to?*—not thinking of anything at all, other than the lock on the front door of her building, her key slipping in.

As she pushed open the door, Brenna had so effectively blocked out her thoughts that she was unaware of the sudden rush of radiator warmth or of the cold wind at her back, or of the first floor tenant, Mrs. Dinnerstein, who was exiting the building at the same time Brenna was entering and nearly ran Brenna down with her shopping cart.

"Careful," chided Ina Dinnerstein, who'd long resented living downstairs from a private investigator, but particularly in the past few months. All those reporters. All those questions and camera flashes and cruel, prying eyes . . .

That woman and her ridiculous assistant, putting the whole building in danger, not to mention that child of hers.

"Sorry, Mrs. Dinnerstein," Brenna said, unaware of Ina's thoughts, or of the visitor whom Ina had turned away this morning, or of the flash of reluctant shame in the older woman's eyes as she said it again, this time with extra meaning:

"You need to be more careful."

2

As she opened the door to her apartment, Brenna was greeted by the sound of a flushing toilet. During the days Maya wasn't with her, Brenna lived alone, so this would have been alarming, were it not for the fact that her office was located in the front part of her floor-through, and that her assistant, Trent La-Salle, had worked the previous two Saturdays due to a backlog of recordkeeping following their recent surge in business. Still, she was annoyed. Brenna had specifically told Trent there was no need for him to come in today, and she hadn't planned on paying him.

"That you, Brenna?" Trent called out.

"Yes, Trent."

"I'm in the can!"

Brenna sighed. "Yeah, I'm a detective so I figured that out."

The bathroom door closed and then Trent was in the room with her—a vision in neon orange board shorts and a skin-tight black T-shirt that read, in red letters, "Orgasm Donor." Brenna winced. In Trent's twenty-seven years on this planet, no one had ever been able to teach him how to dress appropriately for either cold weather or the workplace, and she'd long ago given up trying.

"'Sup?" Trent said.

"I told you, Trent, you don't have to work today."

"You did?" His gaze dropped to the floor. "Guess I forgot."

He moved over to his computer. Instead of leaving, though, he sat down. Trent's chair was draped with Mardi Gras beads. (They multiplied every year, though as far as Brenna knew, he'd never been to New Orleans.) His screen saver, which always changed, was currently a rear view of Kim Kardashian in a bikini. As long as it kept him happy, Brenna supposed, for Trent was smart and organized and a true prodigy when it came to computer investigation. He'd also nearly gotten killed as a result of their last case, and yet he hadn't complained or even spoken about it. If that meant his desk had to look like spring break in Fort Lauderdale, so be it.

"Seriously, Trent, you can go," Brenna said, though she was relenting a little. Brenna still had no idea what to do about Morasco's texts and didn't want to think about what was in the police papers, so the distraction of Trent and his overpowering cologne wasn't entirely unwelcome. But still . . . "I am not going to pay you overtime."

"You don't have to."

"I *don't*?"

"No . . . I . . . uh . . . you mind if I just sit here? Like . . . chillax for a few?"

"Uh, okay." Brenna sighed. "As long as you don't say 'chillax' anymore."

"Thank you," he said, which for Trent was . . . weird. Not just the phrase, which he hardly ever used, but the way he said it, like a chastised schoolkid. Brenna half expected a "ma'am" after it, and it hit her that he'd been acting that way ever since she'd come through the door. Reserved, serious—and, outside of the cheesy getup, very un-Trent-like. When he'd greeted her, he had even called her Brenna—not Spec or B. Spec or Spectator Sport or any of the other stupid nicknames he assaulted her with on a daily basis. Brenna. Her actual *name*. "Trent, is something wrong?"

"No. Why do you ask?"

Why do you ask?

"Oh, wait. I almost forgot. You got some messages." He tapped his mouse, and his sober-looking desktop replaced Kim Kardashian's barely covered ass, as though it were the next thought in someone's very strange stream-of-consciousness. He opened the message file. "Okay, first of all, you got a new client query."

"We can't take any new clients for at least three months."

"I know," Trent said, "but this lady seemed nice. Her son went missing seven years ago."

"What's her name?"

"Sophia Castillo."

Brenna nodded. "I know her."

"She didn't say she knew you."

"She doesn't." Just to make sure, Brenna asked for the woman's phone number and recited it, right along with her assistant.

"Whoa. That never doesn't freak me out."

Brenna closed her eyes, the memory starting to flood

her head . . . "She contacted me five years ago," she said. "February 15, 2005. Her son had been missing two years. A boy named Robert. I did a little research and found out Sophia Castillo had been divorced two years earlier, her husband had gotten full custody and taken the boy to El Salvador, where he's from. It's sad, but it's not a missing child case. I called her back. Told her I couldn't take it."

Brenna could feel the phone pressed to her ear on February 16, 2005. She could hear Sophia Castillo's sad, flat voice through the earpiece, all Xanax and loneliness. *I'm sorry to hear that, Ms. Spector.* Quickly, she pulled the journal out of her bag, and held it. The memory faded. *Thank you, Clea.*

Trent said, "I was working for you five years ago. Where was I during all this?"

"You were right here. You answered the phone when she called, transferred it to me. You were here when I called her back, too."

"I so don't remember that."

"Why would you?"

"But wouldn't she remember?" he said. "Why didn't she tell me that she's already talked to you?"

"I'm sure she doesn't remember that day any better than you do."

"But it's her son . . . Her . . . her own little kid."

"And I'm probably one of a dozen PIs she called. Five years ago. And I turned her down right away. Who, outside of me, would remember that?" Brenna exhaled. So often, she felt one step removed from the rest of the world, as though everyone were watching a movie, but she was the only one who could keep track of the plot.

"Just tell Mrs. Castillo we aren't taking any new cases right now," Brenna said.

"Kay-kay."

"What else?"

"Huh?"

"You said there were other messages?"

"Oh . . . yeah. Well, Faith called."

"Just now?"

"No, this morning. She said she wasn't going to be able to pick up Maya."

"Yeah, right, I got that, Trent, because I already dropped Maya off and Jim was there and not Faith."

"Good, so you got the message." Trent's gaze stayed glued to his computer screen.

Brenna stared down the back of his head. "So," she asked him. "Did you have a nice conversation with Faith?" This was the final litmus test. Trent, the Trent LaSalle who had worked for Brenna for six years, the Trent whom she often saw seven days a week and now knew better than most all her family . . . *that* Trent thought Faith was "smokin' sick hot," and even though she'd given him no reason, he'd recently come to the realization that "on, like, a sub-atomic level," Faith felt the same about him. *That* Trent couldn't resist any opportunity to inform Brenna that her ex-husband's wife of seven years "wanted his bod in the most cougarly of ways" and if it weren't for her loyalty to Jim, Faith would be on him "like hot wax on an Escalade."

"Sure," said Trent. "Faith was nice."

"Okay, what the hell is wrong with you?"

"Huh?"

"You're acting weird, Trent. You're willing to work a Saturday unpaid, and outside of chillax and kay-kay, you haven't said one idiotic thing since I got here. Plus you're being all polite and you're talking in full sentences and I gotta tell you, it's scaring the crap out of me."

"Brenna . . ."

"I mean it."

Trent sighed. Slowly, he turned his chair around to face Brenna, but his eyes stayed downcast. "I . . . I'm scared to tell you."

"That's not my problem."

"But—"

"Listen, if you don't grow a pair and tell me what's going on, you're out of here, do you understand me? I can't work with you like this. It's stressing me out."

"Okay, fine," he said. "You promise you won't judge me?"

"Why does everybody think I'm going to judge them? *I don't judge.*"

Trent closed his eyes, and Brenna noticed, for the first time since she'd known him, a few errant hairs poking out from the bridge of his nose. *He didn't wax his eyebrows today . . .*

"Brenna," Trent said. "I'm going to be a dad."

Actually, Trent didn't know for sure if he was going to be a dad. That was why he was scheduled to take a paternity test in less than an hour.

It had all started—as pretty much everything these

days had—with the Neff case back in September. Solving the high-profile case, involving a twelve-year-old disappearance and more than one highly placed public official in the insanely wealthy Westchester County suburb of Tarry Ridge, had landed Brenna (and Trent) on all the morning news shows, making them, for a time, into local celebrities.

Long before that, though, Trent had longed to be famous. If only he were famous, he used to say, he'd be "crushing more ass than an eighteen-wheeler on a donkey farm." So when the opportunity to be famous finally presented itself, the outcome wasn't hard to predict.

In late October, he'd gone to the wedding of an acquaintance from high school—some guy named Cooper whom Trent had never liked all that much, but hey, it was a wedding and, as Trent truthfully pointed out, "No one crushes it harder than a famous guy at a wedding."

Proving the point, Trent had gotten hit on beyond his wildest dreams—women calling him "hot" and "dreamy," women eyeing his moves on the dance floor and pressing into him as he got himself a drink and slipping their phone numbers into the waistband of his pants, all of them acting as though this happened to Trent all the time, sure it did, he was famous after all and this is what happened to famous guys . . .

But of all the women hurling themselves at Trent in the Staten Island banquet hall where the reception was being held, the one that thrilled him most was Cooper's cousin, Julia. Trent had been in love with Julia back in kindergarten, and he'd never truly gotten over her. And now, here they were, eyeing each other across the crowded room like the final scene in a Nora Ephron movie. (Yes, Trent had watched a couple of those movies with his mom and maybe cried a little, *so what?*)

Julia had approached Trent. "Want to dance?"

And Trent had said yes, their slow turn to a Bruno Mars song resulting in a moment that he would remember for the rest of his life: Julia in his arms in her blue bridesmaid's dress, looking up into Trent's eyes, time skidding to a halt.

Trent, she had said. *I've always kinda been into you*.

Recounting it now, Trent said, "I almost crapped my pants."

"Wow," said Brenna. "That's romantic."

But for Trent, it *was*. Later that night, he wound up consummating that breathtaking moment . . . not with Julia but with her friend Stephanie. ("She has a massive front porch," he explained.) And yesterday, Stephanie had texted Trent, telling him she was three months pregnant, and adding, *It's Maury Povich time*.

"I don't think I'm ready to be a father," Trent said.

He and Brenna were in the waiting room of the paternity testing place that Stephanie had sent him to—ClarkLabs—which, as it turned out, was just five street blocks away from their office.

It was, Brenna realized, her second waiting room of the day, and so much more bare-bones than Lieberman's. A handful of scuffed white plastic chairs, a wiry gray rug thrown over an ancient parquet floor, a couple of magazine racks, stuffed with brochures about fetal nutrition and unplanned pregnancy and STDs.

No beanbag chairs here. No glossy teen magazines or bright colors or stuffed animals staring out of baskets. This waiting room didn't pander to its visitors; it scolded them.

Trent's words hung in the air. *I don't think I'm ready.*

"One step at a time," Brenna said. "You don't even know anything until you take the test."

She glanced at the only other person in the waiting room—a serious-looking guy with big shiny eyes like black coffee poured into white saucers. He was slumped in the corner, either waiting for someone to get tested or waiting to be called, Brenna wasn't sure. He'd come in after Brenna and Trent, but she'd never noticed whether he'd signed in.

He wasn't all that young—closer to Brenna's age than Trent's, and he wore casual Friday clothes—a blue and white striped oxford shirt, khakis, loafers—as though he were coming in on his lunch break from some traditional job, even though it was Saturday. He didn't seem like the type to be an unintentional father. But the truth was, what the man *seemed like* didn't tell her anything. Anybody could be an unintentional father—that upstanding-looking, sad-eyed man or Trent or anybody in between, which proved to Brenna for the millionth time that nature was neither fair nor rational, that life didn't give you what you wanted, or even what you deserved. It just happened, like waves crashing over rocks until they lost all their sharp edges, until they looked more like dull clay and it was pointless to keep battering them, but still those waves kept at it, turning them to sand, and for no good reason at all.

Life just *was*.

Or, as Trent was fond of saying, *It is what it is.* Trent, who, when it all came down to it, would probably make a much better parent than either of Brenna's had been . . .

"Trent LaSalle?" The receptionist's voice cut off the memory.

Trent stood up. "Oh boy," he said, and for a moment, she looked past the spray tan and the "Orgasm Donor" T-shirt (not the ideal thing to wear to a paternity testing) and saw only the frightened eyes of a boy. "You'll be fine," she said. "No matter what happens. You can handle it."

Trent headed toward the waiting lab tech. *A better parent*, Brenna thought, her gaze on his tensed-up shoulders, *because he cares.*

As soon as he was out of the room, the memory reformed—two days ago. Brenna sitting on her bed, Nick Morasco next to her, the envelope in her lap.

"You know what's in here," Brenna says. "You've already read it."

"Yes."

"And you think I . . ."

"You should do whatever you want."

Brenna's mouth is dry. She's aware of the humming radiator and the itchy blanket beneath her bare legs, of Nick Morasco's hand at the small of her back. She wants to brush it all away. She slips the papers out of the envelope, skims over her father's name and address and her mother's name under witness. Her eyes scan the report and settle on one word. Every muscle in her body contracts—her thighs and her chest and her neck and her stomach. Especially her stomach. It

*hurts like a kick and she can't speak, she can't breathe.
All she can do is read the word.*

SUICIDE.

Brenna reached into her bag and pulled out the journal. She could feel Mr. Friday Casual watching her from across the waiting room, his gaze on her shaking hands.

Help me, Clea.

Brenna's breath came back as she opened the diary, words jumping out at her as she flipped the pages: *Ecstasy . . . Dream . . . So beautiful . . . Death . . .*

There were parts of this journal Brenna wouldn't read, parts she'd look at and slam the book shut—the parts where Clea talked about their father.

All these years, Brenna's mother had let her believe that their father had left them, that he'd started a new life somewhere and never called and never written because, as her mother put it, "He doesn't care about our family."

This had hurt Brenna, yes. But to have been lied to. To have been lied to all these years by her own mother about something like this, something this important . . .

Brenna could have looked into it. She was a missing persons investigator, after all. But as dogged as she was when it came to tracking down long-gone prostitutes or little girls who had wandered off from parties, as persistent as she was at finding elderly parents or billionaires who'd faked their own deaths or, for that matter, her own forever-missing sister, Brenna had never tried looking for her father. Not once.

He doesn't care about our family, her mother had said. And as untrustworthy as Brenna's mother could be, Brenna had taken her at her word. *He's gone*, she had thought.

We all believe what we need to believe.

Brenna had been just seven years old when her father had left them, and her memories of him were trapped in that fallible area of her mind from before the syndrome kicked in—everything hazier, growing more so by the year, none of it connecting at all.

Including her father's leaving them. *Especially* her father's leaving them. She had a dimming recollection of that morning, eggs sizzling in a frying pan, her mother in her green terry-cloth robe, her hair pulled back into a ponytail. Her mother's voice, so calm. *You girls are going to stay with your grandmother for a couple of weeks.*

Brenna didn't remember if either of them had asked why. But she did remember Clea asking to go into their father's workshop—a room off the garage where he kept the paints and woodworking equipment. She remembered because of her mother's reaction. *Don't you ever ask me that again*, she had said.

When Brenna and Clea had returned, every sign of their father had been disposed of—his clothes, his papers, every picture he'd been in or had taken. "He's gone," Brenna's mother had said. "He'll never be calling again."

And Brenna had never thought to ask, *How do you know? How can you be so sure?*

She'd sounded so positive, after all. Or maybe that was just the way Brenna remembered it, knowing what she did now. The present informing the past. She couldn't be sure of anything.

We all believe what we need to believe . . .

A year later, Brenna's mother had a huge slab of marble delivered to their house. For weeks and weeks, she'd chiseled away at it, the weeks running into months, months stretching out until finally she had completed her creation: an exact replica of Ammannati's Neptune—naked and muscular and incredibly embarrassing. "What the hell is that supposed to be?" thirteen-year-old Clea had asked.

Their mother had replied, "A man who won't leave."

Brenna's gaze focused on the diary page in front of her—the entry from July 15, 1979. She stared at Clea's handwriting, looping into a word: *Temple.*

"You know what a temple is?" That's what Mom asks me, like I'm five instead of fourteen. She says, "It's that soft part of your skull, right next to your eye." Duh, Mom.

She says, "He took the gun. It was a .45 caliber automatic pistol. He kept it in his workshop. Your father took that gun, Clea, and he pressed it to his temple, and he pulled the trigger, Clea. Right there in his workshop."

She says, "You want to know so badly? That's what happened to him." She says it's the truth, and that as hard as it is, I need to believe her.

Here's the thing, though. She said the same thing to me two years ago, back when she told us Dad had left: "It's the truth, girls. You need to believe me." So either way, she's a liar.

This is my dad, and I will never know for sure what happened to him. I don't know who to believe or who to trust and it kills me. It tears me up inside.

Please, Dad. Please CALL ME. Please call me and tell me you didn't mean to leave us. Please tell me you're alive and that you love me and show Mom for the LIAR she is.

Brenna slammed the diary shut.

She looked up to find Mr. Friday Casual, watching her as though she was insane. Brenna tried a smile. "Lousy book," she said.

The waiting room door opened, and Trent returned to her side. "Dunzo."

"That was quick."

"I know, right? They just scraped my cheek and kicked my ass out of there. I don't get to find out results for two freakin' days."

Brenna stood up. "Well at least you have two days where you don't have to think about it."

"Like that's gonna happen."

"Try."

"Hey," Trent said. "You okay?"

Brenna looked at him.

"You catch something while I was in there?"

"Uh. No."

"Well what happened to you?" Trent said. "Seriously, you look like hell. You'd think it was you that was going to maybe be a father."

The word swirled in Brenna's mind. *Father.*

Your father took that gun, Clea, and he pressed it to his temple . . . "I'm fine," she said. "Just a little tired."

"Me too," Trent said.

"Well in your case, that's understandable."

"Yep. Hey . . . Bren?"

"Yeah?"

"Do you think I'm an idiot?"

"No, Trent."

"I mean, for getting myself into this situation."

"I know what you mean."

"Are you just saying that because you promised you wouldn't judge?"

Brenna sighed.

"Don't answer. That was an unfair question," he said.

"Trent," said Brenna.

"Yeah?"

"You are one of the smartest people I've ever met."

Trent swallowed hard. "I'm . . . uh . . . I'm going to head home, I think. Maybe try and get a little rest. Is that okay with you?"

She pushed open the door, and then they were back on the sidewalk, the weak sun shining down on them, the cold slapping the sides of their faces. Trent crossed his arms over his chest, Brenna's gaze traveling to the lipstick print tattoo, just below his collarbone. God, she hated that tattoo. *Smart people do make stupid choices.* "It's fine with me," Brenna said.

Trent pulled her into a hug. She hadn't expected that, and for a second she was overwhelmed—not just by the sudden crush of waxed muscle and Axe spray and gelled hair spearing the side of her face, but by the very real emotion beneath.

"Thanks," Trent whispered.

He pulled away and sprinted down the street without looking at her. He was at the end of the block and crossing against traffic before Brenna even found the words to answer him.

"You're welcome."

Brenna hurried back to her apartment. The cold was really getting to her now. She had a case she'd planned to work on—a three-years-missing real estate agent from Scarsdale named Debbie Minton. But right now, all she wanted to do was crawl into bed with a blank mind and an Ambien. *Too much in one day*, thought Brenna, as she neared her building. *Too much emotion in one day.*

Too much revelation and danger.

By the time Brenna reached her building, she couldn't wait to sleep, to dream of something other than what her sister had written in her diary, what Brenna had seen in the police papers, her father with a gun at his temple and her mother at the kitchen stove, just hours after. *Hours after she'd found him, and yet so calm, so in control . . .*

Maybe, if Brenna was lucky, she wouldn't dream about anything at all.

Brenna trudged up the stairs. She felt very tired. She was glad, though, for the way her breath and footsteps echoed, the way neighbors' doors stayed closed. Brenna was going to make it all the way back to her apartment without having to speak to anyone, and that was about as good as she could ask for today.

Once she was a few steps away from her door, though, she noticed the bag.

Brenna sighed. Sometimes her upstairs neighbor would search for his keys on her floor, leaving personal items behind. *Really, Mr. Ericson? A bag of groceries?*

She peered into the brown paper bag—not groceries. Clothes and . . . other things . . .

Brenna slipped the clothes out of the bag—an old

pair of girls' blue jeans. Pink tennis socks. A red T-shirt—but pale and tired, as though it had been put in a time capsule that wasn't entirely airtight.

As she placed the T-shirt on top of the pants, Brenna saw the words on the front, the cracked black and yellow letters:

"Elvis Costello and the Attractions. My Aim Is True."

Brenna's breath caught in her chest. Her hands started to shake.

It couldn't be.

Quickly, she pulled the rest of the items out of the bag: A pink and white hair band. A purple Swatch watch, a portable sewing kit, a traveler's map of the U.S. . . .

A faded denim jacket with black lace sewn into the sleeves. *Oh my God.* Brenna knew this jacket like she knew the shirt. Better than the shirt.

Brenna had begged to borrow it for her sixth grade dance . . .

No way, weirdo. You'll spill punch on it, and then I'll have to kill you.

This was a joke. A strange, sick joke and it couldn't be. Not after all these years. Who had put this here? Where had it come from? Brenna said it out loud. "Who put this bag here?" Her voice echoing, the walls closing in . . .

But it could. It was. From the bottom of the bag, Brenna removed the final proof, as dull and faded as the past it came out of. "*Who put this here?*" said Brenna, louder this time, her voice shrill and hurt.

In her hands, Brenna held the driver's license of seventeen-year-old Clea Marie Spector, the expiration date: Clea's birthday, 1991.

3

The grocery bag read "Alpha Beta." Not a store that Brenna was familiar with—and, as she soon found out when she brought it into her apartment and Googled the name, not one that still existed. A West Coast chain, Alpha Beta had folded in 1995. The bag was a relic, along with everything inside it.

Brenna needed answers. Bags of twenty-eight-year-old clothes from long-defunct grocery stores more than a thousand miles away didn't get into locked buildings on their own. Someone had to have seen something, heard something. Someone had to have let this person in.

Brenna hurried back down the stairs. The idea was to start at the bottom of the building, work her way up, but when she got down to Mrs. Dinnerstein's apartment on the first floor, she found the door cracked open, the old woman peering warily out.

"You didn't need to shout," said Mrs. Dinnerstein, whose first name was Ina. Brenna knew this, not because she'd ever introduced herself, but because on February 8, 2005, Brenna had accidentally received a piece of Mrs. Dinnerstein's mail—an "urgent and personal" letter from Macy's credit department, addressed to Ina R. Dinnerstein, that she'd slipped under her downstairs neighbor's door without comment.

"Honestly," Mrs. Dinnerstein said. "It's really inconsiderate." Her voice was barely above a whisper, but still, there was a scolding in it.

A dim lamplight shone behind her, weaving through her thin white hair, making it glow a little. Brenna had lived and worked in this building for nearly seven years. In that entire time, this lamplight was the most she'd ever seen of the inside of Mrs. Dinnerstein's apartment.

Such a dark place to live. The thought made Brenna inexplicably sad. "Excuse me, ma'am. I didn't mean to bother you, but did you by any chance see anyone coming in with—"

"You could have simply knocked on my door, and asked if I'd seen anyone. You didn't need to shout it out to the entire building."

"I was . . . alarmed. Someone left a bag—"

"Some people in the building might be trying to sleep."

Okay, this is getting annoying. "It's two in the afternoon, Mrs. Dinnerstein."

"It's the weekend. A lot of people sleep in on weekend mornings."

Brenna tried not to roll her eyes. "I'm sorry to have bothered you."

"Wait." Mrs. Dinnerstein let out a long, rattling sigh. She was a tall woman—close to Brenna's height, and solidly built, yet she moved and spoke as though she were small and frail. Her eyes were a pale blue-gray, the irises barely distinguishable from the whites—

and never half closed, never sleepy. Frightened, really. That's how they always looked. Or rather, it was the way they looked when her gaze fell on Brenna.

Is she always scared, or is it me who scares her?

Slowly, Mrs. Dinnerstein extended her hand. Between her thumb and forefinger, she clasped a three-by-five card. Her fingers were trembling. "I thought I'd left this with the bag."

Brenna stared at her. "What?"

Mrs. Dinnerstein handed her the card without looking at her. "He was at the front door. He asked for you. I wouldn't let him in. I gave him the card and he wrote down his name and where he's staying."

"He?"

"Mr. Dufresne."

Brenna took the card from her hand. Plain block letters in ballpoint pen: ALAN DUFRESNE, along with a hotel name: PLAZA GARDEN SUITES.

The man's name meant nothing, but the hotel's did, and for a moment she felt herself slipping back into August 12, 2003—3 P.M., *the air conditioner humming at the back of her neck as she taps the number into her work phone, the receptionist answering, the squeaking young voice . . .*

"Plaza Garden Suites, may I help you?"

Brenna squeezed her eyes shut, well aware of Mrs. Dinnerstein's gaze on her, made herself stop remembering.

"Mrs. Dinnerstein?"

"Yes?"

"Why did you let me yell like that?"

"Pardon?"

Brenna looked at her. "Well, if you had this card, and you knew I was yelling about the bag, then why didn't you come upstairs and give it to me . . . you know, before I woke up the whole building."

"I assumed you'd know who left it," she said. "And I wouldn't have to . . . We wouldn't need to talk."

"How would I know?"

Mrs. Dinnerstein aimed the pale blue eyes at her, hard and opaque as marbles. "Because you were expecting him."

"What do you mean?"

Mrs. Dinnerstein took a step back. For the briefest of moments, Brenna saw the inside of the apartment. Her eyes widened. She couldn't help it.

"Mr. Dufresne . . ." The old woman started to say more, but stopped once she noticed Brenna's gaze on her coffee table, on the stacks of yellowed newspapers and magazines, on the curling bread wrappers and empty Kleenex boxes and plastic crates full of garbage, the clutter teetering off the edges of the table, burying chairs near-completely, settling onto the floor in unmanageable drifts . . .

Mrs. Dinnerstein's jaw went tight. She moved forward, blocking the mess with her body.

"Mr. Dufresne." She spat out the name. "He said he knows you."

Before Brenna could ask another question, Mrs. Dinnerstein slammed the door.

Plaza Garden Suites was on Fiftieth and Eighth—a clean, mid-sized modest hotel, frequented by theater-going families and middle management types who'd

missed the last train home. The lobby was dominated
by an electric blue rug and an eighties' modern chandelier that looked to be made of thousands of ice cubes.

Of course, all this information had been gleaned
from a seven-year-old memory—it could have easily
been renovated since August 12, 2003, when Brenna
had taken the 1 train there to meet a client by the name
of Ellie Dunn who had wanted to find her long-lost
father.

But as she sat on the 1 train now, the paper bag
from Alpha Beta sitting in her lap so very much like
the shoebox of Ellie's father's personal effects that
her new client had insisted she take with her, Brenna
couldn't help but feel the plastic seat at her back—not
the one from now, but the one she'd sat on nine years
ago, *Brenna's back sweaty in a yellow gauze sundress
she'd bought a year earlier at the Gap on Twenty-third
and Fifth, and she leans into it, feeling the damp gauze
between her shoulder blades, fighting a memory of
June 9, 2000,* Jim's back to her as he packed up his
suitcase . . .

"Stop crying, Brenna. Maya can hear."

Brenna pulled the journal out of her bag, clutched
it tight until the memory subsided and the electronic
voice announced the stop at Fiftieth Street, and she got
up and slipped out the door, blinking tears out of her
eyes, remembering the bag and what was in it. Remembering only her sister.

"Can you please ring Mr. Dufresne's room?" Brenna
asked the front desk clerk. As she'd expected, Plaza
Garden Suites looked very much the same—that ice

cube chandelier still in place, along with the long, lacquered front desk. But the rug was gone, the wide-planked floor now bare and polished, giving the place a slightly more upscale feel.

"One moment, ma'am," said the clerk, whose face was young and pleasant enough for her to get away with "ma'am."

Brenna's gaze wandered around the lobby, landed on the small faux marble bar, on the man sitting on one of the stools, nursing a lager, staring directly at her.

The clerk said, "May I have your name please?"

"That's okay. I think I might see him."

She turned and headed directly for the man at the bar, the man from the paternity testing lab. Mr. Friday Casual.

"You remember me," he said as she approached, his voice much lighter and more musical than his somber face let on. It was a salesman's voice. Friendly.

"Yes."

He smiled, the saucer eyes crinkling at the corners. "I figured you would. You know. Memory."

"You're Alan Dufresne?"

He nodded. "Your downstairs neighbor is quite a piece of work. I tried explaining to her that I needed to see you personally, but she wouldn't listen."

"You followed me to ClarkLabs?"

He nodded. "I thought I could talk to you then," he said. "I was going to do it while your friend was getting his test done, but . . . honestly you didn't seem much in the mood for talking."

"Well . . ."

"Was that Trent, by the way?"

"Uh . . . Yes."

"Looks exactly like I thought he would." He smiled. "I hope he's okay."

Brenna peered at him, this complete stranger. A man she'd never seen in her life before that exchange of glances at ClarkLabs, and yet his whole attitude—the relaxed posture, the familiarity with which he said Trent's name, the way he smiled so intently at her and lifted his glass—all of it said otherwise. "So good to see you." That, too. He said it as though he knew her well enough to mean it.

Who are you?

Brenna's heart pounded. She closed her eyes for a few moments, got her breathing back down to normal. She tried not to think of the bag in her hands, this twenty-eight-year-old bag, the faint mold-smell of the clothes inside, the feel of the paper, almost silky from age. She tried hard not to think of the long-expired driver's license or what lay with it—the keepsakes of a young girl, Brenna's sister, left for dead in a hotel room by a man who took her diary with him, nothing more. The purple plastic watch. The road map. These items, which, somehow, Alan Dufresne had come to own. *Clea's favorite jacket . . .*

She got all of that out of her mind and leveled her eyes at this smiling man and said something she'd never even *thought* about saying in the twenty-eight years she'd been hyperthymestic: "I'm sorry. Have we met before?"

He frowned. "Pardon?"

"I can tell you for a fact I've never seen your face before today."

"Well you haven't. But still . . ."

"Still, what?"

"You're Brenna Spector, right?"

"Yes."

"Your sister Clea ran off when you were eleven years old."

"Yes."

"You haven't seen or heard from her."

"Right. So?"

"So . . ." He took a swallow of beer. "We know each other."

Brenna exhaled, hard.

Obviously, he'd seen her on the news. He might have even seen her interview on Faith's show, *Sunrise Manhattan*, last fall, during which she'd gone far afield of the Neff case to discuss everything from her relentless memory to her own self-perceived failings as a mother, to Clea, forever-missing Clea, the ghost by her side and in her mind and all over her life. Faith was a damn good interviewer, and for Brenna, that had been a bad thing.

The e-mails she'd gotten. The phone calls . . .

It made Brenna understand why real, full-time celebrities tend toward paranoia. All these people out there, these strangers in their casual Friday clothes with their thousand-yard stares, acting as though they know you intimately—not just acting but truly *feeling* that way. And you've got no one but yourself to blame. How foolhardy is it to share so much of yourself on a screen, in front of so many unseen strangers, even showing them your tears . . . Giving them that much power over you? How dumb is that?

Brenna called the bartender over, ordered a beer, clinked bottles with Dufresne, and took a long, steadying swallow. She wanted to get up and leave him behind, but she couldn't, not now. *Just cut to the chase.*

"Why do you have my sister's things?"

He blinked at her. "You know why."

Nut job. Brenna brought the bottle to her lips again. "Why don't you humor me a little?" she said. "Tell me the whole story. Like we've never met."

He gulped his beer. "Brenna, when you saw me in the lab, you had no idea who I was, did you?"

"No."

"What did you think I was in there for?"

"I . . . well I assumed . . ."

"You thought I was at the lab for the same reason as your assistant."

"Well, yes. Who wouldn't?"

"You didn't think it had anything to do with you."

"Of course not."

"Isn't that strange?" he said. "You can look right at a person. You can look straight into their eyes, and yet still you have no idea what's going on behind them. Windows on the soul . . . what a bunch of crap that is, huh?"

He stared at her. She stared back.

"I'm not sure I understand what that has to do with my sister's things."

"My dad," he said. "I thought I knew him."

"Your dad?"

"My whole life, I looked up to him. I thought he was the most honest man I'd ever known. Turns out he was keeping secrets, right up until the day he died."

"What secrets?"

His huge black eyes settled on her, marble-hard. "You're messing with me now."

"I'm . . . I'm sorry, Alan, but—"

"*The bag.*"

"My sister's things?"

"I never knew he had a storage space. I have no idea how he knew your sister and I never will, because he never mentioned her name to us, not once."

"But he had all of her things."

"For thirty years. Imagine, Brenna. Imagine me getting that delinquent payment notice, addressed to him, four months after he died. Imagining me going all the way there and busting open that lock and finding a girl's clothing. A girl's driver's license."

Brenna watched his face, the dark eyes, brightening from pain. "Where was it?"

"Huh?"

"Where was the storage space?"

He blinked at her. "Utah."

"Pine City, Utah," Brenna said, because it had to be Pine City. Pine City, Utah was the place where Clea's diary ended. The place where, one month after leaving Bill and his blue car behind, Clea had met a boy on the road and fallen in love—only to be left for dead in a motel room.

For a moment, Brenna could feel the diary in her hands again, *the pages between her fingers as she flips to the very last page. Just three sentences, the ink strangely light on the paper, the pen barely touching it:*

Pine City is TOO SMALL. My hands keep shaking. I think I took too much.

"Brenna?" he said slowly. "I understand you want to test me, make sure I'm the same Alan Dufresne. But this is kind of cruel."

"Huh?"

"Why are you acting as if we haven't ever spoken?"

"We *haven't*."

"Maybe not in the real world," he said, that black gaze fixed on her face.

Brenna's jaw tightened. She felt her face going hot. "I'm getting tired of this."

"Tired of what?"

"Cut the crap, Alan. You're not crazy enough. I know those are my sister's things. But you know and I know that we've never breathed the same air before today, and whatever you know or think you know about me on a personal level is a news-created fantasy."

His eyes narrowed. He set his beer down on the bar and stared at it. "The safe deposit box was in Provo," he said, very quietly. "I told you that."

"When, Alan?" Brenna said, frustration rushing through her. "When did you *tell me that*?"

"In my last e-mail."

"*What?*"

"You're the one who needs to cut the crap, Brenna," he said. "We've been e-mailing for the past two weeks. You know it as well as I do."

4

This wasn't the Saturday that Faith Gordon-Rappaport had envisioned last night while falling asleep. Faith was used to that, of course. As much as she was a born planner, her job was, by nature, unpredictable—a fact that, over the years, she'd grown not only to appreciate but to love.

Interviews came through and fell through, front-running politicians dived headfirst into career-ending scandals, children went missing and starlets went crazy and tragedy struck at times and places you could never expect or imagine, never in your worst nightmares . . . And Faith had to stay on top of it all. Not only did it sharpen her skills as a broadcast journalist, it made her heart beat that much faster, made her appreciate the here and now that much more, knowing that, in an instant, everything could go so horribly wrong.

Back when she was a teen and doing pageants, Faith's coach, Kathy, used to call her a "rehearsal addict." "Most girls, I have to twist their arms trying to get them to practice," Kathy used to say. "But you, honey, you're just too prepared for your own good. How am I going to unlearn some spontaneity into you?"

Kathy couldn't, poor dear. Faith was by far the most overprepared, overrehearsed, boring piece of white bread ever to grace the pageant circuit, and she'd have been the first to admit it, even back then.

But Faith's job had succeeded where Coach Kathy had failed. It had taught Faith, once and for all, that a good eighty percent of life is beyond anyone's control, that it never does what you expect it to, and that all those crappy clichés about the best-laid plans are clichés for good reason. It was a lesson Faith was grateful for every day of her life—the ability to just "roll with it" so much more important than any trick or twirl or judge-beguiling answer she'd rehearsed to death during her Miss Teen Georgia days.

But still . . .

Today, Faith had been hoping for some normalcy. It was Jim's and her turn to have Maya for a few days, and she'd been looking forward to time alone with her stepdaughter at the handoff . . . Actually, she'd been counting on it.

It had been so long since Faith and Maya had talked, really talked, and she could feel this part of her life— the one sweet, simple thing she'd always been able to count on—she could feel it turning as unpredictable as the rest.

Last week, she'd twice caught Maya typing furiously on her laptop, only to switch screens and slam it shut when she realized Faith was in the room. Maya, who had never hidden anything from Faith before.

Faith had asked Maya what she'd been typing, of course.

And Maya had replied the way any teenager would: "*Nothing.*"

"Nicolai," Faith said to her cameraman as he took a light reading of her face. "Do you feel like you can tell your parents anything?"

He put the cardboard down and gave her a look like she'd just spoken to him in ancient Sanskrit.

"Are you serious?" he said.

Nicolai's peachy skin was half covered by unkempt dark beard and he wore glasses with thick black frames that Faith had always suspected were clear glass. He had an entire wardrobe of baggy flannel hunting shirts, wing-tip shoes and combat boots, mailman shorts, and brown UPS shirts and dress pants that were probably considered pathetically outré in the late seventies. Nicolai was a spoiled little boy who went to work in costume. Screw him.

"Yes, Nicolai, I'm serious."

"I'm twenty-four years old," he said, as though that was supposed to mean anything. Five years from now, he could *date* Maya, no one would bat an eye.

Faith sighed. "Point well taken."

She supposed she should talk to Jim about this. But maybe not. What if Maya had been writing in a journal, or complaining about her parents to a friend from school? She was a thirteen-year-old girl who had never seriously misbehaved—and with a mother, bless Brenna's heart, who remembered every misstep she ever made. Wasn't Maya entitled to her secrets? Wasn't everyone?

The lights were hot on Faith's skin. Not for the

first time, she felt as though her on-camera makeup were pressing against her, smothering her. There were downsides to this job—the long hours, the pressure, the lack of privacy, which was, of course, ironic. As a nosy, privacy-invading TV journalist, Faith had more stalkers than she'd had as a beauty queen.

None of it was conducive to family. Maybe it was time to rethink this job, take a little hiatus, dedicate herself to being a full-time stepmom . . .

God, Maya would probably hate that, which was sad. Couple of years ago, it would've made her the happiest little girl in the world, which just goes to show, you can't put things off when it comes to kids. If you don't seize the moment and ride it for all it's worth, they'll outgrow you.

They'll leave you behind.

Faith needed to focus. Here she was, thinking of family issues while sitting in the Bensonhurst home of Ashley Stanley, "get" of the year.

Ashley Stanley, who had been held captive for ten years by husband-and-wife sadists Charles and Renee Lemaire. She'd been twenty-three when she was escaped a year ago, and unlike Elizabeth Smart and Jaycee Dugard, she never had the satisfaction of seeing her tormentors brought to justice. By the time Ashley had given the police directions to the home where she'd spent all of her teen years, often gagged and shackled under the bed while the couple entertained unwitting dinner guests, the Lemaires had escaped.

Ashley lived alone. Her mother—her only family—had died four years ago, and with the Lemaires still at large, she'd imposed on herself a new type of captivity:

doors triple-bolted, blocked ID on her phone, natural blonde hair dyed mud brown. She maintained no close friendships, didn't do social media. She didn't even have an e-mail address.

And she had never given an interview. It had taken months for Faith and her producers to coax this poor, terrified girl out of hiding. In fact, Faith might not have had an interview with Ashley at all if, after seeing the sensitive way she'd treated Brenna on camera, Ashley hadn't agreed to have lunch with Faith.

A lunch that, sadly, had turned into yet another horror. Despite taking every precaution possible to keep it under wraps, the two women had been snapped three weeks ago at the Capitol Grille in midtown. The photo had appeared everywhere—and, figuring she had nothing to lose, sad, trembling Ashley had finally agreed to the interview. ("May as well," she'd said.) And here, Faith was secretly angry she'd switched from tomorrow to today?

How selfish could she be?

From behind the camera, Nicolai said, "Makeup says Ashley will be ready in five to seven minutes."

Faith nodded. She thought of the thick scar down the left side of Ashley's pretty face and wondered how makeup was doing with that.

She looked around the living room of Ashley's small, pine-scented apartment as if she were seeing it for the first time—blond-wood furniture, blue cloth couch, polished floors. No personal pictures, no artwork. A bookshelf that was bare, save for a few pastel candles in votives and an empty ceramic vase that looked as though it had been bought out of the same catalog as everything else, and at the same time, too. Everything simple and spotless and not in any way personal.

Anyone could live here. Anyone at all.

"Rosella says you have a call," Nicolai said.

Rosella, Faith's assistant, was waiting outside with the rest of the crew. Ashley had wanted only Faith in the apartment for the interview, relenting only for Nicolai because someone had to work the camera.

"Can she take a message?"

Nicolai shrugged. "She says it's one of Maya's teachers."

"On a Saturday?"

He shrugged again.

Faith got up and smoothed her suit. She had an odd sensation, a fluttering in her stomach, a weakness in the knees as though the ground was shifting beneath her, something changing and she couldn't stop it . . .

Why was Maya's teacher calling her at work? Of course Maya's teacher would have no idea Faith was at work—it was just a cell phone number, pure and simple, on file with the school for when she couldn't be reached on the landline.

But . . . *why?*

The image fluttered back into her mind: Maya, slamming her laptop shut. That look in her eyes . . .

What is she hiding? Is she in some kind of trouble?

Outside Ashley Stanley's freshly painted front door, Rosella was waiting on the stoop, looking up at Faith with her dark, seen-it-all eyes. The rest of the crew was buzzing around the news van and trailer, parked at the curb. Faith stole a quick glance at the trailer, where Ashley was getting her makeup done.

"Maya's teacher?" she said.

Rosella nodded, handed her the phone.

Faith took the phone and said her name into it.

"Faith Gordon-Rappaport?" The voice confused her. It was either a man's, soft and lilting, or a woman's, deepened by years of smoking. Either way, she'd never heard it before. And Faith was sure she'd met all of Maya's teachers. "We have to talk," it said.

Faith cleared her throat. "Is there something wrong?"

"Maya. She's a sweet girl." *A woman*. Faith was ninety percent sure.

"Which teacher are you? I don't believe we've spoken before."

"You shouldn't let her out."

"Excuse me?"

"She'll ask to go out. She thinks she's old enough. She's not. Keep her home."

She looked at Rosella. "Did she *say* she was Maya's teacher?"

The girl nodded. "Math."

Maya's math teacher was a man. And British. Faith glanced at the screen. It read "Restricted Call." "Who is this?"

"I see you with her. I know you love her. You're a good mother."

"Who *are* you?"

"I watch you, so I know."

Christ. Another stalker.

"Don't let her go out. It won't be good for anyone if you do."

Faith said, "Listen. I don't know how the hell you got this number . . ." but then she stopped. The line was dead, the call ended.

For several seconds, Faith felt a dead weight in the pit of her stomach, chills up her back. The lingering feel of a stranger, saying her daughter's name. She stood there, staring at the phone, letting the feeling pass. This stalker hadn't been the first to know of Maya, and she wouldn't be the last. Faith couldn't help but feel a little shaken, but compared to some of the other calls she'd gotten, this one was kids' stuff. Some old chain-smoking prude who'd seen pictures of Faith and Maya in one paper or another, asking her favorite TV host not to let her daughter go out in the world. *I see you with her . . . You're a good mother.*

Rosella said, "Are you okay?"

Faith smiled at her. "Sure, honey."

"That wasn't her teacher, was it?"

She shrugged. "Nope," she said. "Loyal viewer."

"I'm so sorry."

Faith held a hand up. Rosella had only been working for her for a few weeks. "No worries," she said. "No more calls though, okay? If it's the pope, take a message. Ashley needs my undivided attention."

She nodded.

Almost as an afterthought, Faith stole a quick glance up and down the sidewalk. An older woman pushing a baby carriage, huddled against the cold. Three teenage boys in baggy clothes, talking to a friend in a parked car. No one of note. No one "watching." Of course not. That caller was full of it. Talking about Maya as if they were best pals. *Honestly, they read one* Ladies' Home Journal *article, these creepy fans think they know everything about you.*

Including your cell phone number.

Before she opened the door, Faith closed her eyes. *Deep breath. Out with the bad, in with the good . . .* She exhaled first, then inhaled very slowly. It was something a Pilates teacher had taught her years ago, and she could swear it lowered the blood pressure, increased the flow of serotonin and whatever other chemicals the body produced to make the brain relax enough to do its job. One more breath—a cleansing breath, the teacher had called it—and she was focused. Here, now. Faith couldn't care less how the caller had gotten her number, and the only safety she feared for was that of Ashley, her interview subject.

If they only knew how much power they had, Pilates teachers. Faith swore they could run the world.

In her room at Dad and Faith's, Maya made sure her door was locked before she went online and logged onto her chat room. Immediately, LIMatt61 said, **Where the hell have you been?** Because he was like that, always pouncing.

Of course, Maya couldn't blame him. She hadn't been on in days.

Sorry, she typed. **I've been hanging out with a new group of kids.**

LIMatt61 typed: **And, that makes a difference because?????** *Five question marks? Really, LIMatt61?*

NYCJulie cut in with: **What did your mom's shrink say?**

Maya typed: **I couldn't figure out how to ask.** She knew she should say more before they all started giving her advice, or, worse yet, scolding her. (One of the biggest drawbacks to being the youngest person in a chat room. Everybody treated you like a kid.)

Sure enough, Matt typed in: **You would have been more prepared if you weren't spending so much time goofing off with your friends.**

Maya sighed. She typed: **Sorry.** She started to type that she wanted to get to know the psychiatrist first before she started asking him probing questions about her own mother, but then her phone burped. She cringed.

Maya had picked out the burp text tone when she'd gotten the phone—her then-best friend Zoe had discovered it and played it for her, the two of them laughing hysterically for probably ten minutes straight. She'd downloaded it on the spot, but for the past week, Maya had been torn between not wanting to hurt Zoe by changing it, and living in fear of getting texted in front of Lindsay.

She switched the phone to vibrate, then checked her screen.

A text from Lindsay. *Want to sleep over tonite?*

Maya stared at the words. Lindsay Segal. Asking her to sleep over. She read it three more times, just to make sure she hadn't gotten it wrong.

The problem was, she already had plans to stay at Zoe's. Zoe had invited her two weeks ago.

Maya texted Lindsay: *Don't know if I can.*

On her computer screen, another text: *Come on pleaseeeeeee? No parents! Just us girls!*

Whoa. Maya thought of Lindsay, typing in all those Es. And *just us girls?* Why didn't she have a date with

Miles? Maya almost texted her that question, but she quickly thought better of it. Lindsay seemed like the jealous type—not that she would ever think to be jealous of someone like Maya.

Maya's computer beeped. She glanced at it, to see a private message from NYCJulie: **Don't listen to Matt. You're young. You deserve to have fun. Spend time with your friends while you still have them**. Maya smiled. She liked NYCJulie so much.

She wrote her back: **Lindsay wants me to stay over tonight.**

The popular girl? Awesome! And don't worry. We'll still be here when you get back.

Maya thought for a few moments, then texted Zoe: *I can't come tonite. Dad making me go to family thing. :(*

Zoe replied right away: *Srsly?*

Yep.

No answer.

For good measure, Maya sent another sad face.

Still no answer.

Maya got a third text from Lindsay: Three question marks.

She typed: *I'll be there.*

Yay! Get over here nowwwww

Maya's heart pounded. She had a bag all packed for Zoe's, but she emptied it out, going over each item of clothing individually—the boring pajamas, the boring jeans . . . Maya grabbed the pink sweater she'd bought at Forever 21—the one Nikki had said looked cute on her—and changed into it, along with her tightest pair of skinny jeans. Then she started going through every-

thing else in her closet, looking for something, anything that was remotely Lindsay-worthy.

Nothing. But she did have some clothes that at least
weren't embarrassing. As she searched for them and
threw them in the bag, Maya forgot about everything
else in the room, in her life. She didn't notice the computer beeping, her chat room friends asking where the
hell she'd gone off to, NYCJulie explaining, LIMatt61
more irritated than ever, but ClaudetteBrooklyn20 de-
fending her: **Give her a break, Matt. She's only a kid**.

And, once she was fully packed and she'd logged out
of the chat room, once she'd shoved the phone in her
pocket and grabbed her bag and her favorite blue coat
with the brass buttons that her mom had bought her at
Urban Outfitters three weeks ago after so much begging, once she'd gone through the obligatory exchange
of hugs and explanations and phone number with Dad
(who really didn't seem to care who Lindsay Segal was,
deep as he was into some newspaper story he was writing), once she'd rushed out of the apartment, down the
elevator, through the lobby, and up Seventh Avenue
toward Lindsay's apartment, the sun already starting to
set . . . Once Maya had done all of that, only then did
she stop in the middle of the sidewalk and take a few
moments to think about what was going on in her suddenly, weirdly, out-of-the-blue exciting life.

"Amazing," she whispered.

But Maya didn't let herself think for too long. After
all, she had a sleepover to get to.

Just us girls.

She took off fast toward Lindsay's, determined not
to be late. So determined, in fact, that she didn't notice

the blue car tailing her up Seventh Avenue and then left at Twenty-sixth, the cold wind blowing in her face as she wove around slow walkers, her breath quickening, her face easing into a smile. She didn't notice the driver, watching. Watching it all.

"Are you sure you want to do this?" Faith said. She heard Nicolai let out an exasperated sigh and somehow managed to restrain herself from getting up, walking over to the camera, and slapping him across the face. If he was ever going to form a relationship with something that didn't have a lens cap, this child needed to work on his empathy skills. Big-time.

Ashley Stanley trailed a hand across her eyes. A tear trickled down her scarred cheek. "I'm sorry," she said. So strange. Ashley was a grown woman, but she still had the high, frail voice of a little girl—as though the Lemaires had trapped her voice inside her, stunted its growth. "I didn't know it would be this hard."

"Of course it's hard, honey," Faith said. "You take as long as you need."

Ashley breathed, the breath filling and leaving her chest in halted gasps.

Faith wanted to look away. How horrible it felt, to watch another person cry like this, a fragile young girl, and not be able to hold her.

"At night, I keep seeing their faces. I can't sleep without dreaming about them. It's like they're still with me. Just like they said they'd be."

"The Lemaires."

"Yes. They said no one ever leaves them. Not really."

Faith swallowed hard. "No one."

The girl nodded.

"So there were others? Before you?"

"I think so."

"With you?"

"Can we do the interview again?"

Faith nodded. She handed Ashley a Kleenex and waited till she gave her the signal, and glanced over at Nicolai. Her own hands were trembling now. Her stomach felt weak. The way Ashley's voice sounded, the lilt of it . . . at certain times, she sounded so much like . . .

"Rolling," Nicolai said.

Ashley said, "You can ask me that question again."

"Are you sure? We can skip it if you like. Move on."

"No. Please. Ask it. I need to answer it."

Faith placed her hand over Ashley's. She looked into the blue eyes and felt tears coming. Faith, the complete professional, the planner. Faith, who had never cried, not even when she won Miss Georgia. Not even on her wedding day to Jim, or when the doctor told her she'd never be able to have children of her own . . . Faith, who didn't cry, not ever, because crying was for the weak.

Faith shut her eyes. She took a few Pilates breaths and told herself that when she opened them, she'd be looking at Ashley Stanley, a grown woman and a stranger. Not a child. Not her little girl.

Not Maya.

Ask her the damn question.

"Ashley," Faith said. "What made you get into the Lemaires' car?"

"I was lost."

"I know," Faith pushed on. "Let's retrace that day, okay?"

She nodded.

"You'd gone to the movies with your friend and her boyfriend, but you felt like a third wheel."

"Yes."

"You snuck out of the theater, and you figured you'd walk home, but once you were into the mall parking lot, you realized home was a lot farther away than you thought it would be."

"Yes."

"And it was getting dark."

"Yes."

"Then, out of the blue, Mrs. Lemaire pulled up."

"Yes."

"She was the only one in the car."

"Uh-huh."

"So, tell me, honey. You're a smart girl. When she rolled down the window and asked if you needed a ride, what was it about this woman—this stranger you'd never seen before—that made you get into the car with her?"

Ashley shook her head. "I *had* seen her."

Faith looked at her. "Excuse me?"

"I'd seen her before, at the same movie theater. I'd seen *Notting Hill* and my friends were teasing me because I cried. She told me not to listen to them. She was crying, too. She was . . . she'd gone with her . . . her husband. Date night, she said . . . First date night since their baby was born . . ."

"Oh my God."

"Yep," Ashley managed a weak smile. "She lied about having a baby. Wish I could say that was the worst thing she'd done. But when she pulled up in the car . . ."

"She wasn't a stranger."

A tear trickled down Ashley's cheek. She brushed it away.

"You felt safe with her."

"Later . . . at her home . . . she said they chose me that night. When she saw me at *Notting Hill*, when she saw my friends making fun of me, she told Charles . . . She said she told him, 'She's the one.' She said, 'We chose you, and you're happy now.'"

Faith's mouth felt dry. She needed to move on to life in the Lemaires' house of horrors—she only had fifteen minutes with Ashley, and had to give her viewers what they wanted. But all she could think of was that young girl, a girl Maya's age, shedding a few tears over a romantic film. A girl in a movie theater with her friends, a normal child, completely unaware that her life was about to be destroyed by that nice lady on her date night—that lady who told her it was okay to cry.

Faith made herself say, "I'm gonna ask you a few questions about the house." But she couldn't wait until her fifteen minutes with Ashley were up, and she could escape. *I'm so lucky*, Faith thought. *I need to be more grateful.* And she wanted to show it. She wanted to take off this thick TV makeup and hurry home to her apartment and to her beautiful little family. She wanted to feel her husband's arms around her—have a date night of her own. But first she wanted to catch Maya before she went to Zoe's for her sleepover. She just had to hug that sweet girl for all she was worth.

5

Alan Dufresne wasn't lying about his father. On one of the computers in the Plaza Garden Suites business center, he logged into his e-mail and showed Brenna the correspondence he'd exchanged four months after his father's July death with the credit department of WeKeep Storage in Provo, Utah, the representative informing him that Roland Dufresne had indeed maintained a space there since October 2, 1981.

"My mother had no idea he'd even *been* to Provo," Alan told Brenna. "She asked me to go there and open it. I have two other brothers but out of all of us, I was closest to my dad."

"So you did."

Alan gave Brenna a look, as though traveling from his home in Sacramento, California, to Provo on a moment's notice to check out the contents of a storage space was a no-brainer, which, of course when Brenna thought about it, it was.

"What was your mom afraid she'd find in it?"

He shrugged. "Gifts from some secret girlfriend probably."

"Nothing worse?"

Alan turned to Brenna, the saucer eyes deep and sad. "My dad was a truck driver. He was gone a lot of the time, and you know what they say about truckers on the road. But he wouldn't *hurt* anyone. My mom knew that and so did . . . I *still* know that. My dad was a great father and a good man."

He'd already said that—not to Brenna but to the person who'd been writing him for the past two weeks, claiming to be her. *I know it sounds bad, Brenna. But my dad wouldn't hurt anyone. He was a great father and a good man.*

He'd shown Brenna those e-mails first—a steady exchange of them, increasingly friendly and confidential, between himself and BrennaNSpector@hotmail.com. It was not Brenna's e-mail address—she'd never had a Hotmail account. But her middle name did begin with the letter N. And sitting there behind the closed glass door of the hotel business center, reading the e-mails one by one, the real Brenna Nicole Spector had felt as though the floor beneath her had dropped away, and she was sinking into something thick and deep and inhospitable. A quicksand of confusion. It had become hard for her to breathe. It was hard still.

This person knew things about Brenna. Personal things. I *know you've never met my assistant, Trent,* she'd said in one e-mail, *but trust me. He's a real character.* In another, she noted that she had "a very close friend" on the police force in Tarry Ridge. In several she mentioned Maya. Most of the information, of course, could have been gleaned from the media over the past couple of months.

But not all of it.

Brenna's eyes were focused on the credit department e-mail, but her mind was scrolling back, into a
memory from just fifteen minutes ago, of reading the
sixth and final e-mail from BrennaNSpector, sent just
yesterday . . .

*Alan, I know how hard that must have been for
you—discovering that your father kept secrets. My
father kept secrets, too. He tried to be a good father,
and I remember him that way. But I've since found out
he was deeply disturbed. A sad, sick man . . .*

Brenna whispered, "How does she know *that*?"

"Who?" Alan said. "The credit rep from WeKeep?"

She blinked. "No. I was talking about the person
who was e-mailing you. The one pretending to be me."

"Oh."

"That stuff about her father."

"It's true?"

"It may be." Brenna exhaled. She looked into the
dark, sad eyes of the son of Clea's . . . *Lover? Abductor? Trusted friend? Killer?*

And it hit her that this man—not Nick Morasco,
not Trent, not even her mother—this corporate lawyer
from Sacramento, whom Brenna had met via a bag of
her sister's belongings, would be the first person she
would say the words to out loud.

"My father committed suicide when I was just seven
years old," she said. "I have the police papers."

"I'm sorry."

"That isn't the point, though. The point is, I only
found out about it when I *read* the police papers. That
was two days ago."

"I don't understand."

"My mother lied to us. I'd always believed he'd just left home."

He frowned at her. "So this person . . . The one who's been writing me—"

"Knows more about me than I do," Brenna said. "Or at least, she's known it for longer."

"Or he."

Brenna cleared her throat. "It could be a he. Could be anybody."

Alan shook his head. "It's a brave new world we live in."

"Huh?"

"Internet hacking, identity theft . . . Heck, if that person could break into that Snapfish page and change your e-mail contact info, then who's to say they couldn't go into the police records and find out about your dad before you were ever able to read them?"

"Snapfish page?"

"Um . . ."

"What Snapfish page?"

"You're joking, right?"

She leveled her gaze at him. "I haven't joked once since I got here, Alan."

"I'm talking about the missing persons Snapfish page," he said, very slowly. "The one you posted the picture of your sister on."

Brenna stared at him. *"What?"*

Without saying any more, he logged onto Snapfish and called up the page: a collection of personal photos titled, "MISSING LOVED ONES." He scrolled down the page, photos of tiny children and smiling brides and strapping young men, the captions slipping fast up the screen like movie credits. So personal, so full of loss. *Beloved Dad . . . Missing since 2001 . . . 1995 . . . Have you seen our daughter? We think about him every day . . . Gone from our lives but not our hearts . . .*

Alan stopped scrolling at a picture of a smiling blonde girl.

Clea.

Brenna couldn't speak. Her eyes stayed fixed on the screen—on the picture of Clea, aged sixteen or seventeen, standing in their kitchen back in City Island, smiling in front of their mother's light blue cupboards. Robin's egg, their mother had called the color. She'd always been so specific about it.

In the photo, Clea's long hair was in a ponytail. She wore a red T-shirt with a pink heart on it, the collar cut off. She wore her favorite denim jacket with the black lace sewed on. Brenna felt the weight of the grocery bag in her lap, the weight of that same jacket. "My God," she whispered.

"I never went to the police to find out who she was. I was too . . . My dad . . ."

"I understand."

"But I did go online a lot, looking for missing persons pages. There are hundreds of them. When I found this one, I recognized her immediately," Alan said. "You could just imagine my reaction, especially when I saw what she was wearing."

There must be an explanation, Brenna thought. *Something simple I'm overlooking. There has to be, please . . .*

"Brenna?"

"I didn't post that picture. I've never seen that page before."

He gaped at her, saying nothing.

Brenna just nodded. *Thanks for not asking me if I'm kidding.*

"Who could have done this?"

"I wish I knew."

"So strange," Alan said. "I never let . . . that person . . . know that I was coming to New York. It was a last-minute trip—a client flew me out. I had told her I'd send her the bag, but she still hasn't e-mailed an address."

"Can you give me the address once she sends it?" Brenna said.

"Sure."

"And can you do me another favor?"

"Yeah?"

"Keep writing her. Act like nothing's wrong."

"That will be hard."

"I know."

"Wish I could ask her where the hell she got that picture."

Makes two of us, Brenna thought, all the while slipping into August 31, 1990, *lugging her heavy, dark blue vinyl suitcase to the front door of their house on her way to freshman orientation at Columbia. A car horn outside their door: Two honks, short and polite.*

Brenna says, "Must be the cab."

"Wait," Mom says.

Brenna doesn't want to. The air-conditioning's out again and the air in the house is slow and thick and hard to breathe, and besides, she hates the idea of saying good-bye to Mom. Not of leaving her. The actual act of looking into Mom's eyes and telling her good-bye.

She turns. Mom is standing closer than she thought. Brenna tenses up, and Mom pulls her into a hug.

Brenna hugs her back. Maybe I don't have to say it. Maybe I don't have to say anything at all.

Mom's skin feels cool and sticky. She presses her cheek against Brenna's and it's wet. Brenna wonders whether it's sweat or tears. In her mind, Brenna asks: Do you love me?

"Here," Mom whispers. She slips something into Brenna's hand.

Brenna pulls away to see it—a slim white envelope. She opens it up. There's a check inside. Five hundred dollars.

"That should get you through the first quarter."

"Thank you, Mom."

There's something else in the envelope. A picture. Brenna sees Clea's face in it and looks up, into Mom's eyes.

Mom nods.

"I didn't know you kept that picture."

"Of course I kept it," Mom smiles. It's a hard smile. "You took it, Brenna. I've saved every picture you've taken."

Alan said, "Brenna?"

She dug her fingernails into her palms, and she was back in the present, staring at the picture, at the caption: "MISSING SINCE 1981."

"Had you ever seen that picture before?"

She turned her gaze to Alan. "I was the one who took it."

Once she got home, Brenna tried to remember taking that picture of Clea. Like all of her memories of her older sister, though, it was dim in her mind and fading still. Clea stopping to pose in their mom's kitchen on her way out to . . . what? A birthday party, maybe? A night out with friends?

Clea hated to be photographed, Brenna remembered that much. Used to throw her hands in front of the camera like a movie star evading paparazzi. Of course, it could have just been *Brenna's* camera she wanted to evade. In her teens, Clea had found her little sister so annoying that their mother used to scold her for it—and you could actually *see* it in the kitchen picture, the way she stared down the camera: the flat eyes, the too-wide, get-it-over-with-already smile. *Was I too young and dumb to notice, or did I just not care?*

Brenna put the bag of Clea's things down on her work desk, along with the business card Alan Dufresne had given her. Then she started through the kitchen, down the hallway, and into her bedroom, all the while lapsing back into a memory she knew would never fade—September 30, 2009. Just last fall, returning home and getting ready for bed after her first meeting with her then-client, Nelson Wentz . . .

Brenna slips her black sweater over her head, lays it on the bed and folds it, Wentz's voice still in her brain, the insistence in it, the powerless anger.

Carol doesn't have anything she wants to keep from me.

Brenna has the same thought she had an hour ago, in the Wentzes' sad, pristine house. How hard does someone have to work to be in that type of denial?

She yanks off her boots, unbuttons her jeans, slips them down to her stockinged ankles, and kicks them off. As she folds them, Brenna allows herself to think of the photograph on the far left side of in the slim drawer at the top of her dresser, empty save for the photo and small stack of envelopes.

She pads over to the dresser and slips out the photograph, looks at it for the first time in eight months. Such a frail thing, this photo, dull and faded as Brenna's memory of taking it. She runs her thumb over Clea's face. She doesn't look annoyed anymore. In fact, she barely looks human, the features so time-softened that she's almost two-dimensional . . . a drawing.

Brenna places the picture in the drawer, slides it all the way to the back, pushes it shut. Maybe I'm in denial, too, *Brenna thinks.* Maybe Clea isn't alive and out there somewhere. Maybe that's just something I tell myself, like Nelson Wentz tells himself that his wife has nothing to hide . . .

Brenna was in her bedroom now. She dropped her handbag on the bed and slid her hand in to touch Clea's journal, to bring herself back. Then she walked up to her dresser and opened that slender drawer for the first time since September.

She let out a gasp.

The thing about having a perfect memory is, you always remember where you put things. Exactly.

Brenna often wished she had a dollar for every person who said, upon hearing of her disorder, "If I had your memory, I'd never misplace my keys again." (And while we were at it, why did so many people keep misplacing something as important as their keys?) But it was true. Brenna always knew where her keys were. She always knew where everything was . . . or at least, where it was supposed to be.

On September 30, 2009, Brenna had put the picture of Clea in the very back of the drawer. It was now at the front of it.

"It's Brenna," Jim was reading off the caller ID screen, and his voice tripped over the name. Faith had just gotten home, Ashley Stanley all over her brain. She'd hugged her good-bye. Ashley hadn't hugged back. Faith was pretty sure Ashley wasn't a big fan of bodily contact, a sweet girl like her, so deserving of a hug. And that made her situation even sadder. Ashley had so many worse scars than the one on her face.

Saying good-bye to Ashley, Faith had thought again of Jim and Maya, her beautiful, healthy family. For a moment, she'd flashed on the phone call she'd gotten before the interview: *She'll ask to go out. She thinks she's old enough. She's not* . . . But she'd quickly dismissed it.

She'd hopped into a cab and gone home without even bothering to take off her stage makeup, envisioning it all in her mind—the warmly lit apartment, her husband and stepdaughter waiting for her. She'd pictured herself rushing in and hugging them with all her might, holding them close, telling them how lucky she was to have them in her life . . .

Only to hear that Maya had already left for her sleepover. Why didn't anything ever look the way you'd planned it in your mind?

"How did the interview go?" Jim had said. And then, before she could answer, the phone rang.

"Hi Brenna."

"Hey, Faith. Listen, I need to talk to Maya."

"Get in line."

"Huh?"

Faith sighed. "Nothing. Just . . . rough workday."

"I hope your interview went well."

Faith took a breath, thought about explaining but realized she couldn't, that swirl of emotions in her head, none of it logical . . . "Brenna," she said. "Is everything okay with Maya?"

Brenna sighed. "Yes. Yes, I'm sure she's fine. I didn't mean to sound so dire. It's just . . . something was misplaced in my apartment and I wanted to talk to her about it."

Faith's turn to sigh. Nothing against Brenna. But that memory of hers . . . Honestly, when Faith was Maya's age, she had a bottomless supply of binder paper reinforcements, an alphabetized CD collection, and a color-coded closet, but if her mother had known for a fact every time she'd misplaced something and *called her on it* . . . well, let's just say there just wasn't enough Xanax in the world . . .

"Sorry, honey," Faith said. "Maya's at a sleepover at her friend Zoe's. But if you want to call or text her, I'm sure she'll get back to you."

"Okay. Sorry to bother you."

Faith frowned. Had she sounded curt? "You never

bother me, Brenna," she said. "And I'll tell you what, I wish she was around, too. That girl's been spending too much time with her friends lately."

"Agreed," Brenna said. "Take care, Faith . . . and say hi to . . ." Her voice trailed off.

"I will, honey."

Faith hung up.

"What was that about?" Jim said.

"I guess Maya misplaced something of hers."

"Ah."

"And she told me to tell you hi."

A look passed over Jim's face, an emotion Faith couldn't quite define.

Interesting, ever since she'd married Jim, Faith had spent so much time trying to make things easier on his ex-wife. Knowing how much the sight or sound of him hurt Brenna, Faith had positioned herself as a go-between, discussing everything that needed to be discussed about Maya, dealing with the joint custody handoffs, careful to never even say Jim's name out loud around her.

And then, last December, Brenna and her assistant had gotten carjacked and nearly killed. Maya had found out about it and called Jim and when Brenna returned home, her ex-husband had been there, waiting for her with her daughter.

Faith had been on assignment, but when she'd called Brenna's place, all she could think was *Oh, poor thing. To have her life threatened like that and then come back to Jim . . .*

But she hadn't thought about how Jim had felt. What had the sight of Brenna done to him? He'd never talked about it, other than to say how relieved *Maya* was to see her, which, when Faith thought about it, was strange. Wasn't it? He goes face-to-face with his ex-wife for the first time in easily seven years, and doesn't tell his current wife one word about how it felt? Faith recalled the way his voice had cracked when he said Brenna's name, then shook the thought out of her head. *Some ideas need to be killed before they grow into anything.*

"Lindsay, not Zoe," Jim said.

"Huh?"

"Maya's plans changed at the last minute. She's staying at her friend Lindsay's. She left the number."

"The one she helped with that art project?"

"An older girl—a junior I think. Kid's getting so mature."

"I still see her as a six-year-old, though," Faith said. "I guess I've got to work on that."

"Me too." He smiled. "Or maybe she'll just have to deal with it."

Faith looked into his eyes, the warmth. It had been Jim's eyes that first hooked her and Jim's eyes that had her hooked still, the way they glowed, as though someone had lit candles behind them.

"Faith?"

"Yes?"

"You look kind of sad."

Faith took a breath. "It's just that interview I did."

"The kidnapped girl?"

She nodded.

"It was hard?"

Another nod.

"You want a hug?"

Faith smiled. She moved closer to Jim and gazed into his eyes and felt that warmth. *He's yours. He always will be.* "I do," she said. "I really do."

"So what do you like," Trent said, by way of answering the phone. "Daddy? Poppa? Pops? Mack Daddy?"

Brenna said, "Aren't you jumping the gun a little?"

"Hey, my baby mama's due in like six months."

"You don't even know if you're the father."

"My philosophy is, be prepared."

"That wasn't your philosophy three months ago."

He sighed. "Haters gotta hate."

"Well, regardless, fathers-to-be are usually trying to think of what they'll call their children. Not what their kids are going to call them."

"Oh, I already have names picked out."

"I'm not surprised."

"Do you want to hear them?"

"No."

"Oh. Uh . . . you sure?"

"Listen, Trent, sorry to bug you on your day off, but how hard is it to find out who posted something on a Snapfish page?"

Trent took a breath. "Impossible."

"Damn."

"Kidding. Nothing's impossible when you're me, who happens to have a certain female Snapfish contact, who happens to think I'm USDA prime man steak."

"Can you get in contact with her?"

"Affirmative."

"Please don't say or do anything to make her go vegetarian."

He sighed. "What's the page?"

Brenna gave him the URL. "Scroll down close to the bottom," she said. Then she waited.

"What the . . ."

"I know."

"So . . . uh . . . you didn't post this."

"No, Trent. I didn't post it."

"And do you have any idea who might have?"

"Somebody who knows my middle name," she said. "Someone who knows who you are and who Maya is and . . ." *Someone who's had access to both the police papers and that picture.*

"And what?"

"Probably someone who's been in my apartment over the past two weeks."

"Dude, are you saying it was me who did this? Because it so *was not*."

Brenna sighed. "No," she said. "I'm not saying it was you."

After she'd finished the conversation and hung up with Trent, she texted her daughter: *Honey, can we talk? Call me anytime.*

But even as she typed the words, there was something about Maya creating the Snapfish post that didn't add up. Yes, Maya lived with Brenna for half the week and had access to both the photograph and the police papers. Yes, she'd let crazy DeeDee Walsh and her knife into the apartment on December 21 because DeeDee had claimed to be her long-lost Aunt Clea. But Brenna doubted Maya had been very happy to see her, even before she'd pulled out the knife. Brenna was having another memory now. December 19, two days before

DeeDee, Brenna had woken up from a nightmare about her sister to find her daughter in her room . . .

"*Mom?*"

Brenna feels a hand on her shoulder. Clea shifting into focus, into . . .

"*Mom.*"

"*Maya.*"

Maya steps back, her face scrunching up, hands grasping each other. "Uh . . . *You told me to wake you up at eight.*"

"*Right,*" *Brenna says. She struggles into a sitting position. Maya's face shifts into focus.* "*Was I talking in my sleep?*"

"*Yeah, a little.*"

"*Sorry. Weird dream.*"

"*About Clea?*"

"*Good guess.*" *Brenna's eyes feel sandy. She runs a hand over them.*

"*Hey, listen, Mom?*"

"*Yeah?*"

Maya sits down on the edge of the bed. She does it very lightly; Brenna can barely feel the weight of her daughter. She picks at a fingernail. Brenna watches her. God, sometimes she looks so like a little girl.

Maya says, "*What happens if you do find her?*"

"*Lula Belle?*"

"*Clea.*"

Maya's head is bowed and Brenna feels the urge to comfort her. She moves next to her, smoothes her soft blonde hair. "*That's a good question. I'd want to find out if she's okay, first.*"

"*Sure. But then what?*"

Brenna shrugs. "Talk to her, I guess."

"What if Grandma is right about Clea, though? What if she's crazy and destructive and stuff?"

Brenna puts a hand on her shoulder. "Maya," she says. "Grandma says a lot of things to make herself feel better."

"How would it make her feel better to say her own daughter is a nut job?"

"Maybe it helps her to stop wondering why Clea ran away and never called."

"Okay, I get that . . . But Mom? If you do find Clea . . ."

"Yeah?"

"Do I have to talk to her?"

Brenna touched Clea's diary—the diary Maya wanted nothing to do with on the day it had arrived in their mailbox in a plain brown envelope. *Oh great, Mom*, she'd said when Brenna had ripped open the package. *Something else to help you live in the past.*

Maya didn't want to find Clea. She had enough trouble with Brenna's obsession with her long-lost sister as it was, and it wasn't helped by the fact that her grandma had fictionalized her into some kind of bogeyman. Why would Maya post a picture of Clea on a missing persons page? Why would she pretend to be Brenna in order to glean more information about her?

Whoever did post Clea's photo had to have some degree of obsession—with Brenna, with her search, not to mention an investigative thirst that rivaled Brenna's own, and a need to take that search into their own hands, to take control of it.

Brenna knew someone like that—someone whose

need to protect sometimes struck her as a need to control. Someone who had been in Brenna's apartment several times within the last couple of weeks and who had such intimate knowledge of the police papers that he'd known what had happened to Brenna's father, weeks before she'd read about it herself.

Her own words echoed in her head. *It could be a he. Could be anybody.* And a feeling struck her—the same one she often had at the moment she solved a case—as though a thin skin had been peeled off everything—all of it suddenly, unexpectedly clear . . . And so much less pretty.

Brenna grabbed her phone, clicked on her text messages, scrolled through them until she found that last one from Nick Morasco:

I'm here if you need me.

Brenna swallowed hard, clicked reply, and typed, *Can you come over? We need to talk.*

6

Life is like a jigsaw puzzle, Sophia Castillo's mother used to tell her. *One piece goes missing, the whole thing loses its meaning.*

At the time, when she was young and unbowed, Sophia had thought the analogy overblown, especially considering her mother had used it when talking about Sophia's father—a useless puzzle piece, even during the few short years he'd been around.

For years, Sophia had believed herself far more resilient than her mother. She had allowed friends and lovers into her life knowing full well they'd eventually leave it, never feeling their loss so fully as her own capacity to survive it.

But then she'd given birth to Robert. Looking into her baby's eyes blinking their first blinks in the bright hospital light, feeling the slick weight of him against her chest, Sophia had experienced a love so overwhelming, it changed how she looked at the world. He had reached out to her, her Robert—tiny fingers grasping for her hair. Sophia had held him close, and in his heartbeat, she had found meaning. *I'll do anything for you*, she had thought. *Anything.*

And then came January 16, 2003—the one date she would always remember. On January 16, 2003, Sophia's then-husband Christopher had left her, taking Robert with him. Robert had just turned thirteen—tall for his age, as Sophia had always been. He had his father's big brown eyes and teeth that stuck out and a whole closet full of those ridiculous baggy pants the boys liked to wear back then, baggy shorts that came down past his knees and voluminous Yankees T-shirts. Jeter was his favorite.

Seven years had passed since then, but Robert still lived in Sophia's mind in his baggy pants, that shy, gap-toothed smile, forever thirteen. A missing puzzle piece, Sophia's whole life collapsing in around it.

Sometimes, now for instance, on the seventh anniversary of Robert's disappearance, Sophia would close her eyes and try hard to envision the twenty-year-old man he had become. Did he still love baseball? Had he learned to tolerate raisins, or did he still pick them out of his oatmeal cookies and line them up on his plate? Had he gotten over his Batman obsession, or did he still have that tottering stack of comic books he used to keep in the back of his closet, and if so, had he taken them with him to college? Was he in college?

Did he ever think about his mother?

Sophia's eyes started to well up. She swatted at them with the back of her wrist, hating her memory and her unanswered questions and her whole caved-in life.

Stop it. Stay focused.

The building loomed over her—a blocky prewar she'd probably passed a hundred times within the past year, but had never thought about, not until an hour ago, when she'd followed Maya here.

She grasped the steering wheel and gazed up, wondering which apartment Maya was in and how she could possibly get her to leave it, alone.

Not that she needed to. It didn't have to happen tonight, on the actual anniversary. Sophia took very little stock in that type of symbolism, and if Maya left this building tomorrow morning dazed and sleepless after a night with her new friends, if she left alone to walk home, then that would be fine.

An eye for an eye, an only child for an only child. Harsh words, yes. But life was harsh, and it was unfair, too. And it had no meaning unless you put it there yourself.

When Robert was very young—five or six maybe— the three of them were sitting at the kitchen table, eating dinner. Robert had been unusually quiet, and when Sophia turned to look at him, she saw that his eyes were closed. Sophia asked him what he was doing, and he replied, "Imagining."

"What are you imagining, honey?"

"I'm imagining that the kitchen floor is a cloud. And we live on it. And you and me and Daddy are the only people in the world."

Sophia let herself remember, but only for a short time. Brenna Spector's thirteen-year-old daughter was somewhere in that building and so Sophia needed to wake up, leave the past behind. She needed to focus on the here and now. *An only child for an only child . . .*

She turned off the ignition. Listened to the car go quiet. Waited.

* * *

"You okay?" said Nick Morasco. He was standing in Brenna's office area, looking not so much like her friend of three months or her lover of three weeks but like a stranger at a memorial service, paying respects.

Was Nick Morasco a stranger? He'd barely been in her life for a season, but facing your own mortality can make you cut to the chase relationship-wise—a big mistake for anyone, particularly for someone who won't ever be able to forget it.

Since meeting Nick, though, Brenna had faced her own mortality three times—and suffice it to say she'd *jump*-cut to the chase three weeks ago. First time she'd been with a man since May 8, 2006, and it hadn't felt like a mistake at all . . . Quite the opposite actually. Until now. Until the missing persons page on Snapfish.

Waiting for him to show up, Brenna had run so many scenarios through her mind, searching for any reasonable excuse Nick might have had to go into her drawer, pull out her personal photo, and post it on an obscure missing persons Web page, then masquerade as Brenna once he had a reply. The best she could come up with were *He wants to help*, *He doesn't think I can handle this*, and *He wants to protect me*. She hated all three.

"I'm okay," she said.

"Are you sure? Because . . ." His voice trailed off. Or maybe she just stopped listening.

Brenna recalled the first time she'd laid eyes on him—September 30 in this very office in those glasses of his and with that messy hair, such a surprise for a cop. Wearing a tweed jacket with elbow patches. His dad's jacket. Brenna hadn't known at the time that the jacket had been his father's, but she knew it now and that knowledge not only brought her back into the room with him, it softened her feelings a little—the closet full of his late dad's clothes, the soft, myopic eyes, the dated references he kept making (*a Jimmy Hoffa joke? Really?*) the way he sometimes stumbled over words when he got excited, as though his brain was moving faster than his mouth. The chinks in the armor drew Brenna to him still, but the armor itself, the shining armor . . . that was what pushed her away. "Don't you think I can take care of myself?"

Brenna hadn't meant to say that. Not so soon anyway, with his overcoat still on and "Hello" barely out of their mouths.

"What are you talking about?"

"Let me take your coat."

"Brenna . . ."

"I can't do this in here."

He gave her his coat. Let her lead him into the living room and sit him down on the couch. "I didn't go searching for those papers," he said.

God, he thought she was still angry about the police papers. "I know."

"And the only reason why I read them is that Grady Carlson told me what they said. He said he helped your mother cover up your father's death."

"Suicide."

"He didn't say suicide."

"It was in the police papers."

He looked at her. "I know. But Detective Carlson didn't say it."

Brenna closed her eyes. "Nick," she said. "Nick."

"I'm sorry, Brenna. I really am. I guess your mother thought it would be better for you and your sister not to know the truth. But I don't understand that logic any better than you do."

"My father . . . That isn't what I want to talk about."

"It isn't?"

Brenna sat down next to him. She slipped off his glasses and got close enough to him so he could see her without them. She could read him this way. She'd done it before—on December 29—and the knowledge that she was repeating the same behavior made her feel more comfortable.

"I know about the Snapfish page," Brenna said. "I'm not going to ask you why you did it because I think I know. I think you've got caring about me confused with *taking care* of me. I think you've had so much loss in your life that's been beyond your control that you have the urge to take control of other people's lives, solve their problems for them. It's why you're a cop. It's why you open doors for me and you come running even when you're not asked to come and you tell me I should call you for backup in situations I'm perfectly capable of handling on my own."

"Brenna . . ."

"I understand all that. I get why you posted Clea's picture. I get why you didn't tell me about it—you probably assumed no one would reply, and you didn't want to get my hopes up. All that feels like trying to help. But you crossed the line with Alan Dufresne."

She stared into his eyes, searching.

"What?" he said.

"Why did you pretend to be me, Nick? What were you trying to do?"

"I have no idea what you're talking about."

Brenna moved closer still. On December 29, she'd watched him like this after he'd drifted off on her and she'd noticed it again—that look that would spring into his eyes every so often.

"What are you thinking?"

"Nothing."

She slips off his glasses and moves closer, so close she can feel his breath on her face. He starts to kiss her, but she holds him off.

"I've seen this look in your eyes before."

"When?"

"November 20, 10 P.M.; December 19, 8 P.M.; December 23 . . ."

"Ask a stupid question."

"What are you thinking?"

"Are you interrogating me?"

"Yes."

"I don't want to talk about it."

"Too bad."

"Do you have to look at me like that?"

"Yes."

He looks down and sighs and Brenna feels it—a softening, a surrender. He looks back up at her. "What do you want to know?"

Nick had told her then about his son, Matthew, who was always on his mind but about whom he never spoke. Matthew, who'd died of SIDS at just seven months old and whose death had broken up Nick's marriage and then stayed with him always, the ghost of his own failure to act, to see, to help . . .

He'd given her that. He'd shown her what hurt him most. He'd said, *I trust you.*

"Nick . . ."

"I swear to God, Brenna. I don't know what you're talking about," he said now. "Who is Alan Dufresne? What Snapfish page?"

She looked for that glint, but she couldn't find it. There was no softening in his eyes. No surrender. She ran a hand through his hair, confusion barreling through her. She wasn't entirely sure whether she believed him. But she did know that she *wanted* to believe him, very badly. For now that was enough.

"I believe you."

"Good. Now can you explain?"

She did. She explained everything. And then she showed him the Snapfish posting.

"Why?"

"I guess someone else wants to find Clea," she said.

He shook his head. "And thinks they'll have more credibility if they use your name?"

"Yep."

"Who would do something like that?"

"Someone else with access to that picture . . . which is in my dresser drawer, so . . ."

"No other copies?"

"None that I know of."

A look passed over his face, a deepening concern. "Well . . . That narrows it down, I guess."

"My point."

He cleared his throat. "I can subpoena Snapfish for you. Find the IP address it was posted from."

"That takes weeks, doesn't it?"

He nodded. "No way around it."

"Thanks. Go ahead." Trent was, of course, a "way around it," but Brenna didn't say that. The way Trent got information for her wasn't always entirely legal and usually involved hacking, and, as far as Nick Morasco went, she'd learned that "don't ask, don't tell" was the best approach when discussing the activities of her assistant.

"I'm sorry," he said.

"For what?"

"All of this. The past few days."

She shook her head. "I'm just trying to figure out who else would know that about my father." She gave him a long look.

He met it without flinching. "Your mother?"

Brenna's heart sped up, but just for an instant. "My mother wouldn't be able to post something on a Web site," she said. "She doesn't even know how to use e-mail."

"How do you know that?" he said. "How do you know anything about anyone—other than what they *want* you to know?"

She gazed at him for several moments, her reserve softening still. *Would he say something like that if he had anything to hide?* "You want to order in some dinner?" she said.

Then her phone rang. She recognized the number and answered fast. "Alan?"

"I just thought you might like to know, I got another e-mail from BrennaNSpector."

Brenna kept her eyes on Morasco. "What did it say?"

"She'll be out of touch for a little while." He sighed out the words. "She hopes she can drop a line eventually about where to send the bag, but for now, just hang on to it. And don't tell anyone. This is so confusing, by the way. Should I be referring to her as she? Or they? Or you?"

"Out of touch?" Brenna said. "Why?"

"You're gonna love this one."

"Oh yeah?"

"Yep. Just for sheer absurdity."

Outside Brenna's apartment, the sky opened up, rain smashing against the windows. From the way it had felt outside, Brenna would have figured on snow.

"Wow," Alan said. "You hear that rain?"

Brenna nodded. "Weird weather. And speaking of weird . . ."

"Right," Alan said. "BrennaNSpector."

"Yes."

"Well apparently, you're not going to be e-mailing for a while because you're in the midst of a family crisis."

The rain came out of nowhere, soaking Maya's hair, her jeans, her stupid pink sweater. She'd started crying again, she wasn't sure when, but her tears were hot on her face and the rain was freezing and in Maya's whole life, she'd never felt this wet before.

She was scared she might catch pneumonia. *Would they care? Would those bitches care if I wound up dying on the street?*

She'd left her new coat with them. She'd left her

overnight bag, too. After spending so much time trying to figure out the best clothes to pack. *God, I'm such an idiot.* Right now, Lindsay, Nikki, and Annalee were probably going through her bag and laughing—probably still had the webcam on.

A couple rushed past her, a coat held up over both their heads like an umbrella. Maya wasn't sure how it was warm enough to rain, but she didn't care. It fell in line with everything else, the whole world punishing her—and for what? What had she done?

Maya thought of her dad—the way he'd looked up at her and smiled as she left. *Do I need to speak to Lindsay's parents? Firm everything up?*

No, Dad. All taken care of.

Was that what she was being punished for? Telling her dad that Lindsay's parents would be there?

Dad, Zoe . . . She'd lied to a few people. Mom, too. Not about this, of course. But about the shrink. Why she'd wanted to see him. Maya promised herself she wouldn't lie to anyone again, ever.

I'm so sorry . . .

Her stomach still felt terrible—hollow and weak from the blackberry brandy. She hated those girls so much. Why had she ever wanted to be friends with them? That seemed the really punishable thing—bad judgment.

And Miles. Especially Miles.

She remembered the way he had looked at her, so solemn. She remembered how he'd said, *It will be our secret, Maya, our secret always . . .*

And he'd been in on it. He'd been in on it the whole time, even as he touched her face, even as he . . .

Maya was breathing in cold water now. Her sweater stuck to her and her whole body was shivering, numb . . . and she hadn't been watching where she was going. She'd missed her block and now she was practically at the West Side Highway, cold wind pushing into her wet face, burning her wet eyes. *Why?* The word was loud inside her. She wanted to scream it. Wanted to fall down on the sidewalk and sob.

They were going to post that video on YouTube. Maya had heard Nikki say it. They would post it and everyone at school would see it and her teachers and her parents and . . .

"Maya."

My life is over.

"Maya!"

She stopped and looked over her shoulder, and saw him coming toward her in a windbreaker, the hood up. She saw his feet pounding the sidewalk, splashing in the puddles, his stride quickening, becoming a jog. He said her name again and yelled at her to wait and that's when she knew this was real, not in her head.

Over.

Maya turned away from him. She ran and ran, fast as she could.

Part Two

Today I left my family forever. I put City Island in the rearview and drove off with my Great Love. We're heading West, because that's where people always go to make their lives better. Bill says that. He writes poetry, too. He has a big, leather-bound book of the most beautiful poems I've ever seen. Someday, all of his poems will be about me.

I know I've never mentioned Bill in here before, which is WEIRD. We're going to spend the rest of our lives together. He's all I think about, and still this is the first time I've written his name on one of these pages. But it's like Bill says: Life works in strange ways. Sometimes you don't see your future until you're heading straight into it. Sometimes you don't know you're in love until it swallows you whole.

From the diary of Clea Spector
August 21, 1981

7

Evelyn Spector woke up with her heart in her mouth. She could have sworn she heard the phone ringing, but it must have been a dream. Evelyn's brain playing tricks on her again. She looked at her digital alarm clock: 3 A.M. Every single night for the past week she'd woken up at 3 A.M. sharp. It was almost as though she had a ghost in her house, jolting her awake. And in a way she did, didn't she?

Jack Spector. Grady Carlson. Evelyn had more than one ghost. Clea.

Two weeks ago, her younger daughter's boyfriend had called her. Evelyn had been pleased to hear his voice. She'd heard about Brenna on the news, of course. That woman breaking into her home, that man killing himself, right in front of her . . . Such a dangerous job she'd chosen for herself, and these days it seemed more dangerous than ever.

But outside of a brief phone call (with Evelyn calling Brenna, no less) they'd barely spoken since. She'd had to get almost all the information about the break-in from her granddaughter—the only one in Evelyn's family who could be bothered to tell her anything.

Perhaps Brenna and her boyfriend are inviting me for dinner, Evelyn had thought when she'd heard his voice on the phone. *After all, it is their turn.*

But Brenna's boyfriend hadn't been calling for social reasons. Quite the opposite, actually. "I thought you should know that Grady Carlson is dead," he had said. "He told me what really happened to your husband. He left me the police papers. I gave them to Brenna."

Who does that? Who calls a lonely seventy-five-year-old woman past suppertime and smashes her whole life to pieces without warning? Who does that, without even having enough sensitivity to say, "I'm sorry"?

Evelyn had wanted to say so many things to him. She'd wanted to shatter that righteous tone of his, to teach him a lesson about minding his own business, to tell him, *Some secrets are secrets for good reason.* But her own politeness forbade it. "Thank you for calling," Evelyn had said.

Would it have killed him, this young man she'd invited into her house and served a dinner she'd spent the whole day preparing? Would it have killed him to offer a seventy-five-year-old woman a few words of apology before destroying what was left of her family, all in the ridiculous name of "honesty"?

Evelyn had never liked Brenna's ex-husband, Jim, very much. He had a sarcastic streak, plus she'd long suspected he'd been seeing that anchorwoman before he and Brenna got divorced. But even Jim Rappaport would've had the social skills to say, "I'm sorry to have to do this, Evelyn . . ."

The one thing Evelyn did know: Brenna and her boyfriend—Nick, that was his name—were perfectly matched. Both of them so young but not knowing it, both so convinced they were right about everything when they still had so much to learn.

Brenna had always been like that, even when she was a little girl. Forever arguing her case until she wore you down, until it was easier to just give in and say, *You know what? You're right.* So convinced of her own correctness, Brenna was, even *before* coming down with that memory disease. After, of course, she'd become insufferable.

If you only knew, Brenna. If you only knew the real truth about your father. If you only knew, you wouldn't be so quick to judge.

The young these days were far too confident. Evelyn couldn't recall a time in her life when she thought herself so above it all, so damn moral and *perfect* that she'd do what Nick had done. *I thought you should know*, indeed.

And don't even get Evelyn started on Detective Carlson. Because of him and his deathbed confession, she'd spent the last two weeks trapped in this slow boil of a panic. A woman her age who probably should be on high blood pressure medication—an artist too exhausted to create, a slab of granite in her studio, untouched for two weeks because she'd been waking up every morning at three, her daughter shrieking at her in her mind: *How could you, Mother? How could you lie to me?* Detective Carlson had shortened Evelyn's lifespan by *years*, she was sure. Detective Grady Carlson, who couldn't even *die* without causing her trouble.

What drove this selfish desire to confess? Evelyn didn't understand it. She could keep a secret until her very last breath if she had to, if she knew that things would be better that way . . . *Envision a small, metal safe in a windowless room. Place the secret inside. Lock it up. Close the door to the windowless room. Never open that door again.* Was Evelyn that much stronger than everyone else?

Don't forget to say good-bye first.

The phone rang.

Evelyn realized that it had been ringing all along; it hadn't been a dream. Her heart beat hard enough to shake her whole body. *My God . . . It's time.*

She picked the phone up fast. "Brenna?"

But she heard only static.

"I think we have a bad connection," Evelyn said. "I can't hear you."

More static, then, for a half second, a break in it . . . a peal of a woman's voice, a girl's . . . *"Please . . ."*

"Brenna?"

The line went silent.

"Hello?" Evelyn said. "Hello? Brenna? I'm sorry. Please don't be mad at me. I can explain."

No answer. The connection was dead.

"Brenna. I did it to protect you."

Before she hung up the phone, Evelyn checked the caller ID. *I'll call her back*, she thought. *I'll tell her the whole story.* But the name and number on the screen didn't belong to Brenna. They belonged to Maya.

Brenna dreamed of thick, bristly ropes tied around her—one pressing against her neck, the other coiled around her waist. Brenna tried to break free, but then the ropes turned into venomous snakes. The one at her

neck—a cobra—reared back, fangs bared and gleam-
ing, dripping deep red poison. It lunged at her face. She
forced herself awake before the bite . . . to find Nick
sleeping with his arms curled around her—one at her
neck, the other at her waist.

Probably shouldn't tell him about that dream.

She slipped from his grasp and looked at the clock:
7 A.M. Early to wake up on a Sunday, but that wasn't nec-
essarily a bad thing. The fact was, Brenna hadn't done
anything on the Debbie Minton case yesterday. She
could use some of the morning for online research . . .

Or maybe she was just making excuses to get out
of bed. Brenna felt cold. She grabbed her bathrobe
from the hook on the bedroom door and threw it over
her naked body, then stole another glance at Morasco,
sleeping, his chest rising and falling with his slow
breath, his arms still stretched around the lack of her.

Last night, while they were making love, she'd fallen
into a memory. The first time that had happened since
she'd started sleeping with Nick, and it hadn't been a
good memory, either . . .

Brenna shut her eyes tight. Clea's journal was in the
other room, out of reach, and so she recited the Pledge
of Allegiance in her head until the memory of the
memory went away.

Too much stress, that's what it was. Too much of the
past, shoving its way into the present. Brenna's sister's
thoughts, fresh and alive in the journal, her father's
decades-old suicide a new thing—new to her, anyway.
The man in the blue car, named at last. *Bill.* Clea's
earthly possessions in the next room—souvenirs from
a twenty-eight-year-old road trip and an OD that may

or may not have been fatal, which had somehow made their way into the hands of a trucker, now deceased, unable to answer any questions, a part of the past as well.

And someone, pretending to be Brenna, exchanging e-mails with the trucker's son.

She'll be out of touch for a little while, Alan Dufresne had said last night, paraphrasing that final e-mail. *She hopes she can drop a line eventually about where to send the bag, but for now, just hang on to it. And don't tell anyone . . .*

Why the sudden stop to the correspondence? Why, unless . . .

Brenna cracked open the door, her mind traveling back to her living room last night, the phone in her hand, Dufresne's voice in her ear, her eyes trained on the floor, avoiding Morasco's face. *"Well apparently, you're not going to be e-mailing for a while because you're in the midst of a family crisis."*

"Alan?"

"Yes?"

"What time was that e-mail sent?"

"Hmmm . . . Let me see . . . It says 5:56 P.M."

Brenna feels Morasco's gaze on her. She glances over at him, she can't help it. He mouths a word: Anything?

She shakes her head. Heat creeps into her face, so she looks down again. He can't see her getting flushed. He'd notice it. He'd ask why.

Why can't she trust Nick? Timing doesn't prove anything. She's been an investigator long enough to know that.

But in this case, it also doesn't disprove *anything.*
BrennaNSpector sent the e-mail to Dufresne at 5:56
P.M.—ten minutes after Brenna texted Nick, telling him
they need to talk.

Alan says, "Brenna, are you still there?"

Brenna raked her fingernails against the inside of
her arm, bringing herself back and punishing herself
at the same time.

She wanted to believe that Nick hadn't lied to her,
wanted so to believe that it wasn't he who had written to Dufresne. Last night, she'd wanted it more than
anything in the world. But the truth was, wanting and
trusting were too different things. And both were a lot
harder to do in the morning.

She drew the robe against her body, shivering. Was
it really that cold in here, or was it her mind, edging
into January 8, 1996. The worst blizzard in 128 years,
the newscaster on NPR had called it. Brenna could feel
the cold creeping in, the announcer's voice buzzing
out of the kitchen radio as she stood at the big window
of their apartment on Fourteenth Street, snow coming
down in bucketfuls, Jim's arms wrapped around her . . .

She leans her head into Jim's broad chest, her eyes
closed.

"You remembering something?" he says, his voice
so soft it's a thing she feels more than hears.

"No. I'm thinking about something new."

"Yeah? What? The weather?"

She shakes her head, feeling herself smiling.
"Newer."

Jim says, "How can it be newer than something
happening right now?"

She tilts her head up, gazes into his deep brown eyes, the gold flecks in them. She thinks, I hope the baby gets those . . .

"Newer? Brenna . . . are you telling me . . ."

Brenna dug her fingernails into her palms. "Four score and seven years ago," she whispered, coming back . . .

" . . . oh my God, Bren . . ."

"Our forefathers brought forth on this continent . . ."

Funny, most people believed life was so much simpler for the young. But that wasn't really true—it was just the soft-focus, selective way that most people remembered their youths. When every single day is clear in your mind, you know how many of them are difficult, how confusing it really is to be young, how the best times are almost always fraught with dark shadows.

Almost always.

There are some rare moments that are so pure they shine—moments like that one at the window during the blizzard of '96. Moments so simple you can sum them up in one small word: *Joy. Love.*

They made Brenna glad for her memory, those moments, but they also made her sad for it. Fourteen years ago, while watching the falling snow from the window of her old apartment on Fourteenth Street, she'd told Jim she was pregnant, and yet it felt like . . . Well, of course Brenna's memories always felt like they were happening now. But still. *Fourteen years.* So long ago, for everyone but her . . .

Brenna sighed. She'd found her way into Maya's room, and through the open door to her own bedroom, she could hear Nick Morasco, sighing in his sleep. She closed Maya's door.

It wasn't Brenna's habit to go into her daughter's room when she wasn't around. Nights Maya was here, though, Brenna would sometimes stand in the doorway, listening to her heavy sleep-breathing. *Proof of life, and something more.* To her, there was no sound more comforting. It sometimes made her worry about what would happen once Maya left home. Would Brenna still stand in her doorway when she felt stressed and fearful? Would the memory of her daughter's breathing be enough to sustain her?

Brenna looked around. Maya kept her room un-usually neat for a young teen. It wasn't spotless, but her bed was always made, clothes folded and placed into drawers or hung in her closet without Brenna ever having to ask.

Brenna could of course recall in perfect detail the mix of dirty and clean laundry that littered the floor of her own room when she was Maya's age, the unmade bed, the Nestlé Crunch wrappers and empty Chee-tos bags on the nightstand. And so she thought about it a lot, her daughter's neatness. She suspected it was the transient nature of her life that made her so orderly; the idea of having two furnished bedrooms in two different apart-ments, neither of which she could fully call her own. Maybe that was one of the things Maya had wanted to talk to Dr. Lieberman about. Had she let crazy DeeDee Walsh into Brenna's apartment because on some level, she figured it wasn't her door to keep locked?

Brenna sighed heavily. Overthinking things, as usual . . . But it was easier than dealing with the man sleeping in her bed, trying to figure out whether he was telling her the truth.

Brenna sat on Maya's bed, gazed at the squat book-shelf braced against the wall. There were a few new things on top—a folded up bag from Forever 21, a pair of striped thigh-high socks, still in the package, a bottle of perfume called Citrus Splash. *When did Maya start wearing perfume?*

The shelves were packed, mostly with Maya's manga books and sketch pads, though there was tradi-tional literature thrown in for good measure—*Treasure Island*, *Little Women*, the Hunger Games trilogy, the Harry Potter series . . . and in the back of the shelf that housed the Harry Potter books, Maya's carefully guarded secret.

Brenna slipped her hand behind the books, felt for the thin spine . . . There it was. *The Very Hungry Cater-pillar.* Rescued from a library donation box on Novem-ber 19, 2004, without Brenna's knowledge, the book Maya had learned to read with, swiped from the box by her daughter and stashed away at the back of these shelves for years—a cherished souvenir that Brenna hadn't discovered till December 12, 2009, when she'd caught sight of it while dusting.

Brenna slid the book out. She knew she shouldn't—this was her daughter's secret, after all—but she needed something, just a few seconds of simplicity to escape Morasco, her growing suspicions. If he'd posted Clea's picture on the Snapfish page to help her, why hadn't he simply told her the truth? If he'd been corresponding with Alan Dufresne, pretending to be her, wouldn't it have been easier to just explain why?

Brenna ran her hand over the book's cover, Maya's

name scrawled across the white space in purple Magic Marker, along with a star, a tree, a princess in a pointy hat drawn right over the caterpillar's face . . . She recalled January 13, 2001, Maya reading to her from this book, chubby little hands on the pages, struggling over the word, *Cat-a-pil-lah*. She shut her eyes, coming back, smiling. Did Maya have that memory, too?

She opened the book, knowing that if she were to see the large print on the page, the colorful Eric Carle illustrations, it would bring on the full memory—another simple one. She needed that.

From the center of the book, four folded pieces of sketch paper dropped onto the bed. She stared at them. Were these the real secrets? The book just a hiding place?

She should just put them back, replace the book, and either get to work on the Scarsdale case or talk to Morasco. The poor kid was right to think this room wasn't hers if she couldn't even hide a few pieces of paper in an old book without her mother finding out.

But instead Brenna found herself edging one of them open, smoothing it . . . This was bad, she knew, but she couldn't help herself. She wanted to see.

It was a charcoaled profile of a young man, gazing out a window.

Brenna remembered this boy, of course. The Justin Timberlake look-alike for whom Maya, a nonsinger, had joined the school chorus. The douchebag-in-training who, after chorus practice on October 1, 2009, jumped all over that older girl in the skintight jeans, right in front of everyone, as though the world were

an *American Pie* movie and the two of them had top
billing. *Miles*. As in, *Miles to go before he grows up*.
Brenna had thought Maya hated him.

Miles and Maya had been partners in art class last
fall, assigned to draw portraits of each other. Brenna
knew that much. She'd come home to their voices
behind Maya's closed door and, of course, over-
reacted.

But why on earth had Maya kept this sketch? Brenna
opened another—a close-up of Miles's face, his eyes
soulful and glistening, his lips parted, as though
coming in for a kiss . . . *Oh man. She does not hate
him*.

And then the third one, not a school assignment at
all but an all-out fantasy—Miles, dressed as a pirate,
his arm around the waist of a blissful young maiden
in Renaissance garb with her eyes closed and her head
thrown back and a face that looked suspiciously like . . .
Well, it was Maya.

"Oh, honey," Brenna whispered. "What are you
thinking?"

On the bright side, what her daughter lacked in judgment, she more than made up for in artistic talent. This
was better than any romance novel cover Brenna had
ever seen. *Put these sketches back. Don't mention them
to her. Hope and pray she grows out of it. It's all you
can do.*

There was one more folded paper. No doubt more
Miles, dressed as a cowboy or Prince Charming, or
maybe he was wearing a tux, handing the final rose to
Maya on *The Bachelor*.

It wasn't worth looking, but still she had to. Before

putting the other sketches back, Brenna smoothed it open. Her breath went away.

"Brenna?" Morasco called out from the other room. "Where did you go?"

She couldn't answer. *You never really know anyone. Not even those people you love more than anything. They'll never know you, you'll never know them. Everyone has secrets. Their minds are their own. You never know anyone, not even your own child.*

The last picture—painstakingly drawn—was not of Miles. It was of Clea—an exact copy of the smiling photograph that Brenna had kept in her drawer, only with one difference. In Maya's drawing, there was a bullet hole in Clea's forehead, blood pouring down her face.

Brenna didn't tell Nick about the drawing. She'd had no right to look at it in the first place, let alone discuss it. So when she emerged from Maya's room visibly shaken and he asked her what was wrong, she came back instead to Alan Dufresne, the e-mails from BrennaNSpector.

"Brenna," he said.

"What?"

"You still think it was me who did that?"

"I don't know."

"You know *me.*"

She sighed, shook her head. "I don't really care either way." She realized, as she said it, that it was true. It didn't matter. We believed about others what we wanted to. Friendship, love . . . it was all based on fiction. No one told the complete truth about anything, especially themselves—which was no wonder because when you scratched anyone's surface, *anyone's* . . . you got some degree of crazy. Look at Clea's secret journal, look at Maya's carefully hidden drawings, at Brenna's father, sobbing against the steering wheel, forgetting his two young daughters in the backseat, thinking he was alone . . .

A gift for destruction that runs through their veins, Brenna's mother had told Nick on November 19 after too much wine. She'd been referring to both Brenna and Clea, saying they'd inherited it from their father. But she could have been talking about anyone. We all had a gift for destruction, didn't we? We were all hurtling toward the finish line one way or another, telling ourselves stories along the way.

Brenna said, "Do you want to see it?"

"See what?" Nick said.

"The bag." She stared at the floor. "Clea's bag."

"Okay."

She walked down the hall and into her office and he followed. Once they got there, she took the clothes out of the bag, followed by the map, the hair band, the purple Swatch, the sewing kit, and the driver's license, which Morasco held carefully in his hands, examining the picture. "She looks a little like Maya."

Brenna nodded. "A lot."

He placed the license back down on Brenna's desk. There was a reverence to the gesture, a gentleness that Brenna appreciated, especially now, with Maya's drawing still in her brain. "I can put Dufresne's father's name through NCIC and the sex offenders registry," he said. "See if he has any kind of a record."

Brenna stared at the license, at the picture, taken on Clea's sixteenth birthday because she couldn't wait one day, as she'd said, "to be free." "Do you think Clea's dead?"

"I have no idea," he said. "Do you?"

"I want to say no, because that's what I've been saying to everyone, ever since she disappeared. If she were dead, I'd feel it."

"But . . ."

"But if the past few months have taught me anything, it's that my intuition is crap."

She looked up at him, the hurt in his eyes. *Not about you*, she wanted to say. But she couldn't.

There was a knock on the door.

"You expecting someone?"

Brenna shook her head.

From the other side of the door, a voice. "It's your mother."

"Great," Brenna whispered.

She opened the door on Evelyn Spector, bundled up in a heavy black coat, cheeks flushed from the cold, pale blue eyes moving from Brenna to Nick and back. She had lost an inch or two in the past couple of years, but she was still an imposingly tall woman—reedy and beatniky and frizzy-haired, a Jules Feiffer cartoon come to life.

That was the thing about Brenna's mother; as much as the world turned and changed around her, she retained the same shape, the same style—as constant as the house in City Island where she still lived, the Neptune statue still watching over her from the tiny backyard, both of them preserved and as unchanging as Brenna's memories.

Brenna hadn't seen her since November 19, but it might as well have been later the same day. Evelyn wore the same black turtleneck, her graying curls pulled back into the same silver barrettes, the same black liner around the light eyes, which somehow made them look accusing. "Oh good," Evelyn said flatly. "You're *both* here."

A memory flicked into Brenna's mind—April 4, 1989, Brenna in the bedroom of her City Island home, four weeks before prom, slipping Clea's black silk prom dress over her head, tying the bow at the waist, spinning around to show her friend Carly.

"Wow, it fits you perfectly," Carly says.

"You think?" But she knows. The dress is so cool and light, it feels like vapor. It's been in the back of her closet for six years, covered in a garbage bag, hidden from her mother. She stole it out of Clea's closet when her mom was throwing out all her things and brought it into her room to keep. She still hasn't figured out how she'll get her mom to accept her wearing it to prom, but she figures if her mother doesn't see her in it until the actual night, she'll have no other choice than to say okay.

Brenna hasn't tried it on till now, and the way it fits, the way she feels like she looks . . . it's almost as though Clea is here, too, as though she bought the dress six years ago with Brenna in mind, as though she wore it to her own prom only to break it in . . . "You think Graham will like it?" But Brenna knows he will. She knows.

"Are you kidding?" Carly says. "You look amazing!"

A knock on the door. "Brenna, what are you doing in there?"

Brenna's heart jumps. "Mom? I . . . I thought you were out."

The door opens.

"Hi, Mrs. Spector." Carly spits out the words like she's just been choking on them.

Mom doesn't answer.

Brenna can't look at Mom, but still she can feel those blue eyes on her, burning. "What are you doing in that dress?"

"I . . . uh . . ."

"Take it off, young lady. Take it off and throw it away right now."

Brenna's mother was saying, "Mrs. Dinnerstein. The woman downstairs." The name yanked her back into the present.

She turned to Brenna. "You were remembering, weren't you?"

Brenna nodded.

"Well to keep you up to speed, I was just telling Detective Morasco that I didn't break into your building. I was let in by your very nice downstairs neighbor."

"Evelyn, I never said you broke in."

"Well it sounded to me as though you were implying it."

Brenna sighed heavily. "What brings you here, Mom?"

"You know." She turned to Morasco. "He knows."

"Evelyn—"

Brenna said, "Would you like to come in? Sit down?"

"I can say what I need to say right here."

"Okay . . ."

"I love you very much, Brenna. I always will. I may have made mistakes, but everything I've done, even the mistakes, all of it has been in order to make your life as easy as possible."

Brenna looked at her.

"You were such a little girl. Clea was older but you still had a chance. You didn't need to know what he was like. I wanted you to forget, and you did. What is so wrong about wanting to protect your own child?"

Brenna stared at her. "What do you mean?"

"See?" she said. "You don't remember."

"You're talking about Dad."

"Of course I am."

Brenna closed her eyes. "Mom. I wanted this conversation to be on my own time. Not yours. You've lied to me for thirty-two years. Don't you think you could at least give me that?"

"What did he say to you?" Evelyn said, not to Brenna. To Morasco. "What did Grady Carlson say to you about me?"

Nick looked at her for a very long time. She returned his gaze, and something seemed to pass between them—a moment Brenna didn't fully understand. "He said," Nick told her, "that you were very unhappy at home."

Evelyn closed her eyes as though bracing for a blow. For a moment she looked so frail, so worn out, it was as though someone had lifted a veil, showing all the change in her, showing everything that had been taken away.

"Brenna, your father was not right in the head."

"He was depressed, Mom."

She shook her head. "He was hospitalized more than once."

"What?"

"Forcibly hospitalized."

"No . . ."

"There was a time, when he was driving you girls home from summer camp, that he stopped in the middle of traffic. You don't remember this, but Clea . . . Clea did, and she never got over it. He had some kind of breakdown. He was arrested . . ."

"Arrested?"

The image again, that hazy, pre-syndrome memory . . . Brenna's father, his head against the steering wheel, the broad shoulders, heaving. The long, wet sobs . . . Car horns blaring. Someone yelling, *Move it, asshole!* Clea saying, *Dad what's wrong?* Her father, getting out of the car, slamming the door . . .

"I protected you," Evelyn said. "I didn't want you to know. But that was when I first met Detective Carlson."

Brenna said, "A gift for destruction . . ."

"What?"

"Nothing." She felt Morasco's hand on her shoulder, and a thought came to her. She looked at her mother. "How did you know?"

"About your father?"

"No," Brenna said. "How did you know that I found out? How did you know about the papers? I hadn't called you yet."

The pale eyes narrowed. She cast a glance at Morasco. She said nothing. But she didn't need to. Brenna stiffened. She moved away from Morasco.

"Brenna," he said.

"No," she said. "No." She couldn't look at him.

"I should leave," said Brenna's mother. "I have errands in the city."

"I'll call you soon, Mom . . . and . . ."

"Yes?"

"Thank you for coming."

Her face relaxed. "You're welcome." She gave her a quick, tight hug. Brenna could feel the bones in her spine.

She opened the door, then stopped. "Oh, and also, Brenna," she said, "you know I wouldn't tell you how to raise your child, but did you know that Maya is staying up till all hours?"

"Huh? Well, she was at a sleepover last night . . ."

"Oh," she said. "That explains it."

"Explains what?"

"I got a call from her at three in the morning . . . I think she may have dialed my number by accident. We had a terrible connection and I could barely hear her. But . . . well, she sounded awfully wild."

"Shouldn't she have called by now?" Faith asked Jim.

"Who?"

She looked at him. He was focused on the TV. "Maya."

"Oh," Jim said. "She texted me earlier. Asked if she could go see a movie with Lindsay and some other girls. Said she'd be home by six. I'm sorry—I thought I told you."

Faith sighed. "When was the last time that girl actually spoke into a phone?"

Jim didn't reply. They were watching the Sunday

edition of *Sunrise Manhattan*, which was actually called *Weekend Manhattan* because it aired at 4 P.M. Already, it was getting dark outside, which gave Faith the creeps—she hated winter.

Ashley Stanley's face filled the screen, the scar on her left cheek glimmering under the hot lights despite the makeup team's best efforts. Offscreen, Faith said, "So, tell me, honey. You're a smart girl . . ."

Faith winced, right along with Ashley. Nicolai had told her he'd cut in for a close-up here, but she hadn't realized it would be this close. She could see pores, tear ducts, as though she were looking at the poor girl under a microscope, which, when you thought about it, she was. "Honestly . . . that tight shot . . ."

"It is very close," Jim said.

Faith shook her head. "The girl is so scared, she spends a year in hiding. She disguises herself, makes no friends, barely leaves her house . . . and we respond to that by showing the whole world her damn X-ray?"

On screen, Ashley said, "I *had* seen her."

"For what it's worth, invasive camera work aside," Jim said, "you are a terrific interviewer."

Faith moved closer to him on the couch. "You think?"

Ashley said, "I'd seen her before, at the same movie theater. I'd seen *Notting Hill* and my friends were teasing me . . ."

Jim nodded. "Sensitive, kind, patient . . ."

"What movie?" Faith asked.

"Huh? *Notting Hill.*"

"No, hon. What movie was Maya seeing?"

"She didn't say."

Faith looked at him. "That's weird."

"What do you mean?"

"Well, when she texts me about going to the movies, she usually tells me which one. You know, to make sure it's appropriate. Also so I can find her."

Jim shrugged. "Growing up."

Faith flashed on Maya, typing furiously on her laptop, then slamming it shut when she caught sight of her. "I guess."

"I'm sure she picked a good movie," Jim said. "She's Maya, after all."

Faith knew what he meant, and he was absolutely right. Maya had a very low threshold for on-screen violence. Last year, she'd walked out on *Avatar* during one of the first battle scenes, dragging her friends Zoe and Larissa out with her. When Faith had met them at the theater a whole hour early, the other two girls had been understandably peeved. ("There wasn't even any blood!" "How can you get that upset when everybody is eight feet tall and blue?") Faith had to take them all out to Serendipity, just to make up for it.

"You are right about that." Faith smiled.

On screen, Ashley brushed a tear from her face. "She said, 'We chose you, and you're happy now.' "

"We raised a sensitive girl," Jim said.

She nodded. "Wouldn't hurt a fly."

Her gaze returned to the screen, to Ashley. Danielle, Faith's executive producer, had said the interview was brilliant. "Barbara Walters, move over." Danielle had actually used those words with Faith over the phone this morning—*major*, seeing as Danielle hardly ever praised anyone, ever. Faith liked to think she was too seasoned to bask in compliments, but in this case, she'd packed on those words like a spa treatment, let them sink in good. Of course she'd been unaware at the time of the invasive camera work. Right now: a close-up of a tear, winding its way down the scarred cheek. "High def from hell," she whispered.

"Makes me glad to be in print," Jim said.

"But you'd look cute in an extreme close-up." She gave his hand a quick squeeze. "Maybe I'll interview you next."

Faith felt a vibration on the couch beside her. Her cell phone. She picked it up, glanced at the screen: "Restricted Number."

She thought of the last call she'd gotten from a restricted number. The cigarette-damaged voice—woman or man?—calling in on her cell just before the interview. *I watch you every day. I know you're a good mother.* On screen, Ashley wiped away another tear.

She hadn't told Jim about that call. Hadn't told anybody. Honestly, what was the point? *Just another stalker*, Faith had thought. If Jim knew how many calls she got that sounded exactly like that one . . . If he'd seen some of the e-mails sent to her work address . . . Well, he'd probably beg her to quit.

But still . . . the mention of Maya. *She'll ask to go out. She thinks she's old enough. She's not.* That had been new, and while Faith always made it a point not to give those freaks any power by responding with fear, she had to admit that she didn't like the way the caller had focused on her daughter like that. It had made her want to reach through the phone, punch her in the face.

The phone vibrated again. She stared at the words:

"Restricted Number," and made a quick decision. She hit the voice recorder app. *Portions of this call may be taped, darling. Hope you don't mind.* "Yes?"

"Faith?"

The air rushed out of her. It wasn't the stalker. It was a child. "Ashley?" Faith said.

"Yes."

"Honey, how are you? I'm watching and you really—"

"I'm scared."

"Don't worry."

"How do you know?"

"Excuse me?"

"How do you know I shouldn't worry?"

"Sweetheart, you come across honest and sympathetic and very strong," she said. Fudging the *very strong* part.

"You should have put me in shadow or something, Faith. You should have altered my voice. That's me on TV, Faith. My face—for the whole world to see, including . . . including . . ."

"Ashley, they can't do anything to you now, don't you see? The more famous you get, the more you put them in the spotlight, too." Faith took a breath. "They have everything to lose. You have your whole life ahead of you."

"Stop acting like that." The childlike voice had a sharpness to it, an edge.

"Like what?"

"Like you care."

"Ashley."

"If you cared about me, you'd have talked me out of

doing this interview. Now they're watching me. Charles and Renee are watching. They're watching me cry."

Faith gave Jim a helpless look, but he didn't return it. He was on his phone, reading a text.

She took a breath, closed her eyes. "Ashley," she said. "I want you to listen to me."

Jim said, "Faith."

"I know it's frightening, coming out of hiding like this. But you just can't live the way you were living. You'll feel better and better. You'll be able to live a normal life."

Ashley said, "Do you think?"

"I know, honey." Faith stared at the image on the TV screen as though she were right there, in the room with Ashley, and then she spoke, not just to convince Ashley, but to convince herself. "By getting out there, by telling the world what happened, you're taking control of your own life again. You're seizing power back from two awful people who don't deserve to have any power, over anyone, ever."

"Faith hang up the phone now!"

She turned to Jim. *Are you insane?* she thought, but one look at his face and the thought dissolved.

"I need to go." Faith ended the call without waiting for a reply.

"What happened?" Faith heard her own voice as though it were coming out of someone else—weak, helpless . . . more childlike than Ashley's. "Is it bad?"

He nodded.

On screen, Ashley ran a hand through her dyed brown hair. Faith hit pause on the DVR and for the briefest time everything seemed frozen—the girl's image on TV, the sun setting outside the apartment window, the tropical fish in the aquarium Maya had requested but never took care of, Maya who had always wanted a dog and would only think of the fish as a consolation prize. Jim's shell-shocked face.

Why didn't we get her a dog? Faith thought, and the thought felt frozen, too, suspended in this moment, these few seconds before knowing.

Then Jim moved toward her holding out the phone, and everything sped back up again and life continued, much as she didn't want it to, not like this, not with the way Jim was looking at her.

"Maya sent a text," he said.

8

"I didn't know what to do," Nick Morasco had said, just after Brenna's mother left. "I was so surprised by what Grady Carlson had told me . . . I just couldn't fathom what she did and so I called."

"You wanted to see how she'd react."

"Yes."

"Interrogate her."

"Well, not really interrogate . . ."

"Question her."

"It was just a brief call."

"I understand."

"Good, because—"

"I just don't get why you didn't tell me that you called her."

"You hadn't . . . I didn't know when you were going to read the police papers."

"So you thought you'd give her a heads-up?"

"It sounds strange when you phrase it like that."

"It *is* strange, Nick."

"I'm sorry."

"I just had to have a conversation that I wasn't at all ready for."

"I know. I'm so sorry."

"You told her, without letting me know. You put me at a disadvantage, and you're supposed to be on my side."

"I am, Brenna."

"Maybe we should just talk later," Brenna had said.

After he'd left, it had taken Brenna a good hour to close the door on all of it—her increasingly twisted personal life, Morasco's control issues, her father's mental illness, her daughter's hidden but now obvious hatred of Clea. All these strange secrets, worming their way into the light . . .

She'd made herself a salad for lunch, texted Maya again, read the Sunday papers online, walked to Balducci's and spent too much money on fresh pasta, imported Parmesan, fresh basil, and sun-dried tomatoes, and cooked it all up for later before diving into her work—in this case going through Debbie Minton's old credit card bills, a process she found oddly soothing.

The last charge, which she was looking at now, had been from a convenience store in Provo, Utah, of all places—but by now Brenna was so focused on the job at hand that she didn't even think or care about the fact that Roland Dufresne had stored Clea's clothes in that very same town for nearly thirty years. Brenna only thought about the last purchase Debbie Minton made—a Diet Coke and a turkey sandwich. According to her husband, Debbie had been a vegetarian.

Brenna's landline rang. She checked the caller ID: Trent.

"Hey," she said.

"Kanye."

"Huh?"

"That's what I'm calling the kid if he's a boy. Kanye. See how I did that? You didn't want to know, but I just slipped it in there, and now you do know whether you want to or not."

"Is that seriously why you called me?"

"Well . . ."

"Because I'm doing work here, Trent."

"You like the name?"

Brenna sighed heavily. "Yes. I'm sure he'll sell a million records."

"He can be KayKay for short."

"No. No he can't."

"Okay, fine," he said. "You can chill now because that's not the reason I called."

"Thank you."

"I called," he said, "because my Snapfish slice came through."

"Really?" said Brenna. "That was fast."

"Like I told you, she wants me."

"What information did she give you?"

"She says Clea's picture was posted by a member who goes by the same name as the Hotmail address on October 6, 2009."

Brenna sighed. "Recent."

"Yep."

"The day after my *Sunrise Manhattan* appearance."

"So Clea was a hot topic then. It could have been anybody."

"The picture wasn't a hot topic. I own the only copy."

"I wish it had been up there for a couple of years," he said. "You know, so you'd be able to rule out people you . . . uh . . . only met a couple months ago."

Brenna smiled. A mind reader. Or maybe she was just as easy for Trent to figure out as he was for her. Six years, Trent had been working for her. Six years of those clothes and that cologne and that desk decor and all those myriad irritating habits, yet thinking about him changing in any way made her feel uncomfortable, lost even.

"Do me a favor," he said. "Don't judge Nick Morasco until you know for sure. I say this as a guy who just got an e-mail from Stephanie titled 'Child support.' "

"Trent . . ."

"I'm serious. The dude's saved your life."

"No he hasn't."

"Well, he would have saved it if you gave him half a chance . . ."

"That doesn't even make any sense."

"I like him, okay? He's nice to you."

Brenna sighed heavily. "You never told me your girl name."

"You want to hear? Really?"

"Yes. Kanye for a boy and for a girl . . . what? Beyoncé?"

"Brenna."

"Yes?"

"No, dude. That's my girl name. Brenna. You don't like it, I don't care."

"You're . . . you would name your daughter after me?"

"Duh. Hello? You're the most awesome female I know."

Brenna's face warmed, her eyes clouding. Genuinely moved. "Thank you."

"Don't tell my mom I said that. She's awesome, too."

She heard Morse code: SOS. Her text tone. She reached for her phone, opened it. It was a text from Maya—sent to both her and Jim. *That's strange . . .*

She clicked on it. The text was long. The first line: *Dear Mom and Dad*. She started to read it. *No*. The word filled her mind, getting louder, repeating itself over and over. *No, no, no . . .*

Trent was saying, ". . . I mean Stephanie likes Nevaeh, so it's not a done deal, but . . ."

"Trent, I'm really sorry, but I can't talk now."

Brenna hung up. Her hand was shaking so bad that she dropped the receiver to the ground, the battery spilling out. She didn't bother to pick it up. Just read the rest of the text, her breath shallow, the word louder in her head, a real prayer. *No, no, no, no, please no, anything but this . . .* Wishing it were a dream, wishing it were a joke . . . Her whole world shattering, crumbling. Gone.

It didn't sound like her. None of it sounded like her. None of it sounded like any teenager texting her parents. But especially not Maya, with her loving sarcasm and her colon-and-parenthesis smiley faces. Brenna read the text five times, each time a blade, plunging deeper, hurting more.

Dear Mom and Dad,

I am sorry to hurt you but I am not happy with you. I have found new friends, a beautiful new life. Please don't try to find me. It's better this

*way. As the years go by, it will get easier. Please
take comfort in the fact that I am happy.*

> *Love,
> Maya*

Brenna texted back: *Maya please come home now!*
She called Maya's number. It went straight to voice
mail. She read the text again, her breath stuck in her
throat.

New friends . . . What did that mean? Maya had
stayed with a friend last night. Zoe, Jim had said. But
Zoe wasn't a new friend. Maya had been close to her
since second grade. Brenna picked up the phone, recalled December 2—the last time Zoe had phoned
Maya on the landline—and tapped her cell number in.

Zoe answered after a few rings. "Yeah?" She
sounded cold, strange.

Brenna took a deep breath. She tried to steady out
her voice. "Zoe?"

"Oh . . . uh . . . hi, Ms. Spector. I thought you were
Maya."

"Maya isn't there."

"Uh . . . no."

"Sorry to bother you, but this is very important. Did
she act strange during your sleepover last night?"

"Huh?"

Brenna had an urge to throw the phone across the
room. She closed her eyes, breathed in . . . "If you could
think back," she said it very slowly. *Stay in control.*
"Try and remember anything she might have said that
sounded strange last night. Anything. About . . . about

new friends. Or any plans she might have for today or—"

"Maya didn't spend the night last night."

"*What?*"

"She was supposed to, but she told me she had plans with her family. That wasn't true, huh? I didn't think it was."

"She canceled on you."

"Yeah."

"Yesterday."

"Yes. So you guys didn't have—"

"She didn't have family plans, Zoe," Brenna said. "She didn't come home."

"Oh . . . I'm . . . Wow, I hope she's okay."

Brenna had that feeling, as though she were slipping down the side of a cliff, fingernails scraping rocks, nothing to hang on to. She stood up. *Keep it together. Just for a few more seconds.* "Zoe, if you hear from her, please call me immediately and tell me exactly what she says."

"I will. I promise."

Brenna cleared her throat. "Thank you."

"Hey," Zoe said, "Did you try Lindsay?"

"Who?"

"Lindsay Segal."

"I don't know who that is."

"She's like Maya's new best friend. She's been eating lunch with her, and Nikki Webber and Annalee Lambert." She cleared her throat. "She . . . uh . . . she never mentioned them?"

New friends . . . "I've never heard her say those names."

Zoe said, "They're juniors."

Juniors. Brenna's thoughts went to Maya's hidden pictures. "Miles," she said.

"Huh?"

"I don't know his last name, but he's in the school chorus. About six feet tall. Trying to grow a beard. He's a junior, too, right?"

"Uh-huh. I know Miles. He's Lindsay's boyfriend."

Brenna stared at the front door, the scuffs down the side of it from all the times Maya had closed it too hard, coming home from school. "Lindsay's boyfriend," she repeated. The image ran through her mind: Maya's crestfallen face after that September 30 chorus practice, her eyes following Miles and the girl with the tight jeans and the wild hair. *Is that the same girl? Is that Maya's new friend?* "Zoe," she said. "Do you have Lindsay's phone number?"

"No," she said. "Lindsay has no idea who I am. Ms. Spector?"

"Yes?"

"Is Maya going to be okay?"

Isn't that the question of the hour, the minute, my whole life, please be okay, Maya, please, please . . . "Yes," she said. "I just need to find her. That's all."

Brenna heard her door buzz. She said good-bye to Zoe and hit end and flew for it, falling on the button, hoping only for Maya's voice, her Maya, telling her the text was a mistake, a joke . . . *Please, please, please.*

But it was Faith's voice who responded, weak and stunned as her own: "It's me, Brenna," she said. "It's us."

*   *   *

Faith stood in Brenna's doorway. She wore a puffy white coat, her hair pulled back in a ponytail, mascara streaks down her face. Her lips looked white.

"Where's Jim?" Brenna said.

"One flight down."

She closed her eyes. "Come up," she called out in a voice that sounded like it was coming out of someone else.

Brenna recalled seeing Jim yesterday morning, in front of the Magnolia, Maya rushing up to him, throwing her arms around his neck. At the time, Brenna had focused only on Jim, on the deep green jacket he wore and the memory he triggered—a memory of Jim and baby Maya—but she should have been watching thirteen-year-old Maya, the way her blonde hair swung, the way she trotted across the street and hugged her father . . . She should have been watching to see if that hug was sincere.

I am sorry to hurt you but I am not happy with you . . .

Had she really typed that? Did she really mean it?

Brenna heard footsteps and then Jim was next to Faith, wearing the same dark green jacket he'd worn nearly twenty-eight hours earlier, when his daughter had hugged him hello. His eyes were aimed at the floor. "It will be okay," she said.

He looked up and into her eyes and in them Brenna saw only pain. Only the present. "I hope so."

Never in her life had Brenna felt this way, this kick-to-the-gut feeling, this fear that if she were to cry or even think about crying, she'd break down and fall to the floor and never be able to get up again. In the past few months, she'd been knifed twice. She'd been punched in the face and kicked and shot at, and yet none of that . . . She'd take it all again and worse, if only . . . She'd give her life, if only . . .

"We called the police," Jim said. "Missing Persons Unit. We gave them Maya's picture. They're also tracing her cell."

Brenna said, "She wasn't at Zoe's last night."

"No," he said. "She was at Lindsay's."

Brenna drew a breath. "Miles's girlfriend."

"Who?"

"We called Lindsay's apartment before we came over," Faith said, "but no one answered."

I have found new friends, a beautiful new life.

"She texted me a couple of hours ago," Jim said. "Told me she was going to the movies with her friends."

"Just a couple of hours ago?" said Brenna.

"Yes."

"Did she say which movie?"

"No."

"Maybe they're still at the movies," Faith said. "Maybe some kid got hold of Maya's cell phone and found your numbers on her contacts and decided to play a prank. These kids never talk on the phone. You can't hear their voices, they can all pretend to be each other, it would be easy . . ." Her gaze darted from Brenna to Jim and back, begging for agreement.

Brenna nodded. "What did the police say?"

"Well," Faith said. "You know the police."

"They didn't think it was a prank," Jim said.

"They need to . . . You know it's true, Brenna. In order to perform their jobs effectively, the police need to . . . they have to assume the worst." Faith smiled. Then she started to cry, a few tears spilling down her cheeks, then more until she was sobbing, her body racked, doubling over. It was the first time Brenna had ever seen Faith shed even a few tears, and it killed her, the love this woman felt for Maya. Same as her own.

Jim put his arms around Faith and held her to him, Faith sobbing on his shoulder, his hands puffing into her white down coat.

Brenna wanted to hug them both, to cry along with Faith, but instead she looked away. *Keep it inside. Find her now. Cry later.*

"It's possible, right?" Faith said. "It could be a prank?"

"Anything's possible," Jim whispered.

Brenna looked at him and he met her gaze as though he were telling her, too, as though he were telling himself. *Anything's possible. Everything is going to be all right.*

Brenna said, "What time did she leave for the sleepover?"

"Around six," Jim said. "Maybe a little after."

"Did she text you last night at all?"

He shook his head. "The first I heard from her was the text about the movies."

"Police have your cell numbers?"

Faith nodded. "Yours, too."

"Good," Brenna said. "Let's not wait here."

Faith said, "Where do you want to wait?"

She grabbed her coat out of the closet, threw open the door, then turned to them. "Lindsay's place," she said.

"Doesn't seem like anybody's there," the doorman at Lindsay's building said after buzzing the Segals' apartment. He was balding and rosy, with bushy silver eyebrows and a slow, friendly way of talking—Clarence from *It's a Wonderful Life* meets the Ghost of Christmas Present.

Brenna would have found him pleasant under normal circumstances, but now his friendly manner felt like mockery, and Brenna wanted to hold him down and slap the smile off his face, to yank the words out of him. He gave her an elaborate shrug. "Sorry." His eyes twinkled. Brenna hated him.

"Listen," Jim said, "our daughter came over last night. She was spending the night with Lindsay—" His voice broke. He grasped Faith's hand.

The doorman nodded. "Yes? And?"

Brenna pulled out her wallet, slipped out Maya's ninth grade picture. Showed it to him. "Have you seen her?"

"No, ma'am. Haven't seen anybody. My shift just started a little while ago." He smiled.

Brenna wished he would stop smiling. "How about last night? Did you see her come or go?"

"Nope. Wasn't here. I'm the Sunday guy. I wish I could help you more, but—"

"Who was here?" Brenna said.

"Excuse me?"

"The Saturday night guy. What's his name?"

"That's . . . Hmmm . . . New guy. Don't remember his name. Glenn? Gary? He trades off with me, which means he'll be in after my shift's over. Three A.M." He smiled yet again, this time at Maya's picture. "Cute kid."

Brenna sighed. "Who are her parents?"

"I thought you said you were."

"No. Lindsay. Tell me about her parents. What are they like?"

"The Segals?"

No. Lindsay's other fifteen sets of parents.

"Yes," Faith said.

"Very nice people."

Brenna said, "Have you seen them at all since last night?"

He blinked at her. "No, ma'am."

"Okay."

"The Segals are out of town all week."

"*What?*" Jim spat out the word. "No . . . that can't be true."

"It is, sir," the doorman said. "See? There's a note right here from Mrs. Segal. We're supposed to hold the big packages. Keep an eye on their daughter . . ."

"Who is out somewhere," Brenna said. "You have no idea where."

"I told you, ma'am. I just got here."

Faith stared at Jim. "I thought you said—"

"Maya told me Lindsay's parents would be there."

The doorman shrugged. "Kids."

Brenna's fists clenched up. She wanted to grab the doorman, slam his head into the marble-topped desk. "No. Not *kids.* Our daughter . . . She wouldn't . . . She doesn't just lie."

"How old is she?"

"Thirteen."

He gave them a knowing nod. "They grow up fast." He started to go through a stack of papers on the front desk. Brenna told herself not to get angry about the nod, the smugness. They'd never told him about the text Maya had sent. Far as he knew, they were just a group of overprotective parents, pissed off because their daughter *hadn't* texted.

"You never talked directly to the parents?" Faith was asking Jim.

"I didn't," he was saying. "I was on deadline and I didn't . . ."

"There ya go," the doorman said.

Brenna gave him a look. "Excuse me?"

He looked up at her, the smile beatific. He thumped his hand on the stack of papers. "This is last night's log," he said.

Brenna looked at him. "And?"

"What I was trying to tell you earlier, ma'am. We don't always know our kids."

Jim said, "What the hell do you mean?"

"The night doorman had three noise complaints about the Segals' apartment last night. Last one was at two-thirty in the morning," he said, studying each of the three faces as though he were mining for a smile. "They claimed the girl was having some kind of loud party."

Brenna flashed on her mother, standing in her doorway three hours ago, just about to leave. She recalled the chastising gleam in the pale eyes as she told her about the phone call she received from Maya. At 3 A.M.

*I think she may have dialed my number by accident.
We had a terrible connection and I could barely hear
her. But . . . well, she sounded awfully wild.*

Brenna looked at Faith. "Maybe someone put her up
to it at the party," she said. "Maybe they got her drunk
and they dared her to type it."

"Maya doesn't drink," Faith said. "She's only thirteen."

Brenna couldn't even bring herself to glance at the
doorman. "Peer pressure, Faith," she said. "These kids
are juniors and they're popular. She looks up to them."

Jim said, "At Maya's age, you think upperclassmen
are gods."

"Right. That's what I'm saying."

"And if those upperclassmen are misbehaving . . ."

"Yes."

Jim turned to Faith, then Brenna. There was a spark
in his eyes, a hope. "That text could have been in her
drafts."

"Yes," Brenna said again.

"She could have forgotten to delete it. It could have
accidentally gotten sent while she was at the movies."

"Yes," she said again, to Jim and Faith both. "Yes,
exactly." A smile crossed her face, twitchy and desperate. She was grasping at a straw, she knew. She was
holding on for all it was worth. But she wanted them so
badly to hang on with her. Hope was so much harder
when you did it alone.

"She's been keeping secrets," Faith said quietly.
"She's been typing on her computer, and then she hides
the typing . . ."

Brenna heard doorbell chimes—Maya's ring tone.
Her heart leaped, then soared for one irrational moment

(*She's in the lobby with us. She's been here all along and her phone is ringing . . .*) before she realized it was coming from Faith's bag. "You guys have the same—"

"Yeah."

Faith answered it, Brenna's gaze heading back to Jim, watching Faith with such fear and hope.

"Okay," Faith said. "Thank you."

She ended the call. Looked at them both. "That was the police," she said. "They've located Maya's cell."

"Where is it?" Jim said.

Faith turned to Brenna, as though she'd asked the question. "They found it," she said, "in Tarry Ridge."

9

"You want Chinese?" Baus asked Morasco. "I'm buying."

Nick Morasco looked up from his desk. Baus was leaning against it, fluorescent lights glinting off his glasses so you couldn't see behind them. It was almost as though Baus had positioned himself this way, but Morasco didn't need to look him in the eye to figure out what was on his mind. Baus was one of the most transparent guys Morasco had ever met. When Baus said, "You look tired," it meant *he* was tired. When he was in a bad mood, he whistled, loudly. And when he offered to buy dinner, it meant he wanted something from you. "What do you want, Baus?"

"How do you know I want something?"

Morasco sighed. This, too. When it was an extra big favor he wanted out of you, Baus got all evasive about it. It occurred to Nick now that maybe Baus wasn't all that transparent. Maybe it was just that after working alongside him at the Tarry Ridge Police Department for almost fifteen years, Nick had learned to read him, the same way you learn to read a spouse. The thought depressed him immensely. He didn't even like Baus that much.

"Shrimp lo mein and a couple of egg rolls," Morasco said.

"You got it, champ."

Baus returned to his own desk—which was two over from Morasco's in the squad room—and called the Chinese place. He'd be back in a few minutes asking for the favor, Morasco knew. "Champ" was another huge tell.

For a few seconds, he let himself think of Brenna, how angry she was at him. Some of it was his fault, some not, just like pretty much any fight he'd ever had with a woman. But with other women, he'd been able to explain himself. He'd gotten tongue-tied with Brenna. Nothing had come out like he'd planned it in his head. And when she'd asked him to leave, he'd done so without protest, afraid of screwing things up even more.

It wasn't like him, the fast retreat. But Brenna wasn't like other women. It was the memory thing. When a woman asks you for an explanation, and you know she'll remember that explanation thirty years from now, word for word . . . Well, let's just say it puts the pressure on.

Driving back to Tarry Ridge, Nick had replayed their conversation in his head. He'd thought about what he'd have said to her if he'd had the chance. In his thoughts, he'd spelled out the real reason that he'd called her mother after giving her the police papers. He'd said it clearly, choosing all the right words. He'd let Brenna know that he was on her side, that he always would be.

But he hadn't driven back to her apartment and said those words in person. He hadn't tried to make things right with Brenna, when he could have done it;

there was no one stopping him. If Nick was going to be honest with himself, really honest, he'd also have to admit that in some ways, getting away from Brenna today had been a relief.

Maybe he didn't want to make things right with her.

He pushed the thought away, went back to his computer. He had already gone through what few open case files there were. Now he was checking the status on the weekend's calls, forwarded to him by the desk sergeant, Sally.

The chief hadn't come in today, which put Nick, as ranking detective, in charge of assigning anything new that came in to the three other detectives and the dozen uniforms who were on duty. It wasn't much of anything. Sundays were slow crime days here in Tarry Ridge, especially in winter.

So far today, someone had called in a domestic dispute, which had turned out to be two elderly sisters fighting over who was going to clean out the litter box. There had been a lost dog call, too, plus a fifteen-year-old prep school kid had shoplifted some beers from the A&P on a dare. The kid was still in the holding cell, waiting for his parents, who apparently felt that three hours behind bars on the taxpayers' dime was preferable to taking their own child home and grounding him.

"Hey, champ." As predicted, Baus was back at Nick's desk. Seriously, he could set his watch by this guy.

"What do you want from me, Baus?" Baus's first name was Ehrlich. It was a family name. He didn't like it much, but he loved his last name, which was pronounced "boss." *Even the chief calls me boss*, he'd say. Baus loved that joke.

Baus said, "Can you talk to Mrs. Rowell for me?"

Morasco closed his eyes. Mrs. Rowell was one hundred and three years old—Tarry Ridge's oldest resident. The *Tarry Ridge Times* did a write-up on her every year for her birthday. She lived alone, was healthy and, for the most part, lucid. That is, except for believing that her husband, who had been dead for twenty years, was still alive. Every couple of weeks or so, she'd realize she hadn't seen him in a while, and come by the station and ask to speak to a detective. "When is she going to be here?"

"She's here."

"What? Where?"

"Interview room."

Morasco stared at him. "You just left her in there and came out to shoot the breeze and take Chinese food orders?" He got up from his desk, headed across the squad room toward the closed door.

"Dude, her husband isn't really missing!" Baus called after him.

"She doesn't know that."

When he opened the door to the interview room, he found Mrs. Rowell huddled up in the one of the hard metal chairs, hugging herself. She caught sight of him and unfolded. "I know you," she said. "Detective Morasco."

"Hi, Mrs. Rowell."

Mrs. Rowell gave him a wary smile. She wasn't any bigger than an eight-year-old. She wore a heavy black coat that looked about five sizes too big and puffy pink snow boots that didn't quite touch the floor.

Mrs. Rowell broke Nick's heart a little. She looked

smaller every time he saw her, as though she were leaving the earth slowly, one inch at a time. "My husband's missing, Detective Morasco," she said. "My husband, Charlie."

Nick sat down in the chair across from hers. "I'm so sorry, ma'am." There was a steno pad and pen on the metal table. He took them. Wrote down the name so she could see him writing. *Charlie Rowell.* Then he looked up at her, pen poised. "Can you tell me where and when you saw him last?"

Her eyes were bright and wet. "No," she said. "I . . . I can't . . . remember."

Morasco put a hand on hers. "It's okay."

"It's not. How can you find him if I can't remember when I saw him last?"

"Tell me about the best time you ever had with him."

"How will that help?"

"I could get to know him better," he said. "That always helps."

Mrs. Rowell watched him for a while, her expression softening. "*Queen Mary.* 1950," she said, finally. "What a wonderful place to ring in the New Year."

"Did you dance?"

"Till three in the morning. There were champagne glasses in a pyramid. The band played 'Near You.' Do you know that song? So romantic . . ."

Morasco smiled. He watched her for a while, let her take in the memory. "Can you describe him, physically?"

"He has sandy blond hair and brown eyes. Very white teeth."

Morasco wrote it down. *Bl hair. Br eyes. Very white teeth.*

"He's five-foot-eleven."

"What was Mr. Rowell wearing, when you danced?"

"Gray pin-striped suit. Red tie. Gold cuff links that are shaped like ladybugs. I gave him those."

Morasco smiled. "Thank you, Mrs. Rowell. This is all very helpful."

"Will you try to find him?"

"Yes." He said it without hesitation. "I will." It didn't matter, after all, whether there really was a light at the end of the tunnel. What mattered was seeing it shine. "We'll do all we can."

Mrs. Rowell stood up. She took one of Morasco's hands in both of hers, which were dry and cool and tiny. She looked up at him, eyes like glowing coals. "You are a very nice person," she said.

He opened the door to the interview room, led her through the squad room and to the front door.

"Bye, Mrs. Rowell!" Baus called out.

She shook her head. "He left me in that room for the longest time."

"He's an idiot," Morasco said.

He pushed open the front door for her. Her driver waited in front, the engine of his glossy town car running. An icy wind slapped the side of his face, but Mrs. Rowell, in her big coat, didn't even seem to notice it. "As long as there are people looking for Charlie," she said, "he's not really gone."

He smiled, and she smiled back. She'd forget him in a week, a day, an hour, he knew. But for now they were old friends, sharing a secret.

Baus is such a tool.

Morasco pushed open the heavy door to the station house. As he passed the front desk, Sally signaled him.

"What's up?" he said, and only then did he notice the strange look in her eyes.

"We got a call from the NYPD—Missing Persons Unit," she said. "A teen runaway they've tracked here."

"Okay, forward me the info. I'll get somebody on that."

He started into the squad room. She held a hand up. "You also got a call from Brenna."

"Okay, thanks, Sal—"

"No." She frowned, her face coloring. "You don't understand."

"I don't?"

"Brenna's call," she said. "The call from New York. They're about the same girl. Brenna's daughter."

Morasco couldn't find a squad car fast enough, but the good news was, Maya wasn't far. Police at the Twentieth Precinct had pinged her phone, narrowing its location to the corner of Van Wagenen and Main, which was just about ten miles away from the station. Everything in Tarry Ridge was fairly close. Though it had quadrupled its population within the last fifteen years, the town had grown up, not out—a dense but small bedroom community, bursting at the seams, but all of it accessible. When there wasn't much traffic—and on a cold Sunday evening post-Christmas season, there was hardly any—you could get to most places within Tarry Ridge in twenty minutes or less.

Morasco was on the way now, Danny Cavanaugh

driving, with his partner, Rich Cerulli, in the passenger's seat, Morasco in the back, calling Brenna's cell.

"I'm on my way," Brenna said by way of answering.

"Me too," said Morasco. "I'll meet you there."

"Nick?"

"Yeah?"

"Do you ever pray?"

"Not really."

"Me neither."

"Don't worry. She is okay. Drive safe."

"I'm not driving."

"That's good."

"I don't think I could drive. I'm shaking so bad."

"Brenna, listen to me. Maya is fine."

"I don't know her . . . I thought I did, but . . . I don't know anything."

"Believe it, okay? She's fine."

Morasco heard a slow intake of breath, a shaky release. "She's fine," Brenna said.

"You're on your way to pick her up."

"I am."

"You're going to hug her and scream at her. Then you will take her home and ground her for the next five years."

Another deep breath, in and out. "Thank you. Thank you, Nick." Brenna ended the call.

Morasco felt turned around, twisted inside.

Cavanaugh was flooring it, siren blaring. He ran a red light, swung into a left on Main, and then they saw it, four blocks down, the Lukoil station on the corner.

Cavanaugh said, "Detective Morasco, isn't that where the Wentz murder weapon was found?"

"Yep."

Of course, Morasco had thought of that as soon as he'd heard which street corner Maya's phone had been traced to. Back in the fall, a knife had been found there, in that same gas station's garbage can. It had tied Nelson Wentz to his wife's murder—a major turning point in the case that had made Morasco something of a hero to Danny Cavanaugh, a third-generation cop and a law enforcement fanboy if there ever was one.

More importantly, though, that same case had first brought Nick and Brenna together. Whether this was a significant fact, or whether it was pure coincidence, Morasco didn't know. Just like he didn't know what had prompted Maya—a reasonably happy kid from what he'd seen—to pick up and leave her parents without warning. To send them a text like that . . .

A detective from the NYPD's Missing Persons Unit had read it to him over the phone in a matter-of-fact, seen-it-all voice. *Take comfort in the fact that I am happy.*

It says that? Morasco had asked.

Word for word, Detective.

But Missing Persons didn't know Maya. Maya would never say those words, let alone type them out and hit send. Maya would never *think* them.

Danny Cavanaugh said, "Are you getting déjà vu, sir?"

"Huh?"

"You know. From the Neff case."

"Oh . . . no."

Cavanaugh pulled in to the Lukoil station and Morasco got out of the car. The street was dark, the stores closed. Tarry Ridge wasn't exactly known for its hopping night life, especially on a Sunday night of a nonholiday weekend.

The gas station, too, was nearly empty. Only ways you'd know it was open at all were the lit up sign and the soccer mom who stood in her fitted black coat, pumping gas into a shiny blue Lexus. Morasco jogged up to her, flashing his badge, Danny Cavanaugh and his partner Cerulli right behind. Words flew out of all their mouths at once. "Ma'am, have you seen a blonde girl, about five-foot-nine . . ."

"Excuse me, Miss, have you seen a thirteen-year-old . . ."

". . . any strange activity involving a blonde girl . . ."

The woman's eyes widened. She clutched the pump. Morasco's eyes went to the back bumper of her car. The peeling sticker: "My Child Is an Honor Student at George Washington Elementary." Then back to her face—tasteful makeup, terror flickering across the features, the mouth twitching. Morasco doubted she'd been this close to danger in her entire life. He thought of her kid, her elementary school honor student, probably at home right now with Dad, his face buried in a biology book, safe and warm and free from fear . . .

"Is something wrong?" she said. "What happened?"

They all three started to speak again, but Morasco held up a hand. He felt somebody watching him. Across the street, a figure stood outside a closed Starbucks, hiding in the shadows. A man. "Finish up," he said to Cavanaugh, then he headed across the street, fast. Behind him he heard Cavanaugh saying, "Missing girl," Honor Mom saying, "Oh my."

The man turned fast, started heading up the sidewalk, shoes clicking. Morasco followed. "Hello," he said. "Sir? I need to ask you a few questions."

The man kept walking, as though he had an appointment to make. He was a couple of inches taller than Morasco, and broad. A big man. He wore a long, dark coat.

"You and I are the only people on the street," Morasco said. "How long are we going to keep this up?"

The man stumbled a little. His hands were straight out at his sides, fists clenching and unclenching.

"You know who I am," said Morasco. "You saw me back there."

The man started to slow.

"Police. Halt." Morasco didn't shout it. He didn't have to—it was that quiet. A car buzzed by—Honor Mom's Lexus, the only car on the street.

The man stopped, turned around. "Yeah?" he said.

The light from a streetlamp hit the side of his face—clean shaven but wet with sweat. His eyes were half closed, the mouth slack. *Pills*, Morasco thought. He felt the weight of his gun at his shoulder holster. "Can you please put your hands up where I can see them?"

"On what grounds?"

"On the grounds that I want to see your hands."

The man slowly raised his hands. "I wasn't doing anything," he said.

"I didn't say you were."

Morasco leveled his gaze at him. He slipped his hand beneath his coat, touched the .45 in his shoulder holster, making sure the guy noticed.

"It's okay," the guy said. "Takeiteasyofficer." The words slurred out of his mouth, bumping into each other. From where he was standing, Morasco detected an acrid, BO smell. Beads of sweat swelled on his upper lip, rolled down his face. "It's okay," he said again. "I wasn't trying to piss you off. I was just walking."

"Have you seen a young girl around here? Thirteen years old? Blonde hair?"

"I haven't seen any girls."

Morasco heard something, a sound coming out of the guy's coat. Doorbell chimes.

The guy started to shake. "Oh shit," he whispered.

Morasco rested his hand on the .45. "Keep them up," he said. He moved closer. The chimes echoed on the quiet street. "Ring tone?" he said.

The smell was worse close up. Under the coat he wore a white button-down shirt, the collar dark with sweat. His eyes were wide open now, the irises huge, eclipsing the pupils. "I don't know, man."

Morasco slipped his hand into the guy's coat pocket, pulled out the slim thing as it chimed.

The phone's case was encrusted with pink glitter.

"This is your phone?" he said.

"Yeah."

The hell it is. Morasco turned over the chiming phone, looked at the caller ID screen: "Mom," it said. Next to the word was Brenna's picture.

Morasco froze. Anger burned through him, bubbled in his veins. *"Where is she?"* he shouted. *"Where is Maya?"*

It happened as though in slow motion: the sweating man turning around and moving, knocking the phone out of Morasco's hand, the phone flying into the gutter, splashing into a puddle from the previous night's rain, the ring dying along with it. Then Cavanaugh and Cerulli running across the street, the wet crash of their shoes on the wet pavement, another squad car arriving, siren blaring, screeching to a stop.

And the asshole was running now, full-on racing up the street, faster than any drugged man should know how to run, big legs powering forward, coat flapping behind him.

"What's going on?" said Danny Cavanaugh, as Cerulli bent to scoop up the ruined phone and Morasco took off after the running man. His feet thudded on the sidewalk, he pushed hard, but the black coat was that much farther up the block, then crossing the street . . .

"Stop!" Morasco shouted, the word a rasp.

The man was slowing, drugs and ill health kicking in, and still Morasco strained forward, gaining on him, close enough now to smell his sweat.

The man faltered, slowed more. Stopped. Morasco could hear his breathing now, hard and wet.

"Turn around!" Morasco's voice echoed up the dark street.

His whole body moved with each breath, shook with it.

Morasco kept his hand on his .45. "Turn around," he said. "Put your hands up."

The man turned. He reached under his coat.

"Put your hands up!" Cavanaugh shouted.

The man grabbed something and pulled it out, his fist clamped around it . . .

"Drop it!"

Maya, just a kid.

"Put it down!" Cerulli said.

Morasco heard a loud crack. And then the freak was spinning again, spinning to run, he thought for a split second, but then he was falling, face to the pavement, Cavanaugh chanting, "Oh my God. Oh my God. Oh my God."

Morasco heard Brenna's voice saying his name, Brenna rushing up to him, her hands on his arms, his face, in his hair. "What's happening," she was saying.

And only then did Morasco see the blood on the sidewalk, pooling under the man's head. Only then, with the smell of gunfire in the cold air and the sound of it still pounding in his ears, still numbing him to every real sound, every word, only then did he realize that it was his own gun he'd heard. Only then was he aware of his hands, still wrapped tight around the .45, still aching from the force, his fingers still resting against the trigger.

10

"You think Brenna's gotten to Tarry Ridge yet?" Faith said.

"Seems like she should have."

"Do you think they'll find Maya there?"

Jim said, "Yes." But he didn't sound like he meant it, and he wouldn't look at her. Jim never could look Faith in the eyes and lie, which was usually a quality she appreciated, but not now. She could have done with a little lying now.

They were sitting on a very uncomfortable couch in the cold, marble lobby of Lindsay Segal's building, waiting for Lindsay to come home. That had been the plan. When police had arrived, and they'd said they could take one parent along with them to Tarry Ridge, the three of them had agreed Brenna would go. (It had been a no-brainer, what with her job and her connection to Detective Morasco.)

Jim and Faith had agreed to stay here, on the chance Maya really was at the movies with Lindsay and someone had simply stolen her phone. That had easily been an hour ago, maybe more. And with no call from either the police or Brenna, no more texts from Maya, and no Lindsay, Faith was feeling increasingly tense.

The doorman's station faced the couch. He was reading *The Secret*. Every so often, Faith would steal a glance at him, wonder what he was thinking—which is what you do when you can't stand your own thought process. It's like being at a restaurant and not liking what you order. You pay more attention to what's on everyone else's plate. You envy them, simply for having chosen differently.

"Good book?" Faith asked the doorman. She never had gotten the doorman's name, and since she was past the point of politely asking him for it, she'd secretly nicknamed him Happy. "I've heard lots of good things about *The Secret*."

Faith could feel Jim cringing next to her. He'd never much appreciated her habit of starting conversations with strangers—particularly now, she imagined. And she and Happy had already talked at length—about the weather, about how they'd spent their Christmases, about which movies they thought deserved Academy Award nominations . . .

Jim got quiet when under stress. He closed up into himself, spinning his own cocoon. Faith assumed that was part of his being an only child, and that was fine. For him. Faith, on the other hand, had three sisters and a brother, and too much silence got her spooked. Her mind would fill in the blanks, in this case crafting images of Ashley Stanley at thirteen, blonde as Maya, smiling at Renee Lemaire as she first pulled up in her car.

I have found new friends, a beautiful new life.

Faith gritted her teeth. She dug her heels into her shoes, pushed away the bad thoughts. She needed to talk to someone, anyone—and if that made Jim feel uncomfortable, she didn't care. "I've had several friends who have read *The Secret* and adored it," Faith said, a little too loudly.

"It's terrific," Happy said. "This is the third time I've read it."

"Isn't it about the power of positive thinking?"

"Not thinking." He adjusted his glasses. "Believing. There's a big difference."

Faith looked at Jim. He was staring down at the marble floor, his hands clasped together. If you didn't know him, you might think he was praying.

Happy said, "Belief is a lot more powerful than thought."

Faith's white coat lay across her lap. She smoothed it, feeling the cool fabric under her palms, wanting that to be true.

"Has it worked for you?" she said. "Do you have any *Secret* success stories?"

Jim stiffened. "Jesus, Faith," he whispered.

"I need this," she said, between her teeth. "I need something."

Happy said, "I really hope you folks find your daughter."

"Can you *believe* we will?" Faith said. "Can you believe we'll find her soon?"

He put his book down. "Yes."

"Believe it with all your heart," she said. "Please."

"Sure," said Happy. Happy, looking sad. "I can believe that."

The door pushed open. The doorman's chin lifted. His thick eyebrows went up, and for a few seconds, Faith thought, *Our prayers are answered. Maya, standing at the door.* Happy said, "Miss Segal, there are people here to see you."

Jim and Faith both stood up at the same time and turned toward the door, where a baffled teenage girl stood, holding hands with a tall, scruffy boy of about the same age. Maya was not with them.

"Lindsay?" Jim said.

The girl dropped hands with the boy—or maybe it was the other way around. "Yeah?"

Strange, when Maya had told Faith that she was helping a junior with an art project, Faith hadn't expected the junior to look so . . . well . . . trashy. Faith wasn't sure whether it was all the makeup or the bubblegum flatness of her voice or the way she regarded her, the pink mouth hanging open, the blackened eyes half closed with a boredom that looked as though she'd practiced it in the mirror. Or maybe it was just the fact that Maya wasn't standing there with her. Maybe that was it.

Faith sucked in her bad feelings, stuck out her hand. "This is Maya Rappaport's dad, Jim," she said. "I'm Faith, her stepmother."

The boy was the one to shake it. "Hi," he said. His hand felt a little moist.

She looked at him. "I didn't catch your name."

"Sorry. I'm . . . uh . . . Miles." He said it as though he'd actually forgotten his own name for a few seconds.

"Nice to meet you, Miles." She saw something in his eyes, a hint of recognition. She got this a lot from strangers—that don't-I-know-you-from-somewhere look. Such was the C-list level of her fame, but while she usually helped people out by telling them she was on that morning TV show they sometimes watched, she didn't care to do that for this scruffy boy (didn't anyone shave anymore?). Not if he wasn't going to help her.

"Lindsay," Jim said. "Maya never came home."

The girl's eyes widened, the gimlet glaze slipping out of them.

"We were hoping she'd be with you."

"No . . . um . . . She's not."

"And you don't know where she is?" Faith said.

"Sorry."

Faith's stomach dropped. It wasn't as though she hadn't expected that answer, but she'd been hoping. Believing. She closed her eyes for a few seconds. Jim was right. At times like this, it was better to close yourself off, weave that cocoon, protect yourself . . .

Jim said, "She texted this afternoon that you guys were going to the movies . . ."

"We . . . we didn't go to the movies, Mr., uh . . ."

"Rappaport. I figured. But my daughter is missing, so any help you might be able to give . . ."

"*What?*" Miles's voice cracked on the word, his face flushing. Lindsay shot him a look.

Faith trained her eyes on him. "That's what we've been trying to tell you. Maya is missing," she said. "I'm sure the police will be talking to you as well, but we just wanted to know if you had any idea where she might be."

"Missing," Miles said.

Lindsay said, "The police?"

"Maybe she mentioned something at the sleepover . . . Do you remember Maya saying anything that seemed strange or out of the ordinary?" Jim said. "I hear there was a party here last night, and maybe—"

"She wasn't here."

"Excuse me?"

"Maya was never here?" Lindsay said it like a question. "I did have a party, but she . . . um . . . She wasn't invited."

"You're being serious with us," Jim said.

"Yes. No offense or anything," Lindsay said. "Right, Miles?"

"Uh . . . no. I mean yeah."

"She's just a freshman. I don't know her that well."

"She never came to your apartment yesterday."

"No."

Jim stared at her for several seconds, saying nothing.

"I'm sorry, Mr. and Mrs. Rappaport," Lindsay said. "We have a test tomorrow and we have to study." She took Miles's hand. "I really hope you find Maya."

Jim and Faith watched them go, Miles glancing over his shoulder briefly as the elevator doors opened.

Jim exhaled—a long, slow breath that seemed to drain everything from him—life, hope. "She could be in Tarry Ridge," he said. "They might be with her right now."

Faith could feel Jim turning to look at her, but she didn't meet his gaze. She stayed focused on the closed elevator doors, on the spot where the boy, Miles, had turned to her. She'd seen something in his eyes then, something crumbling and sad.

"I hope so," Faith said.

* * *

"Help me," Lindsay told Miles. She was taking everything out of the overnight bag Maya had left, and she was shoving it into a black plastic garbage bag. She looked psychotic. "Do you hear me?"

"Yeah."

"Well?"

"Well what?"

"Give me that coat."

Maya's bright blue coat was draped across a chair in the corner. Miles picked it up and handed it to her, thinking of Maya, standing at his door in this coat, her hair pulled back in a ponytail. Two weeks ago. Not even. A week and a half, and now she was . . . Where was she? This was surreal. This stuff didn't happen to people. Not in real life. Miles needed to wake up from this. He wished so badly that he would just wake up and it would be three weeks ago and then he'd know. He'd know what not to do.

"You can't do that," Lindsay said. "You can't check out on me." She stuffed the coat in the bag along with everything else, pushing the arms in, as though the coat was alive and fighting with her. "You're as much a part of this as I am."

"You lied to her parents."

She stopped what she was doing. "You want me to tell her parents what we did to her . . . what *you* did to her?"

Miles swallowed hard.

"I'd be glad to do it, Miles. You want me to?"

"No."

"I didn't think so."

Lindsay finished stuffing the coat into the bag.

"We have to delete the video," she said. "Did you record it?"

He stared down at the rug. Lindsay had cleaned it, but you could still see the puke stain. "No," he said.

"I thought you said you wanted to."

"I didn't record it."

"Okay . . ." She frowned at him. "Well . . . whatever. We're good then. It means I have the only copy." She moved over to her desk, squeezing around Miles, slipping her hands around his waist to move him.

He heard her behind him, tapping on her keyboard as she called up the video. Lindsay's voice slipping out of the speakers. *"And anyway, Miles said you liked to party . . ."*

Lindsay click, click, clicked. Miles stared at the far wall, at a framed poster from the American Ballet Theater—pink ballet shoe against a black background. He thought of all the time he'd spent in this room, on that bed, looking up at that poster. Strange how you can be in the same place, looking at the same thing, yet feel so differently.

"Done." She spun around, started across the room. "Now we have to take her stuff out to the incinerator."

"What?"

Lindsay stopped. "You heard me."

"But . . . what if there's some clue in there. Maybe . . . like . . . a note from somebody or a receipt or . . ."

"Listen to me," Lindsay said. "Maya Rappaport was never here."

"They're going to find out."

"No they won't."

"You texted her, didn't you?"

Lindsay stared at him, blinking. "Whatever," she said finally. "I'll tell them someone stole my phone."

"Come on," he said. "There could be something important in her overnight bag."

"Stop it, Miles."

"We could leave it at the police station anonymously. No one has to know it came from us . . ."

"There's nothing in this bag other than clothes and stuff." She gave the coat one more push, then tied it off at the top. "Look. We played a little joke on her. It wasn't a big deal. Just because she showed up over here and booted on my carpet, it doesn't mean we're required to participate in an investigation."

"But she *is* missing."

"*I didn't make her disappear,*" Lindsay said. "I'm not going to freak out my parents by getting involved with the police. I'm not going to have cops in this apartment making me feel like this is all *my fault* when it *isn't.*"

Miles had never noticed how pale Lindsay's eyes were. He'd only noticed her shiny hair and her tight body and the way she smelled, like fresh flowers. But the way she was looking at him now, they reminded him of ice shards, or maybe lasers. Something so pale and cold it hurt.

"All we did was talk," he said.

"What?"

"That's all we did. She came over. She said she was in the neighborhood. We talked about art class. She told me she might drop chorus. That was it."

"Bullshit." Lindsay pushed the garbage bag at him. "The incinerator is down at the end of the hall."

Miles took the bag and left her apartment. He could

feel the brass buttons on Maya's blue coat through the thin plastic. Again he thought about her at his door a week and a half ago, the way she shifted from foot to foot, her teeth dragging against her lower lip. He remembered the earrings she was wearing and how she tugged on one of them, twisting it around. *I like your earrings*, he had said.

Thanks. My grandma gave them to me.

He remembered how nervous she'd seemed, how obvious it was that she'd worked up courage to come see him and how flattered he'd been by the thought of that. He remembered how he'd stared deep into her eyes as she talked to him, trying to make her more nervous, liking that feeling.

Miles threw the bag into the incinerator. He closed the door and headed back to Lindsay's apartment, trying to keep himself from thinking about her, about Maya, poor Maya, and how he'd made her disappear.

The squad car yanks itself away from the curb and hurls up Twentieth Street, the siren burning Brenna's ears. Her stomach drops with the sharp movement. Forty minutes, *she thinks.* Forty minutes and I'll be in Tarry Ridge and so will she. *The uniformed officer in front of her shifts in her seat. She has cornrowed hair, and when she moves the beads in her braids click against one another. A comforting sound. The seat squeaks as Brenna shifts her weight and the beads click and the siren blares, every sound pushing against her, echoing in her ears. Her heart, too. That echoes, too.*

"You okay, Ms. Spector?" *says the cornrowed officer. Officer Benoit, she's called.*

Brenna nods. She realizes how hard she's been breathing.

"It will be okay, ma'am." *Her voice is very calm. Her partner turns onto the West Side Highway, the car making a wide arc. She closes her eyes. She pictures Maya, standing next to the pump at the Lukoil station on Van Wagenen and Main, Maya spotting the car and rushing up and racing into her arms.* I'm sorry, Mom. It was a dare. I didn't mean to scare you . . .

Brenna bit her lip hard, coming back to the chair in the waiting room at the Tarry Ridge ER.

"Are you okay?" said Detective Plodsky, which made Brenna miss Officer Benoit. It made her miss two hours ago, riding in the squad car, feeling that hope.

"Just thinking."

Detective Plodsky was from the Missing Persons Unit—a thin, no-nonsense woman with a gunmetal bob and pursed lips and eyes like a gate slamming. She'd shown up at the gas station in her own car just as the ambulance was leaving and followed the squad cars to the hospital.

During their first hour together in the waiting room, Plodsky and Brenna had barely exchanged three words, but she seemed to be making up for it now, as though she'd just remembered she was supposed to question her. The mother of the missing girl. *The runaway.* That's how Plodsky had referred to Maya when she thought Brenna wasn't listening. She'd said it to Morasco just as they arrived at the hospital. *How much do you know about the runaway?* she'd said.

Plodsky said, "Ms. Spector?"

"I didn't hear your question."

"Has Maya's schedule changed at all in the past few weeks? Maybe she signed up for a new class, or activity . . ."

"She's in the school chorus," Brenna said.

"And that's new?"

"Since September."

She nodded. She had a steno pad in her lap. She wrote a word on it.

Brenna wished Morasco was here instead of Plodsky. Morasco, of course, was being questioned himself, his gun taken away, suspended from work while Internal Affairs investigated him as they would any police officer who had discharged his firearm. The man he'd shot—the only man who might know what had happened to Maya—was in surgery right now. He'd grabbed for something under his coat, yes. But as backup units discovered, the *something* had been a small white envelope containing half a gram of cocaine. He'd wanted to throw away his drugs, not shoot three cops. And while Cerulli and Cavanaugh had both agreed that there was no way of knowing what this obviously intoxicated guy was going to pull out from under his big black coat on a dark street after attempting to run away from police, Morasco had been the only one who'd fired.

The bullet had been found on the sidewalk, which was good—shots to the head tend to be easier to survive if there's an exit wound. But Brenna hadn't been able to find out whether it had gone through his brain. Last time she'd checked, doctors were using expressions like "touch and go" and "not out of the woods yet."

Plodsky said, "Does Maya like to sing?"

"No."

"Then why did she join chorus?"

"Because of a boy."

"A boyfriend?"

"No. A crush."

"Does Maya tell you about all her crushes?"

Brenna turned. Looked at her. "How would I know that?"

"Pardon?"

"If she didn't tell me about one of them, how would I know that she hadn't told me?"

"Has she been acting differently? Since she had this crush?"

The image floated through Brenna's mind—*The Very Hungry Caterpillar* book, the folded-up sketches fluttering out . . . She pushed the thought away. The thought was irrelevant. The question was irrelevant. All of these questions . . . *The runaway.* All of it.

Plodsky needed to stop. She needed to leave. Brenna turned to her. "There's a man who's getting operated on right now. I doubt he has anything to do with Maya's crush or her school activities, but he has her goddamn cell phone in his pocket so maybe it's him you should be finding out about. Not . . . *school gossip.*"

Detective Plodsky gave her a look. To Brenna, it registered as a blend of pity, condescension, and disdain. "These questions are necessary, ma'am."

"I think I just need a little quiet right now."

Plodsky nodded. "Take all the time you need." She didn't sound like she meant it.

The man, the man whom Morasco had shot, the man who was getting operated on. His name was Mark Carver. They'd learned that from the driver's license, along with his place of residence (2920 Woodhall Road, Mount

Temple, New York) and his age (thirty-five). He owned an American Express card, a Kohl's card, a membership to Planet Fitness. No business cards. No phone of his own. Save for his wallet, which had held the aforementioned items, as well as twenty dollars in fives and tens, nothing else had been found in Mark Carver's pockets. No pills, which was rather surprising. Morasco said he looked like he had swallowed a medicine cabinet's worth.

Detective Plodsky said, "Has Maya been behaving differently at all?"

Brenna sighed. *I suppose you've decided that's all the time I need.* "Differently?"

"Aside from signing up for chorus, does she have any new, out-of-the-ordinary activities or habits?"

"She asked to see a psychiatrist," Brenna said it very calmly. "I took her to one yesterday."

Detective Plodsky's jaw dropped open. "Do you have any idea why?"

"She was held at knifepoint a few weeks ago."

"Are you . . . *what*?"

"We managed to keep that part out of the news. It was DeeDee Walsh. The senior detective on the case was John Krull. Sixth Precinct." She turned to Detective Plodsky. "Do you think DeeDee Walsh might have anything to do with Mark Carver?"

"I don't know."

"Maybe you should ask her." Brenna glanced at her notepad, then back at her face. "Maybe you should write it down."

Plodsky returned Brenna's gaze, held it long enough to make her feel uncomfortable. "Ms. Spector."

"Yes?"

"How does your daughter feel about your job?"

"What?"

"I don't want you to take this the wrong way, but has your work as a private investigator made her feel . . . unsafe?"

Brenna stared at her. "What are you saying?"

"Has she ever said she'd be happier somewhere else?"

She swallowed hard. "All teenagers say that."

"Has *she*?"

Brenna turned away from her. She tried to focus on the sounds of the ER waiting room—the hum of the electric lights, the fuzzy voice over the loudspeaker. "*Dr. Clark, you are wanted in surgery . . .*" She stared across the room, at the portrait of the older woman on the wall—Lily Teasdale, same as at the police station, the gold plaque beneath it, the cream walls, the clean, pinkish floors . . . But she still felt the radiator-warmed air of her own apartment on October 1, the garlic-laced scent of the spaghetti Bolognese she'd made for dinner, a memory of her former boss invading her brain and Maya standing over her, Maya's sad, cracking voice, yanking her out of it.

"*You know what's weird, Mom?*"

Brenna sees Maya standing feet away from her, her dish in her hands, but she's still got her foot in the memory. "What . . . what's weird?" Brenna can see the way Maya watches her, the sadness in her eyes, the start of tears. But in her mind she is still in October 23, 1998. She is in a diner with her old boss Errol Ludlow. She is hearing his voice . . .

Maya says, "In order to get your full attention, you have to be something that happened in the past."

Brenna slipped her hand into her bag, touched Clea's journal. As always, the feel of it brought her back. But it didn't soothe her. She still held on to the image in her mind—her daughter standing over her, thin fingers wrapped around her plate, the lost look in her eyes, and the way Brenna had seen her that night, *as though through glass* . . . "Not my job," she said to Plodsky.

"Pardon?"

"Maya may have been unhappy with me. But not because of my job."

"Did you have any arguments recently? Any times when—"

"Please. Stop."

"I'm trying to help find her."

"I know." Brenna got up. "I'm sorry." She walked up to the front desk, another image in her mind: Maya's drawing of Clea, shot in the head and bleeding. Brenna tamped down the thought. "Any word on Mr. Carver?" she asked the nurse.

"No, ma'am," she said. Her eyes were large and clear and very blue. Like Clea's. Like Maya's. "I'll let you know as soon as I hear."

"Brenna."

She turned around to see Nick Morasco, standing behind her. She exhaled, some of the tension draining out of her. "Hi."

"Hi."

"Through being questioned?"

"For now," he said. "There'll be more tomorrow." He looked pale, very tired, his eyes bigger and darker than usual behind the wire-framed glasses. "Any word on Carver? Is he still in surgery?"

She nodded. "I think so."

"Brenna. I'm so sorry. I couldn't help it. Seeing her phone . . . Maya's phone on him. He said it was his, and it rang and I saw your face on the screen . . ."

"He reached into his pocket, Nick," she said. "He could have been grabbing for anything."

"I know," he said quietly. "But."

"I understand."

"I wasn't thinking."

"Nick," she said. "I understand."

He put his arms around her and she hugged him back. They stayed like that for a long time. Holding each other up.

"I'll stay here," Morasco said, finally. "You go home. Danny Cavanaugh is in a squad car outside. He said he can take you."

"But I don't think I can . . ."

"If Maya comes back home, you need to be there."

Brenna pulled away. She looked into his eyes and touched his face. For a few seconds, she flashed on earlier today, her mother at the door. She remembered how angry she'd been at Nick, felt the anger again, running through her veins. But only the memory of it, not the reality. *Why,* she wondered. *Why get so upset over something so small when hours later, the whole world . . .*

"We're going to find her," Nick said. "Or she'll come home. Either way, she's going to be okay." He said it as though he knew it, as though he wasn't just hoping.

"Thank you." Brenna cast a quick glance at Plodsky, writing in her notebook. She kissed Morasco softly, and slipped out the door.

11

Officer Danny Cavanaugh was only seven years older than Maya. Brenna had met him back in December, while working on the same case that had brought DeeDee Walsh to her home on December 21, but he was kind enough not to mention the case as they drove. Kind, or clueless. Brenna was grateful either way. She needed quiet—she'd take it any way she could get it.

She was sitting in the back of the squad car. Every so often, her flip-book of a mind would shift back to other rides in other squad cars she'd taken while working on cases—January 12, 2008; March 29, 1999 . . . She'd touch the journal in her bag and then she'd again recall the ride earlier tonight, Officer Benoit's clicking braids, the siren blaring, the hope . . .

"You comfortable, Ms. Spector?" Danny said. "Do you want me to turn the heat up?"

Danny Cavanaugh's hair was safety-cone orange. He had a round, freckly face and wide-set eyes. In his uniform, he reminded Brenna of one of those plastic LEGO dolls, Little People. Brenna had given Maya a box of them as one of her Christmas presents back in

2002—a firefighter, a construction worker, a doctor, a nurse, a policeman . . . all so cherubic and sweet. Christmas had fallen on a Wednesday that year, but Brenna and Maya had celebrated on Thursday morning, December 26, Maya having spent Christmas Day as she always did, with Jim and Faith. First thing Maya had done after opening the box of Little People was to marry the nurse and the firefighter. *I now ponounce you husband and . . .*

"I'm fine," Brenna said.

Which was a lie, of course. She wasn't fine. She was confused and upset and guilty-feeling, her heart pinging around in her chest, her stomach hollow. She wanted to cry but she couldn't. She wanted to fix things, but she couldn't. She wanted to punch the seat until her hand broke, but instead she flipped open her phone, reread Maya's text message, and that hurt more. Had someone forced Maya to write that text, or had she written it herself, of her own free will?

Or had Mark Carver written it, when he was alone, after . . . Brenna shut her eyes. *No* . . . This was the way Brenna's mind usually worked when she was on a case, running through all scenarios, considering every possibility. But this was Maya. Her own, only Maya. There were some possibilities she couldn't consider.

"Anything you need, let me know," said Danny, who just one month earlier had saluted her outside an abandoned building in Mount Temple as they prepared to search for the body of a very nice woman's only son.

"Thanks Danny," she said, then corrected herself. "Officer Cavanaugh."

"Ms. Spector?"

"Yes?"

"I just wanted to say that . . . um . . . what happened with Detective Morasco."

"Yes."

"I was there, and . . . you know . . . It was a very tense situation."

"I'm sure it was."

"I mean, I know from reckless and Detective Morasco was definitely not. That guy may not have had a gun, but he was under the influence and . . ."

"I would have shot him," Brenna said, "whether he had a gun or not."

Danny Cavanaugh nodded. He stared straight ahead. "I hope you find your daughter," he said.

Brenna's phone rang. She flipped it open, looked at the screen. Faith. She'd spoken to Faith three times tonight already, but of course she understood. Everyone handled situations like this in their own way. Faith needed to talk.

She hit send. "He's still in surgery, Faith," she said. "I'm on my way home. Nick's supposed to call me with any news."

"Faith's asleep. She took a pill. She had to."

"Jim." First time she'd spoken on the phone with him since May 1, 2000, a Monday. The day their divorce became final. But Brenna didn't go back to the date. Jim's voice sounded so different now, drained and flattened.

"She told me she was going to Lindsay's," he said. "She gave me Lindsay's address and phone number. But I never called the parents. I never okayed the overnight with anyone. If I had done that . . ."

"I know."

"It's my fault."

"It's not."

Jim breathed into the phone. Brenna kept her eyes on the back of Danny's head, his orange hair against the dark blue of his police shirt. She looked at his chubby hands on the wheel and she stayed here in the car, her ex-husband on the phone with her, breath shaking. "I could have . . ." His voice trailed off.

Earlier tonight, Faith had told Brenna what Lindsay had said: Maya had never showed up for a sleepover. She'd never even been invited. And even if she had . . . *Lindsay's parents weren't even at her house*, Faith had said. *They're out of town all week. Can you imagine?*

"Maya has never lied to you," she told Jim. "When she said she was going to Lindsay's and that her parents would be there, you had no reason not to trust her."

"Brenna," he said. "I could have stopped it."

Such pain in his voice. Stretched thin enough to break. Brenna closed her eyes. "You didn't know. You can't stop things that you don't know are happening."

"I should take a pill. I should try to sleep but I can't."

"I know," she said.

"If I could trade myself for her, I would. If I could take twenty years off my life, I would, just to bring her back right now . . ."

"I know. I would, too."

Jim said nothing. Brenna pressed the phone to her ear. She listened to his shaky breathing, and for a long time they stayed like that, sharing the silence as the squad car rolled along. She felt as though they were in the same dark room, standing over something dying, watching it slip away.

Stay with me. Stay with me, please . . .

Danny took the turnoff for the Cross County Expressway. Traffic was very light—only a few other cars on the road. They'd be in New York City in fifteen minutes at the most. "I'm sorry, Jim," Brenna said.

"About what?"

"About me. My memory. I'm sorry I've made things so hard for you and for Maya. I'm sorry I spent so much time in the past that I was never fully there with you when we were married. I know that's the real reason why you left me. I know it wasn't because I did that job for Errol."

"Brenna—"

"It was because you knew I'd never change, and I don't blame you. I haven't changed. I can't change."

"Stop."

"I think it's the reason why Maya left, too."

"No," he said. "That's not true. Maya loves you so much."

Danny's eyes were visible in the rearview, aimed straight at the highway. Brenna hoped he was lost in thoughts of his own. She didn't want him to hear this.

"She loves me," she whispered. "But she isn't happy with me."

"Brenna . . ."

"Yes?"

"Maya needs you. So do I."

Brenna swallowed hard. He'd used the present tense. For both of them. Brenna hung on to that. "Okay."

"Let's not give up," he said. "Please."

"I won't," she said, looking out the window, at the dark, empty highway, at the city lights in the distance. "We won't."

There was something about the way Jim had spoken to Brenna, the hushed tone of his voice, the worry in it. It brought on a recent memory—sitting in the lobby of Lindsay's building with Faith and him, Faith saying it, nearly under her breath.

She's been keeping secrets. She's been typing on her computer, and then she hides the typing . . .

"Have you gone through her computer?" Brenna had asked.

"Faith and I read her e-mails," he had said. "Nothing but homework questions and confirmations of iTunes purchases."

"Facebook?"

"Yes."

"And?"

"Looks the same." Which had meant *nothing worth looking at*. Maya had just gotten her own Facebook page a month earlier and so far, she'd added no friends beyond Faith and Trent (Brenna and Jim weren't on Facebook). She'd posted one status on December 12: *"Here I am on Facebook!"*

"I want to look at everything, too." Brenna had asked Jim to copy the contents of Maya's computer onto an external hard drive, put it in an envelope, and leave it with the doorman of his building. She'd picked it up on the way home.

Yes, the police would surely be going through that laptop tomorrow with tweezers and magnifying glasses. But Brenna hadn't wanted to leave all of that up to the Missing Persons Unit. She'd wanted to see for herself what Maya had been typing. She'd wanted to get a jump on Plodsky and her cohorts and start finding her daughter now. Also—and probably more importantly, if she was going to be honest—she'd wanted something to occupy her mind, to stop it from churning and remembering and fearing for the worst.

Back at her apartment, though, when Brenna took off her coat and turned the light on, the first thing she saw was the bag full of Clea's belongings on top of her desk: Brenna's fears staring her straight in the face— the twenty-eight-year-old clothes of someone she loved, a disappeared girl. She heard the hum of the radiator and felt the hollowness of her home and all she could think of was Maya's empty room at the end of the hall.

Stop. Get to work.

She switched on her computer. Checked her bank balance. Maya had an ATM card but there had been no withdrawals since January 15, and Brenna had been the one to make it. She checked her credit card. No new charges, either.

"Where are you, Maya?" She said it to no one, said it into thin air.

Brenna took a breath. She checked her texts and saw one from Trent: *Read your e-mail.*

Trent. He didn't know. She hadn't told him. She texted back:

Maya's gone

She waited. No response. Probably asleep. It was late, after all. Past midnight, and tomorrow was a workday.

She opened her e-mail. The only new one was from Trent, and it was titled "BrennaNSpector." She stared at the name—the name of the person who had been e-mailing with Alan Dufresne—both Dufresne and those e-mail relics from another time. Souvenirs from before everything fell apart. She opened it.

Queen Bee,

Didn't find out much about the Hotmail addy. The "name" listed under the account is 3434. I was able to hack in though (the password? "Password." For real. Who does that?) Anyway, here's what I found: Besides that correspondence with Alan Dufresne, the only e-mails to that account have been from missing persons pages, verifying the address. Turns out 3434 has been posting pictures of Clea on pages like that Snapfish one for at least two years (account is set to automatically delete e-mails over two years old) then taking them down between two and four months later. The pics never stay up longer than four months.

But two years, Spec. Two. Years. You know what that means? (It means Nick is off the hook. Just in case you need me to spell it out for you. Which you usually do.)

Yolo,
TNT, aka Mack Daddy

Brenna read the numbers: *3434*. A thought passed through her mind, but then she pushed it away. It wasn't possible. And even if it was, she didn't care. She took the external hard drive out of the envelope, attached it to her desktop, and saw the icon come up on her screen—a folder, labeled "MAYA'S COMPUTER."

She choked up at the name. Her daughter's name. She double-clicked on the icon, and Maya's desktop appeared—a manga character, a girl with spiky purple hair and huge searching green eyes, and for the briefest of moments, Brenna slipped into a memory. February 2, 2009, curled up on the couch after dinner, Matthew Ryan on the stereo, Maya squeezed next to her, laptop open.

Maya clicks on a folder marked "Art," then a file marked "Untitled" and a manga-style image fills the screen—a girl with spiky purple hair and huge eyes, green and searching.

"She's cool," Brenna says. "Where did you find her?"

Maya turns to her. She smiles. "I drew her."

"You did?

"Yep."

"That's . . . how did you get so good?"

Maya shrugs. "It's not bad, I guess."

"You have a name for her?"

"I'm thinking Yoru."

"Yoru?"

Maya stares at the face on the screen, the light from it reflected in her sad, clear eyes.

"It means 'night' in Japanese."

"Yoru," Brenna whispered. There was a cluster of folders to the left of the screen. She double-clicked on the one marked "English homework." A collection of files appeared, and she clicked on the most recent:

"Book Report: Tess of the D'Urbervilles—January 19, 2010."

The due date was this coming Tuesday. She'd last worked on it yesterday morning at 10 A.M.—one hour before her visit to Dr. Lieberman. Would she have really completed a book report if she was planning on leaving?

Brenna thought of Maya's hands on her keyboard, typing, her green-eyed screen saver, Night. *"Why Night?"*

Maya shrugs. "Because she never lets you see all of her," she says. "She keeps you in the dark."

I have found new friends, a beautiful new life.

Had Maya composed the text in her mind before writing the book report? Had she known Mark Carver? Had they been planning her getaway for weeks, just like Clea had no doubt planned hers with Bill?

No. She wouldn't. Would she?

The first sentence of the book report read: *A beautiful love story is at the heart of Thomas Hardy's* Tess of the D'Urbervilles. *But it is a love story that is born of sorrow.*

Sorrow. The name of Tess's ill-fated child, Brenna remembered. She wondered if Maya had been making a pun and imagined herself asking her, wishing she could. Wishing she could know all of her, some of her, any of her.

There was a knock on her door. Brenna headed for it fast, pressed her face up against the peephole, feeling a split second of hope . . .

Trent.

She opened the door. He wore the same clothes he'd

been wearing earlier, though he looked as though he'd just woken up from a deep sleep, his hair banged up on one side, his shirt rumpled. She tried to smile, couldn't. "Took you long enough."

"I was out for a walk in the area," he said. "Maya's gone?"

"Yes."

"Where?"

"I don't . . . I don't know."

"Oh my God."

"She texted. Said she's found somewhere where she's happier."

"What? No, that's impossible. Maya's a happy kid."

A tear slipped down Brenna's cheek. Then another.

"Aw crap," he whispered.

Brenna had never cried in front of Trent. Even when he was in the hospital and fighting for his life, she'd saved her tears for the waiting room. He was her employee, after all, and besides that, he was *Trent*. And so she'd always kept her emotions in check with him.

But right now, she couldn't. She felt herself crumpling, caving in, each tear building on the next. She hadn't cried all night, not with Nick or Jim. She hadn't even cried at the sight of Maya's ruined phone in an evidence bag. But now she was crying and she couldn't stop.

Trent put his arms around Brenna. "It's okay," he said, "It's okay," like the friend he was, and Brenna buried her face in her assistant's chest, her tears becoming sobs, deep and painful and never ending.

* * *

Morasco had never met Diane Plodsky before tonight, but after spending three hours in the ER waiting room with her, drifting in and out of sleep as she subjected him to bursts of pointless questions, he felt as though he'd known her for years, and not in a good way.

"Does Maya approve of you?" she was saying to him now as he sat, eyes fixed on the nurse at the front desk, willing her to announce that Carver had come out of surgery. The nurse glanced up at him, then went back to her computer.

"I have no idea," he said. "I haven't spent a lot of time with her. Brenna is trying to introduce us slowly."

"Why is that?"

"Maybe she doesn't want Maya to get too attached."

"Before you, did she have a lot of men in her life, coming and going?"

"I don't think so," he said. "Of course, I never knew her before I met her."

He gave her a smile. She didn't smile back.

"Detective Plodsky, look. I've had a really tough night here."

"I know."

"And I understand that I'm the only witness you've got right now. But I've already told you all I know. If you want to find out more about Maya, I'd suggest you check out both her homes."

"Believe me. I will."

She said it like a threat. Morasco let her words hang in the air for a little while. He looked at the assortment of magazines on the table: *People, Atlantic Monthly, Highlights* . . . All ridiculously out of date. His gaze went to *People*—from August 24 of the previous year. Brad Pitt and Angelina Jolie on the cover, plus a Kate Gosselin exclusive: "I Cry All the Time." Morasco wondered if she still did.

"Detective Plodsky?"

"Yes?"

"Maya didn't send that text of her own free will."

"I know you feel that way," she said. "But you have no way of knowing."

He turned to her. "Back in December, her mom got carjacked. Maya had happened to call Brenna while the event was happening. She heard everything, as it was taking place. Maya had the foresight to call me on her landline. I contacted the precinct up in Inwood Park and got them to ping Brenna's cell, but I stayed on the phone with Maya. I talked to her until her dad got there. I told her everything would be okay."

"And . . ."

"And I've been a cop more than fifteen years. I've said 'everything will be okay' a lot, because I've been with a lot of people . . . a lot of family members . . . who needed to hear those words. But no one who needed to hear them as badly as Maya did. She loves her mother very much. She was terrified at the thought."

"Well, any child would be terrified. It was a terrifying situation."

"You don't understand," he said slowly. "She was terrified at the idea of having to live her own life, without Brenna."

"She told you this?"

"Yes," he said.

"She used those words."

"Yes." He looked into her eyes. "So, I do have a way of knowing."

A guy in scrubs was talking to the front desk nurse. Morasco couldn't make out what they were saying, but they kept glancing over at him and Plodsky.

"Look," she said. "I get what you're saying. But from what I've heard so far tonight, Maya was held at knife-point and witnessed her mother's carjacking, all during the same month when most kids her age are thinking about what they're going to get for Christmas. Whether she loves her mom or not, Detective Morasco, doesn't it make sense that she might think about escaping that life?"

"It might *make sense*," he said. "But it isn't what happened."

Morasco was aware of the guy in scrubs, making his way around the desk and through the waiting room.

"Hi, I'm Dr. Clark," he said, standing over them now. He had a chiseled, overly handsome look, more like a soap opera doctor than a real-life one, and a golden tan, despite the time of year. For a moment, Morasco imagined that none of this was real, that they were all just characters in someone else's script, wearing costumes and saying lines, unable to change things. He made himself smile at the doctor. "Everything okay?"

He smiled back. His teeth were, of course, blindingly white.

"Mr. Carver is out of surgery," Dr. Clark said. "He seems to be stabilized."

Morasco and Plodsky exhaled at the same time.

"Thank God," Morasco whispered.

"Will we know when he's conscious?" Plodsky said.

"He's conscious now," said the doctor.

Morasco blinked at him. "How can that be?"

"The bullet only grazed the outer left portion of his skull. It didn't affect the brain. We were actually more concerned about the significant amount of opiate and cocaine in his system. Combined with the stress of the encounter with you, it led to a pretty massive spike in his blood pressure, which affected his heart . . ." His gaze went from Plodsky to Morasco. "Anyway, he pulled through."

Plodsky said, "Do we know when he's ready to talk?"

The doctor stepped back. "He says he wants to talk now," he said. "He wants to get it over with."

Plodsky's eyebrows went up.

"That okay with you?" Morasco asked him.

"It's fine. Just for a few minutes though. He's still weak. We don't want him too stressed."

"No problem," said Plodsky. She slipped her notebook into her bag and stood up, but the doctor stopped her.

"Sorry, ma'am," he said.

"But I thought you said . . ."

"No." The doctor looked at Morasco. "He said he only wants to talk to you."

"Me?"

"That's right. In his words, he wants to talk to the guy who shot him."

12

"Killer." Carver said it just as Morasco entered the room. His head had been shaved and wrapped with a large white bandage. He wore a hospital gown, the white sheet pulled up to his chest, his arms, surprisingly pale, outstretched and taped with several IVs. An oxygen tube was fitted at his nose, dark eyes swimming in blanched skin. He brought to mind a big white spider, belly up to the sun. "You gonna shoot me again?"

"Don't have my gun," Morasco said. "So the point is moot."

Dr. Clark cast him a worried look. "I'll be right outside the door," he said.

As soon as he left, Carver said, "I don't know where she is."

"But you saw her."

"No."

"What did you do to her?"

"Nothing."

"Nothing?"

"We . . ."

"What, Mark?" Morasco drew a breath. Let it out slowly. "It's all right. Tell me."

"My head hurts."

"Tell me."

"We partied a little."

Morasco's jaw clenched up. "You partied a little."

"Yeah."

"You gave her drugs."

"We shared."

"I don't believe that."

"It's true," he said.

"What kind of drugs?"

"Oxy."

"Oxycodone."

He gave Morasco a look, his eyes flat. "Yes that's the full name."

"Where did she get oxycodone?"

"How would I know that?"

"Where did you meet?"

"I want some water."

"Where did you meet her?"

"I can't talk." He stared at Morasco.

"Yes you can. You're talking now."

"My mouth is dry. Dehydrated. The doctor said. It's the . . . uh . . ."

"What?"

"Anastasia." He laughed a little. "No, that's a princess."

"Anesthesia."

There was a pitcher of water next to his bedside. Morasco took a deep breath. He walked over to the nightstand and poured some of the water into a plastic cup. Carver was still chuckling over his princess pun.

Out of it. Christ, what a loser. *Don't get angry* . . . He held the cup out to him. "Here."

"Can't hold it." With his big, insect eyes, he cast a deliberate glance at his arms. "IVs."

Morasco held the cup up to his lips. He sucked at it for what felt like a long time, too long. He drained the cup.

Morasco said, "Tell me how you met her."

He muttered something.

"I didn't hear that."

"Craigslist."

"*What?*"

"Craigslist. She was looking for pills. I was selling."

"Bullshit."

"It's the truth. We met. Partied a little. I sold her the bag."

"What did she pay you with?" he spat out the words. "Her allowance money?"

"The phone. She gave me the phone."

Morasco glared at him.

"The phone. A little cash. Some coke, too. An eight-ball."

"What happened to her?"

"Fuck should I know where that bitch went?"

Morasco's back stiffened. His fists clenched, and his jaw tensed, every muscle in his body coiling, the tiredness draining out of him until he was all anger. He wanted to punch Carver in the face. But he didn't want to stop there. He wanted to beat him senseless and rip out his IVs and kick him in the stomach until he bled to death. He took a breath. Stepped back.

"Why did you run?"

"I need more water," Carver said.

"No."

"Thirsty."

"You'll get water if you tell me the truth." Morasco kept his voice down as he said it, his gaze focused on the dark, swimmy eyes.

"I am telling you the truth. We partied. Said she liked danger. 'I'm into danger, Mark. How far will you go? How close to the edge?' Kinda hot. She cooked the oxy, blew the smoke in my mouth . . ."

Morasco took another step back. He gritted his teeth. "You're sick."

"Huh?"

"She didn't tell you that. She didn't do anything like that. You didn't meet her on Craigslist."

"Yes I did."

"*She's thirteen years old!*"

"No . . ."

"She didn't give you an eightball, you asshole. She didn't blow smoke in your mouth. She's *a kid*. You fed pills *to a little girl*."

"I need water."

Morasco grabbed the pitcher, his hands shaking. He poured it into the cup and jammed it up against Carver's mouth and upended it, spilling it over his face, down his chin. Carver started to cough. Morasco pushed the cup against his jaw, kept pushing. The plastic cracked and sputtered, water spilled out the sides. The oxygen tube pulled loose from his nose. "Tell me the truth," he said, "Or I swear to God I'll kill you."

"*Doctor!*"

Dr. Clark hurried through the door.

Morasco stepped back. "It's okay," he said. "Everything's okay," as Carver stared up at him, wheezing and dripping.

"You need to leave now," Dr. Clark said.

Morasco closed his eyes. "It's okay. It's fine."

"No." Calm and cold. "You need to leave now."

Dr. Clark opened the door, waited, and Morasco moved toward it, hating himself, the way his anger ruined things, his emotions. Behind him, he could hear Carver's labored breathing. Clark telling him, in hushed tones, to "just relax please . . ."

As he reached the door, though, he heard Carver's frail voice. "Wait."

Morasco turned, looked at him, this weak, wheezing man, soap opera doctor hovering over him. "What?"

"I wasn't . . ." He coughed. "I wasn't partying . . . with the girl."

"Then what were you doing with her?"

"Detective."

"I wasn't partying with the girl," Carver said again, as Clark adjusted his IVs. "I was partying with her mother."

Brenna cried for a solid five minutes into Trent's chest. Then she stepped back, pulled herself together. Trent walked over to his desk, slipped open the top drawer, and removed a small pack of Kleenex. "My mom gave me a huge box of these when I moved out of the house," he said. "She's like, 'Have one of these with you on all times. You never know when a lady might be crying.'" He ripped open the pack and handed Brenna a stack of tissues.

"You're actually the first lady who's ever used them," he said as she dabbed at her eyes. "I guess I'm more a make-'em-laugh kind of stud."

The Kleenex, like everything else Trent owned, stank of his cologne. Brenna didn't mention it, didn't care really. In a weird way, the smell was comforting. "Making 'em laugh is a good quality," she said.

"Uh, not always."

"Well."

"So."

She looked at him. "So."

"Let's find your kid."

"Okay."

And that was it. Amazing how the most intense grief can dissolve in the face of hope, any kind of hope at all. "Do you have Maya's computer?" he said.

"I've got a copy of it. Jim loaded it onto an external hard drive."

His eyebrow went up at the mention of Jim's name, but all Trent said was "Awesome."

As always, Trent had been carrying his camouflage-drag man purse (or as he insisted it be called, a messenger bag). He dropped it onto his desk. "I keep all my essentials in here," he said. "Axe spray, gel, lip balm, a bottle of rubbing alcohol in case one of my piercings gets infected because that happens sometimes and let me tell you it is *so* not fun . . ."

"Is this leading anywhere?"

"Yes, boss, it is." From the depths of the bag, Trent produced a small laptop. "This baby's an essential. 40 gigabyte hard drive. If I could marry a piece of equipment, and, you know . . . sex robots weren't on the table . . . she'd be wearing my ring."

He moved over to Brenna's computer, replaced the external hard drive with his own, and copied the Maya folder onto it, then attached it to the laptop. "Maybe she's been chatting with someone online who she shouldn't be chatting with. Maybe she e-mailed or instant messaged a friend about her plans."

When he was done, he moved back to his desk. "You go through her regular files," he said. "I'll check out her online history."

"Faith told me she's walked in when Maya's been typing on her computer, and then Maya hides what she's typing."

"Okay."

Brenna moved over to her computer, ran her gaze over the cluster of folders, feeling, if not better, then a little more in control. "Trent?" she said.

"Yeah?"

"Thank you."

He looked up at her. "We'll get her back," he said. "Kanye's gonna need a babysitter."

Brenna smiled a little. She went back to the screen. She clicked on the folder marked "Pictures." "Missing Persons Unit already has her ninth grade picture, but I'm going to find a few more. I'd like you to send them to . . ." Brenna couldn't get herself to say hospitals, police stations, morgues . . .

"The usual places?"

She nodded.

"Yep. Will do."

There was a big collection of folders—downloaded manga covers, an assortment of glamour shots of Justin Bieber from two years earlier and a *GQ* photo shoot of Taylor Lautner, downloaded last November. There were silly shots of Larissa and Zoe, posing next to the lions at the Midtown Public Library, pictures of shoes and ice cream sundaes and a folder filled with head-shots of young TV and movie actresses, marked "Hair-cuts," which made Brenna smile a little. Maya's hair nearly reached her waist. She kept saying she wanted to cut it short, but every time Brenna had obliged her and taken her to the salon, Maya had chickened out when she was getting shampooed. *I don't think I'm ready*, she'd say.

There were folders dedicated to manga characters and "cute animals" and then one, unmarked, that con-tained just one picture of Maya, cuddling with Zoe's cat. The cat's name was Bananas and for a moment Brenna remembered Maya chasing him across Zoe's living room on the morning of June 3, 2007, when Brenna was picking her up from a slumber party. *"Come back here Bananas and give me a hug!"*

Brenna wanted to enlarge it, if only to look at the smile on Maya's face, proof that she was a happy kid, that she *is* a happy kid . . . when she noticed a separate folder, marked "Shopping: 1/14." Three days ago.

Brenna opened it.

Inside, a whole series of pictures of Maya at a store, modeling clothes and posing with the same three girls—a willowy blonde; a tanned, petite girl with bone-straight black hair and mean eyes . . . and the girl who had rushed into Miles's arms on September 30 after chorus practice. The same girl.

Lindsay. Brenna clicked on one of the photos. "Wow," she whispered.

Maya was wearing a skintight, bright red bandage dress that made her look at least three years older. The dress wasn't Maya, not the Maya Brenna knew, and her smile looked just as uncomfortable—big and plaster-bright and not really happy at all. Standing next to Maya was Lindsay, wearing the same dress but in cobalt blue, making up for Maya's lack of confidence with a surplus of her own. Lindsay, sticking her chest out, working it, her smile relaxed and knowing. It reminded Brenna of one of those "who wore it better" spreads in the gossip magazines. Lindsay in her glittery statement earrings and platform pumps. Maya wearing Converse sneakers and the diamond studs her grandmother had given her for her thirteenth birthday along with a note that read "Welcome to Womanhood!" (Oh, how the poor kid had cringed over that . . .)

Brenna clicked on another photo—all four of the girls, outside the store, holding bags. She enlarged the picture so she could see the logo on the bags: Forever 21. Same bag as in Maya's room, the perfume and the thigh-high socks, bought to impress, then stashed at home, unused, still in the wrappers they came in.

Brenna opened a third picture—Maya and her three new friends, the older girls making kissy faces, Maya smiling that same pained smile—thrilled and terrified and achingly awkward. *She wants to impress these girls so much.*

She recalled Jim on the phone, the pain in his voice. *If I could trade myself for her, I would. If I could take twenty years off my life, I would, just to bring her back right now . . .*

She went on to her e-mail, composed a new one, addressed to both Jim and Faith, and attached the folder.

In case you guys haven't come across these yet, she wrote. *I wouldn't be so quick to trust Lindsay over Maya re: sleepover.*

"You finding anything?" said Trent.

"Sending you an e-mail," said Brenna. She clicked on her own browser and sent Trent the bandage dress shot and the one with the cat. The two faces of Maya.

Trent opened up his e-mail, stared at the pictures. "You want me to crop out Heather, right?"

"Yeah." Brenna gaze locked with that of the girl on the screen. Miles's girlfriend. Lindsay.

He nodded at his laptop. "BTW, I'm gonna have to run a bit-by-bit transferal on this hard drive. See if she's deleted any files . . ."

"You think Maya's deleted files?"

"She might have," he said. "Looks like she's been erasing her browsing history—unless she's been to only two sites in her whole entire life." He glanced over at Brenna. "Do you know her e-mail password?"

"Yes. Of course. So do Jim and Faith."

"Not much point in checking it then. Your private eye mom and your journalist dad and stepmom all have your e-mail password, you're not gonna use it for anything other than homework assignments."

"And confirmation of iTunes purchases."

"Uh, sure."

Brenna exhaled. "What about the two sites?"

"Yeah, we got those at least. Apparently last time she was online, she forgot to clear her history."

"She was probably in a hurry to get to her friends," Brenna said, staring at the screen, hating those girls. Something had happened. Either they'd stood her up or they'd kicked her out or inviting her over had been a joke. But something bad had happened, and if Maya was taken away afterward, or if she'd been so upset she'd decided to run away, to take Carver up on his offer, just so she could disappear . . . Brenna shut her eyes tight. *Put it aside. Keep it together.*

Trent said, "So you want to know which sites?"

She opened her eyes, took a breath. "Of course."

"One was Wikipedia, where she looked up . . . um . . . Thomas Hardy?"

"Yeah," Brenna said. "She did a book report on *Tess of the D'Urbervilles.*"

"Gotcha," Trent said. "But the other one was Chrysalis."

Brenna stared at him. "The search engine?"

"Yep."

Chrysalis. The search engine that was also home to dozens of chat rooms, on one of which Nelson Wentz's wife had been a regular, impersonating the mother of a missing girl . . .

Brenna turned to Trent. "Had you ever heard of Chrysalis before the Neff case?"

"Well, yeah . . ." he said. "But that's only because I've heard of everything."

"I hadn't heard of it," Brenna said, very quietly. "And I'll bet you anything, neither had Maya."

To get to Chrysalis.org's chat rooms, you had to go to "Other Services" and then click on a "plus" icon. Once you did, you were given three choices: ChrysBlogs, ChrysForSingles, and ChrysChats. Brenna clicked on ChrysChats, found the category marked "Living," and then, under all the hobby chat rooms and senior citizen chat rooms and chat rooms for infertile couples and cancer sufferers and victims of violent crime (*Living indeed*, she thought now, just as she'd thought on September 30 at 12:15 P.M. . . .), she found the heading marked "Families of the Missing." They were arranged regionally. Brenna scrolled down to the chat room she'd trolled on September 30 in search of Carol Wentz: "Families of the Missing, New York State."

After the Neff case had made the news and the Families of the Missing, New York State chat room was mentioned in a Huffington Post piece, the room had gotten so overloaded with traffic from reporters and murder fans that the server broke down.

Administrators had shut all the chat rooms down for a week. But that was back in October—ancient history by today's news cycle standards. The chat room was back, the heading looking just the same as on September 30, when Jim, chatting with Brenna via instant message the way he used to every night back then, had urged, **Go to the other services, and click on the bottom icon.**

Even without hyperthymesia—because anyone would have remembered—there was no avoiding the comparison . . . How very far her life had come since September 30, since last month, since this morning. How very far down . . .

"You on?" said Trent.

"Not yet."

"Dude."

"I have to think of a screen name."

"How about SexyBack88? That's mine. I mean that's the one I use for . . . uh . . . other types of online experiences."

"Subtle."

"It is! I could have gone with SexyBack69 but nooo. See? I'm classy."

Brenna sighed. "The Families of the Missing chat names tend to be a first name and an area of the state."

"Uh . . . EighthStreetBrenna?"

"I need something shorter," she said. "And less true. I don't think they're huge fans of mine in there."

"Right. How about KarenStatenIsland? That's my mom. Everybody likes her."

"Sounds good." Brenna created the identity SIKaren and entered the room. There were ten people in there, and she recognized quite a few screen names . . . LIMatt61, ClaudetteBrooklyn20, SyracuseSue . . . They were involved in a conversation about the Jets winning the playoffs—no mention of missing family members. Brenna thought about that—these people, joined together by a grief so lasting that it had become part of who they were. This could have just as easily been a chat room for knitters or senior citizens or people with blond hair. A group of friends, with something in common—only instead of a hobby or a hair color, it was a pain, deep and enduring, a part of them. They didn't need to talk about it. It was always there.

ClaudetteBrooklyn20 typed: **Hi Karen! New here?**

Brenna closed her eyes, opened them again: **Yes,** she typed. **My daughter is missing.**

SyracuseSue: **So sorry**.

ClaudetteBrooklyn20: **How long?**

Brenna typed: **Today.**

SyracuseSue: **Oh no! Police are helping, I hope.**

Yes and no, Brenna typed. **I'm actually on here because I think she may have visited this room before she went away.**

LIMatt61: **Sorry, Karen, but how do we know who you really are?**

She is thirteen years old, Brenna typed. **She is my daughter and she's gone.**

SyracuseSue: **That's a good point, Matt. No offense, Karen. You're new, and you have to be here a while to gain trust.**

WoodstockJackie: **Most people don't find this chat room until their loved ones have been missing for years.**

ClaudetteBrooklyn20: **Yes, who would come on here after just one day?**

LIMatt61: **We've been trolled before.**

"I'm blowing it," Brenna said.

Trent leaned over her shoulder. "Don't give up."

Brenna typed: **Just please tell me if there's been a teenager in here, and if she's said anything unusual in the past few days.**

SyracuseSue: **We've had teenagers come and go.**

LIMatt61: **Don't tell her anything more. I just checked and she doesn't have a profile.**

Brenna cringed. *A profile* . . . The last time she'd been in this room, she'd used the screen name of an established member. Of course she should have thought about creating a profile of her own. She should have made a profile for SIKaren and logged on and discussed the Jets with them first. She should have claimed someone else in her family was missing, had been missing for years. She should have said that she'd heard about this room from a friend's daughter. *Do you know her? She's thirteen. Not sure what screen name she was using . . .* Too late now. Desperation was turning her into a bad investigator, just as it had made Nick fire at Mark Carver. She needed to take a step back, get rid of her emotions. She had to, if she was going to find Maya, and she needed to find Maya.

Trent said, "Tell 'em you're sorry."

She did.

No one replied. They didn't even speak to each other. It was almost as though the screen had frozen.

"Tell 'em you watched the Jets, too."

She did.

ClaudetteBrooklyn20: **I'm sorry, Karen. You aren't welcome here.**

"No . . ." Brenna whispered.

Trent sighed heavily. "Dude, don't worry. I can find out who the site administrator is. Request transcripts from the last month."

"But how long will that take?" Brenna said.

"Depends."

"You know the first forty-eight hours someone goes missing are crucial, Trent. *You know that.*"

"And how many times have we proved that wrong? Come on, Spec, please." He put his hand over hers. "Don't freak out. Stay with me . . ."

Brenna heard a beep. On the bottom of Brenna's screen a message appeared: **You have a private chat request**.

Brenna shot a look at Trent, clicked on it. It was from someone in the room: NYCJulie.

If you would like to private chat, the message read, **Go here.**

"NYCJulie," Trent said. "She's from here."

"Maybe," Brenna said. "Or maybe she's from Staten Island and her real name is Karen."

"Yep."

Brenna clicked on the link—a chat room for two appeared, NYCJulie's screen name blinking, waiting . . .

Brenna typed: **Hi**

NYCJulie: **Hi Karen**.

SIKaren: **Sorry I invaded your chat room, but I really am telling the truth.**

NYCJulie: **I believe you.**

SIKaren: **Thank you.**

NYCJulie: **I just didn't think she was from Staten Island.**

Brenna let out a gasp.

"Whoa," said Trent.

"Let's not get ahead of ourselves. She could very easily be full of crap."

Brenna typed: **You know my daughter?**

She waited, no response. Brenna gave Trent a look, then typed: **Sorry, but I'm going to need some proof.**

The screen said: *NYCJulie is typing.* Brenna held her breath . . .

NYCJulie: **Spirited Away is her favorite movie.**

She used to like Justin Bieber, but now not so much. She likes to draw.

More typing. "Okay," Brenna whispered. "Okay . . ."

NYCJulie: **She has mixed feelings about her missing aunt.**

Brenna and Trent leaned forward at the same time, Brenna remembering Maya's drawing of Clea, the bleeding bullet hole . . .

Trent said, "Maya's been to this site."

"We don't know for sure."

Brenna typed: **That all sounds good. But lots of kids have missing aunts. And lots of them have mixed feelings.**

There was a pause, then finally . . . *NYCJulie is typing*.

The words appeared. Brenna and Trent stared at the screen.

"I think that's your proof," Trent said.

Her screen name is NYCYoru, NYCJulie had typed, **But her real name is Maya.**

Diane Plodsky was good at waiting. Her ex-husband, Bruce, used to tell her she was like a spider, and in a way he'd meant it as a compliment. *You've got patience, Diane*, he'd say. *Endless amounts of it.* Truth. At the end of their marriage, Diane had waited in the parking lot of the Starlite Motel in Tenafly, New Jersey for three hours, just to catch Bruce leaving a room with their neighbor, Laurel Farkus.

Endless amounts.

That patience had served her well at work—both in

her current job with Missing Persons and in her previous incarnation as a precinct detective in Brooklyn. She could question a suspect for hours, probably weeks if it were allowed. She could wade through the most tedious and extensive case files, learn them thoroughly. And when it came to stakeouts, well, that went without saying. Diane didn't need much sleep. She stayed alert, focused. She could outlast anyone, and for the most part she even enjoyed the wait.

So she didn't mind sitting in the Tarry Ridge ER for five hours, waiting for Mark Carver to come out of surgery. She didn't mind the brush-off answers she got out of Maya's mother or her boyfriend Detective Morasco. They were agitated and she wasn't and so of course extended questioning was going to unnerve them, of course it was going to make them snappish. Sifting through snappishness to pluck out real info had long been a part of her job. And so she'd learned to appreciate it . . . Well, anyway, she didn't *mind* it.

But she did mind this doctor. She minded him a lot.

The thing about Diane's endless patience: It demanded a payoff. When a suspect would crack, when the thickest, dullest case file would finally yield a piece of useful information—hell, even when her ex-husband had come out of the motel room with his belt undone and his hand on Laurel Farkus's infinity-shaped ass—Diane would get this strange but powerful sense of relief, the feeling that all her waiting had been for something.

Not so tonight. "Mr. Carver has been sedated," Dr. Clark said, standing over her. "He can't have any more visitors."

"Are you serious?"

"He became agitated with his previous visitor. We can't risk any additional strain to his heart."

"Great."

"Check back in the morning. Hopefully he'll be out of the woods."

"I thought he was already out of the damn woods."

He stared at her without saying anything for several seconds. Then he walked away.

Outside, Detective Morasco was heading into the parking lot, tapping a number into his phone, but Diane managed to catch up with him before he completed his call.

"What the hell did you do to him?" she said.

He stopped.

She glared at him. "What did you say to Carver?"

"Nothing." He sighed. "I got mad at him."

"Shooting him wasn't enough for you?"

"I know Maya Rappaport. Everything he was giving me was complete crap. It was like he was purposely trying to mess with me."

"What did he tell you?"

"A lot of things."

"You know, Detective, a little specificity would go a real long way with me right now."

"Fine," he said. "Carver said he smoked oxycodone with Maya's mother, and that she was the one who gave him the phone."

She gaped at him. "He said he was smoking pre-scription drugs with Brenna Spector?"

"He said he met her on Craigslist."

"How do you know he didn't?"

He shook his head. "That'll teach me to be specific."

"Okay, maybe that's going too far," Diane said, "but you're too close to this case. You're not seeing it from every angle."

He shot her a look, a familiar one. Bruce used to look at her the same way whenever she beat him at Scrabble. "Good night, Detective Plodsky," he said.

He started to walk away.

"Did he refer to her as Brenna Spector, or did he just say, 'her mother'?"

Morasco stopped, turned.

"Did he physically describe Maya's mother?"

He watched her, sleepy eyes widening as realization dawned. "No," he said. "He didn't describe her. He didn't name her."

"So . . ."

"So she could have been anyone. Any woman could have had Maya's phone and given it to him."

"You see what I'm saying?" she said. "You would have gotten that right away if you weren't so close to the case."

"Any woman could have abducted her. Any woman could have claimed to be her mother."

Diane thought it and said it at the same time. "Or Maya could even see her that way. This woman could be one of the 'new friends,' she mentions in the text. Part of the new family she's found."

"No. I told you already. You don't know Maya, so—"

"So I can be objective."

He started to say something, then stopped. He looked a little disgusted with her.

Honestly, Diane wasn't sure why she kept pressing the runaway thing. Yes, it was a very real possibility.

If there was one thing she'd learned during her twenty-five years in law enforcement, it was this: Everybody's got secrets. Doesn't matter how young or sweet or squeaky clean you are on the surface.

But that didn't mean Morasco was going to believe that anyone would leave his perfect girlfriend—most of all her young, sweet, squeaky clean daughter. "Sorry," she said.

He exhaled. "Fine."

"Did Carver tell you where he met up with the woman he said was Maya's mother?"

Morasco shook his head. "She dropped him off near Van Wagenen and Main. That's all I know."

"Did he say anything about her? What kind of clothes she was wearing? Where she was from? Her job?"

Morasco stared at the pavement. "I wish I had another chance with him."

Diane looked at him. "Me too."

He really wasn't a bad guy. Probably not a bad cop, either. Just pussy-whipped. Diane's felling of Bruce notwithstanding, being in love wasn't good for investigative work. It made you impetuous and opinionated and sloppy. "I'll try and get at him," she said.

"Thanks," he said. "Good night, Detective Plodsky."

Morasco headed to the far end of the parking lot, beeped open a car door, and slid in. Diane stared after him, thinking.

Half an hour into Brenna's conversation with NYCJulie, Trent produced a twenty-ounce Red Bull from his messenger bag and cracked it open. Brenna looked at the clock. 2:30 A.M. Julie told Brenna she was getting sleepy, which was understandable, and so they said their good-byes, Brenna mulling the information Maya's online friend had given her, running it through her head.

Maya had joined the chat room in early October in the wake of the Neff case. It was around the same time Julie had joined—Maya having heard about it through Brenna's involvement; Julie, of course, through the news. They had similar senses of humor and NYC in their screen names and so they bonded, despite their varying ages, Maya revealing feelings about the aunt she never knew, Julie discussing her lasting grief over her son, who'd gone missing nearly a decade ago.

Brenna had typed, **How does she feel about her aunt?**

Honestly? She kinda hates her, Julie had replied. **Well, not her aunt so much as her aunt's effect on you.**

Brenna cringed at the memory of the words. She'd known Maya felt as though she was in competition with Clea—with the lack of Clea, actually—and that she was always on the losing end. But she didn't know Maya felt it that deeply.

She was trying to look for Clea, Julie had typed. **She felt like if she found her for you, she'd finally have your full attention.**

Brenna had thought of it immediately—the communication with Dufresne. But Trent had been the one to put it into words. "You think Maya is 3434?"

"Maybe," Brenna had said. But for her it wasn't a maybe. Brenna was nearly certain that Maya had been 3434, BrennaNSpector, whatever you wanted to call the person who had claimed to be her, who had been posting that picture on missing persons sites for the past two years at least, who knew that the picture was in Brenna's drawer and had taken it out at least once since September so she could sketch it . . . and kill it (figuratively, anyway.)

It had to be Maya, which, when she recalled how BrennaNSpector had broken things off with Alan, made the type of sense that was chilling.

Well apparently, you're not going to be e-mailing for a while because you're in the midst of a family crisis.

Brenna had asked Julie: **Do you think Maya was unhappy enough to run away? Do you think she planned this ahead of time?**

I don't know, Julie had typed.

Brenna thinks, *You do know though. Don't you? You just don't want to say . . .*

"I'm going to check my e-mail—see if I got anything in response to the pics," said Trent, perked up from the Red Bull. He moved over to his laptop, gulped from the can some more, and flipped it open.

When the chat room reopened following the server overload and shutdown, Julie and Maya had both sought it out again, mainly to find each other. When they did, they greeted each other like old friends, and before long, they were private messaging regularly, their conversation topics moving from their missing relatives to books and movies, to Maya's school friends, boys, hopes and dreams and fears for the future . . .

Brenna had typed, **Maya ever mention a man named Mark?**

NYCJulie: **A man? Not a boy?**

SIKaren: **Man.**

NYCJulie: **She told me about a boy named Miles. No men.**

SIKaren: **What did she say about him?**

NYCJulie: **She said he's a great singer. Apparently, he's got a whole room full of studio equipment in his apartment, and she thinks he'll be famous. She clearly had a crush, but I was skeptical.**

SIKaren: **She was in his apartment?**

After a long pause, NYCJulie had replied: **For some class project, I think. They had to draw each other.**

SIKaren: **You were close. She could confide in you.**

NYCJulie: **It's tough being an only child. I'm one, too. So I get it.**

Yes. Brenna had typed. She hadn't been able to type anything more. "I should have gotten it, too," said Brenna, an only child, too, but for her sister's gaping memory. "I'm sorry."

"Huh?" Trent tapped at his keyboard.

"Nothing," said Brenna. "You want me to make up the couch for you? It's getting late."

Trent shook his head. "Nah." He took another swig of Red Bull, images flashing on the screen. "Sleeping's for wussies."

Brenna looked at him, his eyes lit from the glowing screen. "Thanks."

"She deleted a lot of song downloads," he said. "I still don't get why she stopped liking Bieber. His new stuff is good."

"Kids change." Her eyes went to the kitchen area, a memory seeping into her mind, February 16, 2009, 3:30 P.M. Maya closing the refrigerator door and turning to her. *"I forgive you, Mom."*

"For what?"

"Not getting cheese sticks."

"Crap, I didn't have a chance. Work was . . ."

"It's okay."

Maya brushes past her, trailing a flowery scent. Justin Bieber's Girlfriend perfume. She stops, kisses her on the cheek. "Don't beat yourself up, Mom, Jeez. It's only cheese sticks."

"People change," Brenna said.

"I still love you, Mom."

The phone rang.

Brenna hurried into her office, checked the screen before answering. "Nick," she said.

"Hi."

"Anything?"

"Good and bad."

"Good first."

"Carver pulled through."

She breathed out. *Thank you . . .* "Now the bad."

"I talked to him, Brenna. But not for very long because I got pissed off again and he went schizo. Now they won't let anybody in to see him."

"Did you get anything?"

"Just . . . He said he got the phone from a woman."

"A girl."

"No," he said. "Not a girl. Not Maya. A woman, who he seemed to think was Maya's mother. He said he partied with Maya's mother, and she gave him the phone."

"Do you believe him?"

He took a deep breath. "When I was talking to him, I didn't at all," he said. "But now . . ."

"What changed your mind?"

"Danny Cavanaugh slipped me Mark Carver's social," he said. "I looked him up."

"And?"

"He's not on the sex offenders registry. Never been arrested for a violent crime. One drug arrest—dealing hash. When he was eighteen—that's half his life ago. He got probation. A few years back, he was questioned in his brother's death."

"He was a suspect?"

"It was an overdose, Brenna. They both took a shit-load of heroin. Carver's brother died. He didn't."

"Oh."

"He just . . . He doesn't seem the type to steal a kid off the street." He exhaled. "He doesn't set off that feeling in me. Not now. Not on paper."

"But he does seem like the type to party with some random woman and take a phone from her, no questions asked."

"Yes," he said quietly.

"I get it."

"I wish I'd known about him earlier. I never would have fired. I wouldn't have—"

"You know about him now," Brenna said. "That's something. He's going to be okay. That's something, too."

"Brenna?"

"Yeah?"

"I wish . . . I wish I could make this all better."

Brenna closed her eyes. She listened to his breathing. "I know you do," she said.

They said their good-byes and hung up. Brenna stared at the phone, thinking about what he'd said. She punched in a number: Her mother's.

She answered after several rings, her voice fogged from sleep. "Brenna?"

"Mom. When you got that call from Maya in the middle of the night . . ."

"Maya?"

"Yes, you said she called you by mistake last night."

"Brenna, is something wrong?"

"I need you to tell me exactly what you heard."

"What? What are you . . ."

"Did you hear a woman's voice? A man's?"

"I . . . I heard static . . ."

"And something else. You said Maya sounded wild."

"I *said* that?"

Brenna gritted her teeth. "*Yes*."

"Are you sure?"

"Mother, I'm always sure. Of everything. Always. You *know that*."

"I . . . don't know, Brenna. It was very late at night. I heard static. I thought it was you at first. I thought you were calling about your father . . ."

"Did you hear Maya's voice?"

"Just static. What's going on, Brenna? Why are you calling me at three?"

"I'm sorry to have woken you," Brenna said. She hung up.

Brenna headed for her bedroom, hopelessness closing in around her. On the way in, she stopped in the bathroom. Stared into the mirror. "Where are you, Maya?" She said it to her reflection, but in her mind she could see only her daughter. Her daughter's face, her daughter's scared, shy smile. Her daughter out there somewhere in the freezing cold night, somewhere crying for help . . .

"*Where are you?*"

Brenna headed out of the bathroom, through the kitchen, and into the office area, where Trent still sat at his computer. "Anything?" she said.

He shook his head. "Homework mostly. She downloaded a birthday party invitation."

"Larissa's?"

"How did you know?"

"It's coming up. February 2."

"You're a great mom."

"Knowing dates doesn't make me a great mom," she said. "It just makes me weird."

He looked up from the computer. "I didn't say it because you knew the date."

Brenna squeezed her eyes shut for a few seconds, ignoring the heat at the corners, at her throat. "You're a good guy, Trent."

She looked at her watch. Two fifty-five, it read, which made her recall that jolly bastard of a Christmas angel she'd talked to, back when she'd thought there must be some mistake, that Maya would be home any minute, that this had to be a dream, a bad one, and she'd wake up soon ... *"Don't remember his name. Glenn? Gary? He trades off with me, which means he'll be in after my shift's over. Three A.M."*

Brenna threw open the closet, grabbed her coat and bag, opened the door.

She heard Trent's voice behind her, "Where are you going?" She didn't turn around to answer.

"Lindsay's place."

"Whose?"

"The Heather. From the picture. I'm going to talk to her doorman."

* * *

Mark Carver couldn't sleep, and he couldn't stay awake, either. His nose ran and his shaved head itched, bandages clinging to it, hairs already starting to poke through the skin. He wanted to slough it all off—the bandages, the hospital gown, the IVs, this whole night and his life and everything that came with it. His heart pounded. He was hot, then cold, then hot. He'd felt okay earlier, but that was because he'd still been under anesthesia.

That doctor. *Only acetaminophen for the pain. No morphine. No opiates.* That's what he'd said. *Your heart will thank me*, he'd said.

I'm not thanking you, asshole.

This was killing Mark, this need. It was destroying him one molecule at a time. He wished he had told the doctor the truth, that he'd been doing oxy every day for the past couple of weeks—no, months—upping the numbers more and more because it took more and more to get him off or to even feel anything at all. But he didn't want to get in trouble. Scratch that. He was in trouble. Big trouble. He didn't want to get in any more trouble than he was already in. He saw the hate in their eyes, all over their faces, even that cop they had guarding the door to his hospital room, looking at him as though he was . . .

What do they think I am?

Mark thought about that other cop, the detective, the one who had shot him. He thought about the girl and how her phone was in his pocket and how that must have looked. Why hadn't he explained? Why hadn't he tried to explain instead of running?

Where is she? The cop had asked. And all he could

think of was that girl's face, how frightened she'd looked . . .

"I don't know her." He said it out loud, his voice echoing in the hospital room. "I don't know that girl."

Weird, when the detective was in his room earlier, Mark had so much he wanted to say, but he hadn't gotten any of it out. Mark had still been coming out of anesthesia. That was part of it, but there was also the way the guy had come at him with his eyes. The *hate*. Mark could feel the burn of it, when the thing was, the thing he wanted that detective to understand . . . Mark wasn't a bad person. He wasn't a monster. He'd asked to talk to the guy for a reason, for lots of *good* reasons, and he wished . . . he wished he'd been able to find the words . . .

An emotion barreled through him. Not a good one. He felt tears pressing against the inside of his skin. His nose ran. His eyes welled up.

"I didn't hurt that girl." Mark's voice cracked and broke. "I'd never hurt anybody. And when you came up to me on the street, I swear . . . I didn't even know where I was . . ."

"Who are you talking to?"

Mark looked up. Most of the lights in the room were off, but there was one on right behind her. His eyes were blurred from tears and so he couldn't make out her features. She looked like a shadow with a halo.

"Have you had visitors?"

"Yes."

"Did you tell them my name?"

He couldn't remember her name. "Why are you wearing a nurse's uniform?" he said.

"Because I am a nurse."

She slipped the blanket off him, undid the front of his hospital gown. Her movements were brisk, efficient.

"What are you doing?"

"Did you tell them my name?"

"No."

He felt a ripping sensation at the center of his chest, like a Band-Aid being yanked off. Then another, a little lower.

"What are you doing to me?"

"Did you tell them about Maya?"

Rip, rip . . .

"No, I swear."

Rip, rip . . .

He winced.

"Just a few more," she said.

He said it again. "What are you doing?"

"Taking you off the monitors, then turning them off," she said. "We don't want any alarms."

"*What?*"

"Sssh." She put a hand over his mouth, cool and firm. He cried out, but the hand clamped tighter. She removed something from her pocket. It glistened in the dim light. A needle. Mark didn't like needles. Not anymore. They made him think of his older brother. When Mark closed his eyes sometimes, he'd remember waking up and seeing Steven on the floor, white and still. He'd remember the needle next to him, like some bug who'd had its fill of Steven's blood, and now it was just lying there, sated. And then he'd have to take pills to make the image go away.

"No needles." He said it into her hand.

She jabbed it into his neck. He felt a hard pinch, like

stitches being pulled too tight. "You'll like this," she said.

He didn't like the pinch or the sting. But he liked the familiar warmth, running through his veins, filling his body. She brought her face close to his. Her eyes were clear and kind in the soft light. "I'll stay with you till you're gone."

Her hand came away from his mouth and stroked his arm, and Mark remembered sitting in the front seat of her car, just as the oxy was kicking in. It had been earlier tonight, and, *really? Only tonight? Feels so long ago . . .*

When you smoked it, it had such a sweet smell. "Are you a happy person?" she'd asked him, and he'd cast a glance at her daughter in the backseat, the gas station light illuminating the dried tears on the girl's face. This had been before she'd caught the girl using her phone, before she'd taken the phone away and put the girl in the trunk and . . . How far had they driven? How long before she'd needed to go for gas?

She took his hand in hers. Her grip was strong. "Let go," she said. Mark thought of his brother again and how he'd cried over Steven's body, how he'd said, "Don't leave me" to Steven, even though he was already gone.

She brushed her hand over Mark's eyes, closing them. He wished he could remember her name.

Blackness poured into his ears, his mouth, his head. There was nothing Mark could do but what she'd told him to do and so he did. He let go, thinking of the slight smile on his dead brother's face and the tears on the girl's face and the girl's lip, how it had trembled, how she had mouthed the word, *Help.*

All he wanted was for everyone to be okay.

13

"Maybe," said Geoff, the late-night door-man in Lindsay Segal's building. He said it to Maya's picture, Brenna holding it out in front of him, her hand trembling from nerves and fatigue and swelling frustration. She realized how unfairly she'd judged the other doorman, who'd at least tried to be friendly. This guy made him look like a superhero.

Brenna clutched her wrist to steady it. "Could you please look at this a little closer?" she said. "This is my daughter. She's missing. This apartment building may be the last place she was seen."

"Yes, you told me all that." He said it as though Brenna were asking him about a missing set of keys. Maybe the ennui came from too many late-night jobs in the city, or maybe he was on too much medication. Maybe he was just an asshole. He wore glasses with very thin silver frames. He adjusted them languidly, the frames glistening like spiderwebs in the soft lobby light. "She doesn't look familiar," he said.

"Are you sure?"

"Yes."

"Why didn't you say that to begin with?" she said. "Why did you say maybe?"

His gaze went to a framed picture placed on the front desk—a long-haired dachshund, posing on a carpety lawn. "There was a party here," he said, addressing the dachshund, not Brenna. "Kids coming and going all night. Neighbors complaining. I don't remember your daughter's face. But that doesn't mean she wasn't here."

"Do you have surveillance videos?"

"Maybe," he said again.

Maybe? Really?

"Can I look?" Brenna said. "I would need last night from around 6 P.M. to . . . about twenty-four hours' worth."

"I'd need to talk to my supervisor about that."

"So talk to him."

"It's three in the morning."

Brenna moved closer to him, her whole body filling with anger, vibrating with it. "Maybe you didn't hear me when I told you my daughter is missing."

"I heard you," he said. "But I'm not going to wake up my supervisor at three in the morning over some girl who's probably at her boyfriend's place. It hasn't been that long since the party, lady, and you're not the first parent I've talked to. You're not the first parent who's complained, only to call back later and—"

"Here's the thing," she said, very quietly. "If you don't let me see those surveillance videos *now*, I will scream loud enough and long enough to wake up your entire building. *Maybe* get you fired. *Maybe* even get you arrested."

She locked eyes with Geoff. Still with the ennui.

Still without the slightest hint of concern behind the spiderweb frames. "You're not going to do that and we both know it."

"How do we both know it?"

"Get some rest, lady."

In the real world, Brenna had long been known for her interrogation skills. Her memory had always been a plus in this area, allowing her to trip up her subjects with their own perfectly recalled words or actions while enabling Brenna to stick to the facts, to keep her own emotions at bay.

But this wasn't the real world. The world hadn't been real since 6 P.M., when she'd read the first word of Maya's text, and it had been getting less and less real ever since. Brenna wasn't herself, and so she had no other choice than to be the broken, desperate person she'd become—to be that person, for all it was worth. Brenna kept her eyes on Geoff. She took a breath. She screamed.

In Faith's dream, her mother was screaming. Faith was back in her old house and she was getting her books to go to school and her mother was in the kitchen, shrieking like a scared cat.

"What's wrong?" Faith said.

Her mother pointed at the door, at Maya running out of the house, into the street, an eighteen-wheeler roaring down their quiet suburban street, headed straight toward her. Faith fell to her knees as the truck sent Maya flying and Faith's mother shrieked, "I told you not to let her out!"

I told you!

Faith woke up in a sweat, shaking, thinking not about her mother but of the call she'd gotten, just before her interview with Ashley Stanley. The phone call from that weird female fan.

She reached out to touch Jim, but he wasn't there. "Jim?" she said.

No answer.

She said it louder, and he said, "In here!" Faith got out of bed, followed the sound of his voice to the room he used as a home office. He was on his computer, a picture of two young girls in bandage dresses filling the screen. Faith blinked a few times before she realized one of them was Maya.

"Where did you get that?" she asked.

"Brenna sent it," he said. "She sent both of us a whole series of them. They're on Maya's computer, taken two days before she . . . before she told me she was going on the sleepover."

Faith peered at the girl in the cobalt blue dress, fingers curled around Maya's waist. She looked at the way she leaned her head into Maya's, Maya wearing an identical dress, standing beside her in front of a three-way mirror. In the photo, the other girl's smile was so big and friendly Faith nearly didn't recognize her at first. But then she looked at the made-up eyes and it all came together. *Lindsay.* Lindsay, that trashy girl who had told Faith and Jim she barely knew Maya, that she was just a freshman . . .

"She was invited on that sleepover," Faith said.

"My thoughts, too. I mean . . . whether she showed up or not is a different matter. But Maya didn't lie to me."

He turned and looked at Faith. His eyes were blood-shot and full of pain.

"Honey, you should take a pill. Try to sleep. It's best in the long run."

"I know," he said. "But I feel like if I let go for one minute . . . If I don't sit by the phone and watch the computer and . . ."

"I understand." She swallowed hard, her dream in her head again. *I told you not to let her out . . .* "Jim?"

"Yeah?"

"I got a phone call when I was interviewing Ashley Stanley. Someone telling me not to let Maya out because if I did, something bad would happen."

Jim swung away from the computer and stared at her. "Are you serious?"

She nodded.

"Well . . . why didn't you say anything earlier?"

"I get lots of calls like that. E-mails, too. All the time."

"About Maya?"

"About all of us."

"Jesus."

"I figured it was someone who knew I was inter-viewing Ashley, someone trying to scare me. The person said they like to watch me. I get that a lot, too."

"How did they get your cell phone number?"

"I guess they called the station. Claimed to be Maya's teacher."

"Was it a man or a woman?"

"A woman," she said. "I think."

"Faith."

"I know."

"Honey."

"I know, Jim. Let's just . . ."

"You get these calls all the time?"

"Jim."

He closed his eyes. Faith's phone was in the kitchen. She grabbed it, along with Detective Plodsky's card.

"What are you doing?" he called out.

"I'm calling that detective."

She tapped Plodsky's number into the phone. She moved back into Jim's office before hitting send.

The call went straight to voice mail. "She's got her phone off. Can you believe that?"

She hit redial. "Seriously, what if this was some-one important? What the hell am I talking about, *I am someone important.*"

Voice mail again. She ended the call.

Jim looked up at her. "Call Brenna." She shouldn't have noticed the readiness with which he'd said Brenna's name, the look in his eyes as he said it . . .

Faith was messed up. Brenna being back in both their lives after all these years was made less strange by the awful situation—but it still did feel strange, incredibly so, as though someone were rearranging the foundation of a structure that had stood just fine for years . . . *Should I ask Jim how he feels about that?*

She shook the thought out of her mind. She hit redial and got voice mail and left a message for Plodsky asking her to please call. "Honestly. There's a child missing and what? She wants her beauty sleep?"

"Are you going to call Brenna?"

"It's 3 A.M., Jim," Faith said. "She's as emotional as we are, and if she's managed to get to sleep at all . . ."

"I bet she's up," he said. "She's a night owl. Like me."

"How do you know that?"

He shrugged, looked away.

Faith swallowed hard. "I mean, are you talking about when you were married to her? Because that was a long time ago and you were both a lot younger . . ."

"Forget it."

"Okay."

She turned back toward the bedroom, and then Jim was up, putting his arms around her.

He said, "It isn't a big deal."

"What isn't a big deal?"

He exhaled. "A couple of times last year, I was up late working on one assignment or another and she was up, too, and so we . . . we instant messaged each other."

She pulled away from him. "You . . . what? Seriously?"

"We talked about Maya, work . . . stuff like that."

She shook her head. "I thought she couldn't talk to you without getting hit by some memory."

"She couldn't. She couldn't hear my voice or see me. But instant messaging was different." He sighed. "Don't look at me like that, Faith. It was just a way to catch up. And we only did it a couple of times."

She forced a smile. "God bless modern technology," she said, thinking, *If it wasn't a big deal, then why didn't either of you tell me?*

He put his arm around her, and together, they walked back to the bedroom, but they stopped at Maya's room, her empty room. They stared into the darkness, at the moonlight pouring in through the window, resting on the neatly made bed. Maya's bed.

Faith rested her hand on his shoulder and closed her eyes, hot tears forming under the lids. She put her arm around his waist and held him tight. Too tight. "What will we do?" she whispered.

He didn't answer.

Diane Plodsky was listening to a rebroadcast of *Prairie Home Companion* when—after two hours of her sitting in the parking lot, waiting—she saw Dr. Clark leaving the ER. *Thank you.* Even though NPR had long been Diane's stakeout soundtrack of choice, she preferred Harry Shearer or *Wait, Wait Don't Tell Me*, or even the *BBC News Hour*. Lake Woebegone had always worked like a tranquilizer on her, and between the car heater, Keillor's voice, and the fact that it was past three in the morning, Diane had been thisclose to surrendering to sleep when Clark finally strode across the parking lot, got into his car, and drove off.

"Hurry home," she whispered, shaking off the drowsiness before stepping into the cold night.

There was a new nurse at the front desk. A confused-looking little thing with chubby baby cheeks and granny glasses who practically fell out of her chair from shock when Diane walked through the door. *Piece of cake.*

Diane smoothed her hair. She squared her shoulders and leveled her gaze at the girl in the sternest of ways, heading for the front desk without hesitation.

"Can I help you?" the nurse said.

Diane slipped her badge out of her jacket pocket and showed it to her. The girl's mouth dropped open.

"What room is Mark Carver in?" Diane asked.

"Did you want to—"

"C-A-R-V-E-R."

The nurse tapped at her computer. "Seven-oh-one East?"

"How do I get there?"

"Take the elevator up to the seventh floor, go all the way down to the end of the hall, and make a right." The nurse looked at Diane as though she were a train speeding toward her and there was no time to jump off the tracks. Amazing how far a badge and a little confidence can get you at three o'clock in the morning—*especially* at three o'clock in the morning, when no one expects an oncoming train. For the umpteenth time in her adult life, Diane realized, her patience had paid off.

"Thank you," she told the terrified nurse, and headed straight for the elevator, hit floor seven, and walked down the hallway with a stride so deliberate, no one bothered to stop her—not the two doctors, going over files at the first nurses station, or the group of orderlies who came up behind her, wheeling a gurney full of medical equipment, or the blue-eyed nurse who passed her as she neared the end of the hall, her gaze just as hard as Diane's.

A lot of the detectives Diane knew—the ones who worked out of the precincts like she used to before she'd gotten divorced and decided her whole life needed changing, the ones investigating homicides and acts of grand larceny and all those other crimes that involved real people rather than the lack of them—those detectives tended to be condescending toward Missing Persons. They dismissed Diane and her ilk as pencil pushers who filled out the appropriate forms and went home at 5 P.M. *Bureaucrats*, they'd say. *Not real cops.*

If they could see her now, though, those precinct detectives. If they were to get a load of the swagger and the don't-mess-with-me glare on Diane Plodsky, moving like a champion through these hospital corridors, wide awake and all-powerful at three o'clock in the morning. If they could see her now, those detectives would surely regret every dismissive thought that had ever dared pass through their narrow little minds.

If Bruce could see her . . . Well, Bruce probably wouldn't be all that surprised.

Diane caught sight of room 701. There was a uniformed guard in front of it, half asleep. She flashed her badge at him and opened the door quickly, slipping in like she belonged and then shutting it softly behind her. One fluid movement.

Mission accomplished.

"Hi, Mark," she said, once the door was closed and her breathing had slowed.

No response.

The lights were dimmed, the room very quiet. He was sleeping, she figured. But that was fine. More waiting was fine, long as she was in the right place. She could stay awake. The stress of getting up here and looking confident doing it had shaken the sleepiness out of her and besides, this quiet, deathly though it was, was a better stimulant than *Prairie Home Companion*. She sat in a chair near the door, folded her hands in her lap. "You go ahead and rest, Mark," she said. "Don't mind me."

Diane sat waiting for a few more moments before that old cliché movie tagline flashed in her brain. *It was quiet. Too quiet.* It *was* too quiet. And when she looked around the room, Diane realized at last that there was a distinct reason for this: All the equipment had been turned off.

Diane switched on a light. Carver looked very pale, very still.

She moved toward his bed, rested her fingers against his neck . . . "Oh no," she whispered, pressing the call button, jamming her fingers into it. *"Oh no, no, no . . ."* She pushed her hands into his chest, attempting CPR, but he didn't budge, and as the door flew open and medical staff rushed in, Diane noticed the note pinned to the front of Carver's hospital gown, pinned there with a tiny, glittering diamond stud earring.

It read, "She's happy now."

Part Three

Mom just told me, "I don't know you anymore."
She said it angrily, like it was my fault. I don't get
it. If Mom doesn't know me, why am I to blame?

From the diary of Clea Spector
June 6, 1979

14

"That's Maya's," Brenna said.

It was 5:30 A.M., still dark outside. She was sitting across from Plodsky in the kitchen of Jim and Faith's apartment. She'd been in here several times before, to pick up Maya, chat with Faith, maybe have a cup of tea—an airy room with stainless steel fixtures and a big, photo-shoot-ready island of polished wood, a granite chopping-block top she'd always coveted. But being here in this capacity, sitting around the island on tall stools with Plodsky, Jim, Faith, and Morasco, Plodsky's briefcase placed at the center of the chopping block with the evidence bag on top . . . This was completely unfamiliar. It made her thoughts race around, especially after a night of no sleep—no rest, even— and no food other than Trent's Red Bull. The worst night in Brenna's life, capped off by Plodsky's 5 A.M. phone call and then the cab ride to Jim and Faith's, the briefcase and the evidence bag.

It had been kind of Detective Plodsky to call. It had been very kind of her to offer to come down to Jim and Faith's instead of making them all drive up to 147th and Frederick Douglass Boulevard, where the offices of the

Missing Persons Unit were located. And the fact that
Plodsky had waited it out at the hospital long enough
to find Carver's body the way she did . . . that had been
heroic. This was what Brenna was trying to focus on—
the good. But all she could see was the evidence bag,
what was in it.

Plodsky said, "Are you sure it's Maya's?"

Brenna nodded, tears welling in her eyes, pain tear-
ing at her. It was an earring, like thousands of others.
But as seen through the thick plastic, it might as well
have been a lock of hair, a severed fingertip. "Her favorites," she said. "Her grandmother gave them to her."

"She wore those all the time," Faith said. "She liked
them because her ears had a tendency to get infected
and the posts are twenty-four-karat gold which—" Her
voice broke off. She closed her eyes. "Yes, they were
her favorites."

Jim put a hand over hers.

Brenna said, "Can we see the note?"

Plodsky nodded, and Brenna noticed something
strange in her expression—a softness to the eyes. *Sym-
pathy.* It made her not want to look at the note. It made
her want to get up and run, and she had to steel herself
in order to ask again. "Please," she said.

Plodsky opened the briefcase, removed another bag,
and slid it across the island so they could read the note
inside.

"Oh my God," Faith whispered. She started to
breathe hard and fast, Jim taking her into his arms. "It's
okay," he said.

"No," she said. "No, you don't understand . . ."

Brenna stared at the carefully printed block letters:

"She's happy now." It brought on a memory—February 16, 2005, *phone pressed to her ear, guilt tugging at her as she grasps for the words. "I'm so sorry, but we can't take every case . . ."*

Nick squeezed Brenna's hand, bringing her out of it.

"My thought is that this is a message to you," Plodsky was saying, her voice calm and quiet as Faith caught her breath. "It could be from someone Maya went with willingly, but considering what was done to Mr. Carver, the person is still dangerous. I've recommended issuing an AMBER Alert. My superiors are still considering whether that's the best possible approach in this particular situation. In the meantime, does that phrase, 'She's happy now,' or maybe the handwriting is familiar . . . is there anything about the note that feels personal?"

Faith said, "I know who took her."

Brenna stared at her.

"I got a strange phone call on Saturday, when I was interviewing Ashley Stanley," she said. "A woman with a very deep, husky voice—someone who clearly had smoked a lot of cigarettes. She told me not to let Maya out."

Brenna's eyes widened. "Why didn't you say anything about that?"

Plodsky said, "Do you get calls like this often, Mrs. Rappaport?"

"Yes."

"And that's why you didn't tell us about it earlier?"

She looked down. "Yes," she said. "I get them all the time. They try to screen them at the studio but . . ."

Brenna said, "Mentioning Maya?"

"Mentioning everyone." Faith turned to her. Her eyes looked weary and cold. "After I interviewed you in October, I got quite a few mentioning *you*."

She said it like an accusation. *What is going on with you, Faith?* Brenna thought. She cleared her throat. It had been a long day, a long night, a nightmare they were all still trapped in. It was natural to start bumping against each other, trying to get out.

Brenna said, "Was the call from a restricted number?"

"Yes."

"It can still be traced."

"Please give me your cell phone carrier information and the time of the call," Plodsky said.

"But I think I already know who the caller is," Faith said. "That's what I'm trying to say."

They all looked at her.

"Renee Lemaire is a smoker," Faith said.

"The woman who abducted Ashley Stanley," said Plodsky. "You think she was the one who called?"

"Yes. She's a chain smoker. Ashley told me."

"You think she warned you she was going to take Maya, then took her anyway as . . . what? Why?"

"As payback for putting Ashley on TV and bringing the story into the spotlight. They'll never be able to take her again, so they traded one blonde, thirteen-year-old girl for another."

"Were the Lemaires drug users?"

"Ashley said they sometimes gave her pills. Why?"

"Mark Carver died of a heart attack, induced by an overdose of oxycodone. His doctor had specifically ordered no opiates. The medical examiner noticed bruising at the neck, consistent with an injection. So whoever left the note—presumably the same person who killed him—would have known their way around a needle."

"Listen to me," Faith said. "In the interview, Ashley told me that Renee Lemaire used those exact words with her. She said she told her, 'We chose you, and you're happy now.'"

Plodsky said, "I'll need a copy of the interview."

"I'll have the studio send one over to you right away."

"Ashley said that on TV?" Nick said. "She used those exact words?"

"Yes."

"How would Renee Lemaire know how to find Maya?" Jim said.

"Don't you see? The paps caught Ashley and me having lunch weeks ago. It was in all the papers. Her husband could have found out about Maya. He could have been stalking her for weeks. Maybe she called and tried to warn me, but now she's in it again . . . She's in it with him and they have her."

"Carver did say he was partying with a woman." Jim looked at Nick. "Right?"

Nick nodded.

"That woman could have been Renee Lemaire," Faith said.

Plodsky said, "I suppose it's possible."

"You suppose?" Faith said. "The words on the note were Renee Lemaire's exact words."

"Not anymore."

"What do you mean?"

"They're everyone's words now."

"*What the hell is that supposed to mean?*"

"They were said on a TV show with millions of

viewers," Brenna said. "Anyone who saw her use them could have taken Maya, killed Carver, and left that message."

"That's true," said Jim.

Faith shot him a look, which again made Brenna wonder why. "I don't mean it's not Renee Lemaire," she said. "I was just pointing out that she's not the only one who knows about that phrase now."

"Ms. Spector is right," Plodsky said. "And objectively speaking, a message like 'She's happy now' could mean any number of things. Including exactly what's on the piece of paper. Maya herself said something similar in the text message—"

"That wasn't Maya," Nick said.

"Look," Plodsky sighed out the word. "I understand that all of you have your opinions—"

"It isn't an opinion. It's a fact."

"—and the four of you are more knowledgeable on the topic of police proceedings than most parents, but that doesn't change . . ."

As she continued to talk, Brenna stared down at her hands, seeing them on her own desk on February 16, 2005, a Wednesday. She could feel the dry heat from the radiator in her office space, *her face flushing from it, flushing from nerves, too, because she hates to let her down—poor, sad Sophia Castillo, her pain so deep you can feel it through the phone.*

A mother, just like Brenna. Missing someone, just as she does. Her own son. Her only son.

The clock at the bottom of Brenna's computer screen reads 3:04 P.M. Brenna stares at it, watches it turn to 3:05, all to avoid looking at the open e-mail.

"Ms. Castillo." Her throat is dry, her voice barely audible. "I'm very sorry but I can't take your case."

She takes a breath, waits a few seconds, but there's nothing, no reply at all. "I . . . uh . . . I received an e-mail from a source of mine, within the legal system."

"What source?"

"I can't tell you that, ma'am. But what I can tell you is that I've learned that your husband, Christopher, has been awarded sole custody of Robert."

"But I don't . . . I don't know where either one of them are." Her voice sounds drugged beyond sadness.

Brenna shifts her gaze to the back of Trent's head. She listens to Sophia's shaking breath. She's not sure she believes the rest of Len's e-mail. Lots of things are said in a divorce proceeding that aren't true. Lots of things are said that are out-and-out lies . . .

"Robert is my only child," Sophia says.

"I know," Brenna says, "and I'm sorry. I know how much you must hurt, believe me. I'm the mother of an only child myself—"

"You don't."

"I'm sorry?"

"You don't know how much I must hurt. Your only child is still with you."

Brenna takes a deep breath, lets it out slowly. "I can have my assistant e-mail you a list of qualified private investigators who may be willing to take your case."

No answer.

"In the meantime," Brenna says, "try to focus on the fact that unlike so many other missing children, Robert is probably well. He's happy now."

"You're not going to take my case."

"I'm sorry, ma'am, no. I can't."

"I'm sorry to hear that, Ms. Spector."

"Ms. Spector?" Plodsky said.

Brenna gritted her teeth, shut her eyes tight. When she opened them, she saw everyone staring at her.

"I was just saying," the detective said, "that we need to look at this case from all possible perspectives. This morning, a civilian representative from our community outreach department will be speaking to the other children at Maya's school . . ."

He's happy now.

Faith said, "I have a suggestion, Detective," but Brenna didn't hear it. She was back into February 16, 2005—not to the phone call with Sophia Castillo, but to the e-mail she'd avoided looking at during the conversation. It had come fifteen minutes earlier, from Len Kirch, a former legal reporter for Jim's paper, the *Trumpet*.

Len used to be a very close friend, but on June 18, 2007, they'd gone out for drinks and he'd made an incredibly awkward and unwanted pass. Both of them knowing her memory all too well, they hadn't spoken since.

Back in 2005, though, when Brenna had never heard Len say the words, "My wife doesn't understand my needs," she'd asked him to investigate Sophia after speaking with her on the phone the previous day. The e-mail had arrived on her screen with a shotgun blast— all her e-mails used to make that sound back then . . .

"She's way into my pecs," Trent says into his phone, his voice bounding off the thin walls of Brenna's office area. In a month and three days, it'll be this irritating

kid's one-year anniversary of working here. Brenna shakes her head at that. How could he have lasted this long?

Trent says, "And I can tell she wants to partay if you know what I'm sayin'."

"Trent," Brenna says. "What did I tell you about personal calls?"

"Uh, on my cell phone and during lunch break?"

"Bingo."

"Sorry, boss."

Brenna hears a shotgun blast—a new e-mail, from Len Kirch.

"Dude, I'm gonna have to call you laaaaatah." Trent sings out the last word like it's an American Idol audition. *Brenna rolls her eyes. She moves the cursor to click on the e-mail, then notices the subject: "Re: Sophia Castillo: Yikes."*

She opens it.

"Ms. Spector?" Plodsky said again.

Brenna turned to the detective, the body of Len Kirch's five-year-old e-mail still floating in front of her eyes *as she skims it, stopping at the words "serious danger," at the words "trouble with authority," at the words "psychiatric issues"*. . .

"I was just telling Detective Plodsky," Faith said, "that I am going to make an announcement on air this morning." Faith had a piece of white paper spread in front of her. Her gaze stayed on Brenna, brittle and hard.

Brenna blinked at Faith. "Okay . . ."

"She thinks it's a good idea," Faith said. "And if you can get out of your own goddamn head for a few

seconds, I can *re*read it to you and you can tell me if
you have anything to add."

Jim said, "Take it easy, Faith," and Faith said, "*You*
take it easy," and it was only then that the iciness of her
tone sank in. That phrase: *Your own goddamn head.*
Faith never talked to Brenna this way. She hardly ever
even swore.

"Are you okay?" Brenna said.

Jim said, "We're all stressed."

"Right." Morasco glared at Faith. "We *all* are. And
by the way, this is *Brenna's child* that's gone missing.
You might want to take that into account before attack-
ing her."

"She's *my child*, too."

Brenna closed her eyes, put a hand up. "Please," she
said, not so much to Faith or to anyone in the room but
to herself, to the exhaustion and pain that kept cutting
into her thoughts, her memories, making it so hard to
recall February 16, 2005, and Sophia Castillo on the
phone and the sound of Brenna's own voice, the words
coming out of her own mouth: *He's happy now . . .*

She looked at Plodsky. "I may have a lead for you,"
she said.

"What the hell is wrong with her?" Nick said, once
they'd left Jim and Faith's apartment.

"Plodsky?" Brenna said. That was the only "her"
on her mind. Plodsky, who'd done everything short of
rolling her eyes at the mention of a disgruntled mother
stealing Maya away, seven years after getting turned
down as a client. "I guess for all her talk about explor-
ing all options, she thinks the Lemaires are a sexier

lead than Sophia Castillo. Can you look her up on NCIC? You still have access, right? It's probably a crap lead after all, but maybe it isn't. And I don't trust Plodsky to follow up."

"Sure," he said, "but I wasn't talking about Plodsky."

Brenna turned to Nick. The sun was rising. It cast a pink glow across his face, made it softer, sadder. "Faith?"

He nodded, Brenna noticing the dark circles under his eyes, the way his hair stuck out at odd angles. She ran a hand through it, "I did the same thing to you, you know."

"What do you mean?"

"My father killed himself. My mother lied about it for more than thirty years. When I finally find out, who do I get angry at? You."

"That was different. You're hurting now and she should have some consideration."

"Faith's hurting, too. She's lashing out at me like I lashed out at you. Sure it's unfair, but this whole situation is unfair. It's making us all go a little crazy."

He brushed his hand against her cheek. "You haven't slept, have you?"

"No," she said. "When Plodsky called, I'd just gotten home."

"From where?"

"Screaming at a doorman."

"Oh," he said, as though screaming at a doorman were the most normal thing in the world. No *Why?* No *Are you all right?* No *Why didn't you call me? I could have helped.* Morasco had changed, too. His eyes were stricken. "Did it get you anywhere?"

"It may have," Brenna said. "I'll be able to tell you for sure in a couple of hours."

"Please," he said. "Let me know anything that happens."

"You care about Maya."

"Yes."

"You're scared."

"Yes."

"We're going to find her." Brenna stared into his stricken eyes. More than anything, she wanted him to agree.

"Yes," he said again, his gaze still locked with her own. "Yes we are." As though to prove his point, Nick took a steno pad out of his jacket pocket, and asked Brenna to tell him everything she knew about Sophia Castillo.

What Brenna knew about Sophia Castillo wasn't a lot, but she did have her phone number. For Nick's computer search, Brenna had scrolled back yet again to February 16, 2005, recalled the moment Trent had transferred Sophia Castillo's call to her, and basically read the number to him off a five-year-old phone screen—same as she'd done with Trent yesterday when he'd told her about Castillo's new call.

"You're amazing," Morasco had said to her, just before heading off to yet another Internal Affairs interview.

Brenna had shaken her head. "It's just wires crossing in my brain. You know that."

He had kissed her then, quickly, but with such tenderness. "I wasn't talking about your memory."

After he left, Brenna stood on the sidewalk, wind whipping at her skin, burning it. *Can Maya feel this? Is she cold?*

The number was still in her mind, and so she plucked her phone out of her bag and tapped it in. The call went to voice mail after a few unanswered rings, Sophia Castillo sounding a lot more cheerful than she had five years ago. *Please leave a message and I will call you back!*

"Hi, Ms. Castillo, this is Brenna Spector . . ."

It was a long shot, she knew. But at this point, Brenna would take any shot, she'd talk to anyone. She'd do anything, anything at all.

Faith felt Jim's hand on her shoulder. "I love you," he said. She looked at him, his face so pale and tired, sheen across his forehead from the hot lights. Faith put her hand over Jim's and grabbed it, the way you'd grab on to someone's hand to keep from falling, so tight it hurt, based more on need than on any softer emotion. "I love you, too."

"You guys ready?" said Danielle, the executive producer. Her voice was too cheerful, given the situation, and to Faith everything seemed a little off—a little too bright and professional. Life going on, business as usual . . . nothing could hurt as much as that.

Ashley had said something along those lines during the interview—how her happiest moments were when the Lemaires left her alone, but in some ways they were the saddest, because she'd have time to think about life outside, how it was going on without her . . .

Faith reminded herself that Danielle was doing her

a favor—allowing her to make this announcement—a personal one and quite a downer—before the regularly scheduled *Sunrise Manhattan*, even coming in early to personally supervise the broadcast. That was kind, though the cynical side of Faith's brain reminded her that today's regularly scheduled show was the rebroadcast of the Ashley Stanley interview, and you couldn't ask for better PR than the host's own daughter going missing, probably as a result of *what-you're-about-to-see*.

For Danielle, this was win-win.

Faith pushed the thought away. The klieg lights hummed in her ears and Nicolai counted down, and Faith's gaze went to one of the monitors, Maya's ninth grade picture filling the screen. *Please, please, please* . . . She took a deep Pilates breath, tightened her grip on Jim's hand. *Don't let me fall.*

"Action," Danielle said.

Faith launched in without a missing a beat. "My name is Faith Gordon-Rappaport and this is my husband, Jim," she said. "Our daughter, Maya Rappaport, has gone missing . . ."

"That girl goes to your school," said Miles's mom.

"What girl?" said Miles. Dumb thing to say. Maya's picture was on TV, they were watching TV over breakfast, what other girl could she be talking about?

"The girl on TV, Miles. Her mother just said she's a ninth grader at P.S. 125. Stop texting for a minute and look."

Miles felt like he was in the middle of the worst dream he'd ever had, like he was banging his fists on the side of it, but the dream wouldn't give. It wouldn't let him out. He hadn't eaten any of his breakfast burrito, which was weird. His mom would remark on that soon. He glanced at the phone in his lap, at Lindsay's latest text: *Just act normal.* He took a bite of the burrito. Choked it down.

"Do you know her?" Miles's dad said.

"Kind of. Not really. She's younger. She's in my art class."

"If she's in your art class, that would mean you know her."

"Her poor parents," Miles's mother said.

Miles took another bite. His stomach ached and churned. He felt like he might throw up. "Can I have some water?"

His mother started for the cupboard, but his dad stopped her. "Glasses are by the sink," he said. "Water's in a pitcher in the fridge. You're not paralyzed."

Be normal. "Whatever," Miles said.

His little brother laughed.

"Shut up, Neil."

"Miles," his mother said. "That isn't nice."

"Sorry."

Neil laughed some more. He was six years old. He didn't have a problem in the world that couldn't be fixed with a nap or an ice cream cone. Miles hated him.

He got up from his chair and moved toward the sink. The air around him felt thick, like something swollen. It was hard to breathe. He'd once read a story by Edgar Allan Poe—when was that? Seventh grade. Right. The one about the heart, beating through the walls, pounding in the murderer's head until he has to confess, he has to . . .

"You okay, dear?"

"Uh, yeah, Mom. Why wouldn't I be?" He opened the cupboard, took out a glass. On TV, the image flipped from Maya's school picture to her dad and stepmom. "When I taped the following interview with Ashley Stanley on Saturday, January 16," Maya's stepmom said, "my daughter was at home. She was safe. She left our apartment in the West Twenties that day, sometime around sunset. We don't know where she went after that. But she never came home. Maya is five-eight and 120 pounds. She has waist-length blonde hair and blue eyes and she was last seen wearing a bright blue coat with brass buttons . . ."

Miles swallowed hard, the thick air closing in on him. *The coat.* His phone vibrated in his back pocket. Another text. It was probably from Lindsay. He didn't want to look at it, but it was better that than to look at Maya's parents. Better to look at Lindsay's smiling picture on his screen than to remember the way her face had looked when she'd stuffed that coat into a plastic bag.

The text read: *Stay strong.* The glass dropped out of Miles's hand, shattered to the floor.

Miles's parents stared at him.

"I'll clean it up," he said. "I'm sorry."

Maya's stepmom said, "She means the world to us."

Miles shoved his phone into his back pocket without replying. He grabbed a broom and a dustpan out of the kitchen closet and swept up the ruined glass.

I will clean it up, he thought. *I'll clean it up as best I can.*

15

"What are you doing?" said Annalee.

Lindsay glared at her. "What does it look like I'm doing?"

"Standing in front of Miles's locker?" It almost sounded sarcastic and Annalee had never been sarcastic, not with Lindsay anyway. If this were a normal day, Lindsay would have smacked her down good. But it wasn't a normal day.

Annalee hooked a lock of pale blonde hair behind her ear. "Did you hear about Maya?"

"Sssh."

"What? Why? Everybody's talking about it. Her mom was on TV this morning and—"

"Stepmom. I saw it. Of course I saw it, Annalee, Jesus."

"We're having a special assembly."

"When?"

"Now." Annalee spit her gum into a Kleenex and leaned in close. "Lindsay, I'm kind of worried," she whispered.

"Why? You didn't say anything, did you?"

Fruit gum fumes curled out of her mouth. Lindsay

felt queasy. "I didn't, no. But there were a bunch of people at your place that night. And I could have so sworn I heard Nikki telling Jordan Michaelson about the video. What if she took him into your room and what if she showed him . . ."

"She didn't," Lindsay said.

"How do you know?"

"Because I do."

Lindsay turned away from the gum stink of Annalee. She peered up and down the hallway, skimming the crowd for Miles. Where the hell was he?

Annalee tapped her on the shoulder. "Why are you looking around like that?"

"No reason."

"I'm sure everything will be fine. Forget I said anything."

Last year, when Annalee was dating Chris Kolchek, Lindsay had overheard Chris and his friends talking about her in study hall, Chris bragging that she'd done everything, that she'd gone everywhere with him that he wanted to go. He'd actually called her Anally, which had made Grant Everly and Seth Perkins laugh their asses off. Lindsay had known that wasn't true, but still she hadn't bothered to stick up for Annalee. She'd laughed, too, in fact.

Lindsay felt a little bad about it, but the truth was, she hadn't really liked Annalee since fourth grade ballet class. Annalee was irritating and simpery and she copied Lindsay's outfits, always.

Yet Lindsay had stayed friends with her all these years, *best friends* and, why? Because it was safe. Because it was a habit she'd had for so long, she didn't know how to break it. Because people were used to seeing Lindsay and Annalee together. Because finding someone new would be a pain, and not worth it. Weren't those all reasons why old people stayed in bad marriages?

Meanwhile, her friendship with Nikki was even worse. She'd *never* liked her. If Lindsay was going to look hard at her life, if she was going to be genuinely honest about it, she would admit that she didn't like any of her girlfriends. She would admit that she rarely had any real fun. For the most part, Lindsay would admit, life to her felt a lot like that blackberry brandy on Saturday night. She could stomach it. She could act like she enjoyed it. But really that was all she was doing. Acting.

She grabbed her phone out of her purse, texted Miles: *Where TF R U???* just as the PA system cranked on.

"They probably want us in the auditorium now," said Annalee, oblivious to the way Lindsay had turned away from her, her body language begging Annalee to leave her alone. *How dense can one person possibly be?*

The principal's voice pushed through the speaker system. "Students, please go to the auditorium immediately for a special program regarding a missing student," he said. "Lindsay Segal, come to my office."

"*What?*" Lindsay dropped her phone. It clattered on the walkway, and she picked it up and checked it, her hands shaking. The glass was fine, nothing broken. Still no text from Miles.

Annalee said, "Wow, no way."

Lindsay looked at Annalee. Her eyes were big, but calm and dry.

"I'm sure it's nothing," Annalee said, but she looked relieved that she hadn't been called along with her, and Lindsay wanted to smack her for that, smack her hard. "Probably just . . . like . . . some question about your after-school activities or something."

"Shut up, Annalee."

"Busted," said Ryan Cordonne as he passed.

"Whatever." Lindsay's heart pounded.

A huge group passed her on their way to the auditorium. She saw Nikki among them, but not Miles. Nikki mouthed, *You okay?*, that same look on her face that had been on Annalee's. Relief.

Lindsay shrugged at her elaborately.

Where was Miles? Had Principal Bailey called Miles into his office, too? Or had Miles gone in on his own? Had he told on her? Had he told the principal everything that they had done?

He wouldn't. Miles wouldn't do that.

Miles was into Lindsay—they'd even started to say the L-word to each other. Miles sounded like he meant it, too, and Lindsay thought maybe he did. Maybe they were some kind of real, lasting thing, and whatever had happened between him and Maya two weeks ago was just him being a guy. Hell, Miles wouldn't even admit that anything *had* happened between them . . .

It had, though. Of course it had. Miles was a guy, after all, and he did what any guy would do if any girl were to just randomly show up at his apartment when his parents weren't home. Any girl. Even some dumb little skank like Maya Rappaport, whom Nikki had seen leaving Miles's apartment, her hair messed, that ugly blue coat buttoned up all wrong . . .

And now she was missing. Disappeared into thin air, but it wasn't Lindsay's fault. It was Miles's fault more than hers and Maya's fault more than anything. *You don't just show up at guys' apartments when their parents aren't home. Especially guys who are older than you. Especially guys with girlfriends.*

One night, back in September when she and Miles had first started dating, they'd sat on his balcony and looked into each other's eyes and he had touched her face . . . All he had done was touch her face and yet the way he had touched her, his fingertips tracing her cheekbones, her lips, brushing against her neck, so lightly, as if she were some special, precious thing. All he had done was touch her face and yet she'd never felt so cared for, so loved . . .

Had he touched Maya's face like that, too?

You show up at some guy's apartment, some random upperclassman with a girlfriend he's said the L-word to. You do that, Maya Rappaport, and you get what you deserve . . .

Maybe Principal Bailey had called Lindsay's parents. Maybe they were in his office with him right now, back from their vacation, telling him there must be some mistake, their daughter would never bully anyone . . . *It wasn't bullying, it was what she deserved.*

Lindsay missed her parents. Why did they have to go off to Thailand for a whole week and leave her in the city alone? Maya's parents would never do anything like that—Lindsay barely knew them, yet she could tell. It had been bad enough, seeing them in the lobby last night, but on TV today . . . Lindsay had had to turn them off. That look on the stepmom's face, like the pain was going to break her apart . . .

Lindsay grabbed her binder and her history text-book. She clutched them both to her chest and thought of armor, a shield. *Stay strong.*

She heard her name over the speaker system again and hurried down the hall to the front desk.

"Yes, Lindsay, you can go right in," said the recep-tionist, an old lady whose name Lindsay had never learned.

The door to Principal Bailey's office opened, and he stood there, looking at her. Principal Bailey was chubby and rosy-cheeked and normally friendly, in that corny, superficial way. But you wouldn't know it to see him now.

"Hello Lindsay."

"Hello Principal Bailey," she tried. There was a dark-haired woman sitting at his desk with her back to the door, a bunch of printed-out photographs spread before her. Lindsay wasn't close enough to see what they were of.

"There's someone here who needs to talk to you, Lindsay," said Principal Bailey. And then the woman got up and turned around. She was tall and thin, and though Lindsay didn't recognize her face, she looked at Lindsay as though she knew her.

"Uh . . . hi?" Lindsay said.

"I'm Maya's mother," she said. "And you've been lying to us."

"And we're done," Danielle said. Faith let go of Jim's hand and took a deep breath. It made her a little light-headed, and only then did Faith realize she hadn't eaten since the early dinner she'd had with Jim last night, right before the Ashley Stanley interview broadcast.

"You did great," Jim said.

"Thank you," Faith said. She was normally a breakfast person. She should have grabbed a banana in the greenroom, but the thought of eating anything made her feel so sick . . .

Danielle strode toward Faith and Jim, gathered them both into her arms.

"Anyone with a pulse would have been moved by that." Danielle said it into Faith's neck, and it made Faith uncomfortable, as though she were complimenting her on a performance.

"I hope it works," she said.

"You'll get that little girl back," Danielle said. "I know it."

"Thank you." Faith was grateful she couldn't see Danielle's face.

"I'll leave you guys to each other." Danielle left, Nicolai trailing behind her, neither of them fully looking Faith in the eye.

She turned to Jim, gazed up into his eyes, those warm eyes that had always driven her wild, now so tired and hurt. She said, "When was the last time you and Brenna instant messaged?"

"September."

"What stopped you?"

His gaze left her face, focused on a point just over her left shoulder. "I don't know."

"It's good," she said, slowly, "that we can all talk in person now."

"Yes."

She put her arms around him, rested her head against his chest, listened to his breath, his heartbeat.

"God," he whispered. "I hope Maya isn't too cold."

She pulled him closer. They stayed like that for a while before she noticed the door chimes coming from the nearby greenroom. "My phone."

Faith pulled away from him and followed the sound, hurrying into the greenroom, plucking her phone out of her purse. Caller ID read "Restricted Number."

She answered fast.

"I'm sorry, Faith." Faith's breath died in her throat. It was the same person who had called during her interview. The smoker, the voice so corroded that it was hard to tell gender.

"It's you," Faith said.

"I saw you on TV."

"Please tell me where Maya is."

"Can I meet with you, Faith? Please?"

"Will you—"

"Don't tell anybody I called. This is important."

"Okay."

"You have to promise me. I want to tell you the truth, but I can't do that if anybody knows."

"The truth about Maya."

"Yes."

"Where can we meet?"

"There's a playground on Twelfth and Hudson."

"Okay, when?"

"Twenty minutes."

Faith thought about it. If the subways were on time, she could probably get there in fifteen. "Okay."

There was a sharp intake of breath on the other end of the line. "Come alone," the voice said. "Don't tell anyone."

Faith shut her eyes tight, every muscle in her body tensed, every part of her hoping. "Will you bring Maya?" she said. "Please?"

But there was no reply. The caller had already hung up.

Lindsay Segal clutched her books to her chest and stared at Brenna as though she were a mother bear whose path she'd inadvertently crossed. "I didn't lie to you," she said.

Brenna shook her head. "Sorry, Lindsay," she said, "but that is incredibly lame." The girl's eyes widened. She looked at the principal, as though he were supposed to feed her a line.

"Why don't you come here and take a look at these pictures," Brenna said.

Lindsay took a few timid steps forward.

"You'll never see them from all the way back there."

Lindsay cast a quick glance at the principal, his hands folded across his chest like a prison guard, then moved closer.

On the desk, Brenna had placed all of Maya's pictures from Forever 21, enlarged and brightened courtesy of Trent, and printed out on shiny photograph paper.

It was hard for Brenna to look at the pictures. Larger and clearer on the contact paper, the nervousness in Maya's eyes was all the more apparent, the stiffness of her smile, the way she looked at the other girls, so desperate to please.

She stayed focused on Lindsay. "You said you don't even know Maya," she said, as the girl gaped at the photographs, "but you all look like besties here."

"Oh . . . that was just . . ."

"One day of unseasonable closeness?"

"Um . . . yeah."

"Maya's friend Zoe says you guys have been inseparable for a week. In fact, she's been feeling a little insecure, like you were actually taking Maya away from her."

"That isn't—"

"She initially had plans with Maya for Saturday night, and when Maya canceled on her, you were the first person she thought of."

"Look. Mrs. Rappaport, I don't even know who Zoe is."

"Ms. Spector," she said. "And she knows who *you* are."

Principal Bailey said, "You had better start telling the truth, Lindsay."

"I *am* telling the truth."

Brenna said, "Can I ask you something, Lindsay? It's sort of an opinion question."

"Umm . . ."

"How do you feel about surveillance video?"

"What?"

"Surveillance video. Like they have in the elevators, hallways, and lobbies of almost every New York City doorman apartment? Including your own."

"I . . . Wait. There's video?"

"Do you still want to tell your principal and me that you barely know Maya? That she was never at your apartment on Saturday night?"

Lindsay stared at her, the color draining out of her face. Her gaze darted from Brenna to Principal Bailey and back again, but Brenna kept focusing on her eyes.

"If she'd gone to Zoe's that night," Brenna said, "she never would have left. In the morning, her dad would have met her over there, walked her home, just like he always does." Brenna took a step closer, muscles tensing, anger pressing through her. "She'd be fine, Lindsay. But she changed her plans because of you."

"I didn't do anything."

"Surveillance video doesn't lie."

Lindsay swallowed hard. "I want to talk to my parents."

Principal Bailey said, "Rest assured, they will be called."

The girl's eyes narrowed. For a moment, Brenna thought she was going to turn and make a run for it, but instead she crumpled. Her eyes welled.

"Lindsay," Brenna said. "What happened on Saturday night?"

"It . . . it was just a prank."

Brenna swallowed hard. *Here it comes.*

"We didn't want anything bad to happen to her, we just . . . we were kidding around and . . ."

Brenna stared at her. She gripped the back of the chair very tightly. *Stay calm. Get what you need and then you'll never have to look at her again.* "What was the prank?"

"We . . . we gave her some alcohol. She got sick. We got her on . . . on camera and . . ."

Brenna closed her eyes. "When?"

"Excuse me?"

"When did you do this?" Brenna took a few steps closer. She was at least five inches taller than Lindsay, and she used it, staring down at her, into her eyes until they sparked with fear.

"Uh . . . when?"

"You heard me. *When did you publicly humiliate my daughter?*"

"Umm . . . About 8 P.M."

"And what happened next?"

"She . . ."

"She what?"

"She left."

"Right away?"

"Yes . . . But . . ."

"So she left your apartment at 8 P.M."

"I'm sorry, but . . ."

"What?"

"Didn't it say the time on the video?"

"I never saw any surveillance video."

The girl's jaw dropped open.

"I never said I did. All I said was that most buildings like yours *have* surveillance cameras. You filled in the rest of the blanks."

"No . . ."

"In fact, according to your doorman, your building is actually *between* surveillance cameras as the elevator one has been on the fritz since Friday." She turned to Bailey. "Funny way of putting it—*between surveillance cameras*, like between jobs or between relationships—but you could forgive him the phrasing. He was very agitated at the time."

"Hope they get a new one," Bailey said helpfully.

"Doorman or surveillance camera?" Brenna said. "They could use both."

Lindsay said, "Wait. There wasn't any video of . . . No one saw Maya leaving?"

Brenna shook her head. "You know the good thing about digging your own grave? You always make it just the right size."

Brenna scooped the pictures off the table, slipped them on top of her closely clutched notebook. "I'm going to give you these. I'd suggest pinning them up on your bedroom wall at home so you can take a good long look at the way my daughter is smiling at you girls."

"Can . . . can I . . . please go now?"

"No way," said Brenna, as Principal Bailey buzzed the receptionist, asking her to call in Nikki Webber and Annalee Lambert. "We have a lot more questions for you, and your friends."

It wasn't until Brenna was blocks away from the school and nearing her apartment that Lindsay Segal's words truly began to sink in. Maya hadn't simply left the apartment at 8 P.M. on Saturday, January 16. She'd left the apartment in a state of extreme mortification and despair, after being plied with alcohol and filmed getting sick from it—all for the benefit of Miles, Maya's crush (who, according to a crying, broken Lindsay, had found the whole thing "hysterical"). Maya was dehydrated, humiliated, crying, probably still very drunk. Oh and at that hour, it was also pouring freezing rain.

She could have gone off with anyone in that state. *Anyone.*

Yes, Brenna had drummed *stranger danger* into

Maya's head from the time she first learned how to walk on her own. Yes, Maya knew all the horror stories—from Grimm's fairy tales to Iris Neff to Jaycee Dugard to Ashley Stanley. Yes, she knew to look both ways and stay on the alert and avoid unlit streets and keep her phone in her hands at all times. She knew to scream "Fire," not "Help," because "Fire" made them come running and "Help" did not, and she knew not to make eye contact with strangers, or to speak to them, no matter how friendly and helpful they seemed. And above all else she knew not to get into a stranger's car. But no one is immune to that one dumb mistake. *No one—* especially a child. A poor, hurting, intoxicated child . . .

She pulled her handbag close to her. She felt the bulk of Clea's diary against her ribs and thought of the Boy from the Road, who had picked up her seventeen-year-old, hitchhiking sister twenty-eight years ago in Portsmouth, Virginia, after she'd run away from her "great love" Bill. The Boy from the Road of whom Clea had written, "He can save me," but who had wound up dosing her full of drugs and leaving her for dead in a motel room and *please don't let history repeat itself. Please let Maya be alive and somewhere we can find her. Soon. Now.*

Brenna's eyes started to well. *You have an exact time when Maya left Lindsay's. Eight P.M., Saturday, January 16. Get back to that. Work from there.*

Brenna stepped into the street, narrowly missing a speeding taxi. Its horn blared. Her heart jumped into her throat. *Green light. What the hell is wrong with me?* Brenna stepped back onto the curb, breathing deeply. *Eight P.M., Saturday, January 16. Think.*

Brenna felt a vibration against her side. Her phone. She yanked it out of her bag, looked at the screen. Faith. Probably calling to apologize for being so curt—the last thing she needed right now. She debated letting it go to voice mail, then answered at the last minute.

"Brenna, we don't have much time." Faith's voice trembled like a child's.

"Huh?"

"She called again."

"The woman you thought was Renee—"

"Yes," Faith said. "She called, and she wants to meet me. She wants to meet alone."

Through the phone, Brenna heard a car horn, Faith's breath leaving her in sharp gasps, as though she were running. "Where are you?"

"She wouldn't let me tell anyone. She wants to meet. I'm scared. Do you think she has Maya?"

"Faith," said Brenna. "Where are you right now?"

"I'm on my way to meet her at the playground at Twelfth and Hudson."

"I can get there in five minutes."

"She said to come alone."

"I know. I'll keep my distance. Don't worry."

"Brenna . . ."

There was a pause at the other end of the line. Brenna could hear Faith's breathing, rapid and tenuous. "Yes?"

"Thank you."

16

"I'll meet you back home," Faith told Jim after she finished the call and left the greenroom. "I need to pick something up first." Terrible excuse, she knew, but she hadn't either the time or the brainpower to think of a good one.

"What are you picking up?" Jim called after her as she headed down the hall, straight for the elevator.

Faith pretended not to hear, even though her ears were beyond perfect and Jim knew that. In the old days, the days before yesterday, he joked that in order to fart without Faith hearing it, he had to take a cab across town. But Jim was so tired now and Faith was so tired and they were both different people than they were two days ago.

He didn't repeat the question, or say, *I know you heard me*. And so Faith headed for the elevator without having to elaborate.

Once she got outside the building, she saw that traffic wasn't as bad as she thought it would be, so she reconsidered the subway, stuck her hand out. A cab pulled up fast. Had to be a sign.

"Twelfth and Hudson please." *Please, please, please.*

"I'm in a huge hurry." *Please bring Maya. Please bring her safe and well.*

"Excuse me," said the driver. "Aren't you Faith Gordon-Rappaport?"

She exhaled. "Yes."

The driver glanced at her in the rearview. His eyes were bottle green, beneath bushy copper brows. Faith tried to smile, but could only manage a grimace and pretended to be immersed in the TV screen on the back of the front seat, some maniacally grinning fake reporter singing the praises of the *Spider-Man* musical.

The driver said, "Saw you interview the kidnapped girl yesterday."

Faith nodded.

"Fascinating."

"Thanks."

The cab swung around a truck and zoomed down Broadway, hitting a long line of green lights. Faith's heart pounded. She'd make it on time. She'd make it down to that playground and she'd see that woman *and please let me see Maya. Please let her be all right.*

"I don't get her parents, though," the driver said. "I mean what kid just gets into some car in the middle of the night? Even if it's a woman you had a conversation with once. What kind of kid does that?"

"It wasn't the middle of the night."

"I blame her parents for that," he said. "She had no survival skills. You have to teach survival skills. You teach them to kids when they're young, or else they'll be some teenager like that girl, getting into some pervert's car . . ."

Faith turned back to the screen—Spider-Man gliding over an enthusiastic group of dancers, lights glinting off the wires holding him aloft.

"It's tragic, really. A mother with that little concern about what happens to her daughter, she can't be bothered to teach her the basic skills. What it takes to stay alive."

"Her mother's dead."

"I know that."

"She died of grief."

"Oh come on."

Faith gritted her teeth. "From what I know, she worked hard to give Ashley the best life possible. That's the kidnapped girl's name, you know. Ashley."

"Single mom. Too busy with her career to spend any time with her kid. Ashley probably went off with those two perverts because she was so damn *lonely.* Kids crave a family unit."

Faith's face flushed. She stared at the small screen, at Spider-Man, bounding off the side of a building.

"And how could she have stayed there all that time, you know what I'm saying? Ten years? That couple wasn't around 24/7. If she was raised better, if she was taught survival skills, she would have figured out how to get out of there sooner."

How can wires that thin hold up such a large man?

"When girl goes missing for that long . . . I mean. There's something else going on, know what I'm saying?"

"No."

"Well I—"

"No, let me correct that. I do know what you're saying. And I want you to shut the hell up."

"*What?*"

"How dare you judge a girl you don't know? How dare you judge her mother?"

He cleared his throat.

"I can get off here," said Faith. They were on Hudson, around ten blocks away, but she didn't care. She'd rather run in the cold than stay in this cab another minute.

"I don't know why you're so miffed about this," he said. "I'm entitled to my own opinion."

The driver pulled over. Faith shoved her credit card in the slot and paid the bill and flung the door open. "No you're not."

She slammed the door and hurried down the sidewalk. *How dare he*, she kept thinking. God, she was a mess . . .

But the more she walked, the more her thoughts shifted back to the phone call, how the woman (was it a woman?) had apologized to her, and said please and how she or he had sounded so much kinder than before. That could mean many things, both good and bad. Same with asking Faith to meet alone . . .

Please, she thought. *Please. Good news. Please.* She felt like Spider-Man in that Broadway show, kept aloft by the thinnest, most breakable of wires.

A woman shouted Faith's name and "Love *Sunrise Manhattan*!" and Faith nodded at her, ducking out of pedestrian traffic for a few seconds to grab her sunglasses and scarf from her purse and put them on.

Please, please . . .

She pulled out her phone, stared at "Restricted Number," the last call on the log, it all hitting her. Within twenty minutes, Faith would *know*. That woman from the phone would be Renee Lemaire, or she wouldn't be. She'd either have Maya, or she wouldn't have Maya, but either way, Faith would know what had happened to her stepdaughter. Her daughter. *Her little Maya Papaya* . . .

She couldn't do this alone.

But she couldn't call the police, not without risking that woman's rage. And she certainly couldn't tell Jim, who wouldn't be able to handle this any better than Faith could . . . Her heart pounded. Strange how a turn of events like this one could shuffle the contents of your mind, how it could make you push aside all other feelings, especially the petty ones. Because they were petty, weren't they, her feelings of this morning? Why should Faith even care about Jim and Brenna instant messaging each other? Why should she care about that when her daughter was out there, Jim's daughter, Brenna's daughter, and her own little Maya Papaya? Maya, who, unable to pronounce THs as a toddler, used to call her Mama Fate . . .

She stared at the clock on her phone, time ticking away. She tapped out the number, waited for her to pick up. And when Faith heard her voice—the voice of a friend, a dear friend, after all—she knew she'd made the right choice. "Brenna," she said. "We don't have much time."

Brenna fell into a throng on Tenth and Fifth—a thick swarm of slow-walking building gapers who would not, *could* not move. She wanted to mow them all down.

Five minutes. That's all she had to meet Faith and the woman who had called her—a woman who might

or might not have stolen Maya. A woman with a cigarette voice and a warning to meet her alone, *meet me
alone or else . . .* God, that didn't sound good. Brenna
wove her way around the slow walkers, pushing into
one—an elderly man who spun around with surprising
speed. "*Watch where you're going!*"

She rushed across Sixth Avenue against the light,
nearly sliding under an oncoming bus, but she didn't
care. Brenna didn't care about anything other than getting her daughter back.

Brenna saw a clear stretch of sidewalk ahead of her,
and she hit it running, sneakers piling into the concrete,
Maya's face playing in her mind, her voice, her clumsy
gait, the surprising heaviness of her step and the way
she kept slamming the front door and leaving the refrigerator door open, no matter how many times Brenna
asked her to close it softly please and *please, please,
please . . . please be alive, Maya. Please be well.*

Finally, she caught sight of it. The playground.
Brenna barreled toward it, running with all her might,
her bag bouncing against her hip, searching the area
for a reedy teenager with long blonde hair, arms outstretched, running toward her . . .

She saw Faith, sitting alone on a park bench near the
wrought-iron gate in a scarf and oversized sunglasses,
looking like a femme fatale escaping with the cash.
Faith was alone. There weren't even any kids at the
playground—it was too cold.

Brenna slowed her breathing. From the other side
of the gate, she aimed her eyes at Faith, stared at her
until she got her attention. Faith took off her big, dark
glasses and gave her a nod.

Brenna took out her phone and pretended to be checking it, moved toward the opening in the gate, her eyes scanning the sidewalk. *Show yourself.* The words echoed in her head. *Come on . . .*

"Faith Gordon-Rappaport?"

Brenna turned to the voice—not the cigarette-strangled voice of Faith's woman caller but the crackly voice of a young man. He strode toward Faith, a tall boy in a dark wool coat, black cap pulled over his lowered head. Brenna moved through the gate.

She saw Faith stand up, heard the boy say, "You made it."

Brenna knew the voice. And, as she neared the bench, she saw his face—the scruffy beard, the pink cheeks, the eyes like a shamed puppy.

Her hands clenched into fists.

"Miles?" Faith said. "You . . . You're the one who's been calling me?"

"Yes, ma'am." He took a step forward, then stumbled back when he saw Brenna. "Mrs. Spector? I never wanted this to happen, ma'am. I swear to God, I never—"

Brenna slapped him, hard, across the face.

Miles apologized three more times. Once before Brenna told Faith everything she'd learned from Lindsay Segal, once after. Once more after they agreed to go with him to his apartment and pick up the last footage recorded of Maya before her disappearance.

"That's why I called Mrs. Rappaport," he said, in the media room of his apartment, after showing them the computer he'd called her from, using a microphone and voice-changing software to transform his voice into that of a raspy older woman. "I wanted to warn her."

The apartment was just a block away from the playground, and he'd let them in himself, explaining his parents were both at work and his little brother was, as he should be, in school.

"Why do you have this software?" Faith said.

"It's part of a whole recording suite package. My mom and dad got it for me for Christmas," he said. "Like I was telling Maya, I don't just want to be a singer, I want to be a producer and . . ." His voice trailed off.

Brenna said, "Like you were telling Maya?"

"Yes," he said.

She wanted to hit him again.

"I think you'd better give us that video now," Faith said. "And we'll be on our way."

He shut off the voice changer, and double-clicked on a folder marked "Videos." On the screen, Faith saw a frozen image of Maya, sitting on a pink shag rug with Lindsay and the other two girls from the Forever 21 pictures.

"It was Lindsay's idea. I didn't want her to. I told her . . ."

"You knew all about this?" Brenna said. "You knew it ahead of time?"

"I knew something bad was going to happen. I wasn't sure what." He looked at Faith. "That's why I called you, it's why I told you to keep Maya at home. I figured if you heard it from a stranger, maybe you'd be scared enough to listen." He looked down at his hands. "And no one would know it was me."

"Miles," Faith said.

"What?"

"How did you know something bad was going to happen?"

"Lindsay is a very jealous person."

"What does jealousy have to do with it?" Brenna said.

He took a breath. Both women waited.

"A few weeks ago, Maya stopped by my apartment," he said. "She told me she had pushed the buzzer on a dare with herself."

"She did?"

He smiled a little. "Maya says stuff like that a lot, which is why I like her. She's in my art class." He gave Brenna a nervous smile. "You know that. We were working on our portraits at your house a little while ago."

"I remember." She didn't smile back.

"We're also in chorus together."

"I remember that, too."

Faith said, "So she stopped by your apartment."

"We talked. I showed her all my sound recording equipment and the new songs I'm working on, and she told me she thought it was great. We talked . . . about teachers and classes and stuff."

"How long did she stay?"

"About an hour. I mean . . . nothing happened. But I guess Nikki saw her leaving and told Lindsay and she like . . . assumed something. She said she'd get back at Maya. Before I knew it, they were hanging with Maya, they were inviting her to our lunch table . . ."

"Maya helped her with an art project," Faith said.

"Yeah, that was part of it, too."

Faith looked at Brenna, her eyes sad. "She was so proud of that."

"A setup," Brenna said. "Pretty easy to do with a kid who admires you all so much. Act like you care about her, it's like shooting fish in a barrel."

Miles cringed, visibly. "I did . . . I do care about her."

"Play the video."

He did.

They watched. It lasted around ten or fifteen minutes. When it was done, Brenna's stomach burned and her face throbbed and she was filled with an awful, nagging hurt. She turned to Faith and saw the tears in her eyes, watched her lips part, unable to form words. Brenna looked at Miles. "You went along with this."

"No."

"You were on the other end of the webcam. I heard her talk to you and when I spoke to her at school this morning, she told me you thought it was, and I quote, 'hysterical.'"

"My God," Faith spat out the words.

Miles said, "I wasn't in the room."

"What?"

"I wasn't watching. Once they told me she'd showed up, I left my place and I headed over to Lindsay's. I was going to tell them to stop, but then I saw Maya leaving. I didn't know what to do so I followed her for a bunch of blocks and when I finally yelled out to her, she freaked out," he said. "She started running."

Brenna's eyes widened. "You saw her. That night. On the street."

"She ran away from me," he said. "I don't blame her."

"Did you see where she went?"

"She got into a car. They headed up the highway."

Both women gaped at him.

He opened his eyes. "I'm so sorry."

Brenna said, "What kind of car was it?"

"I don't know. Like . . . Maybe a Subaru or a Volvo or something."

"Did you get the license plate?"

"No."

"What the hell is wrong with you?"

"I figured it was someone she knew." His voice cracked. "Maybe one of you guys. Or her dad."

Faith got her voice back. "Why would you think that?" she said, very quietly.

"The car pulled up. She got in so fast, like she knew them. It was raining so hard and—"

"Jesus," Brenna whispered.

"I'm sorry."

Faith stood up. "Thank you for telling us."

He started up after her, but she held up a hand. "That's okay." She looked at Brenna. "We'll find our own way out."

Brenna nodded, following.

After they left, Miles sat at his computer, staring at the place where Maya's mom and stepmom had been sitting—the same couch he'd been on with Maya two weeks ago when, after half an hour of talking about his new studio equipment and their art class and best and worst teachers and Maya's decision to cut chorus this semester, he'd taken her face in his hands and he'd kissed her.

If Miles tried, he could almost feel her in his arms again, so stiff, and then that moment of surrender, her body melting into him, but just for a few seconds. It was the most honest thing he'd ever felt from a girl. He wanted to think it was just because she was young, but there was something else in the way she'd given in. Something he couldn't look at too hard. *I've got to go*, Maya had said, and he'd let her, with her coat buttoned wrong and her face all flushed and her eyes glowing in that way, like her whole life had changed.

It had been her first kiss. Miles had known that without Maya's saying anything more. He hadn't told anybody. He never would.

Outside Miles's apartment, Faith turned to Brenna. "Two weeks," she said.

Brenna nodded.

"Doesn't it unnerve you a little, Brenna? I mean . . . here Maya goes and visits that boy in his apartment two weeks ago and we'd never know about it if it weren't for . . ." She didn't finish the sentence.

They were facing the playground and Brenna gazed out at it, recalling a trip to a different playground—a cement monstrosity in Battery Park on October 5, 2000, *with the wind easing in off the river and pushing through Brenna's hair and the sun shining, Maya darting over the concrete, heading for the slide. "Watch me, Mama!"*

"That one's too high for you."

"No Mama, watch me! Watch me!"

"You remembering something?" Faith said.

Brenna nodded. "Maya at three," she said. "She was too young to have secrets."

"I wish she still was." Faith stared straight out ahead. "I wish we all were."

Brenna looked at her.

"It's okay," Faith said.

"What's okay?"

"The instant messaging."

Brenna stepped back. She opened her mouth, closed it again.

Faith's sunglasses were back on. "I don't get why neither one of you ever told me you were in contact," she said. "But it's okay."

"How did you find out?" Brenna said, which was the wrong thing to say entirely. "I . . . I mean . . ."

Faith put a hand up. "Thank you so much for coming, Brenna. I don't know what I would have done if you weren't here." She gave her a hug and started away.

Brenna closed her eyes. "You do know you mean the whole world to Jim," she said.

But Faith didn't answer. She was already at the corner, slipping into a cab, heading home.

A few blocks away from Brenna's apartment, she spotted a coffee cart. She bought a black coffee and a kaiser roll with butter and mainlined both—just to keep from passing out. The roll was the first solid food she'd eaten since the pasta she'd made on Saturday afternoon, and it felt strange and tiresome, the whole act of chewing and swallowing. She felt antsy, as though she could find better use for her time, and the truth was, she could.

In her bag, she carried a flash drive, containing the video from Miles's computer—Maya at the lowest, saddest point in her life. Brenna would get rid of the video as soon as she found Maya. She'd make sure all copies were destroyed before anyone else could see them. But she needed the video now, as it was the only record she had of what her daughter had been wearing on the night of her vanishing, of how Maya had looked just before Miles had seen her get into a colorless, make-less car for whatever reason, saw her speed up the West Side Highway to whereabouts unknown.

Nice eyewitness account, Miles, you self-absorbed, unobservant jerk.

Regardless, she needed to get the footage to Trent and to Plodsky so that they could send it around, maybe take a still from it—if a decent one could be found, one that showed her face . . . Tears sprang into Brenna's eyes. She was getting used to this, these waves of emotion crashing through her unannounced, knocking her down again and again.

Keep it together. Keep breathing.

Brenna ran across the street to her apartment building, weaving around pedestrians, feet hitting the pavement hard, practically running over Mrs. Dinnerstein as she reached the door, Mrs. Dinnerstein standing there with her ever-present grocery cart, blocking Brenna's way, her face hard and grim.

"Excuse me," Brenna said to her, but she didn't budge. "Mrs. Dinnerstein. I need to get in, please."

"I heard about Maya," she said. "I saw her father and stepmother today on the TV."

"Yes."

The old woman put a hand on Brenna's shoulder, fear playing all over her features. "I need to talk to you," she said.

"Okay . . . Maybe we could . . ." Brenna was about to suggest going into Mrs. Dinnerstein's ground floor apartment, where at least it was warm. But then she remembered the wall-climbing clutter in there, and the way Mrs. Dinnerstein had reacted to her brief glance at it all. "Maybe we could go into the foyer."

Mrs. Dinnerstein shook her head vigorously. "It's better out here. Where we can see people coming."

"Okay," Brenna said. "But I really am in a hurry."

"Do you remember all the reporters that were here back in December, after that woman broke into your house and you killed that gentleman?"

Brenna sighed. "I didn't kill him, Mrs. Dinnerstein. He committed suicide."

"However you want to look at it," she said. "But last December, Ms. Spector. There were dozens of reporters outside this building every day. It got so a person couldn't leave through this door without taking her life in her hands."

"I'm sorry it was so bad for you, Mrs. Dinnerstein," Brenna said. "Is that what you wanted to tell me? Because I really do have a lot of things to—"

"*No.* This is important."

Mrs. Dinnerstein took one of Brenna's hands in both of hers. The first time she'd touched Brenna in all the years she'd known her, and it took her aback. Her grip was unexpectedly strong. "There was one reporter in particular," she said. "A woman. She kept talking to me."

"Okay . . ."

"She kept asking questions about Maya."

Brenna stared at her. "What kind of questions?"

"She wanted to know about Maya's schedule."

"What do you mean?"

Her grip tightened. "She wanted to know which days of the week Maya was at your ex-husband's and which days she's here. I assumed because she wanted to take pictures, but . . . well, she frightened me. There was something a little off about her. A little too intense for the questions she was asking."

Brenna's palms began to sweat. She had the strangest sensation—her pulse thrumming in the ears . . . as though something irreversible was about to happen and she was trapped here, in the dead quiet before the roar of the avalanche. *A woman.*

"Why didn't you tell me this earlier?" she said.

Mrs. Dinnerstein pursed her lips. "I don't talk to you about things like that, Ms. Spector," she said. "In case you haven't noticed, I really don't talk to you about anything."

"Okay," Brenna said. It was beginning to make sense, though—the way Mrs. Dinnerstein had been looking at Brenna lately—that odd mixture of fear and anger. She'd always known the woman didn't approve of her, but this was different.

"Ms. Spector," she said.

"Yes?"

"I saw her again."

"The reporter?"

She nodded.

"When?"

"A few days ago. She was watching our building from across the street. I know it was her. I walked out of the door and looked right at her. I started across the street to talk to her, but she left very fast. She ran."

Brenna's eyes watered from the cold. She wanted to pull her coat closer, but Mrs. Dinnerstein wouldn't let go of her hand. "It might very well be nothing other than an overzealous reporter," she said. "But I did think I should share it with you."

"I'm glad you did," she said. "I need to find my daughter. And any lead, any lead at all . . ."

"She left her phone number with me."

"Who?" Brenna said. "The reporter?"

"Yes. Back in December. She told me to call it if Maya's schedule changed in any drastic way, or if she were to leave town for an extended period of time." Mrs. Dinnerstein dropped her hand for a moment. She reached into her coat pocket and produced a scrap of paper with a phone number on it. "I save everything," she said, averting her gaze. Then she pressed the scrap into Brenna's hand.

Brenna opened it, read it, her pulse starting to race.

"Her name is Miss Barnes."

Brenna stared at the small piece of paper. "J. Barnes," it said, in block letters similar to the note that had been pinned to Mark Carver's body. But it wasn't the name or the handwriting that made Brenna's hands start to shake. It was the phone number. It belonged to Sophia Castillo.

When Brenna opened the door to her apartment, Trent was sitting at his desk, Maya's desktop on his computer. He started to say something, but she held a hand up, tapped Morasco's number into her phone and hit send. She sighed heavily. "Nick, please call me whenever you get this message. I really hope you were able to do that NCIC search. Sophia Castillo has been stalking my apartment."

Trent's eyes went big and confused. After Brenna hung up, he said, "The lady who called here about her son?"

"Weird, I know," she said. "But I'll need you to get me everything you can on her."

"Okay."

"Did you find anything on Maya's computer?"

He nodded slowly. "I hacked into her Families of the Missing account," he said. "Read a lot of private messages . . ."

Brenna's phone rang. She saw Morasco's name on the screen and picked up fast.

"Hi Nick."

"How do you know?"

"How do I know . . ."

"About Sophia Castillo stalking you." His voice was pulled tight enough to break. "How do you know?"

"My neighbor saw her . . . She asked her about Maya. What Maya's schedule was, when she'd be at my place versus Faith and Jim's. She claimed to be a reporter, but the number she gave her is the same as Sophia Castillo's."

"I'm on my way. I should be there in about ten minutes."

"Wait. Ten minutes . . . You're already on the road?"

"Yes. I'm on the West Side Highway."

"Why? What happened?"

"Call Plodsky. Tell her about Castillo. Tell her what you told me."

"What the hell is going on? Did you check NCIC? Did you find out anything?"

"Yes."

"And?"

"A DUI two years ago," he said. "And four years ago, breaking and entering."

"Wait," Brenna said. "Slow down. Why are either of those things such cause for alarm?"

"It's not *what* her crimes were that concerns me, Brenna. It's *where*."

"What do you mean?"

Morasco took a breath. "The DUI," he said, "was in City Island."

Brenna swallowed hard. "That could be a coincidence."

"The breaking and entering."

"City Island, too?"

"Yes."

"So again, it could be—"

"Brenna, listen to me," he said. "The house Sophia Castillo broke into."

"Yes?"

"It was your mother's house."

17

When their son Robert was a little boy, Sophia Castillo and her husband, Christopher, took him up to Saratoga Springs for the weekend. Robert was just learning how to speak at the time, and whenever he figured out a new word, he'd take that word everywhere with him, tossing it around, repeating it over and over and over again until got sick of it and a new one took its place.

In Saratoga Springs, of course, the word was "horse." The first morning of the trip, they'd gone to the track to look at all the Thoroughbreds before the day's races began, and Robert had stood up in his stroller, pointing at one of the shiny muscular creatures. "What dat? What dat?"

His father had told him, and for the rest of the trip, that had been his chosen word, whether there happened to be a horse around or not. "*Hosse, hosse, hosse!*"

Sometimes, when Sophia went to sleep at night, she could still hear him, so delighted with the sound of the word, leaning on Hs and the Ss. Funny how she could remember the exact sound of Robert's voice at that age. It wasn't like other memories. She didn't have to strain for it.

But still, Sophia wasn't sure why it had come to mind now, as she stood in the bathroom of the Quality Inn near the Mount Temple train station, waiting for Maya to wash the dye out of her hair. "Do you like horses?" she said.

Maya didn't answer.

"My son used to love them when he was little."

Still, not a sound. Maya stayed bent over the sink, water pouring over her head, not even moving. As though she'd frozen that way.

"You're going to have to talk to me sometime."

This wasn't going the way Sophia had hoped it would. She started to say more, but she stopped herself. She tamped back her anger. She was a good parent, after all, and good parents were patient, even with sullen teenagers who refused to say a goddamn word. She'd had Robert for only one of the teen years, and when she looked back on it, she'd felt him pulling away like this, too. It was part of nature. Kids needed to assert their independence in order to grow up.

"You know you don't hate me," Sophia tried. "I'm still the same person I've always been. I'm the one you can talk to. I'm the one who rescued you from the storm, from that boy. Remember that. The nice things I said to you . . . The way I listened."

Still no answer. *Fine.* Sophia pressed the gun between Maya's thin shoulder blades. "That's enough," she said.

Maya lifted her head from the sink and turned off the rushing water. Sophia draped the towel over her and put her hands on it, buffing and plucking at the girl's bowed head.

How many times had she towel-dried Robert's hair like this, when he was a little boy? Sophia had cut his hair until he was eight. Well, most of the time. Robert loved the barbershop at the mall because of the big basket of lollipops, and sometimes she'd relent, maybe buy herself a pair of shoes at the Payless across the way while she was waiting, and if he was a good boy, they'd go for ice cream . . . *Done.* She lifted away the towel.

"Oh." Sophia gazed at Maya's reflection. "Look at you."

Shorn to just half an inch, Maya's hair was now close to black, and in the baggy men's sweatshirt Sophia had purchased with cash at a nearby Duane Reade along with the electric hair trimmer and the package of Garnier Nutrisse color in Deepest Mahogany, Maya looked . . . She looked . . . "You look like my son."

Maya stared at herself in the mirror, her blue eyes bright and glistening sad.

"Do you miss your hair?"

Maya nodded.

"I'm sorry," said Sophia. "But we had to do it. You saw the TV. Your stepmom showed your picture."

Maya said nothing. A tear trickled down her cheek. Sophia longed to comfort her.

"We can make it a different color if you want. Red? Maybe a blue streak?

She smoothed Maya's glossy hair, watching her face in the mirror. "You'll get used to it."

Maya had dark circles under her eyes, puffy red patches on her cheeks from crying, but that would change, wouldn't it? It had to. Kids cried until they stopped crying. It was a fact of life.

"I'm still the same person," Sophia said again. "I'm still your friend."

Trust me, Maya. Be nice to me. It will be easier on both of us if you are.

Sophia wanted pills, and that wasn't helping. She wished she'd remembered this feeling last night before she'd used, or at least before she'd given all the rest of her supply to Carver.

It wasn't that Sophia was an addict—she'd been in recovery for a while. Last time she'd gone to a meeting, in fact, she'd had nearly two years. But that was if you didn't count the here-and-theres. Sophia never counted the here-and-theres, though she did feel their after-math, which was the problem now. Her head pounded, and everything was too bright—the bathroom lights, and the white countertop and the red sweatshirt she'd bought for Maya, the dark hair dye that spattered the sink, her shirt, the plastic gloves in the wastebasket.

All these colors. It brought new meaning to *assault on the senses*. It would pass. It always did. It came in waves, the ache, and then the waves would subside each time they came in, just like changing tides. They'd keep receding until they disappeared, even from her memory. And then she'd be back in recovery again.

Weeks could go by. Months. But then she'd crave again and she'd fall again and then, this feeling. The punishment. Like everything else in life, a cycle. You want. You take. You pay for it.

Sophia's head ached. Her eyes felt too big for their sockets. And Maya was too quiet. This morning had been a real downer, right from the sleepless start of it.

"You look like I feel, Maya." She moved the gun

from between Maya's shoulder blades and pressed it against her temple. She stared at the child's face, her trembling lip. Should she just give up on this whole idea? Would Maya let go as easily as Carver had?

Stop it. That was no way to be thinking. Not after all her hard work, her planning. She needed to give this a chance. Maya needed to eat, for one thing. She hadn't touched her sandwich at the rest stop, and when Sophia had picked her up, she'd just been sick from alcohol— she'd said so herself.

This was the problem: Maya and Sophia were both in need. And if something wasn't done to feed those needs soon, things would get bad around here.

There was a doctor Sophia knew. His office was right near the Metro-North stop at 125th Street. Down the block, there was a pharmacy, and around the corner, a good diner. Every need met, within a two-block radius.

She looked at Maya's reflection, tried a smile. "What do you say we get something to eat?" she said.

To her surprise, Maya nodded.

Sophia breathed a little easier, though she kept the gun in place. She was, as they say, cautiously optimistic. "Okay, great," she said. "But we need to make one stop, first."

Diane Plodsky didn't have a large circle of loved ones. She would be the first to admit that. Yet compared to Mark Carver, her life was a Norman Rockwell Thanksgiving painting, which didn't make her happy. It actually made her disappointed in the world, the idea that anybody could be that much more alone in it than she was . . .

Ostensibly, Diane was at Mark Carver's squalid duplex in Mount Temple to notify next-of-kin, though as she soon found out, Carver had no next of kin. Both of his parents had died ten years ago in a car crash. His brother had overdosed three years ago and, being woefully short on anyone-else-who-gave-a-damn, he'd gone on to live with a succession of Craigslist-gleaned roommates in this duplex, which had been left to him by his parents (though they'd apparently never taught him how to clean it.)

The latest roommate—a big bearded biker type who inexplicably called himself Ethel—was sitting across the kitchen table from Diane, wearing a black T-shirt advertising Mickey's Big Mouth beer, two elaborate Chinese dragon tattoos crawling up his arms. Diane kept her elbows off the table, her hands neatly folded in her lap. Not out of politeness, but out of the knowledge that direct contact with any object in this room could easily result in staph infection.

"So Mark kicked it, huh?" Ethel said this after an uncomfortably long pause. From anyone else, Diane might have hoped for something more profound, but it was pretty much what she'd expected out of Ethel. He flexed his muscles. The dragons shimmered. Diane was pretty sure he thought that was impressive.

"Did Mark have a job?"

"You mean besides selling oxy online?"

"Uh. Yeah."

"Nope."

Diane slipped Maya Rappaport's picture out of the folder she was carrying and showed it to him. "Have you ever seen this girl?"

He squinted at it. "Nope."

"How about a woman? Someone you might mistake for that girl's mother."

"Never saw any ladies come by here . . . except today." He grinned at her. He had a silver front tooth with a gold skull inlay that dared you not to look at it. She tried to accept that dare.

"He never mentioned anybody?"

"Nope."

Diane sighed. "Oookay." With the right type of witness—i.e., one with the potential for having actual information or, at the very least, an IQ higher than that of a piece of paper—Diane was a questioner of infinite patience. But Ethel wasn't that type of witness. *Ethel wins.*

"Okay," Diane said. "I'm going to get out of your hair, but if you don't mind, I'm going to have a look around. I'll need to take a few of Mr. Carver's personal items for our investigation."

"Personal items?" He said it like it was the punch line in a dirty joke.

Diane sighed heavily. "His computer. Cell phone."

"Oh that other lady already took his computer."

She blinked at him. "What?"

"The other lady cop. Left just a couple of minutes ago. I figured she came with you."

"Excuse me, please . . ."

Diane headed out of the house, onto the street. She scanned the area surrounding the house and then ran up the sidewalk, cursing Ethel in her mind for taking so goddamn long to say absolutely nothing. The sidewalk was empty and lined with parked cars. Her own car was double parked; one of the perks of being a cop—

but the other woman wouldn't have had that luxury no matter what lie she'd told . . .

She ran past dozens of town houses and duplexes, all of them nearly as neglected as Carver's, tarry snow remnants pushed up against them, dotting brown, weed-choked lawns. She ran all the way to the very end of the three very long, sad blocks, and that's when she finally saw her—a good forty feet away. A woman getting into a parked blue car, a laptop bag thrown over her shoulder.

"Wait!" Diane hollered.

She opened her door.

She held her badge in the air. "Police."

The woman turned. She stopped and stared at Diane, alarm all over her face.

Diane kept running until she reached her.

"Is something wrong?" the woman said. She wore a long dark coat, her hair pulled back from her face.

Diane squinted at her. She didn't know her. She was sure of that. Yet there was something about this woman's face that seemed familiar.

"Were you just at the home of Mark Carver?"

"Who?" The woman's face flushed. She grasped the laptop tighter.

"Mark Carver." Diane saw an ID tag on the case and pinched it toward her. On it, she saw Mark Carver's name and address. She showed it to her. "See?"

"Oh . . . right." She exhaled hard. "Listen, I'm sorry. I'm Ethel's sister. He owes me a ton of money. He gave me this laptop to partially pay it off."

She looked at her. "Ethel told me you said you were with the police."

She rolled her eyes. "Ethel's a jackass."

Diane had to agree with her there.

"We had a big fight," she said. "I guess you're his way of getting in the last word."

"I'm honored," she said. "But is Ethel really the type of person who would give away his roommate's laptop without even knowing he was dead?"

"His roommate's dead?"

"Yes," she said. "But he didn't know that until I told him."

She sighed. "What a tool. His real name is Edward, by the way." She stuck out her hand. "I'm Janine."

Diane shook it. "Okay Janine, well I'm sorry. But I'm going to have to take that laptop."

"Okay, sure." She handed it to her. Her forehead was shiny with sweat. Odd, considering how cold it was outside and the way she looked otherwise, so neat and put-together and . . . she really did look familiar.

Diane said, "Can I take a quick look in your car?"

"Sure," she said. "But do you mind if I ask what's going on?"

"We're looking for a missing girl," Diane said.

"Seriously?" she said. "I mean . . . I can tell you right now, I'm a mom myself and I would never—"

"I'm sure of it. But you know . . ."

"No stone unturned."

Diane smiled a little. "Yes."

The woman met her gaze. Her eyes were bloodshot. "You . . . You don't suppose Ethel . . ."

"No, ma'am. It's his roommate we were interested in."

She nodded. "Okay, whew," she said. "Sure. Look in my car."

She unlocked it.

Diane opened the front door, and looked inside, then the back. All the seats looked relatively clean, though she did notice three empty water bottles strewn across the backseat. "Yep. You're definitely a mom."

"How do you know that?"

"The water bottles. My partner has four kids. The backseat of his family car looks like a recycling bin."

"I forgot those were even back there."

Diane said, "How old are your kids?"

"I have just one," she said. "He's . . . um . . . thirteen. Listen. Can I ask you a favor?"

"Uh-huh?"

"I mean . . . would it be that big a deal if I kept the laptop?"

Diane frowned at the car floor. "Why?"

"I really need one. And I'm so low on cash on account of Ethel."

Diane pulled herself out of the car, straightened her back. "I can see about getting it to you once we're done going through it," she said.

"But . . ."

"Now if you could just pop the trunk for me, too, I'll take a quick look and be on my way." She started to close the car door, then stopped. On the floor she saw something, a small glittering thing. She pulled a Kleenex out of her pocket and plucked it up, careful not to touch it, her pulse racing.

"Your son have pierced ears?" Diane said. "Because I notice you don't."

Janine said nothing.

Diane turned to face her. As she slipped her hand

into her coat, she glanced down at the woman's shoes. Sensible, white shoes. Pastel nurses' pants under the dark coat. *That's* where she'd seen this woman before. The blue-eyed nurse who'd passed her in the corridor of the Tarry Ridge Hospital at three in the morning, the one coming toward her as she walked to Carver's room . . .

"I know who you are."

Janine socked her in the stomach.

Diane crumpled up, the air barreling out of her, lights flickering in front of her eyes. She tried again for her coat, for the gun in her shoulder holster, but then something crashed into the side of her head, something huge and heavy and mean. She tasted blood in her mouth, and saw a pool of it on the sidewalk, along with three tiny white stones . . . they were teeth. Her teeth.

The pain was blinding.

She went again for her coat, but Janine's arm came up and then down, the weight of her gun connecting with Diane's head.

No chance, she thought.

And that earring, that poor tiny earring in the pocket of her coat as the gun landed on the top of her skull and white light flooded in and she was beyond pain, beyond thought.

18

"Why didn't you tell me?" Brenna said.

"It wasn't anything worth talking about," her mother said.

"Someone broke into your house."

"A drunken woman," she said. "She thought my house was hers, and I called the police and she left peacefully."

Brenna stared at her screen—an article in the *City Island Times*, not about the break-in, but about a car accident two years later, in the earliest hours of morning on August 5, 2007, one that had resulted in the death of one of the island's oldest trees—and ultimately, in Sophia Castillo's DUI.

"She was back in your neighborhood two years later," Brenna said. "She killed a tree."

"Well I didn't know anything about that."

"You didn't read it in the paper?"

"If I did," she said, "I don't recall it."

The newspaper article was one of the few mentions Brenna had been able to find online of a Sophia Castillo from New York state. No Facebook page, no Twitter, no languishing MySpace page. No LinkedIn or Match.com profile . . . Just a five-year-old staff listing at St. Vincent's—she'd worked there as a nurse in the ER—and an eight-year-old White Pages entry in Katonah for Sophia and Christopher. No phone number. Just an address. It was as though she was trying to make as small an impact on the world as possible. Even the article in the paper was brief, with a picture of Sophia's car next to the decimated tree—but no mug shot. No personal photo. Nothing at all of Sophia herself.

"Would you be able to describe the woman? Maybe pick her out of a lineup?"

"The one who broke into my house?"

"Yes."

"*Why?*"

Brenna sighed. "Just please answer me, Mom."

"I never saw her."

"Seriously?"

"I locked myself in my bedroom and called 911 when I heard the window break, Brenna," Evelyn Spector said. "Wouldn't *you*?"

"Yes. Yes, of course I would."

"I mean really," she said. "Why do you even bring this up? It was years ago."

"Mom?"

"Yes?"

Brenna tried to sound calm. "Did you . . . Did you ever hear from her again? I mean . . . a phone call . . . anything?"

"Why on earth would I hear from some crazy drunk woman?"

"No idea. Sorry. I've got to go."

"Brenna, what is going on?"

"I'm on an important case. I'll call you later." Brenna

hung up, grateful in the knowledge that her mother did not know how to work a computer, that she rarely watched TV, and so it would be a long while before she caught wind of Faith's on-air announcement. Hopefully long enough.

"You're not going to tell her?" Trent said.

"I am," said Brenna. "Just not now." *I'll tell her once we find Maya and bring her home and everything is back to normal again.*

Brenna said, "So tell me what you found on the Families of the Missing page."

"Umm . . ."

"Trent, I don't have time to play twenty questions with you. If you found something, if you found *anything*, you can't mince words. You can't worry about the right way to say things. There's too much at stake for that."

"Okay," he said. "Sorry." He cleared his throat. "Maya never cleared her instant message cache, so I've got a couple months' worth of IM exchanges, all of them between Maya and NYCJulie."

"Okay."

"There are a lot."

Brenna nodded. "NYCJulie said they were good friends."

"I'm talking hundreds."

"Well, with an online friend, it's easy to rack up a lot of messages."

Trent gave her a long look. "Brenna," he said. "I don't like these messages."

She got up, moved over to his desk. He tapped the screen—an exchange dated December 23 between NYCJulie and NYCYoru, aka Maya.

NYCJulie: **Your mom's not being responsive to your needs. You got attacked by some psycho because of her selfishness. Who does she care more about? Her dead sister or you?**

NYCYoru: **She doesn't think her sister is dead.**

NYCJulie: **Wow. Way to go off topic.**

NYCYoru: **LOL. She loves me, tho.**

NYCJulie: **How do you know? How do you know her disorder isn't a form of autism?**

NYCYoru: **Who cares if it is?**

NYCJulie: **It might make it impossible for her to focus on you in the way you need her to. She might be incapable of caring.**

NYCYoru: **I don't even get what you're saying.**

NYCJulie: **Her obsession with the past, and with finding her sister, might be the most important thing to her. More important than you.**

Trent put an arm on Brenna's shoulder. "She's full of crap," he said.

"Maybe." She had a lump in her throat. "But she's got some basis in the truth."

The buzzer sounded.

"Can you get that?" Brenna said.

Trent got up and moved over to the door. She heard him talking to Morasco over the speaker system, buzzing him in, but she wasn't listening to what they were saying. She read on:

NYCYoru: **Well what am I supposed to do about that? Go, "Hey Mom. How come you love your dead sister more than me?" LOL**

NYCJulie: **I don't know. Maybe talk to a shrink?**

NYCYoru: **About me or her?**

NYCJulie: **Both. Mostly her though.**

NYCYoru: **Wait! I could go to the one she went to as a kid. I can ask him about her.**

NYCJulie: **That's a great idea, hon. But seriously? What I want you to take away from this is that it isn't your fault. It's never a kid's fault. It's always on the parents. Your mom has a lot to answer for.**

Morasco put a bagel in front of Brenna, along with a cup of coffee. "Eat," he said. "You have to, if we're going to find her."

"Dude, listen to him." Normally, she would have chastised him for talking with his mouth full—a habit he should have broken at the age of seven. But there was no normal now. There was only Maya. The lack of her, and the words she'd left behind.

"I already had a kaiser roll," Brenna said. But she did take the coffee. Her gaze stayed on the screen.

"Did you find out anything about Castillo?" Morasco said.

"An article about the DUI. It's up on my computer. If you enlarge the picture, you can probably see the driver's license."

"Okay," he said. "You talk to your mom?"

She nodded. "Nothing worthwhile."

He kissed her on the forehead. She barely felt it. Hadn't even looked at him since he'd come in and she knew that was unfair, but she couldn't help it.

"How's it going with IA?" she said, still staring at the screen.

"Pretty good," he said. "The guy I was dealing with back in October has been very helpful."

"You going to get your badge back soon?"

"He says forty-eight hours, tops. We'll see how it shakes out." Morasco moved toward Brenna's computer.

She kept at it, scrolling through message upon message, the words "Mom" and "unfair" and "real love" flying past her eyes and then more words still, words she never knew were on her daughter's mind, words she never expressed to Brenna, or maybe she had but they'd gone unheard . . . and thus unremembered.

So hurt . . . no cure for it . . . I just wish we could talk . . . Wish she'd talk to Dad . . . Please don't tell anyone . . . feel so alone . . .

"You don't need to look at all of it," Trent said.

"Yes I do."

Brenna saw Miles's name at January 4, 5:30 P.M. Brenna remembered Maya coming home from school late that day—5:20 according to the clock in the kitchen. *"I've got tons of homework, Mom."*

Brenna glances up from the onion she's been dicing and sees a flash of blonde hair, the bright blue coat, Maya heading up the hall and into her bedroom.

She hears the soft creak of Maya's door as it shuts.

"I'm making chicken and rice," Brenna calls out. "Is that okay?"

No answer.

Brenna sighs. "It better be okay," she says to the onion, "because that's what we're having."

But now, as Brenna pinched herself back into the present and read the exchange between Maya and NYCJulie, an exchange that had taken place moments after she closed the door . . . Brenna's chest tightened. Tears sprung into her eyes and again, she felt herself sinking. *Maya. Oh Maya. You had your first kiss. You and Miles. That day in his apartment. You kissed him.*

"Oh my God," Morasco said.

Brenna swatted at her eyes and turned to him. He was frozen, the mouse clutched in his hand. She got up and moved toward him. "What?"

He'd enlarged the picture so much that the car's bumper filled the screen. Brenna could clearly see the New York license plate, the bumper sticker: "My Child Is an Honor Student at George Washington Elementary."

"When I ran across the street to question Carver, I'd spoken to a woman first—a soccer mom filling up at the Lukoil station."

"Yes?"

"We spoke to her—Cavanaugh, Cerulli, and I. Asked her a few questions, but she looked scared and confused. A waste of time—she'd obviously seen nothing, and there was Carver, right across the street, a drug addict, sweating bullets, Maya's phone ringing away in his coat pocket."

"Nick, why are you telling me this?"

"Because," Nick said. "This is her bumper. This is her car."

"*What?*"

"The woman we let go. The soccer mom. That woman was Sophia Castillo."

The key for Sophia was to not think too hard about it. It was like so many other things that, when focused on too intently, went from second nature to impossible. You do it, you leave. You don't let thought become a part of the process.

And so in this case, what Sophia needed to do was

to take off her coat and throw it in the backseat without thinking about the bloodstains, to twist the cap off the container of gasoline without thinking about the smell, and to spill the gasoline on the coat, on the seat, on the front seat, too, and the dashboard and wherever else it would go, to do all that without thinking about the car she'd owned and loved since Robert was seven.

Don't think. Just do.

She stepped back from the car. The pink sweater that she held still reeked of vomit, but it had dried off by now, and when she held a match to it, the frail, fuzzy thing ignited fast. She tossed it into the backseat and ran away from the clearing and into the woods as fast as she could. She didn't stop running until she reached the tree. Didn't turn around until she heard the roar behind her.

Funny about cars. They're just big hunks of metal filled with toxic chemicals, but we attach such meaning to them, it's as though they're members of the family. Sophia sighed. She listened to the crackling of the fire. The heat bit at her eyes, even from here.

She clicked open her purse, checked her cash supply—she still had plenty. She took out her phone, but before she turned it on again, she caught a glimpse of herself in the glass. Definitely in need of a freshening. Sophia pulled out her lipstick, twisted off the cap, and got angry, all over again. The top of the lipstick was bashed in and flecked with brown bark. She dusted it off, dotted her lips with the color, but very lightly. If she wanted to use the lipstick the way it was intended to be used, she'd need a pack of Kleenex and a razor blade. *Maya.* This had been expensive lipstick, too. What was wrong with that girl?

At least the lipstick can be saved, she thought, watching the car, her beloved car, flames wrapped around it like a cocoon. *Some things can't be saved, no matter how hard you hope.*

Déjà vu, Brenna thought, once she and Morasco arrived at Faith's, where they'd all agreed to meet after exchanging information about Castillo. There they were yet again, Jim and Faith sitting at the island, only this time, instead of Plodsky, they were sitting across from a guy with salt and pepper hair; a thick, ruddy neck; and a shiny brown coat that strained against the bulk of him. A manila folder was sprawled open on the table, a stack of pictures inside.

"Hello?" Nick said.

Tight Sportcoat stood up, stuck out a beefy hand. "I'm Ray Sykes. Detective Plodsky's partner."

Brenna had spoken to him earlier. She recognized his voice from the phone. "Diane's still not back from the next-of-kin call?" Brenna said.

"Traffic must be bad," Sykes said. "We've gone ahead with the AMBER Alert. And we're putting out a BOLO on the license plate, with descriptions of both Sophia Castillo and your daughter." He glanced at Faith. "Thanks to the on-air announcement, we've already gotten a lot of calls on the tip line, and once it hits the news cycles, I'm sure we'll be getting a lot more. The problem is weeding through everything. A lot of nuts call these lines."

"Anything worthwhile?" Brenna said.

"Not unless you believe in alien abductions."

Faith said, "Detective Sykes?"

"Yes?"

"It's been more than thirty-six hours since Maya got into that car on the West Side Highway."

"That's correct, ma'am."

"That's a very long time."

Brenna said, "Have you pinged Sophia's cell phone?"

"Trying."

Brenna didn't say anything. She had a terrible feeling, as though she was thrashing around in deep, churning water with nothing to hang on to.

From the open folder on the table, a mug shot stared up at her. She put a hand on it.

"That's from the 2007 DUI," Sykes said.

She nodded, drew it to her and stared at Sophia Castillo's pale, drawn face, the mud-brown hair, the cloudy, sunken eyes that refused to look at the camera. There was something familiar about the face. But more in the expression than the actual features—which were so different from those of the blue-eyed patrician soccer mom Morasco had described seeing at the gas station. How could they find a chameleon like that? And Maya . . . who knew where she was keeping her, what she was doing to her. Who knew what Maya looked like now?

Sykes was saying, "We're monitoring her credit cards, bank activity . . ."

"Nothing?" Morasco said.

"She withdrew five thousand dollars from her bank account three days ago. Nothing since."

Faith said, "That will probably last her."

Brenna closed her eyes. *Maya is alive. She's healthy. She'll be home soon.*

"What can we do?" said Jim. "How can we help?"

"You're doing everything you can. We couldn't ask for more helpful family . . ." Sykes's cell phone trilled. He looked at the screen. "Be back in a few." He moved out of the room, into the foyer.

Jim looked at Nick. "I don't get it," he said.

"What?"

"When you approached Carver, he was right across the street from the woman he supposedly partied with. Why didn't he just point her out? Why did he run?"

Morasco stared at the table. "Scared," he said. "He was thinking about himself, the coke in his pocket, getting caught. If I hadn't come on like such a hard-ass, maybe he would have talked instead of running."

Jim didn't say anything, but the way he looked at Morasco, it was the same as agreeing. It made Brenna remember Jim on October 23, 1998, the night he'd learned she'd broken her promise to him and done a job for her former boss, Errol Ludlow, the night he'd ended their marriage, no questions asked. He'd given her that same look. That face, like a gavel crashing down . . .

I just got back from Ludlow's office. I know what you did last night.

Faith's voice brought her back. "Did you ever think," she said to Nick, "that Mark Carver could have been scared of *her,* not you?"

Brenna looked at Faith, so pale beneath the TV makeup she'd never bothered to take off, so tired. She recalled the way she'd thanked her outside Miles's apartment, the way she'd gone to her car without saying good-bye. That sadness that clung to her . . . it hadn't been about instant messages. Faith was starting to give up.

"I mean, did you see Maya, Nick?" Faith said. "Did the other two officers see another person in the car when they were questioning that woman?"

"No, Faith. They didn't. But that doesn't mean—"

"How do you know he wasn't too scared to talk? How do you know he hadn't just seen something happen to Maya, something so awful, and he was afraid that if he pointed that woman out, she'd get free and she'd find him and she'd do the same thing to him?"

"*Stop*," Jim's voice was broken, wet.

"No," Nick said. "She had her hidden somewhere. The trunk probably. Maya is alive. I know she is."

"How do you know?" Faith was in tears now. "Because of the texts? Those texts didn't sound like Maya. Anybody could have written them, anybody could have pinned that note to a dead body and used my daughter's earring. *She's happy now.* That could mean so many things. So many terrible, unthinkable things . . ."

"*Please Faith stop it*," Jim said.

Faith started to sob. He put his arms around her and pulled her to him and held her tight, to keep from crying himself, Brenna knew.

Brenna had seen this so many times with clients after she'd given them bad news—arms clasped around each other, huddling together to ward off the inevitable, the grief. The truth.

"She's alive," she said to no one, with too much pleading in her voice.

"I know she is," said Nick. And all she could think of was his infant son, who had died in his crib, and for no other reason than life was unfair, that nothing happened for any reason other than it happened. It *was*.

Please be alive, Maya, Brenna thought, Brenna hoped. Even though she knew that Maya couldn't hear her thoughts, even though she knew that hoping did nothing, other than to make you feel as though you had some tiny bit of control.

Sykes came back through the door, just as Brenna's phone vibrated SOS. A text. She flipped it open and checked who it was from and for a few seconds, stopped breathing. "Her phone is on," she said to the detective. "Castillo. Her phone is on. She just texted me."

"I know," he said. "We have a location. There are already officers at the scene."

"Already?" Brenna said as she opened the text and read it, her skin going cold.

"What does it say?" Faith said.

Brenna slid her flip phone to the center of the table, and Faith grabbed it. Read it. "What does this mean? What is she talking about?"

It read: *I got your message. Too little too late.*

"I . . . I called her earlier. Said I'd be glad to help her find her son."

"Too little, too late," Faith whispered. "My God. My God, no, please no . . ."

Brenna looked at Sykes. "How could the officers be at the scene already? What happened? Where is Maya?"

"I'm not certain what happened, or where your daughter is," Sykes said. "But the officers are already at the scene because there's been an explosion."

19

Ever since she'd hung up with Brenna, Evelyn Spector hadn't felt quite right.

Evelyn often got that feeling after speaking with her younger daughter—a certain uneasiness with herself, with the past. But this was different. Usually, when Brenna brought up events that made Evelyn feel uneasy, it was because she'd been there for them. They were lodged in her allegedly indisputable memory, and thus the world was compelled to face the supposed truth along with her.

The break-in, though. That had been all Evelyn's.

How had Brenna found out about it? It hadn't been in the papers. Evelyn hadn't pressed charges. Specifically, she'd never told Brenna, because she hadn't wanted her to worry, of course—but also because the experience had been so strangely humiliating: Evelyn cowering in her nightgown, alone in her bedroom as that loon of a woman crashed around her house, shouting obscenities. Shouting . . . Evelyn didn't even want to think about what she'd said. And then, the policemen showing up, asking Evelyn if this was "something personal."

What was that supposed to mean—*something personal?*

Anyway, Evelyn had washed her hands of the break-in. She hadn't thought about it for years, but then there was Brenna bringing it up again—out of the blue, and with that tone in her voice, as though she were accusing her of something . . . *Something personal.*

Evelyn needed a change of scenery—a nice brisk walk to clear her mind, and thank goodness, that's just what she was getting. Already, the cold air was making her feel better as she strode up the sidewalk, turning the corner on City Island Avenue and heading toward Bay Street, arms pumping, long legs stretching and flexing. Evelyn didn't brag about it, but she was in terrific shape for a woman her age. Walking on a winter's day reminded her of that fact. It made her feel alive.

The library was one of Evelyn's favorite destinations. There was something about the rounded entrance to the squat brick building that was so inviting, and the smell, that wonderful piney smell . . . The library had undergone a major renovation in the late nineties, doubling in size as a result. But inhaling that combination of furniture polish and books in plastic covers, Evelyn would feel such powerful nostalgia, her mind flooded by images of picture books and puppet shows and story hours gone by, of lives that were young and uncomplicated and, for the most part, happy.

"Hello Evelyn," said Ruth the librarian, a woman her own age who had taught a poetry writing class for children here, back when Clea was a little girl and Brenna was still in diapers. "Did you have a nice walk?"

"Lovely," Evelyn said. "Cold as it is, I can almost feel spring in the air."

Ruth smiled. "Oh what a nice thought."

Clea used to love Ruth's poetry class. She had adored creative writing as a child, and was quite good at it, crafting poems and stories about wizards and unicorns and princesses trapped in towers. Evelyn and Jack used to believe she'd be a famous writer someday. Another Barbara Cartland or Mary Higgins Clark.

When exactly that gift for fiction had turned into a talent for lying, Evelyn wasn't sure. All she knew was, it had happened, both her daughters growing into funhouse mirror images of their parents—Clea with her father's gift for destruction times ten; Brenna with that bizarre memory disease, the extreme version of her mother's inability to let anything go.

"Your computer's free," Ruth said.

Evelyn smiled. Why couldn't everyone in the world be as kind as Ruth? She could still remember the book club Ruth used to host for the local wives. Evelyn had adored that group, especially those times when the conversation veered away from the Philip Roth or John Updike they were reading and got personal. Evelyn would stay quiet while the other women griped about their husbands because at the time, she believed she'd nothing to complain about. Back then, Evelyn had thought Jack's moodiness had stemmed from a poet's soul, his selfishness a raging need only she could understand . . . Oh how stupid she'd been. But happy, so happy.

When Jack had started to turn, the other women

had asked questions. *Is he okay?* they had said after his first arrest. *How are the girls? Do you need any help?* There'd been such satisfaction behind their concern, though—that smugness in their eyes, their tone. *Poor thing*, she'd hear them say when they thought she wasn't listening. *Poor Evelyn.*

But Ruth had never asked questions. She'd never said a word.

To get to the computer room, you had to walk through the children's section and make a right. It was a sunny, airy place, welcoming despite its relative newness. There was rarely anyone in here except when a class was in session. She supposed it was because most people owned their own computers, and that suited her fine. Evelyn was no longer young and stupid. She valued her privacy. She had secrets that were her own now, not her husband's.

Evelyn's computer was in the back row to the far left. She checked her e-mail first. She had three different accounts, and so she went through the first two quickly—deleted the spam and newsletters. When she logged in to Hotmail, though, her heart fluttered, all the more when she saw a new e-mail from Alan Dufresne. She would miss him, she knew that. But she couldn't risk talking to him any longer. After reading his e-mail, she hit reply and typed:

Dear Alan,

Thanks so much for your concern. Things are fine, now. If you could put the contents of the bag into a packing box and send them to the following

address, I would be happy to reimburse you for
your troubles.

> *Sincerely,*
> *Brenna*

Evelyn listed the P.O. box she maintained at JFK Airport, sent the e-mail, then quickly shifted over to the Snapfish page and deleted all of Clea's information. It had been two months, and if Evelyn's secret search had taught her anything, it was that, like it or not, it was sometimes essential to cut all ties and move on.

She went back to the Hotmail account. Before doing anything else, she clicked on the sent e-mails, and reread all the correspondence between Alan and herself, from beginning to end.

Yes, she would miss him very much.

Strange, and sad, too, that in Alan she'd found a kindred spirit—someone who, like her, had been forced to face the truth: You can love someone with all your heart without knowing them at all.

A great father and a good man, he had typed, and she'd known exactly why he'd typed it, exactly how he'd felt. Alan Dufresne was clinging to a lie as hard as he could, just as she had done for so many years. You believe that lie and if you believe hard enough, it becomes . . . well, if not the truth, then something close enough. Something you can live with. Something to keep you from falling apart.

My father kept secrets, too, Evelyn had typed, confiding the truth in this stranger as she'd confided in no one else. Confiding, though, while masquerading as her own daughter. The irony wasn't lost on Evelyn.

Lies upon lies upon hiding upon more lies. That was what Evelyn's life had become. That was what it had always been, she knew now, even back in the good old days. Even if back then, she'd only been lying to herself.

Evelyn deleted all the e-mails, then closed the account. In a few weeks, she'd find another missing persons Web site. She'd start again, and in her new posting, she'd include the name Roland Dufresne. She'd get closer to *this* truth, if nothing else.

Once she left Hotmail, Evelyn's homepage came up—MSNBC News. She was about to turn off the computer and walk home when she saw the headline "AMBER Alert for Missing NY Teen." She clicked on it. She saw the picture.

It wasn't until Ruth came rushing in that Evelyn realized how loud she'd screamed.

About twenty minutes after Brenna and Nick Morasco left, Trent was in the bathroom spraying himself with Axe when the office phone rang. He was so startled he dropped the container and set it clattering across the tile floor, having forgotten for few seconds that this wasn't just the home of his friend's missing daughter, it was an actual place of business, *his* place of business.

He grabbed his spare set of clothes out of his messenger bag, threw them on fast, and ran out to answer the phone.

Trent checked caller ID. The number looked familiar but couldn't place it right away. He cleared his throat, put on his professional voice. "Brenna Spector Investigations."

"TNT?"

He let out a shaky sigh. "Stephanie." All this stuff going on, Trent had almost forgotten about the DNA test . . . *Almost*. He crossed his fingers, though at this point he wasn't sure what he was hoping for. "Is there . . . um . . ."

"I don't have any news, okay?"

"Okay."

"I . . . I probably won't for a while."

"How come? I thought it takes just two business days."

"Yeah, it does."

"But?"

"I chickened out on the amnio. The doctor says it's optional, and so I figure, you know . . . why not wait to do the DNA test till the baby is born? It'll be easier, no needles . . ."

Trent shuddered. He hated needles so much that hearing the word "needles" made him feel like he was going to throw up. "I get it." His gaze moved to his computer screen, where before his shower, he'd been exchanging instant messages with a girl he'd met at an identity theft seminar last year. Actually more of a lady than a girl. A lady named Camille Rogers (who had a nice rack, okay? And he'd noticed it. Being a potential father didn't make him dead.) Camille had promised she'd get him whatever info she could on Sophia Castillo—whose full maiden name, he'd learned, had been Sophia Belyn Liptak. Nothing yet, though.

As Stephanie kept talking, Trent shifted screens, back to Maya's desktop, the messages she'd exchanged with NYCJulie taking shape again in front of his eyes,

so different from the quick back-and-forth he'd just had
with Camille. So personal, so sad.

NYCYoru: **Sometimes I get the weirdest feeling, Julie—like someone is out there, watching me.
Someone I can't see. And they don't know me, but
they're thinking bad things about me. There's nothing I can do and that scares me** . . . *Why didn't she
tell her mom these things? Why didn't she tell me? Why
did she find it easier to trust some random woman in a
chat room where nobody gave their real names?*

Trent's thoughts were so loud in his head, it took
him a few seconds to remember that the mother of his
possible child was talking to him on the phone.

". . . and anyway," Stephanie was saying, "I've decided it doesn't matter."

"What doesn't matter?"

"Are you even listening?"

"What kind of a douche do you think I am? Of
course I'm listening."

"I was saying"—Stephanie sighed—"I'm a big girl."

"Well, uh . . . heh . . . yeah, that's true."

"Jeez, Trent. Is boobs all you think about?"

"Well . . ."

"I mean I'm a *grown-up*. I'm responsible for my own
pregnancy."

"Uh . . . Steph? I kind of had something to do with it."

"We used two kinds of protection," she said. "If we
took all that precaution and I still got knocked up, you
shouldn't have to take the fall."

Trent blinked at the phone. "The fall?"

"I know you don't want to be a dad."

"No you don't."

"What?"

"You don't know that I don't want to be a dad," he heard himself say. "If I don't know it, how can you?"

"Hey . . ."

"What?"

"What are you trying to tell me here?"

"I'm saying that if it's my baby . . . or even if it isn't. I want to know. And I want to help."

"Are you serious?"

"Hellz yeah," he said, surprising himself. "I want to be there for the ultrasounds. I want to see the little guy move around and stuff and coach you with the breathing."

"You do?"

"Yes I do. So . . . like . . . stop being all 'it's my baby,' and 'I can do it on my own.' Because you know what, Stephanie? *It's really freakin' insulting and annoying.*"

There was a long pause on the other end of the line. Trent stared at Maya's words on the screen and heard his own words in his head—words he hadn't known he was going to say until they'd flown out of his stupid, flapping mouth like those doves flying out of the fake cake at his cousin Siobhan's wedding.

Trent thought about taking it all back, about telling Stephanie sorry, he was having a rough day, he hadn't had enough sleep and she'd called before he'd had a chance to gel his hair and he never could think straight with his hair ungelled. Of *course* he wasn't ready to be a dad. Hell, Trent's own dad wasn't ready to be a dad, let alone Trent, who still brought his laundry home to his mom every weekend.

"Actually—" he said. But then he stopped. He didn't want to take it back.

It was a crappy world, Trent knew that much. It was a world that took sweet kids and swallowed them up, leaving nothing behind but sad words on a screen. And if nobody did the right thing, if nobody "took the fall," it would just keep getting crappier and crappier.

"Actually what?"

"Actually, I only knew about one form of protection." She exhaled. "You really want to help?"

"Yes. Duh."

"Okay. You can, then."

"Whatever."

"So . . . like . . . I'll call you? Like when I have my next ultrasound?"

"You'd better."

"Trent?"

"Yeah?"

"Thank you."

She hung up the phone, and Trent hung up and rubbed at his tired eyes, returning his gaze to the screen, trying not to think of kids, how easy it was to fail them.

He started up for the bathroom again so he could gel, maybe work an eyebrow check . . .

Trent was halfway down the hall when he heard a piercing beep—his instant message signal, turned all the way up. He turned around, headed back for his computer, switched screens, where, sure enough, he saw a new message from Camille.

Found something weird, it read. **Check your e-mail.**

"Where is my daughter?" Brenna barely got the words out, winded as she was from running and panic. The phone had been pinged to a clearing in the woods behind the White Plains reservoir, and so she'd had to park her car at the bottom of a hill and run to it, following the smell of smoke, the cluster of emergency vehicles, the black cloud that still hovered in the dull white winter sky.

She said it to the group of uniformed cops who stood in front of the crime scene tape, apart from the firefighters and EMS guarding the smoldering black heap that was still recognizable as Sophia Castillo's 1996 Lexus ES300. They looked at each other, but none answered.

She zeroed in on one of them—a muscular bald guy she'd met briefly at a sleazy Mount Temple nightclub called Heavenly Pleasures on September 12, 2004, when she'd been investigating the disappearance of a stripper who called herself Clarity. He'd been working security at the time and dressed to fit his job and the surroundings, his thinning hair gelled and sculpted, sunglasses at night, a glossy black goatee that matched the shiny shirt, but she didn't flash back to it. She couldn't get lost in a memory when the present felt like this. The air smelled of burning rubber and gasoline and smoke. Like the end of the world.

Her gaze went to the crime scene techs milling around the car wreckage in fireproof white suits, two of them prying open the trunk with a crowbar, her heart pounding. *Please, please, please . . . No, not Maya. Not Maya in the car . . .*

She made herself look away, into the eyes of the ex-security guard. "Where is she, Daryl?" she said.

"Do I know you?"

"My daughter is a thirteen-year-old girl—five-foot-eight-and-a-half-inches. She was with the woman who was driving this car."

"We haven't seen anyone, ma'am."

"What was found in the car?"

"I'm going to have to ask you to step back, please."

Brenna took a breath, tried to keep her voice in check, but still it came out tight, manic. "I'm a private investigator, Daryl," she said. "I bought you a twenty-dollar pack of Corps Diplomatique cigarettes and a thirty-seven-dollar glass of wine on September 12, 2004. I sat at the bar of the crappy strip club where you worked, listening to you complain about your cheating girlfriend Rolanda for half an hour, while you gave me absolutely no worthwhile information about Clarity and tried to get me into the back room, which you referred to as the VIP lounge." Her voice broke. She blinked away tears.

Daryl stared at her, his face coloring. The cop next to him raised his eyebrows at him. "She knows you, all right."

"Shut up."

"I'm looking for my daughter, Daryl. *It's the least you can do.*"

He exhaled. "Okay," he said. "Firefighters managed to put out the blaze pretty quickly. Backseat of the car, we recovered some articles of clothing and what looked like a laptop case. No sign of the driver or any passengers. They're still working on the trunk."

She nodded slowly.

"That's all I got."

"Thank you."

He stared straight ahead, his face still red. She moved away, focused on the crime scene techs, working on the trunk. She thought she could make out the charred remains of the honor roll sticker, still clinging to the bumper.

Brenna's cell phone vibrated. She glanced at the screen, saw her mother's number, hit decline. When the call went to voice mail, she texted Jim, Faith, and Nick:

Here. No sign of anyone. Just the car.

The phone vibrated again: Her mother, again. Brenna turned off the phone, moved around the periphery to a cluster of trees to the left of the wreckage and got a clear view. She saw Sykes on the passenger side of the car, talking to another uniformed officer, scribbling on his notepad as more techs photographed the car. She waved to him, tried to meet his gaze, but he wouldn't look at her. Maybe it was on purpose.

Her phone vibrated SOS. She flipped it open. A text from Morasco:

OK. On my way to Tarry Ridge; getting q'ed by IA for the rest of the day.

Internal Affairs. Could they waste any more time with him?

Another text came in, from Trent:

Important info re: Sophia Castillo.

Call when U can.

She started to call him, but then she heard a creaking noise, someone shouting, "Got it," and she saw the trunk sprung open, a cloud of black dust rising out of it, hanging in the air. She held her breath.

The techs stepped back, covering their faces. "Okay, okay," one was saying.

The other shouted, "We have something!" and Sykes moved around to the back of the car. He backed away, shaking his head . . .

No . . .

"Ma'am!" someone said, because she was running to the wrecked car, legs pumping, breath cutting through her lungs.

"Please step back!" someone said, as she reached the car. She got a glimpse of it—fists clenched, knees bent . . .

She screamed, and lost her footing and felt arms around her, holding her back. "*Nooo . . .*"

The officer pulled her away. She heard, "Looks to be a female . . ."

She heard, "Need some identification . . ."

Brenna couldn't breathe, couldn't move. She heard Faith in her head. *She's happy now. That could mean so many things. So many terrible, unthinkable things . . .*

Her knees gave out and she felt arms around her. She saw Sykes talking to one of the techs, his face a deep red. She focused on his fists, Sykes's meaty fists clenched like the ones in the trunk. And then blackness crowded her eyes and her head swam and for a second, she heard only the sound of her beating heart.

Trent sent the text, waited. No response from Brenna. He stared at the article on his screen—a short one, in the *Deseret News*, May 2, 1970, about a car crash that killed a young family of three—the Liptaks. The daughter, age four, was named Sophia Belyn.

Another instant message came in from Camille: **Did you read?**

Yep.

Weird, right?

I don't get it. Sophia Liptak died like forty years ago?

Camille typed: **All I can tell you is it was a lot easier to get a new identity in the eighties.**

Trent typed: **Right**. He wanted to come up with more words, but he couldn't. It was hard, on this little sleep and this much stress, to put his thoughts together. Man, he needed another energy drink.

One thing he did know though: There was no use looking for another Sophia Belyn Liptak. This one, the forty-years-dead one. This was his girl.

Document-wise, Sophia Belyn Liptak Castillo had come alive at the age of seventeen, when she took and passed the GED. After that, Trent had been able to trace her graduating from the University of Colorado at Boulder, then from nursing school back in Albany. She'd married Christopher Castillo in a small ceremony at the age of twenty-five, and had Robert a few months later. She'd lived in Katonah and worked as an ER nurse at St. Vincent's, right up until seven years ago, when Christopher had dumped her, taking Robert back to his native El Salvador. (Dude was clearly not into the whole visitation thing.)

She'd gone a little cray-cray after the divorce, what with the DUI, the break-in at Brenna's mother's house. She'd lost her job at St. Vincent's and worked at two different clinics in Mount Temple before getting laid off two years ago and filing for unemployment. All those ups and downs of Sophia's life were documented, just as they were with everybody.

What was missing, though, was the prequel. Trent had found no high school records for Sophia Belyn Liptak—no local news articles or sports awards or medical records or stints in juvy. Nothing about her at all before the age of seventeen, her childhood one giant missing puzzle piece.

Trent had no idea what this girl's real name was or what awful turn of events had fueled the need to steal a dead baby's identity and start over. He wished he knew. He wished someone could tell him what sick things Sophia Belyn Liptak Castillo had witnessed—or done—when she was a kid, when she was Maya's age. What was she capable of doing to a girl like Maya now?

Camille typed: **You okay?**

"Nope," Trent whispered to the screen. He typed: **Yep. Just confused.**

I'll see if I can find anything else on her, she typed. **But it may take a while.**

"I don't have a while," said Trent, who had looked for enough missing people Sophia's age to know that the while it would take would be a very long one.

In the sixties, seventies, eighties, most kids didn't even get social security numbers until they were in their late teens. So in other words, Sophia Liptak's social could have been this chick's first and only, and where did that leave him? In the dark.

He typed, **Thanks, CC. Gotta go.**

You can change your identity, you can change your looks but you can't change who you really are. That was one of the first things Brenna had taught him when he started working for her, and it was true. No matter how hard you try to act like someone else, you're still going to be drawn to that one thing you need—whether it's golf or guns or knitting or kinky sex. You'll buy a gun, you'll join a country club, you'll frequent bars and groups and private chats where that need can be satisfied.

What was Sophia's need? Drugs, sure. But what was Trent supposed to do? Post her pic on Craigslist? Start canvassing offices of oxy docs? The drug-dealing community wasn't exactly known for helping out investigations, and he didn't have much time . . .

Sophia had other interests. She *had* to. He wished he'd kept her on the phone for longer when she'd called Saturday morning. He wished he'd asked her more about her life, because she'd seemed in the mood to talk, unlike Trent, who could only think about that freakin' paternity test . . .

He'd even said it, hadn't he? *Your son was lucky. Not everybody who's a parent even wants to have kids.*

Not a day goes by, she had said, *when I don't think about my Robert. He's my everything and he always will be.*

Trent's breath caught. "Wax my ass with a hot glue gun," he whispered. Maybe he *hadn't* needed to stay on the phone any longer. Maybe he'd found out everything he needed from her.

Screw drugs. Screw her real name. Screw everything except the one thing in Sophia Liptak Castillo's life that really mattered. *Robert. Her missing child.* Robert was Sophia's need.

The Families of the Missing rooms used to be a well-kept secret, but for a few weeks this past fall, the Neff case had turned them into a "thing."

So it stood to reason that someone pissed off enough at Brenna to break into her mother's house, obsessed enough with her to take her kid . . . that person would know all about the chat room that Brenna had invaded, right? It made sense that someone like Sophia would join that chat room, make friends there, maybe get extra close to a young girl who sounded so much like Brenna's daughter . . .

Trent found Chrysalis. He looked up the chat rooms. He invented a name for himself: DowntownEnrique. (Sexy, right?) He was about to go into the room, but he remembered the trouble Brenna got into when she tried the same thing. He called up the profile pages, went to "create your profile" and started typing info about DowntownEnrique: twenty-seven, missing a baby sister . . .

Man. They might not have asked for real names, but there were a lot of personal questions on these profiles. Everything from favorite band and celeb crush to "What was the saddest moment of your life?" Maybe it was to weed out the fakes, but filling out this thing could take all day.

Trent scrolled down the list, thinking. *Has everyone in that chat room answered all these questions? Have they answered any of them?*

If that was the case, he might not have to fill one out at all.

Trent looked through the existing profiles till he found NYCJulie's. He opened it up and started reading it, skimming over the favorite band–type questions, going for the gold . . . Missing loved one: **My son. He's been gone for seven years** . . . Biggest disappointment: **Finding out who my real friends are. Not having anyone on my side** . . . He read on, but when he got to one of the final questions, "Do you ever think you'll be able to move on without your loved one?" his jaw dropped open.

"Bingo," he whispered.

NYCJulie had answered: **Not a day goes by when I don't think about my son. He is my everything and he always will be.**

When Brenna's eyes fluttered open, she was lying in a gurney, a man's face hovering over hers. "Drink this." He fell into focus—an EMT worker, round and baby-smooth and with eyes like shiny black buttons. A human teddy bear. He handed her a bottle of water. "You're probably dehydrated," the bear said. "Sip it slowly."

She did, but within seconds, the horror crowded in again, the charred, clenched fists . . . "My daughter," she said. "In the trunk."

"There was one body found in the trunk of the car, ma'am."

"My daughter."

"No ma'am," he said. "It's a middle-aged woman."

Brenna looked at him. She blinked a few times. "Are you sure?"

"Yes."

"Can I leave now, please?"

"I'd rest a bit more . . ." he said.

But she was already sitting up, and he had no choice but to help her. She slid off the gurney and found her way out of the vehicle and back outside. Emptying the water bottle into her mouth, she headed toward the blackened car, to where Sykes was standing, head bowed. She said his name and he turned. "Ms. Spector." His mouth was tight, his eyes clouded.

She looked at him. "Detective Sykes . . . the body in the trunk. The EMT told me it was a grown woman."

"Yes," he swallowed hard. *That face. The shock.* "Some of the clothes are still intact . . ." He didn't say anything more; he couldn't. But Brenna knew.

She said, "Detective Plodsky."

He nodded.

"Oh God. I'm sorry."

"She told me she was going to pick up Carver's computer. See if she could find any correspondence between him and . . ."

He swiped a hand over his eyes.

"The laptop in the backseat. That was Carver's?"

"Looks . . . looks like there was trauma to the head." His voice broke. He ran an arm across his face, and it was as though Brenna had already left, as though he were all alone.

Brenna stepped away. She cast her gaze past the clearing, into the surrounding woods. They hadn't found Maya yet, but that didn't mean anything. The car was charred, and what she'd done to Carver . . . Now Diane Plodsky. Those clenched fists. Trauma to the head. All over a laptop.

The last person to have seen Maya was Miles. She'd gotten into that car nearly two days ago—the car of a woman who had killed two people within thirty-six hours—and while paths had crossed with Sophia Castillo, no one had reported seeing a girl with her. The officers in Tarry Ridge had said her car was empty.

She's happy now.

Please be out there, Maya, she thought, gazing out and past the birch trees, the voice inside her fading. *Please be alive . . .*

At the edge of the clearing, on the pale white trunk

of one of the birches, Brenna noticed a thick, red smear. She started walking toward it, slowly at first, then faster, her heart in her throat. *Could be nothing, probably is, don't think about it, just look . . .*

It was too bright to be dried blood—a true pinkish red. When she got nearer she saw that it had a waxy texture. Lipstick.

She ran her fingertips over it—a long, swooping curve of fresh lipstick, drawn on the trunk if a tree. To the left, she saw two large vertical dots.

Colon and parenthesis smiley face.

She placed a hand on the red swirl, then threw her arms around the tree, tears springing into her eyes, a feeling bubbling up inside her . . . Hope.

20

Brenna sped down the Henry Hudson Parkway and into the city, to her apartment. Once she'd left her Sienna in the garage, she turned on her phone, called Faith as she walked the five blocks to her place.

"Where were you?" Faith said. "We've been trying to reach you."

"I'm back in the city. Any news?"

"No Brenna. No news. If we had any news, we would have told you."

"Of course," Brenna said.

"We're home now. Where have you been?"

"She's alive," Brenna said. "Maya's alive."

"Oh my God, did you see her? Is she there?"

She took a breath. "No . . ."

"Then how do you know? Did the police tell you—"

"The car was burning," Brenna said. "Detective Plodsky was in it. She was the only body."

Her voice flattened out. "Yes, Detective Sykes told us."

"Listen to me, Faith. She left me a sign."

"I . . . don't know what you mean."

"You don't have to," Brenna said. "It's too strange to

explain. Just don't give up hope, okay? Know that we're going to find her."

"Okay, Brenna." She didn't sound convinced. Didn't sound anything other than sad.

"Believe me," Brenna said. "I know it's hard, but please, Faith."

"We have to believe," Faith said, her voice barely audible. "If we stop believing, it's over."

Brenna said good-bye, hung up. Before she put the phone away, though, she noticed that she had another text message, from Trent.

Sophia Castillo = NYCJulie.
Come back. Will explain.

Faith stood in her living room, staring at the phone.

"What did she say?" Jim said it from across the room, and to Faith it felt as though they were both in a thick fog, trying to find their lives again.

Two hours, they'd spent, helping to man the tip line. Two hours of prank calls and bad leads and hopes dashed and crushed to the ground.

Two hours of taking calls that still stuck in Faith's mind, haunting her . . .

I saw her at a strip club.

I saw her at my school.

I saw her on the subway with a disgusting old man.

That chick who took her. Maybe they ran off to-gether. Maybe they're secret lovers or something.

I know it sounds strange, but kids are different these days.

I think they're in on it together. I watch the Investigation Discovery channel, so I know this shit.

It's the Internet. It's ruining our children. I bet they met online.

I'm a psychic, and I'm getting a sense. She's in terrible danger.

Maya's dead. That psycho bitch killed her. She did it right away. She wasn't in any pain.

Faith looked at Jim. "She told me not to give up hope."

He said nothing, just shook his head like someone turning down his last meal.

"I know," Faith said. "I know."

Maya's stomach was so empty it hurt. She felt as though she'd been walking for hours, and maybe she had been, she wasn't sure. After she'd untied her from the tree, Sophia had made Maya walk through the woods for so long. *Can't risk going out in the open*, she'd said. *Not here.* They'd walked in places where there were no paths at all, where plant growth was thick, even in the winter—needly pines, bushes with leaves as sharp as razor blades.

Maya had scratches and cuts all over. Her empty stomach gnawed and burned, but she'd been too scared to complain. Too scared to say anything for fear if she did, it would be like what happened when Sophia caught her with the lipstick.

They were on some highway now. Outside of knowing that she'd never been here before, Maya had no idea where they were. Maya and Sophia, trudging along that long, bleak stretch of road, Sophia stopping every once in a while and sticking her thumb out. Cars whizzed by. They disappeared like wishes.

"Oh look," Sophia said. "I found this in my jacket pocket."

She held out a banana. Maya grabbed it and devoured it. She dropped the peel on the ground.

"Don't litter," said Sophia. Like a mother. A mother holding a loaded gun. Maya scooped the peel up off the ground. Shoved it in the pocket of her big red sweatshirt. For a few seconds, she let herself think of Saturday night—of Miles running toward her, the blue car pulling up.

Maya? she had called out. *It's me. NYCJulie.* And Maya had been so grateful. Her friend from the chat room, appearing like some kind of guardian angel or something, rescuing her from her pain and the freezing rain and the boy she never wanted to see again.

She'd gotten into the car, which had been warm and dry, a jazz station playing on the radio. Sophia had even given her a clean towel to dry off her face, and Maya had felt so good, so safe, telling "NYCJulie" all about what had just happened to her.

You know what? Screw those stupid girls, Sophia had said. *What's important is you. How do you feel?*

Cold. Wet.

Don't worry. We'll get you some dry clothes.

Huh? No, that's okay, I can—

Believe it or not, they actually have some cute sweatshirts at the Sloatsburg rest stop.

What? No, Maya had said. *I live on Twenty-third Street.* And then the car had sped up and Maya had felt the barrel of the gun at her rib cage and it had hit her then—only *then*—that she'd never put up a picture of herself on her Families of the Missing profile.

She'd never even described the way she looked and yet NYCJulie had recognized her anyway, at night and in a rainstorm and on a crowded city street . . .

Stupid.

Another car approached. Sophia stuck her thumb out. It didn't even slow down.

"Damn it," Sophia said. She smoothed her hair, dusted off her nurses' pants, fluffed up the blue parka she'd changed into, back at the burning car. She opened her bag and plucked out her ruined lipstick and dotted it to her lips. She gave Maya a nasty look.

Maya cringed. "I'm sorry." She pictured her mom finding the tree. But she didn't think about it too hard or for too long. She wasn't sure whether it was lack of sleep or food or the actual truth, but she had the very real sense that Sophia could read her thoughts, and she didn't want to risk anything. She couldn't risk anything more. She had to listen to Sophia and learn her rules, or else she'd go like that weird guy Mark, like that poor policewoman with the bashed-in head who wound up taking Maya's place in the trunk.

Don't think about the policewoman. Don't think about her face.

Sophia plucked out a mirror and smoothed her eyebrows and sighed. "I have a bad headache," she said.

Another car came. Sophia stuck out her thumb, and to Maya's surprise, it slowed down, stopping about forty feet ahead of them.

"Finally," Sophia said. "Looks like a good one, too. Red."

They hurried toward the car, Maya a few steps in

front of Sophia so Sophia could hold the gun to her side.

Sophia said, "Why is red good?"

"It means the driver doesn't care about the car getting noticed."

"Right. What colors are not so good?"

"Beige," Maya said. "Black."

"Excellent. What about vans?"

"Minivans are good. Work vans are okay if there's writing on them, bad if there isn't. The worst kind are the ones with no windows in the back."

"Impressive," said Sophia, who had taught her all these things, these weird new truths, Maya listening and learning without asking her how she knew them. If she wanted to live, Maya had to learn without question, without backtalk.

It was Sophia's adventure. That's what she'd told Maya. And on Sophia's adventure, this was how things were done.

Maya could feel the barrel in her ribs, but she knew to act natural. She'd learned this, early on in the adventure. Scream, you get screamed at. Pull away, you get hurt. Cry, you get something to cry about.

Act natural, or you go in the trunk.

A man was behind the wheel of the hatchback. He wore sunglasses, which he took off as Maya and Sophia approached. His eyes were small and sparkly with crinkles at the corners. He was about Maya's dad's age and as he leaned out the window, his face was chiseled and kind and made her feel like crying.

"You're a nurse, huh?" the man said to Sophia.

She frowned at him, obviously forgetting for a few moments that she was still wearing her nurses' pants.

"Oh," she said finally. "Yes, my shift ended a while ago. Sorry . . . it's been a difficult day."

"Okay."

"I had a fight with my husband. He drove off in the car."

"Wow." The man's eyes softened. His gaze fell sort of pityingly on Maya, making her aware of how different she looked in her baggy red sweatshirt Sophia had bought for her at Rite Aid, her now-short black hair covered by the dirty Yankees cap that Sophia had swiped from Mark Carver's house. Maya had dirt on her face and smelled of sweat. It made her feel sick, like Sophia. Beyond hope. "Tough luck, eh, buddy?" he said.

Maya nodded.

Sophia said, "Robert isn't much of a talker."

"Me neither." The man smiled. "Where you guys headed?"

"White Plains train station," she said. "We'll get in the back."

This was something else Sophia had told Maya. *When accepting a ride from a stranger, the back is always safer.* Maya remembered the way Sophia had said it— the caring, patient tone. *Ironic*, Maya had thought, considering that when Sophia had pulled over for her on the West Side Highway, Maya had gotten in front.

I'm not a stranger, Maya, Sophia had said, responding only to the expression on her face. Reading Maya's mind.

Maya and Sophia slipped into the backseat, Sophia staying close to her, pressing the gun into her side.

The man was listening to the radio. ". . . another

chilly day here in the tri-state area," the announcer was saying, "we're looking for mostly clear skies and highs in the low thirties . . ."

"Fucking news radio," Sophia whispered.

Maya frowned. What was wrong with news radio? Had Sophia heard something while she was in the trunk?

"We'll be back with all your headlines at the top of the hour."

Sophia stiffened. Maya glanced at her. There was a sheen to her face, beads of sweat at the top of her lip.

The man said, "How old are you, Robert?"

Maya stared into the rearview. She cleared her throat. "I'm . . ."

"He's thirteen," Sophia said.

"I got a son that age. You play baseball, Robert? I notice you got a Yankees hat and—"

Sophia cut him off. "I thought you said you don't talk much."

Maya glanced at her, then at the man's eyes, watching them in the rearview. She stared into him, thinking it as hard as she could. *Help* . . .

"You okay there, son?" he said, as a car dealership commercial ended, and the announcer said something about the headlines of the hour.

"He's fine," Sophia said. "He's just tired."

"Maybe you ought to answer me yourself, kiddo."

". . . In the New York area, AMBER Alert has been issued for thirteen-year-old Maya Rappaport. She is five-foot-eight-inches, 120 pounds. Blue eyes."

Maya gasped. She couldn't help it.

The man's eyes focused on her, his gaze sharpening. "Oh my God."

"She is believed to have been abducted by a woman by the name of Sophia Castillo. Mid-forties, considered extremely dangerous."

"My God," said the man, as the gun came away from Maya's side, Sophia pressing it into the back of his head. "Pull over," she said.

He gripped the wheel. "I . . ."

"Did you hear me?"

"Please."

"*Did you hear me?*"

"I'm a father," he said. "I have three kids. A wife."

"Pull over," she said. "I'm not going to ask again."

Maya's stomach knotted. A tear spilled down her cheek. She reached into her pocket and gripped the banana peel, same way she used to hold her stuffed dog Patches when she was a little kid, when she used to have nightmares. She'd hold him tight to her chest and she'd imagine him talking to her, telling her she was his best friend and that he had magic powers to help her fight any monsters. It had been so long since she'd thought of Patches. She couldn't have been more than three years old. She'd still lived on Fourteenth Street back then. Her parents had still been married to each other . . .

The man drew a shaky breath, slowed down, and pulled over to the side of the road. He put his hazard lights on.

"Give me your phone," Sophia said.

"I don't have a phone," he said. "I . . . I mean I have one, but I . . . I left it at the office . . ."

"Get out of the car."

"Why don't you leave the kid with me? You can go on ahead. I won't tell anyone, and you can escape. You can take my car."

"Get out. Now."

The man opened the door. He raised both hands over his head. "I have three young children," he said.

Maya couldn't move. Her pulse thrummed in her ears and tears formed in her eyes and she dug her fingernails into the banana peel. She didn't know what to do. She wished someone would tell her, help her . . .

Mom . . .

Sophia grabbed her by the wrist. She opened the back door and yanked her out of the car, Maya's legs giving out from under her, her knees crashing on the pavement at the man's feet, as Sophia dragged her around, next to her.

Maya gazed up at him, his hands in the air, his eyes so sad and kind. "You poor kid," he said.

And then Sophia put the gun to his head and fired.

Brenna ran up the stairs to her apartment, opened the door to find Trent on his computer, looking up at her with sharp, excited eyes. "I'm in the Families of the Missing room now," he said. "They're talking to me."

"And?"

"NYCJulie hasn't been in the chat room since Sunday."

"Last night."

"Yeah."

"She talked to me last night," Brenna said. "Maya was already gone then, so I'm not sure what that proves."

"I know, Brenna, but she had only been on for a short time. They told me. She could have hopped onto a laptop last night. Public computer. Anywhere—just to look like business-as-usual. The people in the room say she's a major regular. This is the longest she's been off since she first started going there."

Brenna looked at him. "This is the only reason why Julie is . . ." The thought faded, bent . . . *Julie.* For a few seconds, Brenna flashed on Mrs. Dinnerstein outside her apartment this morning, handing her the note, the name on the paper, Mrs. Dinnerstein's concerned voice . . . *Her name is Miss Barnes.*

"Julie Barnes," Brenna said.

Trent stared at her. "Huh?"

"Julie Barnes. That was the name of the girl on *The Mod Squad.* I just remembered, when I was a little kid, we used to watch reruns . . ."

Trent squinted at her. "Ookaay . . ."

She blinked a few times, snapped out of it. "Lack of sleep," she said. "Stress."

"Right. Well anyway, that's not the reason why I think Julie is Sophia." He tapped at his keyboard. "Come here. Look at this."

On Trent's computer screen was NYCJulie's extensive profile.

"Look at all her answers." He got up from his chair, and Brenna sat in front of his computer, read the first response.

Missing loved one: **My son. He's been gone for seven years.**

Age of loved one at time of disappearance: **thirteen.**

She glanced at Trent. "Well, the first two answers fit. But a lot of people—"

"You need to look at all of them, Bren . . . Well, actually, scroll past all the favorite song and movie questions and go to the last few."

Brenna started to scroll down, then stopped. *No. That can't be. A coincidence. That's all.*

"It's like you told me," Trent was saying. "You can change your identity but you can't change who you are."

Brenna whispered, "You still like the same things . . ."

"Need. You still *need* the same things is what you said. Hey why are you stopped there? Scroll down to the last few questions. The second to the last answer, Sophia Castillo actually said to me over the phone. She used those exact same words."

Just a coincidence.

"Brenna. Are you listening to me?"

Brenna took a breath, snapped out of it, scrolled down. "Same words exactly?" she said as she read Julie's response.

"Yes," he said, "except she said, 'Robert' to me, instead of 'my son.'"

"That's . . . It makes sense . . ." she said, it all dawning on her. "Sophia befriended Maya so that she could find out more about her schedule."

"Exactly."

"In the private chats, Maya confides in her about the sleepover at Lindsay's. 'The popular girl,' NYCJulie says. Tells Maya to go for it. The same night, Sophia's car turns up near Lindsay's apartment."

"Right," said Trent. "She'd probably been waiting outside. She'd planned it. She knew."

"She knew everything about her," Brenna said. "Not just her schedule." It was true. Maya's closest confidante, her best-kept secret for months, NYCJulie knew about Maya's hopes and fears and deep, painful, wracking insecurities. She knew of her problems with her parents and the first kiss she ever had and Maya's aunt, her long-missing aunt who took up so much of

Brenna's world that Maya hated her, hated the smiling
teenager in her mother's dresser drawer enough to draw
a bullet hole in her head . . .

The smiling teenager, who, on weekdays after she
came back from school, would curl up with her baby
sister on the couch and watch *The Mod Squad*.

Who was this grown woman, who could elicit such
trust in a girl she'd never met, who had told Maya
during one of their chats, **I'm a lot like you**? Who was
this woman who, on her profile, had listed her favorite
album as Elvis Costello's *My Aim Is True*?

Julie Barnes. Clea's favorite *Mod Squad* character.
Don't you think I look like her? Clea would say.

A coincidence, Brenna thought. *After all these
years, it can't be more than that.* And then her buzzer
was going off, Trent jumping up to answer it, to hear
her mother's voice, shouting into the speaker. "It's an
emergency. I need to talk to Brenna *now*."

The doctor's office on 125th Street—the one where
Sophia could get her pills—that doctor's office was
closed. Sophia said that it was just as well, what with
Maya sniveling and crying like a little baby, how could
she take her anywhere, acting like this? Maya was
trying to follow the rules, trying hard as she could. But
it was hard to follow rules when they kept changing
like Sophia's did.

That man in the car had done nothing wrong. He'd
pulled over when she'd said so. He'd put his hands up,
surrendered his car, he'd done everything she'd asked
for and followed all Sophia's rules and yet still . . .
she'd put the barrel to his forehead and . . . Still. Maya

couldn't think of it. She couldn't live that moment again, even in her head. *Don't . . .*

"I had to do it, you know," Sophia had said to Maya, after she'd pushed her back into the dead man's car, after she'd belted Maya in and started it up, the car pulling away with a pained screech, the body left behind, that man's body in pieces at the side of Route 9, when he'd followed all the rules. *He did everything she said to do.*

Sophia was heading up Broadway now. There wasn't a lot of traffic, but she was driving slowly. She was in a dead man's stolen car, and the car was red. She didn't want to get noticed, Maya knew that much.

"I know what you're thinking," Sophia said.

Reading my mind again.

"Do you understand why I had to shoot him?"

Maya said nothing. She didn't know the right answer. In her mind, she started to count down from a hundred.

"He had a spot-on description of us. He would have called the police. He was lying about his phone being at the office. We both knew it. We aren't stupid, are we, Maya?"

Ninety-six, ninety-five, ninety-four . . .

"You want something to eat?"

Ninety-three, ninety-two, ninety-one, ninety . . .

"You have to go to the bathroom?"

Maya stopped counting. Nodded. Some things are needs and you can't help them.

"I can only take you to the bathroom if you stop crying like that."

Eighty-nine, eighty-eight, eighty-seven, eighty-six, eighty-five . . .

"Are you going to stop crying?"

Some things you can't stop, no matter how hard you try. He had three little kids. A wife. He had a nice smile and now he's . . .

Blood, all over the pavement, spattering the tires, the pale blue parka. Blood everywhere.

With a screech, Sophia jerked the car to the side of the road and threw it into park. They were on Broadway and 145th Street. A woman was pushing a baby carriage up the sidewalk, and she stopped and gaped. *Don't look at her, Sophia. Don't see her, looking at you.* Maya pictured a gun to the woman's head, blood on the sidewalk, the carriage, the baby's pink blanket. It made her cry more. She couldn't breathe. She felt as though she was drowning.

"Do you hear me, Maya? Am I getting through?"

Maya took a deep breath. She heard herself say, "Yes," in a strange little voice. A baby's voice. "Yes, Sophia." The first time on Sophia's adventure that Maya had said her name out loud, but it almost seemed as though someone else was saying it, as though this were all part of some awful dream and Maya would wake up from it soon, wake up a little kid again, holding Patches to her chest, calling for her mom.

Maya jammed her hands into her pockets, felt the cool slime of the banana peel against her fingers. She saw the man's sunglasses on the floor of the stolen car and smelled her own sweat, mingling with the scent of the car's clean carpet. *It's Sophia's adventure. I'm just a part of it.* Tears trickled down her cheeks. She was crying again. Sophia didn't like it, she could tell. But that was okay. *Sometimes, you have to give up the fight. Sometimes, there's nothing you can do. Some-*

*times, you have to throw your hands up and surrender
and not think about your parents, how hurt they'll be.
Sometimes, you have to think,* It will all be over soon.

Maya said, "Why haven't you killed me yet?"

Sophia let out a sigh. She took off Maya's baseball
cap and ran a hand through her short dark hair and
looked at her with tired, flat, fed-up eyes. "You've been
such a disappointment, Maya," she said.

"Why didn't you call me back?" said Brenna's mother
after she took the seat Trent had brought out for her, collapsing into it like she was something old and broken.
"I must have left fifteen messages on your voice mail.
Both on your cell phone and at work." She looked at
Trent accusingly. "Do you just erase them without even
checking?"

"No, ma'am," Trent said.

Brenna said, "You've seen the news."

"Yes, of course I have."

"Well then you've got to know why I haven't called
you. I'm trying to find my daughter, Mom. Talking to
you about it isn't my number one priority."

Her mother stared at her. "Wait," she said. "You think
I came all the way here to be comforted over Maya?"

Brenna frowned. "Well . . . yes."

"You don't think I have any information to give you?
Didn't you even listen to my messages?"

"Mom. I've been busy."

Evelyn Spector exhaled hard. Her face was pale and
drawn, her eyes sunken. It was as though the years
had caught up with her overnight. She looked her age.
Older. "I'm sorry if you're offended," Brenna said.

"Offended." Evelyn shook her head. "I need to talk to you." She looked at Trent. "Privately."

"Mother, I'm in the middle of—"

"I don't mind," Trent said. "I need to finish my hair anyway."

When he left the room, Brenna said, "I'm at the end of my rope, Mom. I honestly can't take any more—"

"I need to talk to you about Bill."

Brenna stared at her, the rest of the thought gone. "Bill?"

"You have Clea's diary," she said. "Maya told me you have her diary."

"Maya told you."

"I talk to my granddaughter," she said. "Why do you think she accidentally called me at 3 A.M.? Because my number was on her queue."

"I didn't know."

"Brenna," she said. "There's a lot you don't know."

She took a breath. "Clea's Bill."

Evelyn nodded. "So I'm right in assuming that Clea mentions Bill in her diary."

"Yes . . . Yes, she does."

"What does she say about him?"

"That . . . that she loves him . . . That she got tired of him . . ."

"That's what she said? That she got tired of him?"

"Well, she said he was acting strangely. He gave her a bad feeling."

"What did she do," Evelyn said. "What did she do when she had this feeling?"

Brenna stood up. She felt strange on her feet. Shaky. She moved over to the window, looked down at the street, at the life outside this room. "Mom, I'm confused," she said. "You know about Bill but you never told me? How long have you known?"

"*Brenna.*" Evelyn was right behind her. Brenna spun around to see her mother close, her eyes boring into her skin as though she were trying cut to the chase, to read her thoughts directly without having to ask her questions. "*I need to know what Clea says she did.*"

"She . . . she says she left him." Brenna cleared her throat. "She started hitchhiking. That's when she met the boy on the road. He turned out to be the man you read about in the news, the one who killed himself in front of me, back in Decem—"

"Clea left Bill."

"Yes."

"That's what she wrote. In her own diary."

"Yes, Mom."

"My God," she whispered. "She even lies in her diary." "*Mother, what are you talking about?*"

"Bill was Bill Edwards," Evelyn said. "He's from before your . . . your memory issues. Do you remember that name?"

Bill Edwards. Brenna strained for it, but it was beyond her grasp. "It sounds familiar."

"He taught in Clea's high school. He was the English teacher. He quit after Clea's junior year. A nice young man. Probably twenty-three years old. Twenty-five at the most."

"He was Clea's teacher?"

"Yes. She used to talk about him. Mr. Edwards. He taught them Kerouac. The Beat poets."

Brenna shook her head.

"Anyway, I'm not sure when Clea became involved with him, but he was married. He left his wife for her. No one knew—not his wife. Not you and me. The way she put it, it was her *adventure*. I suppose the secrecy was part of that."

Brenna stared at her. "The way she put it? She told you?"

"Not before she left, Brenna. When we saw the police, I was as in the dark as you were. I thought she'd been kidnapped, I had no idea . . ."

"So, when?"

"A month after Clea left, she called me," Evelyn said. "She needed my help."

Brenna's head was throbbing. All these years. All these years of wondering, of waiting, and yet . . . "You knew."

"Yes."

"When you got rid of all her pictures, you knew she was out there." Brenna's face grew hot, tears rushing into her eyes. She bit her lip, slowed her breathing. *Keep it together,* she told herself, though she was ripping at the seams. "She asked you for help and . . . what? What, you were too angry?"

"It was her," she said quietly. "It was Clea. Clea was not right."

"She had a gift for destruction that ran through her veins. You said she got it from Dad. You told Maya that, Mother. Why did you tell a young girl that her own aunt was evil?"

"Because it was the truth."

"How could you *say* that?"

"She killed Bill Edwards," Evelyn said.

"What?"

"She stabbed him to death and left him in his own car. That nice young man. With a lovely wife and so much to live for."

"Did . . . did Clea say why?"

"She blamed it on drugs, Brenna. Bad acid or something." She took a breath. "She wanted me to take her back, to lie for her. She said, 'You covered up for Dad when he killed himself. Why not me?' You see, no one knew that she and Bill had been involved. He'd left his wife a note and disappeared a full month before he came back for Clea."

Brenna stared at her mother.

"There are some things you can't help your child with, Brenna," she said. "Even the most loving mother has to draw the line somewhere."

To Brenna, it felt as though she was looking at a different person. Someone she thought she had known from birth and whose every facial expression hung in her memory—every snide comment, every smile, every flicker in the eyes from the past twenty-eight years. But still, Brenna hadn't known what was behind any of it. You never really know someone until you see what they've been hiding. Brenna hadn't known her mother at all.

"I couldn't call the police," Evelyn said. "She was in Tennessee where they had the death penalty and what she had done was surely deserving of it."

"So you didn't tell," Brenna said quietly. "You didn't tell anyone. You rid your house of traces of her. You got rid of the evidence. You hoped she'd found a new identity, a new life."

"Yes."

"You thought, that way, she could start again."

"I swore I'd never tell anyone and I didn't intend to. I stopped bothering the police, Detective Carlson. I was relieved when they closed the case. I hoped and prayed you wouldn't find her, what with your line of work and that memory . . . My God, when I heard you found that man she'd been with all those years ago . . . I prayed it would stop. I wanted it all to go away. I wanted for her to stay away . . ."

"Mom."

"I even tried looking for her myself. I thought, if someone finds her, let it be me, not Brenna. I was thinking of you. You have to understand."

"Mom, look at me."

Down the hall, Brenna heard the bathroom door open. She stayed focused on her mother, on her tired, scared eyes. "Why are you telling me now?"

"Because, honey. I saw the news story about Maya. I saw the mug shot . . ."

"Oh my God."

"She colored her hair. She was wearing contacts. She was drunk and on drugs and had aged twenty-five years, but I knew, Brenna. Just like I knew when I was hiding in my bedroom five years ago, I knew that voice. I didn't want to admit it, even to myself. But a mother knows, Brenna."

"No . . ."

"Sophia Castillo," Evelyn said quietly. "That's your sister. That's Clea."

21

"Why haven't you killed me yet?" Maya said.

Sophia took off the Yankees cap, ran her hand through Maya's dark hair. So much like her Robert's, and yet this girl was not like him at all—not stoic, strong Robert. Robert never cried—a little man at ten, twelve, thirteen. He hadn't cried when he had said good-bye, even though she'd known how much he wanted to. She had seen it in his eyes.

Maya, on the other hand. Maya wouldn't stop. She was sobbing now, like a baby, but worse. Babies cry when they need something—food, sleep, diaper change. You fill that need and they stop crying. But Maya wasn't crying out of need. She was crying over something she'd seen happen—the weakest type of crying. "You've been such a disappointment, Maya," she said.

Maya stopped crying. Just like that. She gave Sophia a look, wide-eyed, as though Sophia had just performed some sort of shocking magic trick. It made Sophia think of a time long ago, when Robert was just one week old and she was attempting, in vain, to nurse him. He wouldn't latch on, no matter how hard she tried. Robert was shrieking from hunger, and Christopher kept asking Sophia if she was okay until, finally, it all got to her—the futility, the failure, the incessant wailing of a baby whose need she couldn't fill . . .

Sophia had lost it. She'd burst into tears. And like magic, *like this*, Robert had stopped crying. He'd given her the same look Maya was giving her now, and Sophia realized how similar their faces really were . . .

Anyway, Robert had stopped crying and latched on at last. *Can you believe this, Christopher?* Sophia had said, her baby boy nursing away. *One week old, and already I'm guilting him into doing things.*

She'd only been joking, of course. He hadn't done it out of guilt, or love, or anything else other than need. The purest need. The need to survive.

Sophia looked at Maya—at the cruel trick of genetics that was Robert's face and Brenna's face and their mother's face and Sophia's own. A combination of cells, creating enough of a likeness to pull at Sophia's heart, to make her believe that, in time, this girl might need her, that this hostage she'd taken might recognize Sophia in the way that her own mother had not, even as she crashed around her living room, begging her to come out, to look at her, to see what she'd done to her firstborn child . . .

How naïve had Sophia been to believe that, at some point, Maya might stop crying and look at her, really look at her? That she might say, *I know you. I need you*?

Sophia recalled the dream she used to have—about dying in the arms of a movie hero, a firefighter. In the dream, the firefighter begs her not to go. *Stay with me*, he says. The way they always do in movies. Did people really say that to the dying, or was it just a Hollywood cliché? Was anyone really that poetic, that romantic, when trying to keep someone alive?

Sophia hadn't thought about that dream for years, but it had been on her mind throughout this adventure—the idea that, no matter how much she destroyed the rest of her life, she could still have a death that was perfect and true. How in that moment of leaving this world, there would be someone with her who could give her what she wanted: to feel needed, forever.

But Maya wasn't Robert. She never would be. She had similar genetics, yes. But she wasn't family, not really. When Sophia put out the big light, Maya couldn't be the one to hold her, to beg her to stay.

As Sophia pulled away from the curb, she noticed the cell phone, clipped into the driver's side visor. She grabbed it. *Knew he was lying.* And she knew, too, how this adventure had to end.

She turned to Maya, who was staring at the phone, that same shock still scrawled across her face. "Are you ready?" she said.

"Sup?" said Trent, as Brenna and her mother stood staring at each other, Brenna unable to move, to breathe. "Listen, I almost forgot," he said. "Detective Morasco called. Guess you weren't answering your cell . . ."

Brenna's phone vibrated SOS in her pocket.

"Nothing important. Just wanted to know what was going on . . ."

She pulled it out, looked at it. The text was from a number she'd never seen before. She opened it up, read the first line.

This is from Sophia Castillo . . .

". . . get you anything, Mrs. Spector? Maybe a cup of coffee . . ."

Do not tell anyone about this text . . .

Brenna read on, willing herself not to cry out, not to shake or drop the phone or go ghost white, hoping with all she had that her body wouldn't betray her.

"Where are you going," Trent asked, for she was already at the closet, yanking her coat out, putting it on.

Brenna said, "Don't leave." Her gaze darted from Trent to her mother. "Either one of you. Stay right here until I get back."

"Brenna?" said her mother.

"Where are you going?" Trent said again.

Brenna didn't answer. She was already out the door, she was on the sidewalk, rushing the five blocks to her car with Trent's question stuck in her head and the bag of Clea's clothes in her arms, that moment replaying in her mind . . .

"Where are you going?" Trent asks after her as she hurtles toward the door. She grabs her purse from her desk, then, the tired old grocery bag, the mold smell of Clea's clothes wafting up, Clea's journal pressed into her side. I'm going to see my sister, *she thinks.* And she will give me back my daughter. *And she hurries down the stairs, out the front door,* into the present.

Maya's abduction was the top story on the local news. Faith and Jim sat on the couch, watching it, just as, a century ago in this same spot, they'd watched Faith's interview with Ashley.

They were showing footage of Faith's morning

announcement—again made a century ago, back when Faith thought she was talking to the strange person who had called her, when she thought she was appealing directly to Renee Lemaire and not some silly high school boy. When she thought that she could do something.

When she was able to think.

"Maya is five-eight and 120 pounds," Faith was saying on the TV. "She has waist-length blonde hair and blue eyes and she was last seen wearing a bright blue coat with brass buttons . . ."

Jim stared at the screen. Faith gazed at his profile, the light from the TV flickering in his eyes. He'd barely spoken since they got home, yet in some ways she had never felt closer to him. She could read his mind, now that they shared this awful feeling.

Maya's high school picture appeared on screen alongside that of her abductor—the mug shot they'd seen this morning. Sophia Castillo with her greasy hair and her wild eyes. Something out of a "Crack Is Whack" campaign.

". . . Rappaport and the NYPD are urging anyone who may have seen these two to call this tip line. Castillo is considered extremely dangerous, and is already responsible for one death since Maya's abduction . . ."

"Two," Jim said.

Faith nodded.

"Maybe more."

"Please."

"Faith."

"Yes, honey?"

She turned to find him facing her, his eyes thick with tears.

"I don't know if I can live without her."

She took his hands in hers, and tried to think of something, anything, but the only thing on her mind was the image of Maya, running through the freezing rain, Maya getting into that blue car and closing the door and disappearing forever. How could she comfort Jim, how could they comfort each other when they were both feeling the same hopeless rage, the same budding grief . . . When they could read each other's minds?

Faith put her arms around him. They held on to each other like two people drowning—neither one able to save the other, but neither wanting to die alone.

An hour later, the TV was off. Faith was in the kitchen, waiting for water to boil, listening to Jim's voice, on the phone with Nick Morasco. "No," he was saying, "the tip line has really been pretty worthless, unfortunately . . . yeah . . ."

She heard the click of the phone as, from the bottom of the pot, the first bubbles forced their way up to the surface. She had used the pasta maker. She'd kneaded dough to make homemade pasta because kneading dough and feeding it into the machine and turning the crank were all things she could do. When she dropped the homemade pasta into the boiling water, her stomach growled. She hadn't eaten since . . . She couldn't remember when. She needed to eat. So did Jim. This was something they could do. Eat.

She felt Jim watching her and looked up from the pot to see him in the doorway. He stood there so stiffly that for a moment, he looked like a shamed young boy, which made her think of Miles. It made her gut clench up. *Miles could have saved her. At the very least, he could have done something more than the stupid things that he did.* She slipped the wooden spoon into the boiling water, broke up the pasta. "Did Nick say anything?"

He shook his head. "He was being questioned all day. First by Internal Affairs, then for the criminal investigation into Carver's shooting," he said.

"Technicalities," she said. "A waste of time."

He nodded. "He was hoping we might have news."

"What about Brenna?" It still felt weird to say her name to Jim, but it was getting easier.

"Nick said he hasn't been able to get hold of her. Trent said she'd run out, and she's not answering her cell."

"Weird," she said.

"She does that sometimes."

"Does what?"

"Disappears . . ."

Faith didn't know what that meant. She wasn't sure she needed to know. Not now, anyway.

"The pasta is done," Faith said. Almost a pun. *The past is done.*

She turned the gas off and opened the cupboard that held the colander. When she was bending down to grab it, she heard a knock on the door. She shook her head. *Concerned neighbors.* There'd been a parade of them this morning after the show, with more showing up in spurts throughout the rest of the day, all of them so well meaning, but all so torturous, with their worried eyes and their *We're praying for her,* and *Is there anything I can do?* One woman—someone Faith saw in the elevator maybe once every couple of months—this woman had actually said, "I'm so sorry for your loss." It had been all Faith could do not to haul off and punch her.

The evening news had brought a few more, with Jim politely showing them out and Faith hiding in the kitchen, unable to take it. No doubt this was more of the same. "Jim, can you?"

"Sure," he said.

Jim headed for the door, as Faith poured the pasta through the colander. She heard him say, "Yes?" And then, "*Oh my God.*"

Faith headed out of the kitchen and made for the door. She saw Jim's back before she saw who he was hugging. But she knew, in the tears that spilled down her own cheeks, in the emotion bubbling up through her. *Oh please, please, please, please let this be real.*

She heard "*Daddy,*" before she saw the sheared-off hair, the red sweatshirt, the closed eyes, before she saw the tearstained face buried in Jim's shoulder, the face of Maya. Maya looked up when she saw Faith and threw her arms around her, both of them weeping, unable to stop. Maya was here. Maya had come home.

Brenna's phone trilled when she was on City Island Bridge. She glanced at the screen. Morasco. "I'm sorry, Nick," she whispered. "I can't talk." She put the phone back on her lap, let the call go to voice mail, kept driving. Strange. On other drives to City Island, Brenna could barely focus on the road for all the memories that barraged her. She'd turn on the radio to flood them out. She'd plug in Lee the GPS and listen extra closely to the suave Australian voice, mispronouncing "Dit-

mahhhs Street" and "City Ahland Boolevahd" and all
the other street names of her youth, making them into
different places, exotic spots that didn't trigger memories at every turn.

She'd sometimes call Trent and get him to talk to
her, to describe whatever idiotic thing he was doing at
the time, just to keep her thoughts in check, her eyes
focused on the road as it was now, not then.

But this time, she didn't need to do any of that. She
remembered nothing, the present situation overshad-
owing everything she'd lived before. She was going
to see her missing sister and bring home her missing
daughter, God she hoped that was going to happen . . .

Maybe it wasn't that strange.

She was on the island now, passing the Lobster Box
where she'd had her first date with John Berger on May
24, 1984. But the memory didn't stick. She passed the
Star of the Sea Church, where on June 4, 1997, she'd
served as maid of honor at her best friend Carly Davis's
wedding to Grant Stratton, and the library her mother
had stormed home from on April 5, 1986, telling
Brenna she was never going to talk to Ruth the librarian again. She passed the Mariner's Museum, behind
which she'd smoked her first cigarette with Beth Purdy
on August 8, 1985. But none of it held. She didn't feel
the burn from the smoke in her chest or smell the star-
gazer lilies from her bridesmaid's bouquet or hear her
mother's indignant voice, cursing Ruth's treachery.

She could remember it all, of course, but only in
passing—her senses weren't involved. Brenna turned
off City Island Avenue, onto Carroll Street, her palms
sweating, her lip trembling as she edged toward her

mother's house, where her sister had asked she come alone, tell no one, or else. *This is a serious warning.*

Brenna saw the Neptune statue first, and at the same time, her phone vibrated. A text. "Okay," she whispered. "Okay . . ." She stared at the house, a chill running up her neck. There was a large, street-facing window that her mother had always hated. *It throws too much light into the kitchen,* Evelyn would complain. *It hurts my eyes when I'm having my morning coffee.* The window had been bashed in. A pile of shattered glass sparkled in the flower bed, the window gaping open as though beaten up and in shock.

Clea hadn't needed to do that. Brenna's mother kept her spare key in the same place she always did, the plastic rock in the bed of impatiens on the left side of the front door. *It's still there, Clea. You could have checked. You didn't have to break Mom's window in, it must have made such a sound . . .*

Brenna swallowed hard. She thought of her mother's voice, the sadness in it. *A mother knows . . .* she had said. She stared at the smashed-in window, the cold air rushing in. She felt sorry for her mother, for the first time in a long while.

In Brenna's line of work, there was an adage—one she felt compelled to bring up to most clients before beginning an investigation: Be careful who you look for.

No one is perfect. Some of us are less perfect than others. Still others are better off as memories than they are in the flesh, and these people are better left unfound. It was a fact of life, but Brenna had never thought it would apply to the one missing person who had filled her thoughts for three decades, the person who had guided her life and her decisions and her mistakes, *my God, so many terrible mistakes* . . .

She remembered her phone vibrating and checked her texts. There were two. The most recent, from Sophia's strange new number . . .

Dropped Maya at her father's. I am in Dad's workroom.

Brenna stared at the small screen. *Dropped Maya at her father's.* She checked the other text, from Faith. *SHE'S HOME!!!!!!!!!!!*

Brenna put her head against the steering wheel. She cried until there were no more tears left inside her. She wanted to pull away from the curb and drive to Jim and Faith's, to throw her arms around Maya and hold her tight enough never to let go. And she would, she knew.

But first she needed to leave her sister behind.

Brenna grabbed the grocery bag full of Clea's things, slipped the diary out of her purse, and headed around the back of the house, past Neptune, to the locked shed that used to be her father's workroom.

She looked so different from the way she always did in Brenna's dreams, where she was always seventeen and always leaving, her blonde hair backlit by the dawn sun. Now, she was an adult, an exhausted-looking one, with dark circles under her eyes and sweat beading on her forehead, on her upper lip, her dyed brown hair wet with it . . .

The eyes, though. She wasn't wearing the brown contacts she'd had on in the mug shot, and those clear blue eyes, just like Maya's, those eyes Brenna remembered.

"Clea."

"Sophia," she said. "That's my name. I've been Sophia for most of my life."

Brenna gripped the grocery bag to her chest. "I've missed you. You might not know that, but you've been on my mind. Ever since you left."

"Then why didn't you take my case?"

"I . . . I didn't know . . . I didn't know it was you."

Sophia said, "It's empty."

"What?"

"Dad's workroom. There used to be so much stuff in here. Do you remember?" Brenna looked around the space, which was, yes, completely empty. There was a dull vinyl floor, and cement walls and no boxes, no equipment, not even a rusty chair to sit on. There were dust motes floating in the air, the setting sun catching them, making them sparkle.

Brenna said, "I can sort of remember wood shavings."

Sophia nodded, a vague smile crossing her face. "Yes," she said. "He had a circular band saw. He tried to make furniture, but he was really terrible. His chairs always had these huge seats and short legs. His tables were all uneven. He'd show them to Mom, and she'd roll her eyes and he'd take them in here and saw them to bits. The whole place smelled of wood shavings all the time."

Outside, a car drove by. Brenna heard the roar of it, but she stayed focused on her sister. "Mom never let us in here," she said.

"I know, but a no from Mom never meant much to me. I used to sneak in here all the time." She looked at Brenna. "It's how I found out."

"Found out what?"

Sophia moved over to the far wall and put her hand against it. Brenna moved closer, and that's when she saw it—a series of faint brown spots. They could have been dirt, or faded paint, or . . .

"Blood," Brenna said.

"You can scrub and scrub," Sophia said. "But the truth always shows itself, doesn't it, Brenna?"

Brenna turned to her. "Is that why you did it? Dad's death?"

"I've done a lot of things. Which one do you mean?"

"Changed," Brenna said. "Is that why you changed?"

"Everybody changes, Brenna."

Brenna dug her fingernails into her palms, the same way she so often did to come back from a memory. "You killed the man you loved."

She nodded.

"Why?"

"I don't remember."

Brenna gaped at her. *"You don't—"*

"It was thirty years ago, Brenna. I was high. Not everybody remembers everything."

Brenna closed her eyes for a moment. *Keep calm.*

"I remembered you though," Sophia said. "All these years . . . All this time I haven't been myself, I've kept up with you."

"How?"

She shrugged. "News. Internet. I even bought that book the doctor wrote about you. I didn't want to get too close. Mom made it clear I wasn't wanted in your lives. I just wanted to know you were okay."

Brenna stared at her. "Okay?" she said. "You took my daughter."

"That was after you turned down my case. You have an only child, Brenna. You're my sister. You'd think you'd know how I felt. You think you—"

"Why did you take her?"

Clea looked at her, a sad smile curling her lips. For the briefest moment, she looked so much like Maya . . . "It seemed like a good idea at the time."

Brenna closed her eyes. "Jesus," she said. "I never knew you at all."

"What's that?" She gestured to the bag. "Groceries?"

"No. It's your things."

She handed her the bag. Sophia looked inside. She put it on the floor. "How did you get this?"

"Like you said. The truth always shows itself."

Sophia picked the journal out, and as she looked through the pages, Brenna noticed, for the first time, the gun in her hand. She looked up at Brenna, her eyes welling. "These aren't my things," she said. "They're Clea's."

"You are Clea. You're my sister no matter what you do or who you hurt or how much you try to change. No matter how little I know you, you're my flesh and blood and you always will be."

"Do you love me?"

Brenna said, "I have no other choice."

"Do you need me?"

"I am trying not to."

Sophia threw the journal at Brenna's head. It clipped her in the side of the face, slamming into the wall behind her. Brenna's eyelid stung. She wiped it with the back of her hand. When she brought the hand away, she saw fresh blood. She flashed on a memory, a vague, pre-syndrome one—Brenna on her back in the grass, crying. Clea sitting on top of her, her hands working Brenna's arm, just above the wrist, where the skin is most tender. Brenna remembered the awful sting of it, the tears in her eyes, and Clea laughing. Clea's voice. *"Indian burn!"* Brenna must have been three years old.

Sophia said, "You want a Kleenex?"

Brenna shook her head.

"I'm a good person, Brenna." She raised the gun, pointed it at her. "I just need to feel needed. Everybody does."

Brenna gazed at the gun. She felt three years old again. Helpless. Her gaze went from the barrel to her sister's eyes, and she remembered Clea standing over her bed as she had at seventeen, Brenna just eleven years old, her eyes fluttering awake. She remembered Clea's finger to her lips. "Don't tell Mom," she had said. And Brenna had promised. She swore she wouldn't tell. And then Clea had said . . . why was she only remembering this now?

Brenna didn't care about the gun anymore. She saw only Clea's clear blue eyes, she saw Clea at seventeen, in love and hopeful and starting her adventure. *You'll forget me, Brenna. Just wait and see.*

"I never forgot you," Brenna whispered. "I never will."

A tear slipped down Clea's cheek. "It's good to be wrong sometimes." She placed the barrel of the gun against the side of her own head. The temple. "Tell Maya I didn't mean to scare her," she said. And before Brenna could stop her, Clea pulled the trigger.

Epilogue

One month later

Sophia Castillo's memorial service was held at Temple Beth-El, the same synagogue where both she and Brenna had been bat mitzvahed. Sophia had been cremated, which the synagogue frowned upon, but of course, it also frowned upon suicide and murder, and Sophia had been guilty of both.

In fact, the only reason that the service happened at all was that Evelyn Spector was friendly with the new rabbi, a youngish guy who frequented the library and was a member of the book group she'd recently formed with Ruth.

It was a very private ceremony, as serial killers' memorial services always were. The funerals of storied detective Diane Plodsky and respected businessman and father-of-three Bradley Lowell had drawn spillover crowds and had made the covers of both the *Post* and the *Daily News*. Even Mark Carver's service had attracted a respectable group of gawkers. But Sophia's was cloaked in secrecy and shame.

Brenna was there, with her mother, Nick, and Maya.

No one had wanted Maya to go, but she'd insisted. "She was my aunt," she said. "She was Mom's sister."

"Are you sure?" Brenna had said to her this morning. "It could bring on memories."

Maya smoothes her short, newly bleached hair as though she is feeling it for the first time. "I can handle memories," she says.

Now, she was holding Brenna's hand as the rabbi began speaking about Sophia. She turned and looked at her daughter, both grateful and amazed.

Brenna wasn't sure if Maya's ordeal had strengthened her, or if it was preexisting strength that had enabled her to survive it. But either way, it was a part of her now. It was in the protective way she watched Faith and Jim when she thought they weren't looking. It was in the way she refused to return any of Miles's calls. It was in the way she squeezed her mother's hand now, as the rabbi talked about "a mother, sister, daughter, and aunt who, somewhere along the line, lost her way." It was in the way she whispered to Brenna, "Squeeze my hand back. Sometimes, that helps."

The rabbi spoke on, Brenna thinking not so much about Clea/Sophia but about life, how it never taught you things gently, how it slapped sense into you instead. Live and learn, sure. But why did both have to be so damn hard?

From now on, Maya had said on the car ride here, *I'm going to tell you all my secrets.*

Brenna wasn't holding her to that, though. She wasn't holding her to anything. Her priority was to love Maya, to support her and help her heal and grow up without anyone or anything intruding—especially the past.

Brenna and Maya were in therapy together, with Lieberman. He'd warned them both not to expect instant results, to take it one day at a time. "You've both been through so much," he had said at their last appointment on February 15, *and as he says it, Brenna sees the sparkling dust motes in her father's workroom, the slight smile on her sister's face as she puts the barrel to her head . . .*

"It's okay, Mom," Maya whispered.

Brenna realized she was crying. That happened to her a lot these days. She'd cry tears and not even know it until someone pointed them out. "She was misguided, yes," the rabbi was saying. "But she left behind people who loved her very much . . ."

Brenna's gaze drifted to the door, where a few more people were filtering in: a small group that included Alan Dufresne. Brenna frowned. What was he doing here?

"Oh good," whispered Brenna's mother.

"You know him?" Brenna said.

Brenna's mother gave Alan a slight wave that he returned.

You never fully know anyone.

The rabbi wrapped up his brief speech. He said the mourner's kaddish, and Brenna, Nick, Maya, and her mother stood up, bowing their heads. When the service was complete, Brenna excused herself for a moment, headed toward Alan.

"Your mother invited me," he said.

"Why?"

He shrugged. "She's a nice woman," he said. "I'm really sorry for your loss."

Brenna's mother started toward them.

Alan said, "Did you ever find out how my father knew your sister?"

Brenna shook her head. From what she and Trent had pieced together with the help of one of Clea's old friends, a former motel worker named Clint Lamont from Pine City, Utah, Clea had recovered from her OD with a few extra screws loose. She'd headed out of the motel and down the highway in her nightgown, stopping traffic literally.

It had been Clint who had spotted her. But he had no sooner set her up in a spare room with some money out of the cash register and a set of his sister's clothes than she'd escaped again, hitchhiking for around a month, hanging out at truck stops, quoting Kerouac to the clientele. Back then, she hadn't gone by Clea Spector or Sophia Castillo. She was known to all as Julie Barnes.

"I found some love letters in my dad's things," said Alan. "They were from a woman named Pamela. You know where she was from?"

"Where?"

"Provo, Utah."

Brenna looked at him.

"In one of the letters, Pamela asked him to keep something for a young friend of her daughter's. She didn't name names, but do you think, maybe . . ."

Brenna remembered January 20—two days after Sophia had shot herself. Brenna had opened her e-mail for the first time in days and clicked on a forwarded article Trent had sent her, from the *Deseret News*, dated May 2, 1970. In her mind, she was reading through it again, about the car crash, the doomed Liptak family, the daughter, Sophia Belyn . . . She read it all the way to the last sentence, seeing the words in front of her eyes as she met Alan's gaze: *Mrs. Liptak is survived by a younger sister, Pamela.*

"It's very possible," Brenna said.

Brenna's mother rushed up to Alan. "You two know each other?" she said.

Alan nodded. "So nice to finally meet you, Evelyn."

Strange, thought Brenna as her mother pulled him to the side of the room and chatted with him as though he were her dearest friend—the keeper of her daughter's old identity.

But then, all of life was strange, wasn't it?

Brenna gazed across the room at Nick, talking to Maya, making her smile. Two weeks ago, he'd been reinstated on the Tarry Ridge Police force, but was considering a move, he'd said. Away from the suburbs. Away from the house he'd once shared with his wife and baby son. Back to his old stomping ground—New York City.

Why is it that so many steps forward always involve a step back?

She scanned the late group of guests who had come in with Alan—two older women who looked as though they'd gotten lost, and a tall, black-haired man, standing in the doorway alone, shifting from foot to foot. She stared at him. *Could it be?* He'd been so hard for her and Trent to track down, and even so, he'd never replied to her e-mail.

She walked up to him and he turned—a very young man with brown skin and dark eyes and a somber, unfamiliar face. *I don't know him,* Brenna thought.

And then he smiled, genetics springing into place, refusing to be ignored, explaining everything that words could not.

It was Maya's smile. Clea's smile. "I'm Robert," he said.

"I know," she said, pulling him into a hug. "I'm Brenna. I'm your aunt."

USA TODAY BESTSELLING AUTHOR

ALISON GAYLIN

and she was
978-0-06-187820-6

Missing persons investigator Brenna Spector has a rare neurological disorder that enables her to recall every detail of every day of her life. A blessing and curse, it began in childhood, when her older sister stepped into a strange car never to be seen again. When a local woman vanishes eleven years after the disappearance of six-year-old Iris Neff, Brenna uncovers bizarre connections between the missing woman, the long-gone little girl . . . and herself.

into the dark
978-0-06-187825-1

When Brenna watches footage of missing webcam performer Lula Belle, she realizes the stories Lula tells are of memories that only Brenna and her long-missing sister, Clea, could know. Convinced the missing performer has ties to her sister, Brenna takes the case—and in her quest for Lula Belle unravels a web of obsession, sex, guilt, and murder that could regain her family . . . or cost her life.

stay with me
978-0-06-187826-8

As Brenna relies on her P.I. skills to find Maya, her missing teenage daughter, evidence surfaces showing a possible link between Maya's disappearance and that of Brenna's sister twenty-eight years earlier. Are the events connected, or is someone playing a twisted game?